# BULLY FOR SALE

by

LETA BLAKE

An Original Publication from Leta Blake Books

Bully for Sale Sale Written by Leta Blake
Cover by Dar Albert
Formatted by BB eBooks



Print Edition

First Print Edition, 2022

## Other Books by Leta Blake

### Contemporary

Will & Patrick Wake Up Married
Will & Patrick's Endless Honeymoon
Cowboy Seeks Husband
The Difference Between
Bring on Forever
Stay Lucky

**Sports**

The River Leith

*The Training Season Series*
Training Season
Training Complex

**Musicians**

Smoky Mountain Dreams
Vespertine

### New Adult/Coming of Age

Punching the V-Card

*'90s Coming of Age Series*
Pictures of You
You Are Not Me

**Winter Holidays**

North's Pole

*The Mr. Christmas Series*
Mr. Frosty Pants
Mr. Naughty List
Mr. Jingle Bells

Fantasy

Any Given Lifetime

**Re-imagined Fairy Tales**

Flight
Levity

**Paranormal & Shifters**

Angel Undone
Omega Mine

**Horror**

Raise Up Heart

Omegaverse

*Heat of Love Series*
Slow Heat
Alpha Heat
Slow Birth
Bitter Heat

*For Sale Series*
Heat for Sale
Bully for Sale

## Coming of Age

*'90s Coming of Age Series*
Pictures of You
You Are Not Me

## Audiobooks

Leta Blake at Audible

## Discover more about the author online

Leta Blake
letablake.com

## Gay Romance Newsletter

Leta's newsletter will keep you up to date on her latest releases, sales and deals, future writing plans, and more from the world of M/M romance. Join Leta's mailing list today.

## Leta Blake on Patreon

Become part of Leta Blake's Patreon community to support her indie publishing expenses and to access exclusive content, deleted scenes, extras, and interviews.

## Acknowledgments

Thank you to the following people:

Brian & Cecily

Mom & Dad

The wonderful members of my Patreon who inspire, support, and advise me, especially Susan Buttons

Amy, Stacey, and Emily for their beta reading and their excellent suggestions.

Stacey for proofing

Sue Laybourn for developmental and copy edits

Daphne du Maurier for the inspiration

A random GIF set that inspired Ned

And, most especially, **all my readers** who always make the blood, sweat, and tears of writing worthwhile.

For my Omegaverse fans with all my heart

**Important content warnings:** bullying, family coercion, family emotional manipulation and abuse, difficult pregnancy and birth, consent violations due to family coercion, sexual assault (not between the heroes), knotting, mpreg, omegaverse.

# PART ONE

## Bought and Sold

*In a world where omegas are treated as second-class citizens, and their precious heats are contracted and sold, they have little protection except a flimsy consent law that's rarely enforced.*

*Poor omegas can auction their heats off to the highest bidder. But wealthy men use their omega sons' heat and breeding for an entirely different purpose—to make alliances between powerful families.*

*Should a breeding be negotiated as part of the heat contract, and if a baby is conceived, an omega must live with his new alpha for the full term of the pregnancy—five months—in order to have steady access to gestation stabilizing compounds only the alpha can provide him.*

*The dual biological drives of heat and pregnancy keep these men together for the short term, but while all contracts end with an exchange of money, not all end in love.*

# Chapter One

EZER CHEWED HIS lower lip and employed his eraser with zest. The equation was a tough one, but he knew with persistence he'd conquer it. The concrete bench beneath his bony ass and the hard table under his sharp elbows made him ache all over, but there was nowhere else for him to wait for his da to come home from work. He didn't have a key to the apartment, and he didn't live here, though he visited as often as he could sneak away.

The late winter had dissolved into a soggy spring, and mud

puddles shimmered darkly all around the fenced-in area next to his da's apartment. A few rats squabbled over a crust near the drainpipe at the side of the yard, and there were odd pieces of clothing strewn about, as though thrown from one of the higher windows. Ezer's da's living situation was less than ideal and not beautiful to dwell on, so he'd broken out his notebooks and begun to play with equations to distract himself from it all.

The divorce between Ezer's alpha father and his da, the intimate term used for an omega parent, had been unusual and inequitable. The scandal it'd caused was still the subject of whispers amongst the upper crust of Wellport. Even in their society where omegas were given much fewer rights than alphas, it was unheard of to be as vindictive as George Fersee had been in divesting himself of a no-longer-pleasing omega.

Across town, at his father's mansion, Ezer lived in the lap of luxury with every extravagance lavished upon him, most of the time without him even needing to ask. But here, his da lived on cheap food and wore second-hand, threadbare clothes. Da hadn't been allowed to take anything of value when he'd left, not even his nicer clothes, and Father had burned everything after he was gone. Now Da fought just to dress and feed himself. Ezer often brought baskets of food and always wore his oldest jeans and sweatshirt when visiting. He couldn't bring himself to flaunt his tailored pants and expensive cashmere sweaters when he knew how much his da struggled.

Ezer's alpha father could easily afford to pay for a nicer place for Da to live, not to mention plenty of food for him to eat and nice clothes for his back. In fact, most alphas did just that when they took on another omega after dismissing or divorcing one they'd bred before. But George Fersee wasn't a man known for doing the right thing or taking the high road. He was a man for grudges, and he held a massive one against Amos Elson, Ezer's da, because he'd never birthed an alpha heir. Instead, Da had borne omega after omega—four in total—with Ezer being the last of them. His younger brother Rodan, the fifth child, had been the final straw—*he'd* been born a beta.

So after a horrifying and traumatic scene that'd left all the brothers sobbing, and left literal blood on the wall from where Da had resisted being ejected from his home, it'd been out with Da and in with a very young omega named Pete.

It still sickened him to think about the details.

Shaking memories from his head, Ezer looked up as an older omega with long gray hair stepped through the yard with a loaf of bread and a suspicious eye. He glared at Ezer, as if daring him to try to take his bread, and then let himself into the building with his key, glancing over his shoulder to where Ezer sat at the concrete table.

Ezer let the man go without asking to follow him in. The weather was grim with a hint of damp, but it wasn't raining, and he didn't want to frighten the man any more than he already had by loitering. Roughs Neck was an area known for hooligans who often laid in wait to grab whatever they could from anyone passing by. Ezer knew he was skinny, despite having plenty of food at his father's house, and that his sharp cheekbones gave him a hungry look, which many in his da's apartment building took as suspicious.

Going back to his equation, Ezer worked on it a bit more, getting stumped at the same place. He broke out the eraser again, and rubbed the incorrect numbers away, his mind going back to Pete. Ezer wished he could rub *him* away and things could go back to the way they had been.

But he knew they never would. He shouldn't resent Pete. It was never his fault. Besides, Pete was nice enough and already pregnant, and he seemed to make Ezer's father very happy.

George glowed when talking about Pete and was acting like a doting fool over him during every phase of the pregnancy. For Pete it was all hands and hugs, and sweet nothings in the young omega's ear.

But it was humiliating for Ezer to witness, not only as the son of his father's prior omega, but due to the wretched circumstances Da lived in now. He wondered if Pete even knew how Amos was treated these days? If so, how did he trust George not to use him the same way? Or did Pete imagine himself safe so long as he delivered the desired alpha heir? Ezer didn't know. He'd never asked. He couldn't stomach it.

After all Da'd done for Ezer's father, after the five labors he'd endured, and the promises George had made to him? It was disturbing to see how his father could turn that same affection off when it suited him and redirect it to someone else. Seeing Pete waltzing about the mansion blissfully naked, well-fucked, and large with child, just made it worse.

And, if his father's explanation was to be believed, it was all because Da hadn't delivered a "proper" heir. Despite science demonstrating that gender was determined by an alpha's sperm, despite Da's tears and begging, despite Ezer's as well and those of his brothers, George held fast to that line of reasoning. But Ezer suspected his father had spotted an ad for Pete's first heat and been struck with lust strong enough to decide throwing over his spouse and his family was worth satisfying that primal itch.

"Ugh!" Ezer inspected the torn paper. He'd grown irritated thinking of Pete and his father, erasing too hard. The paper crumpled back, opening a hole, revealing the black cover of the folder he'd placed beneath it.

The creak of the chain-link gate caught his attention, and he checked to see if his da had made it home yet.

"Well, look who's here."

Ezer's jaw ticced as he stared at the interloper. He wondered what Braden Tenmeter was even doing on this side of town, but he wasn't going to ask. He wasn't going to say anything at all to the asshole, nor to his two pals, Ned Clearwater and Finch Maddox, who followed him everywhere.

"It's our class's ugliest cocksleeve," Braden Tenmeter called out, swinging up on the chain-link fence with a nasty grin. So long as he stayed outside the barrier, Ezer was safe. He lowered his gaze back to his paper, trying to act unbothered. He stared at the equation, and for the first time ever, even math didn't make sense to him.

Braden scoffed. "Look at him trying to pretend like he isn't scared. Ha. His chin's wobbling." He laughed. "Such a wimp. Gonna cry, Cocksleeve?"

"I'd cry too, if I had to live here," Finch's voice rang out next.

Ned, always the most cowardly follower, murmured, "Let's go. This place sucks. Why did you even bring us here anyway?"

"You know why," Braden said. "To buy Bright's powder."

"And to get our hands on scrawny omega cocksleeves like this one," Finch said, sucking his teeth.

Ezer willed himself not to look up, to ignore them, but of course his body didn't obey. He glared at his three classmates ranged outside the fence. Braden leaned near the gate, swinging it open and banging it closed. His golden hair glinted in the sunshine, and his muscled arms flexed beneath his tight jean jacket. He wasn't as tall as Ezer, but he was much stronger, and Ezer had endured blows from his hammy fists often enough.

Next to him, Ned stood a full head taller and as burly as a full-grown alpha. His dark blond hair was a shade darker than Braden's, and his brutishly handsome face featured a strong jawline, heavy eyebrows, and stupidly pretty hazel eyes framed by stiff, fan-shaped lashes. As Ezer watched, Ned began to chew on the inside of his lower lip, an insecure, nervous signal that meant danger was ahead. Ezer was far too familiar with all of them from the long days of torment they subjected him to when school was in session. He'd at least hoped to escape their harassment over Spring Break.

"So what's it like living in a slum, Cocksleeve?" Braden asked, licking his thick lips. "Do the rats nibble your tiny dick at night while you're trying to sleep?"

"He's an omega. He doesn't need a dick anyway." Finch Maddox sneered, wiping his ever-dripping nose with the back of his shirtsleeve. "Don't know why they even have one."

Short, scrawny, and angry as hell, Finch was as ugly outside as he was inside. If he wasn't so rich, Braden and Ned wouldn't hang out with him at all. But his father owned the left side of the river, and no one wanted to be on Mr. Maddox's bad side. He was known to take out his son's grudges in the negotiation room, making life hard for entire families just because Finch was a nasty piece of work.

"He doesn't live here," Ned said.

"That's right," Finch said, making it sound filthy somehow. "Ezer just *visits*. His *omega parent* lives here."

"Ah, is that so?" Braden climbed onto the gate, using it like a swing, riding it. Ezer balled his hands into fists and waited.

Finch spoke up again, stepping closer to the fence. "This is all his father allowed his omega after dumping his ass. What do you think of *that*?" His tone made his opinion clear.

"Must be trash," Braden said, nudging Ned hard. "Right, Ned?"

"Sure," Ned agreed, looking pale. It always pissed Ezer off the way Ned went along with everything, never man enough to stand up to Braden and Finch. It was almost worse to know Ned had some kind of conscience but managed to override it enough to participate in his friends' harassment.

"Only ruined omegas get treated like garbage," Finch taunted.

Braden took it further, like always. "Are you trash, too, Cocksleeve? Did your father decide your ugly ass wasn't worth it? Did he send you here to stay with your da instead? Huh? Are you also nothing but a foul, rotten, used-up hole?"

"Shut up," Ezer said before he could stop himself. He didn't care what they said about him, but Da hadn't done anything wrong. It was his father's damned selfish pride and his lust for Pete that had put Da in this position.

"He speaks!" Braden said, swinging off the gate and then moving inside. Ned and Finch followed close behind. He tilted his head, considering Ezer. "What do you think, guys? Does he do more with his mouth? Does he, I don't know, suck?"

Ned flinched at that, and Finch snorted in laughter. "He's just an omega," Ned said. "You can't…" He motioned with his hands helplessly. "Do anything to him."

"Oh, there's a difference between shouldn't and can't, Ned. You know that by now." Braden licked his lips, eyes bright. "So, maybe I shouldn't. But yes, I can."

Ned gripped Braden's arm. "His father is George Fersee. *Your* father won't thank you for making an enemy there."

"Don't wuss out on us now," Finch said, reaching up to slap the back of Ned's head.

Braden agreed. "If George Fersee gave a rat's ass about this scrawny bit of omega flesh, his *so-called* son, our pal Cocksleeve wouldn't be sitting here outside this rat-infested apartment building, would he? He'd be back at his father's place in Cliffside, hanging by the pool with his brothers, drinking mimosas and waiting for the pleasure of his first heat as an 'untouched' omega. Instead, here he is, begging for our attention." He nudged Finch. "Right?"

"Like a slut," Finch added, raising a cruel brow. "Right, Cocksleeve? You're a slut."

The reminder of the fact that Ezer couldn't be sure what his father had planned for his first heat was an unwelcome one. He'd taken his first heat risk assessment test the month before, and the results were disquieting: he was small to carry a child, but hormonally on target for his age. Which meant until he was at the age of majority, it was his father's call whether to trigger his first heat, and his father's choice who he'd spend it with. Ezer had the right to refuse, but few omegas defied their fathers when it came to heats and matches.

His older brothers hadn't been triggered yet. Their father was waiting on the right matches for them, so there was every reason to think Ezer would be allowed to wait until he was much older as well. But there was always a risk of a surprise heat once hormones reached a certain level. Heat suppressants might fail, and an omega might "blossom" early. Ezer doubted his father would want to sell his heat in advance, but he might. His test had shown that while a pregnancy might be dangerous at his current size, he could otherwise support a heat whenever the family was ready. Ezer was *not* ready.

"He didn't deny it," Braden said.

"Looks like Cocksleeve wants dick." Finch grinned.

"Yeah. Just sitting out here hoping to catch this thick alpha cock," Braden murmured, grabbing his crotch to illustrate before stalking toward Ezer.

Ezer's hands balled up even tighter. He held on to the pencil, thinking it might work for a weapon.

"Braden," Ned interceded again, chewing on his inner lower lip, and crossing his arms over his chest. "Let's go. He's not doing anything wrong."

Braden rolled his eyes. "Stop playing a fucking hero. You

don't need to court and woo an omega like him. Don't you get it? He's nothing."

"He's George Fersee's son."

"He's Fersee's garbage," Braden contradicted. "If you want him, Ned, you should just *take him*." He lunged forward and Ezer jerked back, falling off the bench. His back slapped hard on the muddy ground, knocking the wind out of him in a painful rush. Brandishing his pencil in his attempt to get away from Braden's touch, Ezer hoped he could hurt Braden before Braden could hurt him. But then Finch was there, strong and fast, ripping the pencil from Ezer's fist and tucking it behind his own ear like a cigarette.

Braden laughed and loomed over Ezer, grabbing him by the legs. Ned hovered nearby, while Finch held Ezer's waist. "Get his pants down," Finch grunted, as Braden landed a punch to Ezer's gut. "Let's see if he's used up."

Ezer struggled, heaving, vomit rising in his throat. But Finch was stronger than he looked, and once he took hold of Ezer's hands, it was impossible to break free. Braden got Ezer's pants open as he ordered Ned to step on Ezer's shoulder to hold him down. Ezer fought the hands on him while Ned muttered protests but did nothing. And then Ned gave in, his boot landing on Ezer's right shoulder hard enough to hold him still. Black dots swirled in Ezer's eyes, air pumped in and out of his lungs painfully, and he struggled against Finch while Braden tugged at his pants.

"Get off me!" he shouted, trying to kick, but Braden straddled him and kept him on the ground. As his groin and upper thighs were bared to the cold air, Braden and Finch's laughter broke over him like an icy wave.

"You can't do this," Ned said, his voice breathless. He lifted his boot enough to give Ezer room to jerk half upright.

Braden shoved Ezer down again. "Ned, for fuck's sake! Shut up! Hold him!"

Ned's boot hovered over Ezer's chest again, not quite touching, as Ezer struggled, and Braden started to unzip his own pants, his erection stiff and visible through the material.

"Get away from him," Da's dark voice thundered across the yard. There was a metallic clicking sound in the sudden silence that followed.

Finch took off running, and so did Ned.

For his part, Braden took the time to kick Ezer in the side and deliver a threat. "Not done with you yet, Cocksleeve. When school starts? Be ready."

All three assholes hustled out the gate, leaving Ezer dazed and shaking on the ground, with his da pointing a pistol at their retreating backs.

"SO YOU'RE NOT going to tell me who those boys were or what that was about?" Da took off his light brown sweater and put a kettle on the stove. His blond hair held gray at the sides now, and his blue eyes displayed small fans of wrinkles at the edges. Regarding Ezer with exhausted sadness as he waited for the kettle to heat, he pressed, "Nothing?"

The kitchen was as clean as Da could get it, but nothing could get the grime from between the tiles on the floor and walls. It was bad enough that Da had left a pampered life to have to work, but to see that the fruits of his labor garnered so little—it was heartbreaking.

Ezer kept his mouth shut. After a shower to scrub off the dirt and mud, and after cataloging his bruises, he was feeling a little more human, but he still didn't want to burden his da with the details of his situation. What could Da do about it? No one had come to Amos's rescue when he'd been sent away. No friends of status, no relatives had stepped up and offered to help. What good would it do to tell Amos his son was being bullied by the "finest" alphas at his school, when Amos had been bullied by their parents?

Rubbing the towel over his wet hair before tossing it onto the back of one of the shabby kitchen chairs, Ezer shrugged and asked instead, "How was your day at work, Da? You look tired."

Yes, Amos Elson, of the famous Elson Street Elsons, now spent his days on an assembly line, sorting trash into recyclable and non-recyclable piles. When Ezer was a child, his da had been so handsome, with blond, wavy hair, blue eyes and sun-kissed skin from all the time spent idling pregnant by the pool. And he'd always had a strong, straight back, and muscled arms that could lift a squealing Ezer high into the air. Now Amos was gray all over, not just in his hair, and he had the stooped shoulders of a man who spent all day, every day bent low, picking through trash.

*Trash.*

Braden's voice echoed in Ezer's head. Oh, how his da's ancestors must be rolling in their graves. And all for what? For pregnant Pete.

"Son, if you think I'm going to forget that I had to pull a gun on three boys who were attacking you, then you're wrong. Talk to me."

Ezer winced. "Can you just let it go? What good can come from talking about it?"

"It's not as though I can't figure it out," Da said, adjusting the heat beneath the kettle. He rubbed his temples and then added in a horrified, quiet voice, "They were trying to rape you."

Ezer held back a shiver, determined not to let his father see his fear. "It wasn't going to get that far." *Oh, yes, it was, and if not for Da…* He gulped, unable to stop that tic from making its way through.

Da rolled his eyes. "We both know you were outmanned. There's no shame in that. What's shameful is their behavior." He took a seat across the table from Ezer. The expanse of scarred wood felt impossible to cross, until Da reached for Ezer's hand.

"I know, and I'm fine." The bruises sang on his back and shoulders, but he wasn't going to admit to being hurt, even though he was already clinging to his da's fingers like a baby.

Da studied him. "They go to school with you."

Ezer nodded.

"They bother you there, too?"

Ezer swallowed hard, wishing he were a better liar. "Yeah."

"Your father knows." Stated. Not asked.

"He says I should stop being so weird."

Da's jaw tightened and released in a rhythm Ezer remembered well from the days before the divorce, when Father would make a proclamation that didn't sit well with Da, but he would just swallow it down like bad-tasting medicine.

"They wouldn't dare bother you at the mansion, though," Da said, narrowing his eyes. "The guards would keep them from even getting onto the property."

Maybe, but maybe not. Given who these boys were, his father might very well send out open-ended engraved invitations for them to come onto the property and choose one of his four omega sons to enjoy. But it would do no good to let his da know that. "Da, it doesn't matter. I want to see you. I want to be here with you whenever I can."

Da sighed, getting up to pour water from the now-screaming kettle over the cheap instant coffee. He stirred both mugs and came to Ezer with one held out handle-first, taking the brunt of the heat on his palm. "I love having you here, son. I do. But it's not safe. This apartment, this side of town, nothing about it is fit for someone like you."

"Someone like me? What about someone like you?" He couldn't contain his outrage. "This apartment building isn't fit for anyone to live here, Da."

Between the artist with his oil paints and flammable rags on the first floor, and the book hoarder on the second, and the poor dressmaker with her fabrics, and the "chemists" in the attic making Bright's powder by the truckload, the place was a fire hazard. That didn't even take into account the mold, the rats, and the tendency for raw sewage to back up.

"Yes, I know. But some of us have no choice. It's the best I can afford."

Ezer fiddled with the handle of his coffee mug, forestalling further discussion by taking a sip. It burned going down, replacing the icy coldness that had taken hold in the moments when he thought Braden would be successful in getting his pants all the way off, and in whatever else he had meant to do then.

"Why did no one protect you, Da? Not a cousin, not a friend." He'd wondered this so many times in the past but been too afraid to ask. In his mind, his da was the persecuted innocent and his father the baleful bastard, and the possibility he might learn anything different had been too scary. But now, thinking of his da's fierce voice preventing further torment and rescuing him from Braden, Ned, and Finch's attack, he couldn't help but wonder why no one had loved Amos enough to do the same for him when George had used him so badly.

"I burned too many bridges," Da said.

"How?" Ezer had never seen his father as anything other than acquiescent and kind, as well as strong and good.

"It's difficult to explain. There's a certain way for an omega to be. In society." He frowned. "I was…not like that. Though I tried."

"What way?"

"Omegas are happy, pregnant, lustful, and supportive. They don't put their own needs above the needs of their family and never above the needs of their alpha."

"You supported Father."

"I did. But I resented it."

Ezer tried to reconcile these words with his memory of his happy, laughing, pampered Da. "But you were happy? With us?"

"You and your brothers brought me so much joy," Da smiled. "But your father and I, behind closed doors, had words quite often about the raising of you, and the need for an alpha heir, even when there were plenty of cousins to choose from, and, of course, I couldn't stomach the way your father did business."

Ezer couldn't stand it either. "He used the way he treated you to prove to his business associates that they shouldn't test him. That he was willing to do anything to get what he wants."

"I know. And he is. That's part of why it's dangerous being here, Ezer. Being around me? When he loathes me so much? It's not safe."

"I'm not going to abandon you, Da."

"You should," he said, the steam from his mug drifting up around his face. "Your brothers don't visit me, and they've all been very clear about the reasons. I miss them terribly, but I understand. No, more than that: I approve."

Ezer's throat tightened. He wasn't going to dignify his brothers' selfishness by discussing it with his selfless Da. They were assholes, like their father, and that was all there was to it.

"They're protecting their futures. Because reputations matter," Da said, as if Ezer needed it spelled out. "Distancing themselves from me is a good way to stay safe from your father's capriciousness, *and* from the likes of those young men today." Da cocked a brow. "Or better yet, to stay appealing to them."

Ezer blinked. "What are you saying?"

"I know you'd tell me more about what happened out there if they weren't powerful boys. That means their fathers are powerful as well, and *that* means..." Da shrugged. "That means they are heat contract and marriage material. Especially in your father's eyes. Drawing their attention in a negative way, like you have, is dangerous to your chances, to your brothers' chances, and to your father's business goals."

Ezer huffed. "I was only waiting for my da and working out some math problems for fun. How is that a negative way to draw their attention? I didn't ask them to stop and attack me."

"No, of course not. But you have to admit you don't play the games other omegas do, and that'll chafe any alpha, particularly a powerful one."

"You mean an entitled one."

"Perhaps."

There was a long silence as Ezer sipped his coffee, his heart aching, and a stubborn refusal to accept his da's words took hold.

Da spoke again. "Your brothers have a larger outlook than you."

"Do they?" Ezer wasn't going to be any alpha's adoring plaything. If that was what his brothers wanted, then they could take their so-called "larger outlook" and shove it because that life looked nothing more than stunted to him.

"Yes. And your brothers want to make sure they'll make a good match in the future. With your father having moved on with another omega, one who will hopefully provide the alpha heir he's been looking for, they'll need to make a good marriage with someone of substantial fortune if they want to continue to live at the level they do now."

Ezer sniffed and lifted his chin. "I don't care about any of that. They have different priorities than I do."

"Obviously." Da stood to adjust the second-hand quilt, faded from washing, that was pinned on a line over the stove to dry. Then he sat down again, his expression all seriousness. "And what is your plan for yourself, Ezer? If not to make a good match?"

"To auction my heats to the highest bidder. That'll be enough to pay for school." He left off the part about wanting to apply most of his proceeds to helping his da live a better life.

Da would only take offense and refuse to be helped, and Ezer wouldn't have that. Once he had heat money, then he'd find a way to make Da accept.

"And then what?"

"I'm good at math. Reading I'll never be able to do, but my teachers give the tests to me orally now." That had been thanks to Da's input prior to the dissolution of their family. "And so long as I pay attention in the classroom, I learn quickly. I could become a professor. Teach."

Da studied him a long moment and then whispered, "You're very smart. I always told your father you were."

And yet Father had never believed Da, and still didn't. If reading wasn't such a problem, then maybe Father would dislike Ezer less, but, as it stood, between his inability to read and his loyalty to his da, Ezer was his father's least favorite son. "I'll make a career of my own in mathematics, one way or another, and remain alone. I don't need an alpha or a husband. I don't even want children."

Da cocked his head. "Don't you, though?"

Ezer did, actually.

Babies were delicious things he craved the scent of, and children were funny and cute. He wanted the opportunity to have a happy family of his own. Despite all evidence to the contrary, some part of him still believed it was possible to have such a thing.

What he didn't want was to have to submit to an alpha who, depending on the contract worked out in advance, could take legal custody of his children and all his property by default, even if the marriage ended due to no fault of Ezer's—like birthing too many omegas, or his alpha's wandering eye.

Ezer would rather be childless than face any future where he was at an alpha's mercy financially, emotionally, and physically.

And after what his father had done to Da, Ezer didn't know how he could ever trust an alpha again.

"You're angry," Da said, touching his cheek. His fingers were cool, and his eyes were sad. "I understand why. But your life doesn't have to be like mine, Ezer. You could find a good match. With an alpha you care about. Who cares about *you*. You could make a life with him in your own way."

Ezer lifted his chin, remembering Braden's strong hands on his body, Ned's boot on his chest, and Finch's nasty laugh. He remembered his own clawing fear, and how helpless he'd been.

"I do plan to make a life my own way, Da. Alone."

"I suppose there's no reasoning with you then. Just know your father has other plans for you. And by coming to visit me you're cementing them further. I love you, Ezer, but for your own sake, you should go home in the morning and never come back."

Da stood then and left the kitchen, his unfinished mug still steaming, and the heavy, wet quilt dripping onto the hot, hissing stove.

# Chapter Two

*Six Months Earlier*

"SORRY."

Ned flinched, turning toward the low voice issuing an unnecessary apology. Ned had been the one to knock into the small omega—and, hell's bells, no omega was ever so fragile-looking as this one—so he should be the one to offer an apology.

But the words died on his lips as he gazed at the boy. He had the most beautiful eyes Ned had ever seen. Clear as the sky, and big enough to drown in. As he stared down into them, Ned's heart gave a weird thump, and his fingers began to tingle.

The bell rang and the already hectic school grounds fell into chaos. The omega, whom Ned had never seen before, winced, and seemed to brace himself for the flow of bodies, his big eyes growing even wider.

Doubleton Academy was Ned's third school in as many years. There'd been a few scandals in his past, most of them not half as bad as they sounded. Luckily for him, his uncle, the powerful and wealthy Heath Clearwater, had been willing to clear up Ned's scrapes. His most recent disgrace, though, had led to him being expelled from Peay's Elite, along with six other alphas. Two of those other alphas had followed him to Doubleton, and as Ned stared in awe at the strange little omega he'd almost knocked to the ground, those alphas materialized at his side.

"C'mon," Braden said, punching Ned in the shoulder. "Class

starts soon."

Meanwhile Finch spat on the ground, standing there being generally repugnant. Everything about him, from his scent to his smile, made Ned's stomach churn. He wished Braden and Finch's fathers had sent them elsewhere after they'd been expelled from Peay's. Instead, the men had ridden on Uncle Heath's coattails at Doubleton and asked for the same deal for their scandal-ridden offspring.

Lazy assholes.

"Ned, come on," Braden said, kicking Ned's boot and nodding toward the series of low-lying, red brick buildings where they'd spend their senior year. "Bell rang. There're omegas to seduce and teachers to terrorize. No time to lose."

Finch laughed, and it was ugly as always.

The little omega, still standing near Ned, looked between the three of them with cutely knotted brows, and then glanced down at a paper clenched in his shaking hand. Ned's heart quickened. He wanted to take the omega under his arm and guide him safely through his day; he wanted to feed him, nurture him, and kiss him in the shadows behind the school. The impulse was dizzying.

"I'm not sure where I should go," the omega said, sticking out his chin and meeting Ned's gaze in a show of confidence. "I'm new here."

"We're new too," Ned said, but he reached out to take the paper anyway, deciding he *would* guide the omega to wherever it was he needed to be. Braden and Finch jerked him away before his fingers touched the paper.

"C'mon," Finch sneered. "That one's going to end up a useless slut. Look at him. Couldn't birth a decent-sized babe to save his life. Don't waste time on him."

Ned jerked his arm loose and turned back to the omega whose eyes had grown stony and fierce. Words caught in Ned's throat, but as he started to speak, the second bell rang. The chaos turned into a crush, as a swath of young alphas, betas, and omegas raced through the grounds trying to avoid being late to class, cutting Ned off from the strange omega with sky-blue eyes and tiny, delicate bones. There'd been something about him, Ned didn't know what, but he couldn't stop thinking about him for the rest of the day.

IT WAS THE fourth day of school, a beautiful day in the city of Wellport before Ned was able to talk to the omega again.

The cerulean blue sky was full of puffy white clouds that had drifted in. The city was warm at the end of summer, but a soft breeze off the sea kept it from feeling stuffy or stale, despite the ever-growing number of people, cars, buses, ships, and trains, all of which left unseemly detritus behind.

Doubleton Academy was also situated at the top of a canyon, and the views outside the classroom windows were almost as good as the view from Ned's bedroom at home, though not quite as stupendous as the views from the room he'd slept in last summer at his Uncle Heath's home.

Over the summer spent with his uncle, his uncle's omega Adrien, and their son Michael, Ned had changed. He'd come to see his striving life with his father in a very different way. The "truths" he'd taken for granted in the past—*anything you truly want is worth any cost*, for example—no longer made sense, and he'd spent a few days reeling from that realization after he'd first returned. Even now, in the middle of class, he felt torn between the boy his father expected him to be and the man he now knew he wanted to become.

For example, he was seated beside Braden and Finch, like

always, but he didn't *want* to be there. No, he wanted to be sitting across the room beside the new, small, quiet omega who worked equations all day long, even in their literature classes, and during lunch, and everywhere else. Ned had no doubt, after days of observing him, the omega even mentally worked on them during physical education, too.

There was something compelling in the young man's ways. He was quiet, yes, but Ned saw wonderful flashes of defiance on his face from time to time. There was more under the surface of the boy, and Ned wanted to know what he might discover.

"Stop staring," Braden said, kicking Ned's shin.

"What?" Ned asked, denying it.

"If you want to fuck him, I'm sure it can be arranged." Finch never minced words.

"I...what?" Ned blinked, disturbed. "I'm done with all that. I thought we'd agreed that we all were."

Braden laughed. "An alpha who's done with fucking omegas? Please. You and I both know we're just biding our time until we go back to having our fun. There are plenty of omegas here who'll want to play the naked games with us, given a little incentive."

Ned shook his head. He'd already gone that route too many times, and he was tired of it. Before summering with Adrien and Uncle Heath, he'd never known what an alpha and omega could truly be together, what they could have. He'd thought of omegas as existing solely for an alpha's pleasure. Though he'd always known when he was old enough, he'd have to make a longer commitment than a tumble in bed in order to score an heir of some kind, he'd assumed it would be contractual—nothing more, nothing less.

But Adrien and Uncle Heath weren't like that. They were in love. They were happy. They respected each other and were growing a family together. Their life looked like a fairy tale from the outside.

Ned had never known so much laughter, love, softness, and adoration could exist in a family until he'd stayed with Heath and Adrien. Now Ned longed for a life like that, a beautiful one made together with an omega like Adrien—someone smart, loving, and sweet. A man who would be a good da to his children. Devoted.

Ned let his eyes wander back to the new kid. Would *he* be like Adrien? Or was he more like the omegas his father used? Mercenary and cynical?

Those bright eyes met Ned's, and suddenly he had a hard time breathing.

"What's the hell's wrong with you?" Braden bit out.

"We'll get some Bright's powder in him after school, and he'll be fine," Finch said.

Ned shrugged. He didn't use Bright's powder anymore either. Adrien had told him all about how his omega parent, a man named Nathan, had been a fan of the stuff and it'd damaged his heart, cutting his life short. Ned wanted to live a long time, become a strong, successful alpha, and watch his children grow up, see them have grandchildren even. Braden and Finch would call all those dreams ridiculous and stupid, but Heath had called them mature and he'd seemed proud.

"Class, we'll be dividing into groups for our first project. Please change desks accordingly."

Ned couldn't believe his luck when he was put into the new omega's group.

*Ezer.*

Ezer Fersee, the teacher had called him. Which meant that he was one of George Fersee's four omega sons. Ned's heart convulsed with joy. Fersee was in the peerage, too. They were of the same class. That meant whatever Ned was feeling every time he saw Ezer? It wasn't completely hopeless.

Still, he couldn't bring himself to speak to Ezer, and the omega didn't speak to him either. They sat in the same group of four and worked on the project in silence, though Ned couldn't help but notice Ezer never wrote anything down. He contributed his thoughts in a confident, quiet voice, and the rest of the group put them onto paper.

At one point, Ezer dropped his chewed-up pencil on the floor, and Ned stooped to pick it up. Lifting his head, he beheld the wide, sky-blue beauty of Ezer's eyes, and his heart pounded so violently he felt lightheaded and dumb. Too lightheaded to speak as he'd passed the pencil back to Ezer's delicate-looking fingers.

Embarrassed, and sure everyone around him knew what effect Ezer had on him, Ned tried to bury himself in his textbook, feigning a sudden dedication to their project, when he just needed time to figure out why his blood was rushing so hard and, despite taking deep breaths, he still felt dizzy. Was he developing asthma?

"You need to stay away from him," Braden said over lunch, sneering as he picked out the direction of Ned's gaze. They sat with a redheaded alpha named Riley, also new to the school. Braden had befriended him a few days before, and his father was a supplier for Finch's father's business.

"Huh?" Ned tore his eyes away from where Ezer was picking at his sandwich and soup. "Stay away from who?"

"That cocksleeve," Braden said, using the crudest term possible, one reserved for an omega of exceedingly low class and breeding, if not an outright prostitute.

"He's George Fersee's son," Ned said, blinking in confusion. "You can't call him that."

"I can actually," Braden said with a smirk. "And you would too if you knew."

"If I knew what?"

"Everything I know."

"And what do you know?"

Braden shrugged. "Plenty."

Riley piped up between big, ill-mannered bites of his ham sandwich. "He's a transfer from St. Hauers Academy."

Ned blinked. St. Hauers was a school for omegas with severe learning difficulties—Braden and Finch had uglier words for it.

"It's sad, really. I started preschool with him, and he was smart enough then. It's just once we turned seven, and we moved up to kindergarten, he couldn't learn to read." Riley shook his head. "I hear he still can't read or write. Has to take his tests orally."

Braden's lips twisted up in a hateful smile. "Ah. See? So he's stupid *and* a whore cocksleeve's son, making him a cocksleeve himself. Like I said."

Riley frowned. "I wouldn't say that."

"Well, I would."

Riley shrugged, but something about the way his face changed made Ned think he wouldn't be sitting with their group in the future. Smart of him.

Braden went on. "Besides, we know all about him and his da."

"Do we?" Finch said, lifting his brows at Ned. "He clearly doesn't."

"He doesn't need to, either. Look, Ned, stay away from him," Braden commanded like he was the boss of him. "You're too good to wet your dick with that filth."

Ned gritted his teeth. He didn't want to "wet his dick" with anyone. That wasn't what he wanted from Ezer.

Riley caught Ned's eye. "He's not very handsome anyway." He seemed confused by Ned's interest and the other alphas' nasty warnings. He ticked things off on his fingers: "Not bright, not handsome. Rich, sure, but that just means he won't die a virgin." Riley looked pained to have to admit these things. "I've heard some of those greedy jerks talking about him and what he's worth." He nodded toward a table of middle-class alphas Ned's peers spurned. "They're plotting for him."

Of course they were. They'd be happy to take on a "less attractive," "less intelligent" omega for the chance at status and money. And George Fersee had both.

Ned wasn't immune to the lure of status and money either. His father had run through all his inheritance ages ago and constantly asked Ned for access to the funds Heath had set aside for Ned and his future.

Marrying an omega from the Fersee family would put an end to his father's money worries. But Ned didn't plan to marry until well after college, once he could afford to buy the heat of a quality omega. One who would hopefully have eyes like Ezer Fersee.

Though he suspected no one had eyes like Ezer.

That afternoon, leaving the school property on foot, heading toward the subway station to make their way back home, Ned caught sight of Ezer sitting beneath a tree alone, scribbling in one of his notebooks. Palms going sweaty, he dropped back and broke away from Braden and Finch, hoping they wouldn't notice. He made his way toward Ezer alone, pulse thrumming and his stomach tilting. Was he going to throw up?

Ezer chin jerked up as Ned came to a stop beside him, and he squinted into the sun, trying to see Ned from where he sat on the dusty ground. His notebook was covered in equations. Ned squatted next to him and pointed at the page. "That makes sense to you?" he asked.

Great. *Those* were the first words he'd said to Ezer? Ugh. Worse that they were a confession of his own stupidity.

Ezer blinked up at him cautiously. "Yes."

"Ah."

"What've you got here, Ned?"

Ned's hackles rose as Braden's smarmy voice came from behind. "Inviting the cocksleeve to our party this weekend?"

Ezer's expression shuttered, and his jaw clenched. He moved to gather his things, but Finch shot his foot out, putting the sole of his boot against Ezer's small shoulder and shoving him back to the tree trunk.

"Hey!" Ned shouted, moving to protect Ezer, but Braden—bigger, tougher—pushed him aside, and squatted down himself.

"You're ugly, but after a few drinks we'll still fuck you," he said, running a finger down Ezer's cheek, and chucking under his chin. "My father's house. I'm sure you know where it is. Saturday. You can be one of…eh, a dozen."

"No," Ned said, pushing Braden out of the way. He'd promised his uncle no more orgies, no more Bright's powder, and he meant to keep those promises.

"*Yes*," Braden said. "Don't get all prudish, Ned. You've fucked more omegas than you can count on all your fingers and toes. Don't play sweet just to get your dick in this stupid St. Hauers' trash. You're better than that. Better than *him*."

Ezer reached up and shoved at Finch's boot, somehow managing to knock it away. He stood, trembling, his eyes hot with rage. "Leave me alone. I wouldn't fuck any of you even if you held a gun to my head. I'd rather die. Alpha scum. All of you."

"Fine. Have it your way, cocksleeve," Braden said. "You just went from fuckable-*ish* to being on my *super special* list." Ezer stiffened. "Guess what? That won't be fun for you."

"He's going to run to his father," Ned said, his heart pounding. He should put a stop to this. He just didn't know how.

"No, he won't," Braden said with so much confidence that

Ned shuddered. "Will you?"

Ezer glared up at him.

"Because, as it happens, my father is working on a deal with George Fersee. He's investing millions in Fersee's next building project. I'd hate to see what Mr. Fersee would do if that fell through all because his son was a tattletale who decided to cause me trouble."

Ned gritted his teeth.

"Besides, if Fersee thinks his most worthless omega son can't handle being here, he'll just send him back to somewhere he knows he's safe," Braden went on. It drove Ned nuts how much Braden talked while he tormented people. He was like a movie villain, all blah blah blah, like he had all the time in the world to tear people down before slitting their throats. "And this dumb shit here doesn't want to go back to St. Hauers, does he? He wants to stay here where people have brains. Am I right, Cock-sleeve?"

As Ezer's eyes filled with tears, Ned wished he'd never met Braden and Finch.

"Yup," Finch said. "That's your name now by the way: Cock-sleeve."

Ezer's lower lip trembled but he put out his chin. He said nothing.

Braden cooed. "It's a perfect name for such scrawny omega, huh? He'd be pretty tight, yeah? Don't worry. You're still invited to the party…if you want to make some alpha friends." He smirked. "There's no better way to make an alpha like you than to spread your ass open for him. He might even like it enough to take you under his wing at school." Braden eyed Ned. "This one's clearly dying for it."

Ezer snarled.

Bradon stood, grabbing Ned's arm. "C'mon."

Ned jerked free, turning back toward Ezer.

But Ezer's beautiful eyes weren't so beautiful now. They were full of frothing hate and rage. He hawked a loogie at Ned, hitting his uniform jacket with a fat wad of saliva and snot. It dripped down the navy material.

"You did *not* just do that," Finch growled, and lunged.

"Stay the fuck away from me," Ezer gritted out.

As Ned stared at the spit on his blazer, a strange frozen helplessness held him. He looked up just in time to see Finch's fist connect with Ezer's gut. No visible bruises. Finch's usual style. Ned stepped forward to pull Finch off Ezer where he curled on the ground, but the headmaster came out of the main building, shouting, "What's going on over there?"

Braden's grip was strong as he hauled Ned away from where Ezer lay gasping. "C'mon, unless you want your Uncle Heath to have to find yet another new school for us."

Shaken, mind whirling, Ned let Finch and Braden lead him toward the subway station. They jumped the stiles and leapt onto the first train in their race to get away from the headmaster who had come after them in full pursuit.

"He wasn't wearing his glasses," Finch said, laughing. "Everyone knows Headmaster Wendel is blind without them."

Ned *didn't* know that. They'd only been at Doubleton a few weeks. How did Finch and Braden get this kind of information? They always did, though, at every school they'd attended together, and Ned wished he could get away from them for good.

As the train jostled through the tunnels, shame filled Ned. Braden and Finch's giddy laughter at what they'd said and done to Ezer made him sick. He vowed he'd stop being friends with them. He'd sit with Ezer at lunch. He'd sit alone. He'd make himself an outcast, but there was no way he could stomach another second of their crap.

Maybe he'd even turn them in. Come out the hero. Ezer would like him then, wouldn't he? And even if he didn't, maybe Ned would like himself.

That had to count for something.

# Chapter Three

*Present Time*

SIX MONTHS AGO, Ned had promised himself that he was going to end his friendship with Braden and become Ezer's protector, but that hadn't happened. His reasons were shameful and could be summed up with a single sentence: Ned was a coward and a very bad person.

The day after the incident on the fourth day of school, Ned's father Lidell had made it clear that because his brother Heath had cut him off, their livelihood was in the hands of Braden and Finch's fathers and the contracts they held with Lidell's company. He'd praised Ned for keeping in those boys' good graces.

So now, the morning after the shameful event in the courtyard outside Ezer's da's run-down apartment building, Ned lounged by his father's pool, soaking in the light winter sun, and stewing in self-hatred. He chewed his bottom lip and tossed restlessly on the lounger. He should've kicked Braden in the face like he'd wanted to do. He'd been about to. Truly. He just should've done it faster.

Like always, he'd been paralyzed with fear.

Why? He was bigger than Braden, and much bigger than Finch. He could take them both down in a fight. So what if their fathers turned on his? Who cared if making enemies of them could result in his father losing everything?

Who was he kidding? *He* cared about that.

But what Braden and Finch had done to Ezer the day before? *That* had been more than the casual brutality and bullying they sent Ezer's way at school—a nasty comment here, a boot to the ass there. They'd never set out to *rape* him before.

Braden had claimed plenty of times that Ezer was too stuck-up and needed to be made to understand that omegas like him were lucky to get any attention at all from an alpha of the peerage. But Ned didn't know what had changed yesterday, or why Braden had decided to target Ezer sexually.

Ezer hadn't done anything to deserve it. *No one* would have deserved that…

Again, though, who was he kidding? Of course he knew what had been different yesterday. It wasn't Ezer, though. It was Braden and Finch. They'd been cranked up on Bright's powder again. They always got vicious on the stuff, and Ezer had been the unlucky omega to catch their attention. Worse, he was the unlucky omega who had a history of denying Braden and Finch the one thing they craved more than Bright's powder: fearful respect.

It was grotesque. All of it.

But Ned's part in it, standing by, doing nothing of any real use, was sickening. He hated himself.

*Coward.*

"Ned, are you feeling okay?" Earl, his personal servant from childhood, appeared by the lounger, blocking out the pale sun. Paid by his Uncle Heath and married to Heath's own childhood servant, Simon, Earl had been around the family longer than Ned had been alive. "It's too cold to go swimming, dear, or are you just sunning?"

Ned grunted, wanting to unburden himself to his trusted friend, but feeling embarrassed. He'd confessed his sins to Earl sometimes in the past, often leaving out the absolute worst details, and Earl had always helped him to feel better. But Ned also knew Earl would worry if he heard about Ned's expedition to Roughs Neck for Bright's powder, and he'd worry even more if he knew about the bullying of George Fersee's son.

He'd be disappointed, too.

Ned couldn't stand to have Earl disappointed in him.

Earl tapped his leg. "Scoot over, you. Let me feel your forehead."

"I'm not sick," Ned said, moving over anyway, and enjoying the pampering despite his protests. "I'm angry."

Earl's bony fingers were cool and dry on his sweaty forehead. The sun was warm, despite the cool weather. Life in Wellport was considered pleasant by those who lived in the northern, and less temperate areas of the country. A day like today, mild and cool enough to warrant a sweater in the shade, was as bad as winter ever got. No snow, no ice. Ned remembered those cold days from when he and his father, Lidell, had lived farther from his Uncle Heath. But the move nearer to the ocean had been for the best. If he sat and squinted from his father's high patio, he could make out the waves crashing against the cliffs in the distance.

"Angry about what?" Earl asked, smoothing Ned's hair from his forehead and smiling at him. Thin as a whip, and gray on top, Earl had probably been handsome once, but time had taken its toll. He seemed sadder now, too, since Uncle Heath had moved to the outskirts of the city taking Simon, Earl's husband, with him. Simon had been unwilling to abandon his charges (Heath and Adrien's son Michael, plus another babe on the way) so he and Earl saw each other on weekends now. It was clearly a hardship. Ned had thought about sending Earl away to live with Simon so he could be happier. Ned wasn't a baby anymore and could do without a personal servant. But then he would find himself in a situation like this one, and, no, he still needed Earl by his side.

"Out with it," Earl said with that nudge of command that always did the trick for Ned.

He let his hatred out, without regard to Earl's finer feelings. "Fuck Braden Tenmeter! And fuck Finch Maddox! And fuck their fathers, too!"

Earl's brows twitched, but he didn't reprimand Ned for his language. "Indeed?"

"Yes, *fuck* them. If I didn't have to play nice with those assholes for the sake of Father's business contracts—"

Earl tutted. "Something young men like you shouldn't have any knowledge of anyway, if I do say so myself."

"Yes, well, if I didn't have to kiss their ugly asses for Father's sake, I wouldn't hang out with them at all." The clouds shifted over the sun, and Ned shivered on the lounger.

"I should think not." Earl took his jacket off and spread it over Ned's shoulders and chest. The lingering warmth from Earl's body made Ned feel safe. He pulled it closer around and took a sniff of it, too. Cigars and lemon drops. Oh, Earl. He loved him so much. What would he do if he *did* decide to go help with the new baby at Heath's when it came? "Go on, Ned. Tell me everything."

"Finch and Braden, they're…they're such…dicks," Ned finished, wishing there were stronger words in his repertoire, but unsure if stronger words even existed. If they did, he'd apply them to Braden and Finch for sure. "I hate them."

"And you've hated them for a very long time. They've gotten you into all kinds of trouble. Like that orgy last year."

Ned blushed. He hated that anyone knew about that, much less Earl. He'd been such a stupid, horny *idiot.* Fucking a string of omegas at a sex party thrown by Braden's older alpha brother, acting like he was some kind of king, and feeling like one too.

He'd fucked omegas before, but that party had been next level, with gorgeous omegas handpicked from one of the local colleges. He'd been pumped full of Bright's powder and flying high. He'd never felt so powerful, and neither had the other alphas with him.

He and Braden had strutted around school for days afterward feeling like royalty. Only to find out later that in the basement that night, at the same house, during the same party, there had been some deeply disturbing things going on without the omega in question's consent. One of the alphas they were supposed to have graduated with was in prison now. Braden's older brother had gotten off with a slap on the wrist, but there was money behind that decision, Ned knew.

In the end, he'd been lucky Uncle Heath had stepped in and gotten all of that cleared from his record. He'd come so close to having colleges closed to him forever, as well as any decent marriage. And all for a few hours of feeling high on powder and acting as if he could fuck any sweet hole in the world. How stupid was that?

"Heath would like you to be done with those two, Simon tells me."

"Yes, I know. But that comes with a high price." He gave Earl a significant look. They were both aware of his father's situation. No one could live in the house and not be. They'd be high and dry within a month of being cut off by the Maddoxes and Tenmeters.

"It does. So what have they done now?" Earl asked, crossing one leg over the other and twining his fingers in his lap.

Ned squirmed beneath Earl's jacket, unwilling to meet his old servant's eye.

Earl hummed, and then said, "Oh, I see. It's something you've done as well, then, and you're ashamed of it."

Ned gave a sharp nod. "Yes. And it's awful. I hate it. I hate *myself* for it." He flopped back on the lounger, with all the miserable angst of an idiot alpha who had reluctantly participated in the roughing up and near-rape of his hopeless, desperate crush.

"Hmm, well, shame is uncomfortable to endure."

Ned twisted up his face, wishing he had the balls to ask Earl what he knew of shame, just so he wouldn't feel so alone in his badness. But he suspected that no matter what Earl shared with him, it wouldn't take the sting of what he'd done away. And it probably shouldn't.

Earl touched Ned's hair, moving a lock off his forehead. "Is there a way to make up for what you've done?"

Ned squirmed again, a strange, pulsing rush going through him as he imagined going back to the apartment building, finding Ezer there at the table again, and apologizing to him. Perhaps with flowers. And a declaration of intent. A promise to make his life better. To marry him.

Ugh. He was an idiot.

"No. Not really," he huffed. "And I don't know how to make it stop, because it's Braden and Finch, too, and if I don't go along with them…" He spread his hands. "I hate that I have to make nice with them all the time."

"What's the worst that would happen if you stopped hanging out with these boys?"

Ned huffed. "You know."

Earl nodded. "I know what you *think* would happen and what your father *fears* would happen, but are you that important to them? Maybe they'd be content to let you go with just a little bullying. A loss of social status for you, yes, but with Heath's money you're still protected. Your father less so, but—"

"Heath will have two heirs soon. I'm content with what he's given me in trust, but we both know that if my father gets his hands on it—and if he's not making money from those Tenmeter and Maddox contracts, then he will—my accounts will be drained in no time."

"You have to tell your father no, Ned."

"Then how will he live?"

"Angrily."

"How will *we* live?"

"Tightly."

Ned sighed.

Lidell wasn't a heartless man, but he was terrible with money. He suffered from poor judgment and even worse luck. He wasn't a likable man by most standards either. It was astounding he'd been able to keep the Tenmeter and Maddox contracts as long as he had.

Ned didn't think he was being egotistical to think his father keeping the Tenmeter contracts was due, in no small part, to Ned's "friendship" with Braden, and the association that brought with Braden's extended family. Every time he went to Braden's house, his younger omega brother, Ashden, was all over him with smiles and attention. He'd made his desire for Ned very clear, but Ned had never encouraged Ashden to act on it. Everyone knew Ashden wanted Ned for himself. There'd even been hints from Mr. Song, Braden and Ashden's omega parent, that since Ashden would be provided with a good-sized trust, they were in no need of asking a high purchase price for his first heat, making him someone Ned could not only afford to marry, but would financially benefit from marrying.

He remembered Mr. Song whispering in his ear, "We like you, Ned. You've been such a good friend to Braden."

If being a good friend to Braden meant not talking him out of bad choices, letting him sniff Bright's powder, and fucking omegas next to him at stupid high school orgies, then, yeah, he'd been a great friend. If it meant helping Braden to become a better person, then he'd completely failed at that.

But Mr. Song and Mr. Tenmeter didn't seem to notice the difference. They held the Ashden-shaped keys to the kingdom before Ned's face, smiled, and shook them with all kinds of hints about what else they could do for Ned's father, for Ned himself.

Ashden was gorgeous, of course, but Ned wasn't interested in a closer association with the Tenmeter family. The idea of breeding with them was horrific. What if his son turned out like Braden? It would be beyond his ability to stand. But Braden basically considered Ned his brother-in-law, due to Ashden's interest, and told him that his father considered Ned as good as his future son-in-law.

Between his father's need for their contracts and the Tenmeter temper when they didn't get their way, Ned felt trapped in the friendship with Braden, and Braden, he knew, was trapped with Finch. Their fathers were among the most important men in Wellport.

If only Ned could confide everything to his Uncle Heath. He was smarter and more powerful than either of them and could help Ned untangle this mess. But Uncle Heath was still angry about Lidell's financial buffoonery, as well as other ugly family business, and Heath refused to help Ned's father any further. Heath and Ned had mended their differences when Ned had spent the summer with him, but with the condition that Ned never ask him for another dime on his father's behalf ever again.

So Ned hadn't.

Instead, he'd floundered and gotten himself all tied up in some pretty dark things. Even after the summer with Heath, he'd stayed mixed up with dark elements. Nothing quite as bad as what had gotten him kicked out of his last school, but bad enough that he knew he wasn't a good enough person to put an end to it all.

Ned hoped his uncle never found out about half of it. He never wanted to lose Heath's favor again, like he had after he'd behaved so terribly over the birth of Michael, Heath's alpha son. His father, Lidell, had acted like an asshole, and Ned had been a frightened, entitled shit. He could see that now. Funny how hindsight only showed his regrets.

And if Heath found out about the recent Bright's powder excursions, the sex parties he still attended (though he never indulged—everyone else was so high or drunk or busy getting their nut that no one noticed him slipping away to a dark corner to read a book), and now the attack on George Fersee's son? Well, Ned had no doubt he'd be out of favor again.

He was stuck between a rock and a hard place. And he couldn't find a way free.

But, Lidell was right in one important way: without the full backing of Clearwater wealth behind him, Ned would need to sustain other connections to make his way in the world. Or find a wealthy omega mate to marry—like Ashden or Finch's older brother, Roald.

Or like Ezer.

If he could just get the boy to look at him without all that hatred in his eyes.

Ned groaned, and Earl, who'd sat patiently as Ned stewed, sighed. "Well?"

"I loathe Braden and Finch. I had to just stand back and watch them bully some omega they want to fuck—" Not 'some omega', Ezer. "But the omega wants nothing to do with them." It was as close to the truth as he could come.

"What kind of bullying?"

"Calling him names, roughing him up. Trying to scare him."

"And they think this is going to make the boy want to spread for them?"

"No. I don't know. I think they like scaring him. I think they're just bad people, Earl."

"It certainly sounds like it. But you knew this already."

"I know..." Ned rolled around on the lounger, holding tight to Earl's jacket, and wishing he could somehow worm his way into a different reality, where none of this had ever happened, and he didn't have to worry about his father's livelihood or Ezer's safety. "I wish there were more legal protections for omegas."

"With your testimony, I'm sure the police would take him seriously, if he wanted or needed to press charges." The hesitancy in Earl's voice gave Ned pause. He was asking without asking if the omega in question had been raped, and if Ned knew of a real crime.

"No, no, it's not like that." *Yet.*

Earl studied him, and satisfied Ned was being honest, he rose. "So what do you plan to do about it? Pout the day away?"

Ned huffed in irritation, but he supposed Earl was only pointing out the truth. He had little to gain from trying to sun the shame out of his skin. Besides, he was huddled under Earl's jacket now. Not even the sun could purify him like that. "Any better ideas for me?"

"One or two." Earl rose and put out his hand to help pull Ned up. "Starting in the gym. Some exercise will set your mood right. And then we'll begin on some of those extra studies the teachers sent your way."

"Not the math."

"*Definitely* the math."

Ned groaned but followed Earl into his father's big, rented house built into the hill above the sea, and down to the weight room on the lowest level.

# Chapter Four

AFTER WORKING OUT, followed by agonizing his way through several equations with Earl, Ned left the house alone, eager to get some fresh air and shake off the irritation that always descended when he tried to do mathematics.

Why couldn't the numbers make sense the way words did? They simply slid out of his mind into a heap.

As the evening descended, Ned let his feet lead the way to the scene of the crime. Or rather, they led him to the subway, and then to a bus, and to Ezer's omega parent's apartment complex. Getting to Roughs Neck took some dedication, and Ned's unconscious mind had plenty of that. Because there he was, standing outside the creaky chain-link gate, staring at the concrete table where Ezer had sat yesterday looking like a scrawny kitten with dazzling eyes.

Ugh. Why hadn't he found a way to hustle Braden and Finch on by? It was like as soon as Ned saw Ezer his head became stuffed with cotton, and he'd been unable to think of any compelling reason to lure Braden and Finch away. It wasn't that he didn't want to get those monsters as far from Ezer as possible, but his ability to make a plan or accomplish anything at all vanished whenever he was near Ezer. He'd acted like an utter fool last week when Mr. Gregson had assigned them to work on a group mathematics project together. He'd been unable to contribute even the smallest answer. Now Ezer thought he was an idiot *as well* as a total asshole.

"Looking for something?" came a deep, somehow familiar voice from behind Ned. It held an implicit threat, and Ned was surprised when he turned around to find that Amos Elson wasn't pointing the pistol at him again. Instead, his arms were full of groceries, but the hate in his eyes burned like fire. "Looking to buy Bright's powder? Or here to torment my son again?"

Ned's face flamed, and he moved aside, giving the man access to the gate.

Amos didn't take it. "What's your name?" he asked instead.

Ned cleared his throat, scraped his toe on the concrete, and then offered up an unintelligent, "Um, uh?"

"I highly doubt that."

"Please, sir. I didn't mean for things to get that far." Amos scoffed, so Ned tried another tack. "Really, Mr. Elson, sir, I tried to stop them."

"Sure you did."

"I swear. I…I *like* Ezer." His throat grew dry as he spoke the words, and his tongue almost tripped over itself. "I didn't want…I mean, I *wanted* to do something, but…"

Amos glared at him.

"Please, sir, I want to apologize." He *did*, he realized. That was the reason he'd come, though he hadn't known that until now. "I want to say I'm sorry."

"If you know anything about my son, then you know he doesn't live here."

Right. *Right.*

He did know that, actually, but he'd forgotten. The events in the yard here, at Amos's apartment, had been at the forefront of his mind, and he'd thought that maybe, just maybe, if he came back, Ezer would be there at the table again, and he could have a do-over.

"To you, I mean. I wanted to apologize to you." That was a lie, but it was true enough in the moment. Now that Ned was standing here with Amos, he was sorry for what he'd done to his son, and he did think he should apologize for it. "I'll do better in the future. I swear."

"I feel like that's a promise you must make a lot."

Ned flushed.

Amos pondered him, tilted his head a bit, and said, "You're Lidell Clearwater's son, aren't you? Though you look more like Sandrino. He was a friend of mine. Once."

"Oh." Ned didn't know many men, aside from Earl, who'd known his omega parent. He'd been auction-born, which was common enough, but his father had fallen for his omega parent during the pregnancy—rather like Heath had fallen for Adrien. But Sandrino hadn't lived long after the birth. Ned itched to ask questions about the man who'd birthed him, but he also knew this wasn't the time or place. "My da died a long time ago, when I was a baby."

"Yes, he did." Amos studied him through narrow eyes and then heaved a sigh. "Well, come along." Amos pushed some of his groceries into Ned's arms. "Come upstairs. We'll talk over tea and see what's what."

Ned was shocked by the invitation, but even more shocked by the state of things inside the building. Given how grim the outside was, that was saying something. Still, Amos's actual apartment was as neat as possible, and the water damage and obvious evidence of termites and vermin were obscured by his attempts to make the small place into a kind of home.

Ned spotted the black notebook Ezer had been working problems in the day before. He wondered if Ezer had left it here by accident. He entertained a brief fantasy of grabbing it on his way out the door to return to Ezer when school began again after the holidays. He imagined Ezer's face lighting up with gratitude…

He was such a dumbass. Ezer hated him.

Ned watched as Amos put the groceries away, and then let Amos guide him to a worn sofa with a few springs showing. It must have been purchased second-hand or pulled from the trash for free. He was embarrassed for Amos's sake. The man had been an admired omega in society before George Fersee's cruel divorce.

"So, Sandrino's son," Amos said, taking a seat on the threadbare chair across from the sofa where Ned perched. "Why don't you tell me what happened yesterday?"

"Braden and Finch—"

"Tenmeter and Maddox's sons?"

"Yes."

"Go on."

"Well, they've taken to using Bright's powder a lot. They use it for…" He chewed on the inside of his lip, and then forced himself to stop stalling and spit out the rest. "Well, for fun, I guess. I don't like it. It makes me feel jumpy. And stupid." And horny, too, but he wasn't going to say that.

"Mm-hmm."

"But it makes Braden and Finch really mean. And, to be honest, sir, they're already mean enough."

Amos lifted a finger. "Hold your thought right there." He rose and went back into the kitchen. There was the sound of running water, the *clank* of metal on metal, and then Amos came back out and took his seat again. "Go on."

"Ezer is…well, at school he…" How could he put this? His lip was between his teeth again. "He struggles at Doubleton. Socially, I mean. And, I think, academically as well?"

Amos shrugged, as though this was not news to him. "Ezer is peculiar, I know."

"No! Ezer is wonderful." Ned blinked, confused by his outburst. He hadn't meant to say that. Heat crept up his neck. He didn't know how to explain the way Ezer made him feel by existing in the world. Not without coming across like a stalker. Hell, he probably already had come across as a stalker just by showing up here. A violent stalker, even, based on yesterday's events.

"'Wonderful', huh? Funny way to show that opinion. Holding him down with your boot while the others—" A spark of rage entered Amos's expression again.

"Yes, I know how it looked. But I didn't want to!"

Amos rolled his eyes. "Let me tell you a secret, Sandrino's son—"

"Ned."

Amos's thin brow cocked up. "All right, let me tell you a secret, *Ned*. Everything you do? Every last thing? You *choose* to do. Unless there's a gun to your head." He smirked. The memory of the pistol was still fresh in both their minds. "Your choices belong to you alone."

"My choices, maybe, but not my consequences."

Amos leaned forward, the anger in his eyes turning to interest.

"It's not a gun they have to my head, sir, but I have a hell of a lot to lose if I don't stay on good terms with Braden and Finch."

The sound of boiling water came from the kitchen. "Your popularity? Social standing? A wealthy marriage to one of the omegas of their families?"

A dart of anxiety entered Ned's chest.

"I know your father, too, Ned, and I know that he's a financial mess. Always has been, always will be. He could barely afford to buy Sandrino's heat. I told your da at the time that Lidell Clearwater was no Heath, but Sandrino was smitten, and the heat was coming so…" Amos sighed.

"My father is always in dire straits," Ned admitted. "He has no sense of 'enough.'"

Ned didn't know if his father suffered a sick kind of optimism or if it was greed alone. All he knew was that when his father was flush, he spent like he was expecting another influx of cash the next day, and when he wasn't flush...well, he spent the same way.

He decided to be honest with Amos about their circumstances. What did he have to lose? Amos wasn't in any position to spread rumors about them anyway. Who would believe the words of a cast-off omega? Who would a cast-off omega even talk to? He was friendless, based on how he lived. "You know my uncle recently had an alpha son with his new omega?"

Amos's eyes took on a thoughtful look. "I'm assuming you're speaking of Heath? I don't recall Sandrino having an alpha brother. Or any brother at all."

"Yes, my uncle, Heath Clearwater."

"Ah, yes. I'd heard the swirl of rumors before my so-called friends stopped talking to me." Amos smirked. "Something about a scandal, but I never got the details. I'm afraid I don't get much gossip at my new job. Trash tells all kinds of stories, but not that kind, I'm afraid."

The kettle in the kitchen began to shriek, and Amos left the room again to reappear with two steaming mugs. He passed one to Ned, who wondered if he should drink it. Amos wouldn't poison him, would he? For roughing up Ezer? No, the man had done *something* to push George Fersee to cruelty, but he wasn't going to murder the nephew of Heath Clearwater.

"It's good. See?" Amos took a sip of his and hummed in delight before putting it down on the banged-up coffee table without even a coaster.

Ned tasted his, it was woodsy and light. A nice tea, indeed. He wondered how Amos afforded it. Then wondered if Ezer brought it to his da as a gift.

"Now, go on," Amos said. "I've missed the gossip. And I believe you owe me after yesterday's events. Tell me about Heath."

"He contracted a breeding heat with a university omega almost at the age of majority."

"Surprising. I thought he'd sworn off omegas after...well, after certain events."

"He had. I was supposed to be his heir, you see. But something about this omega ensnared him." Ned gave a self-deprecating smile. "He bought a breeding. Together, they had an alpha. No more heirship for me."

"Ah."

"Uncle Heath fell in love with the omega and married him." Ned left out the scandalous bits, because while he had been angry enough about all of it at the time, sharing the news far and wide in a nasty rage, he now didn't see the sense in further besmirching the family name.

Plus he didn't think he'd win any points with Amos by being unkind about another omega. The gender did tend to stick together, though none at Doubleton had befriended Ezer yet. Besides, after a summer in his uncle and Adrien's home, he didn't want to be unkind about them anymore. "Uncle Heath's happy, I think."

"Love. It happens to even the strongest alphas," Amos said, smoothing his graying, blond hair away from his forehead. "We omegas are just that tantalizing, you know. Alphas swoon for us. Especially when we're in heat."

Ned wondered for the first time what Amos did to handle his heats now. Or perhaps he didn't have them anymore? Each omega only had five to eight heats in a lifetime, and it was possible Amos was through with them all. Maybe that was the real reason he'd been dismissed. Some alphas couldn't stomach a barren omega.

But, still, Amos had had five sons with George Fersee, the man deserved better than this, even if none of them had been an alpha. There had to be something more to his shabby treatment.

"Heat crushes are quite real."

Ned squirmed. "Yes." He'd never been with an omega during a heat, though he'd allowed rumors to spread he had done so more than once. Braden and Finch had started them, saying it made them more appealing to the omegas in their school if they sounded experienced in all ways. Stupid. "So I've been told. About love, I mean."

"Told? You seemed quite vehement that my son is, how did you put it? 'Wonderful'." Amos smirked. "Omega wiles."

Ned tilted his head. "Do you believe in those? Truly?"

He'd always thought that the near magical omega wiles so often cited by alphas as their reason for poor behavior with regards to the breedable sex were old men's tales and nothing more. But if Amos believed in them, and he was an omega, then maybe there was something to the stories.

Amos's teeth were straight and bright when he flashed a hard smile at Ned's question. "I believe that alphas are men, and omegas are their special weakness. Not every omega for every alpha, of course, but given the fact that you're here, now, talking with me—the da of the omega you're all twisted up about—I'd say Ezer is your weakness. Am I right?"

"Like you said earlier, *I'm* my weakness," Ned countered, unwilling to put any sort of negative stigma on Ezer, and that included the idea that he made Ned weak or used omega wiles. "I'm the one who makes such bad choices, and I should have to suffer the consequences of them. Ezer is stronger than I could ever be."

"He really is, you know," Amos mused. "Stronger than his

father or I ever realized, I think."

"I wish I could—" Ned broke off from the silly comment.

Amos's thin eyebrows went up and he leaned forward. "What?"

"I wish I had his kind of strength. If I did? Then I'd kick Braden and Finch's asses, and not worry about the outcome."

"I hope you meant his emotional strength, because physically my Ezer is nothing but a bundle of chicken bones held together by rubber bands."

"I did mean his inner strength." Ned hesitated, but Amos's comment had brought up a whole other issue he was curious about. "Why doesn't he eat?" Ned asked, and then wished he could swallow his tongue. It wasn't his business.

"It's his way of staying in control," Amos said. "How did you know about that?"

"At school. At lunch. I watch him."

"Oh my. How far gone you are."

"I try not to let people see me watching him. He's…" Ned tried to think of how to put the next part so that he wouldn't outright offend Amos. Though Amos himself had called his son strange. "Ezer is not well-regarded among my classmates," Ned ventured. Now that he was talking to someone who knew Ezer, he couldn't seem to keep his thoughts to himself anymore. "I don't understand how he got into our school to be honest, sir. I know he went to St. Hauers before, but why isn't he still there? Is it because he can work sums that no one else in the class can handle?"

"He is very intelligent in all ways," Amos said. "But he prefers to take his tests orally. Written exams aren't good for him."

Ned bit into his lower lip, considering. "Socially, he hasn't integrated at all. Omegas avoid him. I don't know why. I thought omegas were the kind to stick together."

"We do. If it benefits us. What do the alphas at the school think of him?"

"Not much."

"And there you have it. Omegas don't want anything to do with an omega scorned by alphas."

"He doesn't flirt with us. He doesn't even want our attention at all. He ignores us."

"So to get *his* attention, you and your friends beat him up?"

"No! Well, not me!" Ned sputtered. "I mean, yes, I was there, and—please, Mr. Elson, don't remind me of what I did."

"Fine, but only because I think your own conscience is doing a fantastic job of that by itself."

Ned nodded. "The others—especially Braden and Finch—they think he's disrespectful of their standing as alphas. On the first day of school, they gave him what they thought of as an opportunity, but Ezer turned it down." Here he stopped, afraid to say what had been offered, to give it form, because then he'd be even more afraid for Ezer, and even afraid for himself. Because who knew what Ned might do if Braden and Finch went for Ezer again?

"You think they want to dominate him because he won't act the submissive part, even though, by all rights, he should."

"I *like* that he doesn't."

"Ah, yes, it appeals to the chase instinct," Amos said, lips smirking. "For some though, it ignites a kind of need to punish, but in others to catch and protect."

"I don't want them to catch him ever again," Ned whispered, fists clenching. "I was going to kick Braden in the face if he got his own pants down. I swear, I was."

"Mm-hmm." Amos offered no more opinion on that.

"What should I do?" Ned asked, after taking several more sips of the hot, woodsy tea.

"School's out for the long spring break, isn't it?"

"Yes."

"I lose track of time these days." Amos stretched, and his back creaked. "By the time school returns to session, things will be different."

"How so?"

"The weeks ahead will make that evident."

"You're not going to take him out of school, are you?" Ned couldn't handle it if Ezer was gone. He needed to be able to see those beautiful eyes and know the omega in possession of them was safe. "I promise I'll never let them touch him again."

"Well, I don't have any control over his schooling now. That's all his father's choice. But considering how I suspect this will play out, I'm going hold you to that promise. Never let them touch him, do you understand? Not those boys, and no other alpha, either. Do you understand? Not a single one."

"I promise."

"Good."

Ned was unnerved by the odd, calculating smile on Amos's face, but they finished their tea together, discussing superficial things, and then Amos let Ned back out onto the rotting staircase to find his way home to the privileged side of town.

# Chapter Five

"I HEARD FROM Amos today," Father said, his teeth grinding together, as he sent a piercing gaze down the length of the table. He was still dressed in his suit from business appointments earlier in the afternoon, and he was as dark and imposing as ever.

Pete wasn't feeling well, pregnancy having worn on him that day, and was missing from the family dinner. No doubt, that was the reason Father was mentioning Da's name at all. He had too much sensitivity for Pete's lingering jealousy over the prior omega of the house to bring him up otherwise.

"Who's Amos?" Eight-year-old Rodan looked interested but clueless, raising his dark eyebrows far above his chocolate-brown eyes until they disappeared beneath his mop of black curly hair. His innocent question pierced Ezer's heart. Had he already forgotten Da? He'd just been gone a year.

"Amos is Da," Yissen replied, his handsome, diamond-cut face blank, as though willing no emotion to show. Ezer thought Yissen, as the oldest, should have taken Da's dismissal harder than he had, but maybe he was too stubborn to let his emotions show. At least he didn't feign forgetting him too.

"Say Da then," Rodan said with a shrug, digging into his broccoli.

Florentine and Shan both continued eating, though they shot each other worried glances. The middle omegas, twins, with long dark hair and nearly pearl-black eyes, were two peas in a pod, and both had sobbed when Da had left. But now they never mentioned him at all.

"No," Father said to Rodan with the kind of coldness that always made the hairs on Ezer's arms rise. But the hidden threat seemed to go right over little Rodan's head, as most subtle social interactions did. "That omega is not to be referred to as anything other than Amos in this house. When Pete delivers, *he* will be Da."

Another look passed between Shan and Florentine, but there was no argument or disagreement voiced by anyone. Ezer bit his own tongue to keep from declaring his father's command to be unfair and disrespectful to Da. He knew his father wouldn't care.

Father's dark eyes slid to him as though he knew what Ezer wanted to say, almost daring him to do it.

Ezer kept his mouth shut, stirring his food around his plate.

When Ezer decided it was safe to take a bite, Father spoke again. "Amos said Ezer has been visiting him."

Ezer froze with his fork between his plate and mouth, and his hand began to tremble a little. How could Da betray him that way? He dropped the fork, his hand going to fiddle with the napkin in his lap, as he shook his head, the denial instantaneous. And the wrong choice.

"Don't lie to me, Ezer."

"I only went—" He stared at his father, heart galloping. "I only went because I miss him."

"You need to get it into your head, Ezer. Amos isn't part of our lives any longer."

"Why?" Ezer burst out. "You made him go, but you never gave us a good reason why!"

Yissen looked ready to join Ezer's protest but held back. He was the most beautiful of them all, but he bore a scar beneath his eye from the one time he'd challenged George. The sharp edge of their father's ring had cut him when he'd failed to duck the backhanded slap.

As omegas, the four older boys were all smaller than their father, but sometimes Ezer wondered why they didn't join forces to challenge him—show him what they thought of him. But all his brothers wanted his father's money to lure good matches, so getting disinherited to make a point wouldn't make much sense to them.

It made sense to Ezer, though.

"I don't owe you an explanation," his father said. "Your omega parent has been dismissed from our lives, and I have retained legal custody of all of you until you're married or contracted long-term to an alpha. He has no place in your lives now."

"Actually, I'd like to know why he went away, too," Yissen said, shocking Ezer to the core. "Was it Pete?"

Father's eyes narrowed so fast Yissen shoved back from the table, poised to run. "Your omega parent was not fit. End of discussion." He turned his ire on Ezer again. "As for you, troublemaker, you aren't to visit him again. If you miss him so terribly, make better friends with Pete."

"Omegas aren't interchangeable!" Ezer exclaimed. He motioned at his older brothers. "*We* aren't interchangeable."

Yissan looked frightened now, and he hissed a low warning under his breath. But Shan and Flo lifted their chins for the first time, meeting their father's eyes with a hint of dark defiance Ezer hadn't imagined them capable of.

"Of course you aren't," Father said, sharply. "It's clear that some of you are quite a bit better than others." His gaze came back to Ezer with a grim look. "No more questions. Amos doesn't want you there. He said so himself."

"Da would never say that." Ezer's throat went tight. *Would he?*

"Well, he did. He says it isn't safe for you to be in Roughs Neck."

"Then it isn't safe for him either!"

"Amos made his own bed, and he'll lie in it. You, however, useless as you are, are my son, and I won't have you ruining the only thing you have of value. He told me about the boys attacking you. I suppose that's why you've been mincing around? I'll have one of the servants look to your bruises. You should have told me about it."

Da *had* betrayed him then. Ezer's heart spasmed with pain. How could Da have done this? When would he ever see him again?

"I'm fine. Da's making a big deal out of nothing."

"*Amos* made it very clear that he was indeed *not* making a big deal out of nothing. It will be a very big problem if those alphas succeed in their attempt the next time. *And* Amos believes there will be a next time, though *why* I don't fully understand," Father said. "You're ugly, Ezer. How long until you get it through your head that you have very little to attract alphas to you? You're skinny, scrawny, with some decent eyes to recommend you. And let's not even discuss how stupid you are."

"I'm not stupid," Ezer gritted out, hands clenching.

Shan and Flo shifted in their seats, looking ready to defend him, but Yissen sent them a sharp, muting glare.

Little Rodan murmured, "Ezer's stupid?" A question, not a declaration, so that was something at least.

"You aren't smart, that's for certain. You can't even read."

Ezer jerked back. "You know why!"

"Whatever the reason, with all of your deficits and defects, being untouched is the only way I'll ever get a decent contract for your heats, much less for a marriage."

"I don't want—"

"I don't *care* what you want." Father snapped his napkin down and glared so hard Ezer was surprised he wasn't impaled by his father's disdain. "You are a thorn in my side, Ezer. Don't think I'm not considering how best to remove you."

Ezer blinked at his father, trying to parse the meaning of that threat. Yissen caught his eye and shook his head.

Watching wide-eyed, Rodan sucked his thumb, something he hadn't done in a long time, and only removed it from his mouth when Yissen reached out to tap his wrist, sending a warning glance. Rodan paled and jerked his thumb from his lips, but he didn't start eating again, his attention darting between Ezer and their father.

For their part, Flo and Shan looked sick to their stomachs, but somehow, they managed to pick up their forks and make the motions of eating. Ezer, deciding that between the bruises throbbing on his arms, legs, and chest, and the pain in his heart, he was done taking a beating for the night, said nothing more, but didn't eat another bite of dinner either.

His father might control his life, but he couldn't make him eat.

THAT NIGHT, SHAN and Flo came by Ezer's room together, holding hands like they always did since they were young. "You have to be careful," Flo said, closing the door behind them, and flopping on Ezer's bed, taking the spot Ezer had been in. Shan sat down next to him, his black eyes shining with fear.

"Why? What do you know?" Ezer asked.

Both of his middle brothers were handsome, but they were so invested in their relationship with each other that Ezer wasn't sure marriages could be made for them. Heats could be auctioned, as could advantageous contracts for breeding, but a marriage would require they let go of their obsession with each other and let an alpha come first in their hearts. Ezer couldn't see that happening.

"Shan overheard Father on the phone earlier. When he was talking with Da."

"He did?"

"Yes," Shan said, twisting his hands in his lap. "We were in the library, in that corner where I prefer to read—"

"I was asleep, which is why I missed it," Flo said.

Of course they'd been together. They always were.

"And Father came in to sit at his desk. I figured that so long as I didn't make any noise, I wouldn't bother him, so I continued to read in the corner. A phone call came through, and Father took it right there, and when I realized it was Da..." Shan swallowed, his eyes growing wet as he fought tears. "I miss him!"

"We all miss him," Flo said, pulling Shan down to cradle against his chest. "He's our da. Of course we miss him."

"Even Yissen?" Shan asked.

"Especially Yissen," Flo said. "They butted heads, but that just makes it worse, doesn't it? He hates that Da left when they were on bad terms."

"Why *were* they on bad terms?" Ezer asked. "I never understood it."

"That's a story for another time," Flo said, in that imperious way he had when he wanted Ezer to feel every bit of the four years between them. "Shan, tell him what you heard."

"I only heard Father's side, but he repeated enough of Da's comments in that angry way of his that I kind of know what he said, too."

"Spit it out then." Ezer sat down at the edge of his desk chair, sweat popping up at his temples. Usually both brothers avoided being seen with Ezer for a few days after he'd had a run-in with their father. If Shan had overheard something important enough for Flo to insist on coming to Ezer's room, that meant it was very bad news.

"Da told him you'd been attacked by bullies, but that these bullies were the from the best families in town. He said one of the young men was obsessed with you and wasn't going to give up on the idea of, well, completing the attack."

"What?" Ezer couldn't imagine that Braden found him anything other than an excellent source of opportunistic harassment. Same for Finch. And Ned was just a follower anyway.

"Like I said, I was just getting the information from Father's responses, so maybe there is some subtlety lost, but that was the gist. And Father said you were driving him up the wall being disrespectful to Pete—"

"I've never been disrespectful to Pete!"

"You have to admit you ignore him most of the time."

"Why shouldn't I ignore him? It's not like he's my da. Besides, I acknowledge him when I'm addressed."

"Father wants us to *like* Pete."

"For heaven's sake, I do like Pete," Ezer said. "I just don't like that he's here instead of Da."

"I feel the same," Flo said, grimacing. "But for whatever reason Father thinks you target Pete, and he holds it against you."

"He's just mad that I won't let him forget what he did to Da."

"It's true you have Da's eyes," Shan said. "The rest of you, not so much, but the eyes for sure."

"And eyes are everything. *Your* eyes especially. Every time he looks at them, he must think of Da. How could he not?" Flo agreed.

Ezer was tempted to turn to the mirror. Would he see what

his brothers saw? He knew he didn't look like either his father or da, being made up of some weird mixture of recessive genes, apparently, but he hadn't noticed that his eyes were so much like his da's. Of course, he didn't spend much time in front of the mirror, not liking what he found there. So perhaps they were.

"I think he's planning to punish you in some way. For being a troublemaker and disobeying him too often. He says you take too many unnecessary risks and that's just asking for alphas to harass you."

Ezer gritted his teeth. "Punish me how?"

"Maybe sell your heat early? He said something about not wanting to risk you being, uh, soiled and lowering your first heat price and affecting the family's reputation."

"What nonsense!" Flo muttered, stroking a tender hand over Shan's back. "Virginity is such a ridiculous double-standard. Alphas are encouraged to have experience, and omegas are devalued for wanting the same."

"Wait," Ezer said, derailing the omega rights direction of Flo's thoughts. "He said he was going to sell my heat? I have to consent first. That's the law. And I won't."

Shan nodded, his eyes dark and worried. "I know, but it's Father. He isn't like other alphas who let their omega sons choose who they experience their first heat with or even let them sell their heats. He wants to control everything, and he always manages it. Please be careful, Ezer. He'll find a way. You know he will. So suck up to him, be nice to Pete, and stop being so weird."

"Next you'll also tell me to learn to read."

"No, because the doctors say that's impossible for you."

"And so are these other things. Except for being nice to Pete. I'm always nice to Pete."

Shan and Flo shot each other skeptical glances, but they didn't argue with him anymore. They rose as one from the bed, leaving the sheets and blankets rumpled, and started for the door. "Now you know the situation," Flo said. "Don't tell Father or Da or anyone else where you heard all this from, or I'll slit your throat in your sleep."

"Always full of threats," Ezer said, rolling his eyes. "I've heard that one since I was able to walk."

"This time I'm serious. I won't have Shan getting into trouble for you."

Then they were gone, the door closing behind them, leaving just a hint of their perfumes—lavender and bergamot—and a pit of dread at the bottom of Ezer's stomach.

# Chapter Six

"George Fersee has made an offer I'm loathe to refuse," Lidell, Ned's father, said over dinner two nights after Ned's visit to Amos Elson's apartment building.

The days in between had been filled with a restless, inexplicable longing to return. As if maybe if Ned talked to Amos again, he'd find a way to be closer to Ezer. Maybe even see him there, too. But when Amos had closed his door on Ned's back, he'd made it clear that Ned shouldn't return.

"Mm," Ned said, not giving his father any kind of real answer. He didn't feel comfortable talking about whatever had Lidell's eyes alight like that. Not at the dinner table anyway, and not while they had company.

His father's latest hired omega, a young man with brown eyes and white-blond hair, sat at the opposite end of the table, eating. Ned had already forgotten the man's name—Henry? Hopper? The man was boring, and he wasn't likely to be around more than a few more days since—Harry? No, *Hunter*'s heat had ended a week ago. No breeding had been negotiated, per his father's customary habit.

So, as usual with these things: pleasure had been had, intimacies exchanged, and when Lidell was tired of Hunter, he'd be sent on his way with money to fund the next stage of his life. And, Ned supposed, to soothe any heartbreak at separating, though he had a hard time imagining any omega falling in love with his father. Lidell wasn't a soft man; he wasn't romantic or interested in being in love. Sometimes Ned wondered how his omega parent—the beautiful Sandrino—had managed to get Lidell to fall for him. So far as Ned had seen, Lidell always kept his heart closed off.

Regardless, Hunter would be gone soon, and his father would be sated for a year or so, until he felt compelled to take on another omega to slake his carnal desires. At which point he'd spend a few weeks studying the auction pages, and then make his choice.

It was a sordid cycle Ned was familiar with and secretly disdained. After seeing how happy his uncle was with Adrien, and getting into trouble over fleeting pleasures in the past, Ned no longer wanted to indulge in short-term connections for the sake of physical gratification. He wanted to mate a single omega for life like Heath had done.

To be fair, he supposed Lidell had once wanted that too with Ned's omega parent. Earl said it was after Sandrino's death that Lidell had changed his focus to obtaining power and money. By shunning love and connection, he'd tried to protect himself from ever losing so much again.

But even Ned knew that was shortsighted.

Ned didn't care that much about power. He'd seen the way his father's desire for it had driven a wedge between him and Heath. And, sure, money was nice, but his father was never satisfied financially and always wanted more.

According to Lidell Clearwater's occasional drunken ramblings, relationships with a definite end date and a set cash incentive never involved the complications of emotions. Ned thought it all seemed empty and sad. He didn't want to make do with short bursts of mutual understanding that ended with nothing but a nice memory and a photograph or two.

"I saw George at the club this afternoon and had a very serious conversation with him alone in the garden. Aren't you curious what he's put on the table?" Lidell asked again.

Ezer Fersee's blue eyes popped into Ned's mind with the ferocity of obsession. His cheeks flushed as he recalled what he'd done just a few hours earlier in the privacy of his room, touching himself while thinking of Ezer's fine-boned face and wide eyes. He'd exploded in ecstasy imagining Ezer's face coated with Ned's juices. But no sooner had he come down from that joy, than the shame had risen again. He'd cleaned up his physical mess, mourning that he couldn't clean up the one he'd made with Ezer. There was no erasing that a few days before, he'd had his boot on Ezer's shoulder, complicit in the boy's humiliation, even if only for a few seconds.

"George Fersee is a wealthy, powerful man. This could be our chance." Lidell cleared his throat, annoyed at Ned's apparent lack of interest.

Ned sighed and took the bait. "What has Mr. Fersee offered, Father?"

"A breeding."

"What?" Ned tilted his head in disgust mingled with confusion. "Mr. Fersee is an alpha."

"Yes, he's an alpha. With four omega sons, and a powerful need to offload a few of them. Beginning with the troublemaker."

A tingle of alarm began in Ned's fingers. "'The troublemaker'?"

His father nodded. "It seems one of his omega sons is a bit too uppity and has forgotten his place in the world. Mr. Fersee plans to auction off his first heat, along with a breeding, early. Get the boy knocked up and under control." Lidell smiled, leaking smarm from his pores as he added, "There's nothing like a pregnancy to calm an omega down."

From the other end of the table, Hunter released a condemning cough.

Ned worried on his lower lip for a moment. "Which son is it?"

"I believe you know him." Lidell smiled as if he somehow knew this would matter to Ned. "He's in your class at school. The name is Ezer?"

Ned's gut twisted. Ezer's small form flashed before his eyes, along with memories of the fear in his face as Braden had held him down, the way he'd struggled. He thought of Ezer's strong-minded lift of his chin, never taking a hit to his pride while taking a hit to his body. Ned hoped his voice was steady as he asked, "Mr. Fersee is going to auction him?"

"That was his original plan," Lidell said, with a lifted finger indicating that Ned should wait for the real prize. "But he expressed some interest in us taking the boy off his hands *permanently*—for a price. And by us, I mean you."

"Me?"

"Yes. Surely you don't think I intend to take on a nineteen-year-old omega and breed him." Lidell scoffed. "Of course it would be you."

His head whirled. The words didn't make sense. "I don't understand."

"There's a price of course."

That made even less sense. "If Mr. Fersee wants money, we have nothing to offer." Without his uncle's backing, they couldn't afford to pay for a heat right now, and there was no way Uncle Heath would approve of this situation. Ned and Ezer weren't even in college yet. He shook his head. There had to be a misunderstanding. "Besides, Ezer is too young."

"George doesn't give a rat's ass about the money, son. He wants his child to stop embarrassing him. The boy is of legal age,

I understand. Eighteen is the minimum."

"That's for *common* alphas and omegas, not people of our class." Ned hoped that by appealing to his father's snobbery, he could get through to him. "Or in the rare case where an omega goes into heat early due to a medical issue."

Ned's heart was racing. He didn't know what he would do if George Fersee auctioned Ezer off. He didn't have the money to buy him, and the idea of any other alpha having him made him feel sick. It wasn't until that moment that he realized he'd always planned, hoped, *believed* he'd find a way to have Ezer for himself.

"It's also for situations where young men of 'our class', as you put it, aren't able to behave and their fathers need to see them settled and safe."

"And that's the case with Ezer?" Ned's ears rang.

"Yes. In fact, George has offered the boy to us, along with a lump sum settlement *plus* an annual stipend that more than makes up for what we've lost from my dear, asshole brother. God bless his infant son," Lidell said.

Ned didn't remind his father that the only person Heath had disinherited had been Lidell himself, and that Ned still stood to inherit a tidy sum, nor did he remind him that Heath still paid for Ned's schooling and promised him a good income when or if he married or bred. All that truth would just send his father over the edge.

"Fersee is willing to pay a great deal to keep his son quiet, and there's no reason we can't be the ones to get that money. It's easy. So long as we can keep this boy Ezer in line, which I have no doubt you can do, we win. Besides..." His father's expression turned crafty. "Rumor has it you have some interest in him?"

Ned ignored that question, asking instead the most important one of all, "What does Ezer think of all this?"

His father waved his hand. "Ezer's opinion isn't important. It seems this decision has been a long time coming, but recently came to a head. George has reason to fear his son is attracting the wrong sort of attention from alphas at school, and he'd like to have Ezer heat-bred and out of school before the new term starts. He believes that will solve all his problems with the boy."

"But Ezer has to consent."

"Yes, and I'm sure he will. His father has legal power over him until he's contracted to an alpha or his father dies. So what does his opinion matter?"

"If he doesn't want it, then—"

Lidell laughed. "Oh, when his heat starts, he'll want it."

Ned squirmed.

"Consent in advance is required," Hunter said from the opposite end of the table. Ned jerked, having forgotten the young man's presence, bombarded as he had been by such a flood of information and feelings. Hunter flicked a blond lock from his eyes. "Legally, a contract must be signed."

"I'm sure this boy, Ezer, will see the sense in it, or he'll be made to," Lidell said, waving his fork.

Hunter shrugged. "Maybe. But there *are* laws to protect us. Not many, but a few. And prior consent, before heat starts is one of them. Unless you'd enjoy seeing Ned in jail for rape?"

"I told you! I'm sure Ezer will be brought around to seeing the sense of it."

"I'm not sure *I* see the sense of it," Hunter went on, pushing his luck. "This omega is not even nineteen yet. Or so I'm assuming, since Ned is only eighteen, and they are in the same class."

"Ned turned nineteen last month, and I didn't ask your opinion."

Hunter frowned, putting his fork down and crossing his arms over his chest.

"I think you'll be on your way tomorrow," Lidell said.

"I think I shall," Hunter agreed with matching coldness.

"Why us?" Ned asked, shaking off the question of consent and the unwanted insertion of the stranger-at-the-table's opinions. It was a pointless discussion anyway. He wouldn't take Ezer without his consent, no matter what their fathers planned.

But what if Ezer *did* consent?

Ned's cock rushed with blood. Those eyes, so beautiful and full of feeling, flashed in his mind. Still, they were both only nineteen, and not even at university yet. They were far too young.

Ned cleared his throat and tried to sharpen his mind. "There have to be other, older men who would want to take Ezer off Mr. Fersee's hands." Though the thought made Ned's stomach turn, and he put his fork down, unable to take another bite.

"No doubt. But during my discussion with him, we agreed that you and Ezer would be well-suited."

Ned coughed. In his fantasies they were, but that was just in his head. The real Ezer loathed him and thought he was a bully.

"It seems that you were part of the group that recently manhandled him." Lidell gave Ned a sharp look. "But it also seems you took it a step farther than the others. *You* apologized to his omega parent in a fit of shame."

Ned swallowed hard, heat slamming through him, so that his cheeks, chest, and even his thighs burned in humiliation. "I…I didn't—"

"Stop. I don't want apologies or excuses. At this point, your behavior, ill-mannered, ill-considered, and stupid as it might have been, may just end up being our salvation." He raised a brow toward Hunter, as if considering whether to say the rest in front of him. "It seems you confessed to Amos Elson a strong—how shall I put this? *Attachment* to this boy Ezer."

So not only had Amos betrayed him, but his father had

known from the start of this conversation that Ned knew exactly who Ezer Fersee was, and even that he had feelings for him.

Lidell smirked. "Imagine my surprise, spending the day with George Fersee, discussing your amorous intentions. He filled me in on your confession to his cast-off omega. And then told me of his son's 'oddities'—really, Ned? The boy hardy weighs more than a drowned rat, and can't read? Must you like them small and dumb?"

"Father, I—"

"Truly, I don't care. It hardly matters, given the sums involved." Lidell took a sip of his wine and then went on, as if this was a normal discussion to be having. "In the course of the conversation, it became apparent that George was a bit worried about whether an alpha as young as you would be able to handle his son. But I mentioned to him your newfound desire to mate and breed for life. I know you think you got the idea from Heath, but it was it was inherited, of course, from your omega parent. Oh, sweet Sandrino. He was a romantic sort as well. Dreamy, always talking of making a large family." He drifted off on memories the way he always did when he brought up Ned's omega parent, forever an angel in Lidell's eyes.

Hunter coughed into his napkin and broke the spell.

Lidell shot him a dirty look. "Fersee liked that about you. Plus he likes that you seem to care for his son despite having attempted to assault him." Lidell tutted under his breath, scolding Ned. "That seemed unlike you, I admit, but apparently, it's the truth. So, I have to agree with George. It'll be best to get you in this boy's life in a way that isn't illegal."

"I didn't assault—"

Lidell talked over Ned. "I get the impression that George cares for his son's happiness at least a little. He wants a dedicated alpha who will keep Ezer in hand. I assured him that would be you. If you're so obsessed with the boy now that you'd attempt assault, then—"

"I said I didn't!"

"—you're already infatuated, and that's halfway to a heat crush, and that, my boy, is halfway to love. Regardless, George said he'd be glad to have Ezer off his hands before Spring Break is over. He doesn't want him going back to school, and he's eager to pay us to do it now, while you're both still legally bound to us, rather than risk waiting any longer."

Ned was in far too much shock to parse the offer—or was it an agreement?—that had been made between his father and Ezer's. Instead, he asked another question, "What's Ezer doing that embarrasses his father?"

"I don't know, and I don't care."

"What if he embarrasses us?"

Lidell scoffed "How could he embarrass us more than my own brother has? Taking up with a scandalous lover? Having a first child at his age? No, believe me. This will be easy compared to dealing with Heath. Omegas like to be taken in hand, and once he's pregnant he'll be submissive as a kicked pup."

Hunter sniffed in disapproval but didn't say a word. Lidell shot him another ugly look. "Hunter might not like my words, but he won't dispute them either. A pregnant omega is a willing omega."

"Until the post-partum drop," Hunter said. "Then we get a bit jumpy. Unpredictable."

"Know that from experience, do you?"

"I bred my first heat."

"And walked away from the baby?" Lidell shook his head. "Unsurprising."

"I had my reasons."

"We all have our reasons," Lidell shot back, waving him off, like a gnat. "Post-partum drops are often difficult, yes, but we'll handle him."

Ned swallowed hard. He didn't want his father handling anything about Ezer, not ever. "I don't know about all of this, Father. Couldn't we just sign an agreement for when we're older? After university?"

Many omegas in his age group had already signed agreements assigning their first heat, usually for a large price, to one of their father's friends, business associates, or the sons thereof. It would be unusual for two age mates to sign a contract of intent for the future, but it wasn't impossible. It had been done before, often when love was involved. But Ned knew Ezer didn't love him.

"No. His father isn't sending him to university. The boy's an idiot, son. I don't know what you see in him. He was only able to transfer from St. Hauers due to some strings his omega parent pulled before he was sent away. George assures me that college would be a waste of money for this Ezer, and I heartily agree. This will be much better for both of you. Ezer will sign the heat and breeding contract, and so will you. He'll be happy and pregnant, and you'll be settled with a boy who will take all your devotion and love. Don't you want him? Was his omega parent mistaken?"

"I do want him," Ned admitted. It sickened him to imagine Ezer with any other alpha, and yet this was all so fast, and they were so young. It was wrong. "He's been my first pick for months now, but..."

"But what?"

Grasping for straws, anything to delay this until he was older and more capable, he said, "Braden and Finch hate him."

"What makes you think that?"

"They harass him. Bully him. It's why I haven't made a move to be closer to him at school. You told me to stay in their good graces, and I have."

"It'll be as good a reason as any for you to pull away from the friendships with the Tenmeter and Maddox boys, I know you loathe them. After this marriage, it won't matter. Fersee will give us more funds than we'll ever know what to do with. This is all we've ever wanted since Heath turned his back on us."

Ned chewed his lower lip. "Maybe, but I think Ezer hates me."

"I'm sure he's wary of you," Lidell said, flicking a look toward Hunter. "Given your behavior towards him as relayed to me by his father. But you will prove to him that you're a strong, good alpha. You'll protect him. He'll never be bullied or harassed again with you by his side, no matter how skinny and ugly he is."

"He isn't ugly!"

Lidell chuckled. "Oh, I see George wasn't exaggerating. You're mad for the boy."

"He's just got a lot of growing left to do. It might not even be safe for him to…to…you know, breed yet."

"George assures me the boy passed the standards at his last medical check-in and was marked as available for potential heats as soon as he turned nineteen, which he did shortly thereafter."

That surprised Ned, since Ezer was so small. His hips were narrower than any Ned had ever seen on a man. "I don't know, Father."

"You don't have to know. The contracts will be signed. Once you see that the boy consents, your doubts will fade away." Lidell smiled. "You'll be a real alpha soon. Servicing your first heat. There's nothing like it. You never forget your first."

Hunter hummed his first agreement of the evening and then rose from the table. "If you'll excuse me, I'm going to go pack my things. It's been an enjoyable time, but tonight has been an interesting dinner that's made it clear to me that this is the end of it. I appreciate the care you took with me and the payment to my account." He turned to Ned. "It's been nice meeting you, and I wish you luck. If you take this boy on, be ready. The small ones are the fiercest." Then he wafted away as if on a breeze, his long robe drifting around him.

Lidell watched him go with a hint of something other than irritation on his face. It wasn't quite longing, but it was bittersweet. Then he faced Ned again. "The contract will be ready by next week. You'll sign it then." He wiped his mouth with his napkin and rose. "I think I'll go help Hunter pack."

Ned finished his dinner alone, taking a very long time in between moments of panic and shots of strange, sordid lust. In the end, he decided he shouldn't contract and breed Ezer. They were too young, and it was too much to ask of either of them.

But if Ezer was willing....

No. It was absurd. They were too young to become parents.

End of story.

# Chapter Seven

"No."

Ezer's father leaned back in his desk chair with a smirk. "Oh, but I think yes."

Ezer had been invited into his father's study after dinner for a "little chat". His brothers, even little Rodan, had all stared after them, frozen in their chairs, all aware nothing good came from a post-dinner "chat" with Father.

Ezer's heart pounded, and blue and green dots swam in his vision. He could barely suck in a breath. He was going to pass out. At least the plush carpet beneath the big chair opposite his father's desk was soft, so if he hit the floor there wouldn't be any bruises. He hoped he didn't piss his pants, though.

Somehow, he managed to stay conscious and gasp out, "I'm only nineteen. Besides, Da won't agree to this."

"*Da* doesn't have a say anymore." How his father managed to make the pet name sound so mocking, Ezer didn't know, but it was infused with layers of hate and disdain.

Clenching his fists and willing his panic away, Ezer thrust his chin up. "But I do. *I* have a say. I must consent. That's the law."

One of the few laws protecting omega rights, and one of the best defenses an omega had against unwanted matings and marriages, was the requirement of a signed contract before a shared heat, and another before a breeding. While it was true some alphas waited until the heat had already begun to obtain signatures on a breeding contract in order to capture an omega when his defenses were down, there was at least always a contract. Without one, an alpha could be prosecuted for rape, one of the rare instances of omega rights trumping alpha lust.

George nodded. "It is the law, yes. And you *will* consent."

"Why? Because you'll force me?" Ezer accused. "That's not consent, and you know it."

George's hazel eyes glinted. "I won't force you, son. I'll incentivize you."

Ezer sneered. "Money doesn't matter to me."

"It does. Just not in the ways you think. Have a look." George flipped his computer around, showing photos of four different homes.

One was a nice apartment complex, a place Ezer recognized as being near the lake Da liked to bike beside in the spring. The second was a cozy home in the heart of the Clearwood park, beside the lake, and not far from some of the finest old neighborhoods. The third was a beach house. The fourth was a mountain retreat. All of them places that Ezer recognized as being former possessions of his da before the marriage had transferred the entirety of his inheritance to George. None of which had been returned in the divorce.

Sweat prickled at Ezer's temples. He felt a bit ill. "What's this about?"

George peered at the photos. "Do you think Amos is happy where he is? In that run-down place you insist on visiting him in?"

Ezer stared at his father, stone-still.

"He used to love his apartment by the lake. He lived there before we met." George expanded the photos of the apartment, showing it off, room-by-room. The furniture was all to Da's taste and had been left as it'd been before everything went to hell. "Do you think he'd like to live there again?"

Ezer swallowed against bile, his heart pounding. "Why are you doing this?"

"Because I want you settled, Ezer. Out of my hair. This is a good chance for you."

Ezer worked his jaw, trying to find words to express the cold horror of his suspicions. "This is to punish me."

"Well, yes," George said without hesitation. "And to punish Amos, too, of course."

"How?"

"It's subtle and nothing you would understand." He smirked. "You haven't got the brains for it."

"I'm not stupid."

"So you and Amos claim. But I'm not stupid either, no matter what your damned da seems to think."

Ezer stared at George.

"The apartment Amos has lived in for the last year is disgusting. Do you want him to stay there, Ezer?"

"No, but Da wouldn't want me to sell myself in exchange for an upgrade in his living situation."

"You don't know him like you think you do." George's lips twisted. "He's selfish." His tone shifted to something more sympathetic as he continued. Though he's always wanted a good match for you. Amos wants you to have children. You're his favorite son, after all."

His words gave Ezer chills. "He loves us all equally."

"No. He doesn't." Still said with that creepy and compassionate tone. "He loves you best, and he wants you to be safe with an alpha who can care for you despite your deficiencies."

"Da doesn't think I have deficiencies."

"You're fooling yourself. Of course he thinks you have deficiencies. Because you *do*. Lying to yourself won't help your situation, Ezer."

"I don't want to sign a lifetime contract at nineteen."

"I'm afraid that's not an option for you."

Ezer let out a slow breath. "Just spit it out. What do you want from me?" He could feel his father's trap about to grab his ankles and hold him fast; he knew it would break him in the process.

George leaned back, steepling his hands beneath his chin, and looking thoughtful. "For each child you give birth to, I'll give Amos a piece of his property back. For each year you please the alpha I've chosen for you, I'll give Amos a stipend that will more than replace what he spent annually when he was my omega." He showed Ezer a number that took his breath away.

So many zeroes. Such a better life for Da. No more living in that run-down hellhole. No more rats. No more trying to put together a decent meal out of hotdogs and corn chips.

"Why?"

"You're an embarrassment. Running around acting like you're not a Fersee, looking like a half-starved rat, getting beaten up by your betters, and just..." He waved at him. "Being weird. Existing as proof of...as proof of your omega parent's deficiencies. This will solve all of that. You'll submit to your place as an omega. You'll use your body to produce heirs for an alpha, a man who deserves them. You'll settle into happy, pregnant oblivion, and I'll be well rid of you."

"And it's worth all that? All that *money*? To be rid of me?" Why did his father hate him so much? He wasn't obedient, and he wasn't what George had wanted in a son, not in any way, but he wasn't a bad person. Not like those awful alphas who'd attacked him.

"Being rid of you is worth more than you can possibly know," George said, his jaw tightening. Then, as if making himself relax, he rolled his shoulders and eased his mouth into a pleasant smile.

"And, as a bonus, I'll have one out of the four of you omegas settled early and well. The other three will be easy to place anyway—they're handsome, intelligent, charming, and mine."

"So you're disowning me?"

George huffed a small laugh. "I'm going to spend more on placing you, Ezer, than I'll ever have to spend on any of them. All of them will bring *me* money in heat payments and marriage contracts. You, however, I have to buy a placement for."

Ezer's mouth clamped shut. Tears stung his eyes.

"No one wants you. I was lucky to find a young alpha of a peerage family in dire enough straits to be willing to take you on in exchange for the right amount of money. But I promise he's a good young man, high-quality with strong priorities. He wants to make a family with a devoted omega, and he has the right family connections, if not the money, to make him a good match. Plus, I'm assured he can keep you at heel, even through a hard post-partum drop, if necessary. If you only knew how much effort I'm putting into you. Effort I'll never have to make for your brothers. Don't accuse me of lack of caring. If anything, I care too much."

"'Too much'? You've never even liked me."

"There are all sorts of ways to care, son. I might not want you in my home, or desire to have you or your offspring in my life, but I don't want you to suffer. I want you to be content in your new life. Pregnant omegas are happy omegas."

"Content in the prison you're sending me to?"

"Amos always liked the house by the beach. One heat and birth from you, and he can have his lake apartment, two and he can winter by the lake, and summer at the beach. He could stop working at that trash line and go back to living a life of ease. He could even, perhaps, meet some hapless widowed alpha and make a putz of the man just the way he did me. It's up to you, Ezer. The rats can keep chewing on his hair at night, if you prefer."

Ezer gritted his teeth. "This is blackmail. If I don't do it, you're going to leave Da to suffer. And what will you do to *me* if I don't agree?"

George shrugged. "Like I said, it's incentive. There's no law against incentive."

Ezer's stomach rolled. "Who? Who have you sold me to?"

His father shrugged. "It isn't a done deal yet. First you have to sign the contract. I had my attorney draw it up today." He shoved it Ezer's way, a sheaf of papers outlining the agreement between him and whatever alpha his father had chosen, indicating his consent to be taken and bred. Every omega signed one eventually, whether it was an independently negotiated trade of nothing more than a heat, or a full-on university-sponsored online auction of a breeding, or a family arrangement like this one for a full life commitment. Ezer's eyes glazed with furious tears as he tried to read it. The letters spun and moved around, something numbers never did, no matter how upset he got. Even squinting, he couldn't make out any words.

"Sign it." George ordered. "What does it matter who's bought your heat? He's a young man of good name and his father says he'll be a good stud for breeding. Plus, he's a romantic type, determined to be faithful. You can't ask for more."

He could ask to be loved, couldn't he? But his father didn't love him, so why would his father think he deserved that? Ezer's throat hurt, his eyes burned, and he tried to read the contract again, but it was useless.

"I don't need faithfulness. I don't even want it," Ezer bit out, wiping his tears with the back of his hand.

"Oh, but I do," George said. Goosebumps rose on the back of Ezer's neck. "I want you popping out babies until you're so blissed out on all the pregnancy and chest feeding hormones that you can't see straight. Until you're out of my hair for good.

Understand?"

"Why?"

"If you're so smart, figure it out."

Ezer rubbed his face and pressed his lips together. He heard his brothers' voices lift and fall in the hallway, a spill of laughter, and an excited yell from Rodan. "You want me out of your lives."

"Yes. And that won't happen if the boy's a one-and-done sort of man. But his father assures me otherwise. This one's a real romantic. He'll want to keep you barefoot and pregnant, high on alpha semen and hormones. And that's the best outcome for all of us. A *kind* outcome for you and for your da. Don't be stupid, Ezer."

Ezer thought of Pete, naked and happy, pregnancy-round, and relaxed, walking around the mansion like a man in a glorious dream, and he shuddered. If that was what pregnancy did to a man…wait, had his own da been that way? He didn't remember much about life before Rodan's birth, but he remembered it being happy. He remembered his da laughing and relaxed, and naked. Yes. He'd been naked and happy, too. Just like Pete.

"Fuck you. *I'm* not like Pete."

"Indeed, you're not," George snapped. "And I suspect your post-partum drops will be hell for everyone, but this boy has a reputation for being willing to do what's necessary to get a job done. So, I think he will be able to handle you." He held a pen out to Ezer. "Sign."

"No."

"Yes."

"I won't."

"Then go pack your things. Head to your beloved da's apartment. Don't come back until you're ready to put pen to paper."

Ezer stared at him. He couldn't be serious. "Can't you give me time to think? This is coercion."

"Sign."

"No." Ezer rose from his seat with shaking legs, walked out of his father's study, and passed the large room where his brothers wrestled over the video game remote controls.

Rodan's squeaky voice rose in defiance, "It's my turn!" But Shan and Flo overrode him with low laughs. Yissen danced and sang along to the video game theme song. No one noticed Ezer.

The servants ducked by him in the hallway with their heads down, cheeks aflame, and a certain scuttle to their walk that gave away they knew more than Ezer himself did about what was happening in his home.

He'd no sooner thrown open the door to his bedroom than one of his father's men showed up in the doorway. "I'm here to help you pack your things. Nothing of value. Leave the laptop, phone, and clothing."

Ezer stared at the man, trying to understand what was happening. He picked up his bookbag, emptied it of his school things, and stuffed three pairs of jeans and a handful of random T-shirts inside. He pulled on his hoodie and hitched the bag over his shoulder.

"This way," the man said. His face was set like stone, no reaction showing at all. Ezer wanted to ask if he understood what was happening, if he knew why, but he couldn't get his mind around any of it. He was being kicked out of his home. This was how Da must have felt when Father announced he had to go. It had been equally out of the blue. He'd fought. There'd been violence. Blood.

Ezer put his shoulders back. He wasn't going to fight. He knew he couldn't win.

He was guided out to the car and put into the backseat. No goodbyes for his brothers. In part because he didn't believe this was forever, and in part because he didn't want to see their faces.

If they cried, he couldn't handle it, and if they didn't…well, he couldn't handle that either.

An hour later, after negotiating evening traffic in Wellport through to Roughs Neck, the car pulled up outside of Amos's apartment. Ezer got out and took the stairs to his da's apartment. He knocked on the door, and it swung open.

Amos took one long look at him, sighed, and gestured for him to come in.

# Chapter Eight

IN AN ATTEMPT to distract himself from his father's mad scheme, Ned had agreed to go with Braden and Finch to Roughs Neck in search of a new supplier for Bright's powder. The one they'd been buying from before had been busted the night after they'd left and the entire operation shut down.

The new supplier Finch had uncovered from some source in his father's household—a beta servant whom Finch had bribed—lived in Amos's building, and while returning to the scene of the crime yet again was awkward, Ned hadn't thought he'd see Amos, or Ezer for that matter.

So far he hadn't.

Inside the supplier's apartment, Ned stood with his arms over his chest, hoping nothing exploded until he'd left the building. Burners were turned up high, chemicals and corrosive liquids spilled everywhere, and there were far too many cats running around in the mess for Ned's liking. The supplier, a mustachioed guy named Guffin, sat at a table with various piles of powder, while his pal, a chemist hopefully, worked with the bubbling, burning pots, pans, and glass tubes. A cat was balanced on his shoulder, and two more perched at the end of the long counter.

Another cat slipped by Ned's ankles where he stood close to the door, eager to escape, and questioning his life choices. He should have stayed home and worked out his anxiety in the weight room with Earl. Then he could have spilled his guts to the old man, received his wisdom, and avoided this shit show altogether.

But he hadn't.

Because if there was one thing he'd figured out about himself in the last year, it was that he was incapable of not getting himself into trouble. Just caring about Ezer had placed them both in a dangerous position, and he hadn't done anything other than try *not* to show how Ezer's eyes made him feel. He'd even gone so far as to act as if he didn't care so much, hoping to put a stop to the bullying from Braden and Finch. But it hadn't worked.

The supplier held up two baggies of powder. Ned dreaded the moment when Braden and Finch took their first hit of this crappy stuff. The source looked pretty sketchy, and he wouldn't trust it up his own nose. Not that they tried to get him to use it anymore. He'd convinced them that the reason he'd stopped using it was because he had a weaker-than-average heart. It'd been diagnosed at his last alpha heat-readiness check-up, where they'd assessed his physical health and ability to support an omega through a heat. He'd scored a ten out of ten, which meant his father could do exactly what he was doing: attempt to arrange heats for him to handle, either for practice or breeding.

Ned had used the testing, though, to lie to Braden and Finch, telling them that while he'd love to indulge in the high from the powder, he didn't want to risk his life for it, or damage his heart so that he couldn't support an omega through a heat. Even Braden and Finch agreed it wasn't worth dying or giving up heat sex for. Though given the shoddiness of this apartment and these suppliers, Ned wasn't sure they believed it deep down. Because this couldn't be good powder. No way.

Braden stood by the window all the way across the too-flammable room, gazing out at the courtyard below, waiting for their powder to be packaged. Finch hovered near the dealer's table, watching as the packets of powder were divvied up based on his and Braden's monetary contributions. They were buying some for the servant, too, in exchange for the information.

As Finch hovered, twitching all over, Ned could practically smell Finch's hunger for the drug. He wondered how often Finch was indulging. It seemed, more often than not these days, he was high.

"Hey, what do you know? It's our favorite cocksleeve," Braden said, pressing his nose to the glass and peering down. "Visiting his whore father again."

Ned stiffened. Ezer was here? He didn't want him anywhere near these pricks, not ever, but especially not now when he had no idea what was going to happen between them in the future. Tension flared in the room, Finch's interest piqued, as he came over to peer down, too. "Cocksleeve has a decent-looking mouth," he muttered. "You know he'd be eager to open it once he was on his knees. He just needs someone to put him there."

"That someone going to be you?" Braden asked, laughing.

"Give me five minutes alone with him."

"No," Ned said, shocked by his inability to hold his tongue.

Ezer wasn't in the room with them, he wasn't in danger right this moment, and by the time they had the powder, Ezer would be safe in his omega parent's apartment, and yet even the thought of Finch having five minutes with Ezer alone made his stomach roil and his pulse pound.

"No?" Finch asked, swinging around. "What is it with you and that scrawny cocksleeve? You got your heart set on his tiny ass or what?"

Braden's left brow went up, calculations happening behind his eyes, and he dropped his arms by his side, a lazy, dangerous smile on his face. "Pretty sure Ned here has a taste for rubbish. Runs in his family from what I hear."

"Shut up," Ned muttered, ignoring the slight to his family, not even sure if Braden was talking about his father's penchant for auction heats, or Heath's scandal with his lover's son, or maybe even his own dead omega parent. "Why do you pick on Ezer so much? He's not important. He's not even shit on your shoe. So what's your deal?"

"Interesting change of pace," Braden said, laughing. "Where's your usual refrain? 'He's George Fersee's son, Braden, you can't do that to him!' Which is it? Is he unimportant or is he important as hell? Here's a scoop for you, Ned. He's no Fersee, that's for sure, and that's why he's trash, and *that's* why we can do whatever we want to him. Don't you get it?"

Ned shook his head.

Finch snarled a laugh. "He hasn't heard. No gossipy omegas live in his house, remember?"

"Tsk, tsk, such a shame. Should we enlighten him?"

"Nah. Let him find out on his own."

Ned worked his jaw and tried to keep calm. He was about to ask more questions when Guffin held up a paper bag with the baggies of powder inside. "Don't use it all at once, boys. Or do. I've got a fresh batch that'll be ready to go day after tomorrow." He grinned as he pocketed their cash. "Feel free to come back."

Finch couldn't even wait until they were out of the building to get into his bag of powder. He opened it on the stairwell, spilling some down the front of his sweater as he took a deep sniff of the white stuff. He hummed and then blew a raspberry through his lips, his eyes rolling up. "Fuck yeah. Let's find a hot hole to share."

"'Share'?" Braden said, laughing. "No way. I don't want your sloppy seconds."

Ned lingered behind them on the stairwell, passing Amos's door, tempted to press his ear against it to listen for Ezer's voice.

He heard rusty door hinges squeal below as Braden and Finch exited. He lingered on Amos's ratty welcome mat. Raising his hand, he touched the knocker, and waited for his heart to tell him what to do.

Another shriek of door hinges screeched up the stairwell.

"Ned!" Braden's voice shouted. "Get your lovesick ass down here. We're getting a car to Show City. Plenty of paid fun to go around."

Ned loathed these boys, loathed their voices, their laughter, their idea of fun. He wished he could knock on Amos's door and be invited in for tea. He'd love to sit there in Amos's filthy but warm apartment, gazing into Ezer's eyes, and making some sort of headway with him, forging a path to forgiveness.

"Ned!" Finch this time. "C'mon!"

Ned dragged his feet but reached the bottom of the stairs with a new determination in his gut. "Go on without me," he said. "I don't feel so well."

"One of the rats bite you?" Braden asked, nudging him manically in the ribs. He'd hit the powder now, too. "Need rabies shots?"

"Yeah," Ned said, and lunged with a growl and grimace, pretending to be infected.

Braden laughed. "Whatever, dude. Just don't go back in that apartment building. Nothing good will come of it. Stay away from that omega unless you plan to use him and lose him. In which case, have a go."

Both Braden and Finch sniggered as they climbed into the car they'd hired to take them to the omega and beta prostitutes of Show City. Ned walked toward the bus stop that would take him to the subway station he needed for his trip home, but he ended up walking around the block instead. Back by the chain-link fence, he stood outside the building and gazed up to the fourth-floor light he knew came from Amos's rooms.

He wondered what Ezer was doing there and if he was all right.

The lights flickered with a pop, and the power in the building went out. Various windows began to light up again with the glow of candles, and Ned hustled down the block as people spilled from the entrance, not wanting to be caught by Amos standing there like a stalker. He'd made it as far as the bus stop again before he heard the shuddering boom.

Heart pounding, Ned turned and ran back toward the apartment building, finding it awash in flames. "Ezer! Mr. Elson!" he yelled, trying to push past the tenants running from the burning building. He rushed to the doorway, trying to get inside.

But there was no way he could. Just as he had almost breached the entrance, he was gripped from behind and hauled back by a tall, strong police officer. "Get back from the building, boy! Out of our way!"

Panting and miserable, Ned huddled in the dirty, stinky crowd of residents and watched, spellbound, as the firetrucks arrived, and the hoses began to pump plumes of water into the raging building.

Gray dizziness sank in as Ned overheard the words of the officers and firefighters nearby: There was no hope for anyone inside.

None at all.

# Chapter Nine

EZER SAT, NUMB and empty, on his da's sofa, the hot cup of tea scalding his palms, but he was too shaken to put it aside.

"Talk to me, Ezer," Da said.

"You betrayed me," Ezer said. "You told Father I've been coming to see you."

Da sighed and wiped a hand over his face. "I know that's how you see it, Ezer, but I'm trying to help you."

"He's decided I shouldn't return to school. He wants me to sell my heat *now*. Make me breed! Marry!"

Da didn't look surprised. Ezer's stomach tightened and twisted.

"Ezer, listen to me. I'm trying to protect you."

Ezer went cold all over, reality bending and distorting as something near to understanding began to dawn. "You planned this with him."

"I don't plan things with your father," Amos said. "He'd never allow that. Not now. But I planted the seeds of certain ideas in his head, knowing how they'd come to fruition, because I know *him*."

Ezer shook his head. "No. You wouldn't have."

Amos put his hand on Ezer's knee, eyes pitying. "But I did."

"Why would you want me to sell my heat now? Breed and marry so young? Why? You're an omega. You know what all that *means*."

"It means you'll be safe." Amos pulled his hand back and sighed. "The boy in question is in love with you."

"What? Who? How? No, don't answer those questions. I don't care. You can't make me do anything I don't want to do. There are consent laws."

Da put his own tea aside and leaned forward. "Ezer, listen to me. There are forces at work in your father's heart that you can't begin to understand. The risk of an auction for your first heat—and frankly ongoing heats—is so much higher than this plan. Who knows who might buy your heat? And for what purpose?"

"I think the purpose is rather obvious, but at least I'd have my own money then. Father is paying to have someone take me off his hands! I won't have a dime to my name. Nothing of my own."

"You're naïve! An auction is full of risk. The bidders are vetted, of course, but once you're alone in a heat house with an alpha, there's no promise that he'll be kind. And once you've agreed to breed with him, there's no promise that he'll be a good father to your children. He might, for example, kick them out of the house in the middle of the night and send them to their omega parent in the slums unless they agree to an early heat with a man of their choosing!"

Ezer shook his head. "You *want* me to do this?"

"I want you in a good situation with an alpha who won't do to you the things your father has done to me. I want you happy, Ezer. You're my baby, my dear son, my favorite."

"Why? I'm not half as lovely as Shan, or as smart as Flo, or as handsome as Yissen, or as sweet as Rodan."

Da's eyes softened. "Is he still sweet? I'd hoped so."

Ezer ground his teeth and said nothing.

"Ezer, haven't you noticed that you're different?"

"Stupid, you mean?"

Da blinked and rubbed two fingers between his brows. “Omegas have between five and eight heats in a lifetime. That’s a limited number of opportunities to reproduce, to have children with the alpha that they love.”

Ezer put his tea aside and stood up. “I know how babies are made, Da.”

“Sit down,” Amos ordered. “Listen to me.”

Ezer sat again, his stomach hurting, and a terrible feeling whatever his da was about to say, he really didn’t want to know.

“When I was a young man, there was an alpha in my hometown whom I cared for very much. He was handsome, and sweet. Small. Not much bigger than me. My father refused to let me consider any sort of relationship with him—not a heat, not a breeding, and definitely not a marriage. He wasn’t considered a good risk. He couldn’t read and he was poor. No future in it.”

A cold finger of knowing slid down Ezer’s neck.

“I never forgot him, though. Not through the first four heats with your father. Two were fruitless and the other two were your older brothers. So when I felt my fifth heat coming, worried it was the last, I did something very stupid.”

“Stop.” Ezer stood again. “I don’t want to know about this.”

“When the signs of the heat started, I left Wellport. I went back to my hometown and found Finn. He was still there. Married to a kind omega with whom he shared three children—two betas and an alpha. He struggled to feed them all. I understood then, when I saw how they lived, why my father had said Finn and I would never have stayed happy together.” Amos’s lips twisted. “But with the heat coming on, with the longing I’d always had for Finn, it didn’t matter to me anymore. Finn felt the same. He still wanted me, too, but we agreed we could never have more than this one heat, and that his omega and George must never know about it.”

"Da..."

"So, I used your father's allowance money to take Finn up to a heat cabin in the woods which I'd already rented for the duration."

Nausea hit Ezer hard. The room spun. The air seemed sucked dry of oxygen.

Amos's expression pleaded for understanding. "I just wanted one heat with him. If you ever fall in love, Ezer, you'll appreciate how it was for me. Love is irrational. It doesn't care about right or wrong, or if the alpha is a good match, or if you're already married."

"No." Ezer didn't believe that.

"Someday you'll understand. It was the best heat of my life—the only heat that I chose my partner for." Amos blushed, his eyes going glossy as he remembered. Clearing his throat, he went on, "Your father—well, George, believed me when I told him I'd gone into an unexpected heat while on my annual solo vacation. He believed me when I said it had come on too hard and fast for me to contact him, and that I didn't know the identity of the alpha who'd taken me in and helped me through it." Amos swallowed hard. "George had no reason to doubt me. I'd been a faithful, devoted omega until then."

Ezer shook his head, his entire life spinning in front of his face.

"Finn grew curious, though. He suspected the heat had ended in pregnancy. He was familiar with the way of it from his own omega's experiences, and he recognized the signs. A few years ago, he came to Wellport seeking answers. He wanted to see you."

Ezer stared at his da, a memory flitting into his mind. Several weeks before Amos had been dismissed from the house, he'd taken Ezer to the shore, and there they'd run into a small but handsome alpha whom Amos had called Mr. Swinton, an old friend from his hometown. They'd eaten ice cream together, just the three of them, and Mr. Swinton had asked Ezer annoying and boring questions about school and his hobbies. After Ezer had finished his cone, Da had sent him on home alone, saying that he needed to run some errands.

"Finn thought you were wonderful," Amos said, with a hint of tears in his voice.

"*No*," Ezer said again, still denying the wreckage of his life.

Amos looked away, a veil of shame falling over his features. "After you and I met with him at the shore, he told me he could stay in Wellport for two nights. The temptation was too great. I stayed those nights with him."

Ezer remembered that as well. He'd been confused as to why Amos had gone to "visit friends," leaving little Rodan to the servants and his older brothers to care for. Normally, when Da traveled, he'd given them much more warning. Father had also been confused.

"It was reckless." Amos closed his eyes and shook his head. "I didn't want to destroy our lives. I was caught up. Finn made me feel so..." He swallowed again, opening his eyes, and gazing at the ceiling. "It was so good, but we knew it couldn't be anything lasting. His omega needed him, and I belonged to your father. We could never be more than the one heat and these few nights. We knew that." His lips curved up sharply. "I daresay it only made it all hotter and more intense for both of us."

Ezer shuddered.

Breaking free of his memories, Amos ran a hand through his graying blond hair, shifted to cross one leg over the other, and met Ezer's gaze again. "Anyway, your father found out about us. Well, not George himself, but one of his hired men. There were photos, and your father recognized the resemblance between Finn and the son he'd agreed to raise as his own out of pity for me."

"So *you're* the reason he hates me?"

Da sighed. "Ezer, he looks at you, and he sees only what I did to him. He wants you out of his house because it hurts his pride far too much to have a constant reminder of my betrayal. He wanted to auction your heat as soon as you turned eighteen, but I talked him out of it. Then he wanted to send you out of the house to live with me, but I pointed out that if he did that everyone would suspect that he'd been cuckolded, and he knew I was right. As it is, most people just think he's a heartless ass."

"And this Finn didn't take you in after Father kicked you out?"

"Finn is poor, and his omega is in love with him." Amos shook his head. "I wasn't about to ruin his life too."

"Just mine then. I hate you."

"I know you do right now, but Ezer—"

The explosion rattled the room and the tea mugs fell to the floor, shattering, as a *whoosh* of flame licked beneath the door, setting the rug on fire. Amos leapt up and grabbed Ezer by the hand, dragging him toward his bedroom.

"Da, we have to go," Ezer said, tugging him the opposite way, toward the front door.

"This way, Ezer. This way."

Outside the window of his da's bedroom, there was a rickety, wooden fire escape. Amos couldn't seem to get the window open, and smoke filled the air behind them from the burning carpet. A glance in the other room showed that the sofa was on fire now, too, and the drying clothes draped over the furniture.

"Help me," Amos ordered, and Ezer leaned in next to him, adding his effort to the window. Both of them groaned with relief when it finally gave way. They climbed onto the fire escape with ash floating down from the upper stories. Several other tenants were trying to scramble down, too, but two stories above, a section of the fire escape had caught fire, and the beta couple was trapped.

Ezer wanted to help, but there was no way and no time. Da tugged him away, saying, "We can't help them now. We have to get you down."

Coughing, they both stumbled all the way down the fire escape, the old wood shaking beneath their shoes, and they held on tight, hoping the steps didn't break. Ezer's heart raced; he felt flakes of scalding ash on his skin. When they dropped into the yard behind the apartment, they ran far away from the blaze, following the others who'd escaped. Once they were safe, in an empty lot away from the heat, Amos drew Ezer close, covering his ears to try to stop him from hearing the cries of the trapped people.

The squeal of fire engines filled the air, and they both fell to a huddle on the ground as the columns of water rose above the building, damping it down.

Too late to do any good, and far too late to prevent loss of life.

Ezer shook, staring at the destroyed carcass of his da's reduced state.

Where would they go now?

Both of them had nothing. Absolutely nothing.

# Chapter Ten

NED RAN AROUND the back, his heart in his throat, and skidded to a stop when he saw Amos and Ezer clinging to each other a good distance from the still-burning apartment building. He breathed heavily, his stomach heaving as the smell of chemicals and burning meat reached his nose. Rats scurried across the scorched grass, racing out in hordes, and cats, too, sped from the basement.

Glancing up toward the windows of the Bright's powder dealers, Ned had no doubt the explosion had come from there. He also didn't think any living thing in that flat had made it out alive. He was shocked anyone had survived given the size of the fireball and the way the ground had shaken beneath him.

The people all around cried and stared, rocking on their heels in shock. Ned picked through them, drawing closer to Ezer and Amos, relief coursing through him. "Ezer! Mr. Elson!"

Ezer and Amos turned to him, astonishment on both their faces, and confusion, too.

"You're okay?" Ned asked, putting his hands on Ezer and pulling him into a hug. Ezer struggled against him until Ned released his squirming frame. "You're okay," he muttered in relief. "You're both okay."

"What are you doing here?" Ezer asked, blinking, sweat slipping down his temples from the heat of the flames. An unspoken *Why are you touching me?* hung in the air, too.

"I was just..." Words fled. Ned had no reason to be here. He had no reason to care.

"Buying Bright's powder?" Ezer suggested. "From the idiots who exploded themselves? And not just them, but half the people in this building?"

"No," Ned said. It was true. "I was just passing by and, um, I..." He shook his head, meeting Amos's eyes. "You're okay, Mr. Elson?"

Amos nodded, staring at him with a stunned but measuring air. "We're fine." Then he glanced toward the charred remains of his home and let out a bitter laugh. "Though where we'll go or what we'll do now, I don't know."

"Won't Mr. Fersee let you stay with him, or on one of his properties, until something is sorted out?" Ned asked.

Amos shook his head. "No."

"Oh." Ned thought quickly. "I can take Ezer home to his father's house, and you can stay with me and my father until we can figure something out. We have plenty of room, and—"

"My father kicked me out, too," Ezer said, glaring at Ned. "And why are you being nice? *Why* are you *here*?"

"I'm just—"

"He tried to assault me," Ezer said to Amos. "He tried to rape me."

"No. It wasn't like that, Ezer. I promise. I've been wanting to apologize to you for all that, but—"

The fire sirens began again, another truck screaming in to help. Police and ambulance sirens also cut their discussion short, and Ned didn't know what to do to assist Amos and Ezer. He stood beside them, watching as the fire razed the entire building despite the fire department's efforts, until, finally, Amos took control.

"Ned, Ezer and I would appreciate it if you could arrange for a car to take us to a hotel. It doesn't have to be a nice one. Somewhere we can feel safe for the night. If you would be so kind as to pay for that for us, I'll find a way to compensate you for the kindness."

Ned insisted, "But there's room at my house. You'll both be plenty safe there, and you can rest for as long as you need." His eyes strayed to Ezer, and he said, "I'll take care of you both. I want to."

Ezer's eyes narrowed.

Amos shook his head. "That offer is kind, but far too much right now. The hotel, please."

Ned looked between Ezer's doubtful expression and Amos's exhausted, pained one before pulling his cell phone from his pocket to order a car. He also found a hotel nearby, just over the line from the slums, in a part of town where Ezer and Amos should be safe to walk the streets at night if need be.

When the car came, Ned held open the door for them to climb inside, and it was all he could do not to climb in after them. But Ezer's continued clear distrust of him, as well as Amos's firm hand on his chest, pushing him back before he could get into the backseat too, kept Ned from insinuating himself into their difficult night further.

Ned had already made a mess of things by hugging and touching Ezer, by even being here at all. Though he couldn't help but be glad that he *had* been here.

As the car pulled away from the curb, a police officer jerked him around by his collar, getting up in his face. "What's a rich alpha kid like you doing lingering around? Looking for Bright's powder, huh?"

"No!" Ned babbled out an excuse and was relieved when the officer released him with only a warning to get back to the right part of town. "Hanging out in Roughs Neck will ruin you, kid.

Got it? A short high from Bright's powder and a cut-rate omega hole isn't worth it. If you're horny, you're better off paying the prices in Show Town. Cheap isn't always better."

Ned trudged to the bus stop for the third time, sticky with sweat and with adrenaline raking through his veins. By the time he arrived back home, he'd missed eight texts from Braden and Finch, half of them foul photos of them toying with omega whores, and two from Amos Elson, thanking him for the hotel and reassuring him that Ezer was safe.

He wished he had someone to talk to, but Earl was already in bed.

Ned entered the room he'd slept in since he was a kid and dropped onto his mattress without even showering. He stared out the window at the view of the city below, feeling pent-up and confined. This room was too small for him now. He needed more.

He needed Ezer.

Ned imagined Ezer at the hotel, lying awake in bed, no doubt, thinking all kinds of thoughts. Was he scared? Was he worried? Was he thinking of Ned, too?

"WHAT IN THE hell was Ned Clearwater doing there?" Ezer asked into the darkness.

The hotel was a decent one. Two beds, a television with all the streaming services, and a warm shower with endless hot water. It was clear Da appreciated that the most. Ned hadn't scrimped in sending them to this place, but he was so wealthy it was probably a drop in the bucket to him.

With no cell phone, Ezer hadn't been able to alert his brothers or his father—ha, his father!—about what had happened, and he didn't know whether he even wanted to. His mind was a blur of new information, and troubled from the shock and trauma of seeing men die in front of his very eyes.

He was alive.

He was homeless.

He was penniless.

He wasn't a Fersee.

To think, that morning he'd woken concerned only about whether he would be able to solve the math problems he'd chosen as a fun exercise for himself, and now…

"I'm not sure why he was there, but it doesn't matter. Thank God he was," Amos murmured. From the other bed the rustle of sheets came across the room. They'd cranked up the air conditioning when they'd first arrived, overheated, but now that they were safe, Ezer felt cold down to his bones. "He was able to help us afford a ride, and he got this room for us."

"He was there buying Bright's powder, I just know it. All those alphas use it."

"Perhaps. Or maybe he came to apologize to you, like he said."

Ezer scoffed. "Why would he even think I'd be there?"

"You *were* there."

"Yeah, but how would he have known that?"

"Ezer. It's late. Go to sleep. Everything can wait until tomorrow. In fact, it will have to. There is nothing we can do about any of this tonight."

The night crept by with the *shoosh* of cars passing on the road outside, and the chatter of people walking down the hallway inside, and Ezer didn't sleep a wink. Instead, he played back the last nineteen years of his life and tried to see it all from a new perspective.

So many puzzle pieces had clicked into place: why his father had never loved him as fully as his other sons, why he'd turned on him too when Da had been cast off, why he'd always been Da's favorite despite being scrawny and ugly by society's standards, and, most importantly, why Da had been sent away so decisively and violently.

"Why did you love Finn so much?" he asked, just as the sun started to rise.

Da shifted in his sleep, but only a slight snore answered Ezer's question.

Why had his da risked everything for a few experiences with this Finn Swinton? Was love really so strong? And was it love or lust? Or the combination of the two?

He didn't know. He'd never felt that kind of stirring for anyone before. He'd never even had a crush, so what did he know about love?

Yesterday had proven Ezer knew very little with regards to his life. He'd been wrong about everything from who his father was to what his da wanted for his future, to the very makeup of his blood and family life. He *knew* nothing anymore. So perhaps he *was* wrong about why Ned had been in Roughs Neck, too, then.

But no.

Bright's powder was the only answer. Ned was a disgusting alpha bully who snorted it and used omegas. Everyone knew that.

And yet Ezer couldn't help but feel a hint of gratitude for the kindness he'd shown them last night. Though he was sure Ned would never have grabbed Ezer, hugged him with relief, and made those magnanimous offers if his wretched alpha friends Finch and Braden had been there with him, Ezer was strangely affected by Ned's display of humanity.

Even stranger, Ezer could still feel where Ned had touched him, as if the apartment building's flames had heated Ned's hands and left Ezer burned all the way through his clothes.

Speaking of…they had no clean clothes. Just the smoky, ruined ones they'd had on. What were they going to do? Where would they go?

Ezer flipped onto his side and stared at the window. Decisions needed to be made, and they needed to be made soon. There was no way around it.

In the pre-dawn darkness, he rose, washed his face in the bathroom, put on the sooty clothes from the day before and shut the door without waking his da. He left behind a note telling Amos not to worry, Ezer would make sure he had a place to go and a roof over his head.

Then he set out to keep that promise.

# Chapter Eleven

"JUST PUT IT on my bill. Yes, I'm sure," Ned said into the phone, as he stared out at the view of the ocean crashing against the shore. He paced the railing at the edge of the pool deck as he listened to the hotel clerk's next question. "Yes, and anything they order from the kiosks, gift shop, restaurant, or room service as well. No limits. Thank you."

Earl exited the house wearing his normal servant attire but looking less put together than usual. He rushed toward Ned and motioned for him to end his call.

"What's the problem?" Ned asked, disconnecting with the hotel where he'd been proud to put up Ezer and Amos the night before.

"Your uncle is in town and wants you to meet him for lunch."

"Uncle Heath?"

Earl nodded vigorously.

Ned understood his servant's excitement now. "I'm surprised he left Adrien. Aren't they're expecting the new baby soon? Won't Adrien need him during this time?"

"Simon said there was an important meeting here in Wellport Heath couldn't escape attending, though, yes, Adrien is pining for him already. Still, it's only supposed to be a day they'll be apart. It should be all right."

"But at this stage of the pregnancy, isn't that hard?"

There were a lot of things Ned had learned as an alpha in his sexual and reproductive health classes at school, but one of the most important was the need omegas had for their alphas during *all* the stages of pregnancy, but especially the final ones. The alpha's pheromones and necessary compounds in the alpha's semen helped ease their omega's anxieties, relaxed their bodies, and even aided in the softening of the womb so the babe could release more easily.

"I'm certain Heath can handle the intensity of their reunion. He's a strong, virile man. But, given how much he hates being away from Adrien at all, and with Adrien being so heavily pregnant, I don't anticipate he'll be in a good mood when you meet him, but he wants to see you all the same."

Ned nodded and followed Earl inside. He dressed in a suit and tie, because Heath wanted to meet for brunch at Estrange, a boutique restaurant by the park.

When Ned arrived, a little later than he'd have liked due to traffic and his driver's distraction at a crowded intersection that caused them to miss their turn, Heath was already sipping champagne with an impatient air.

Ned had to admit his uncle was an uncommonly handsome man, with a dark beard, fierce eyes, and a jawline that spoke of stubborn determination. In contrast, Heath's husband Adrien, who was at home, of course, where a pregnant omega belonged, was a beautiful, pretty thing, and soft-natured as well. It was too bad he wasn't here to smooth over whatever had Heath bristling with irritation, but pregnant omegas were never seen in public.

There were physical reasons for that—the sensitivity of their skin during pregnancy and their usual preference for nakedness to endure it being one of them—and cultural ones, too—alphas didn't enjoy seeing their pregnant, naked, often horny-as-hell omegas anywhere near other alphas. It was brutish, perhaps, but no one ever tried to fight an alpha's intrinsic nature on this, even if, maybe, they could or even should.

"Hello, sir," Ned said, taking the seat opposite Heath when his uncle gestured to it with his champagne glass. "How's Adrien? I spoke with him on videophone last week. He said he's feeling healthy, and the baby's growing well."

Heath's smile at the mention of his beloved omega was exactly the reason Ned had brought him up first thing. Heath could be a harsh man, but he was soft as a cloud for Adrien. "He's very healthy, yes, and the new one is due very soon. Little Michael is taxing Adrien some, but the boy's otherwise a little cherub, so we can't complain too much."

Ah, Michael. The alpha baby who'd taken Ned's inheritance. It was a good thing the kid was so cute and charming, or Ned might hate him.

Heath went on, "Unfortunately, certain business will wait for no man, and I must handle this particular problem before I can get back to Adrien." His eyes clouded. "Time is of the essence. He'll be needing me."

"He will," Ned agreed. "But what's so urgent that it brings you all the way to Wellport when he's at such a delicate stage?"

Heath's expression darkened considerably, and Ned thought he shouldn't have used the word 'delicate.' Heath shook it off. "My business partner, Felix, is trying to arrange a contract and breeding for himself, and it's going badly," Heath said, his brows lowering dangerously. "He's asked for my help in negotiations."

"What's the problem?"

"The omega's father has a prior..." Heath sucked his teeth and then rolled his eyes. "A prior *attachment* to the idea of settling his eldest omega first, and, thus, he wants Felix to consider a very unorthodox arrangement." He shook his head. "Fathers of too many omegas...pfft. Always trying to assert their sons' so-called 'best interests' these days when they should just force them to—"

"Lie back and think of babies while we alphas have our way with them? Doesn't that sound a little barbaric?"

Heath laughed. "I'm sure Adrien would glare at me for even implying it."

Glare at him—yes, that would be about all Adrien would do. He was so mild in so many ways. Ned didn't think he could stay interested in an omega like that. He preferred a man with bite.

Like a certain angry sky-eyed boy he'd heroically saved from having to sleep on the street last night. He looked at his phone, hoping to see a text of gratitude or acknowledgment from Ezer (or even Amos again) but there was nothing.

"Which brings me to this lunch. I wanted to see you while I was in town." Heath's thick brow raised. "I've heard more rumors."

"About me?"

He nodded and leaned back, crossing his arms over his chest. "Out with it."

"Out with what?" Ned hadn't done anything recently that could get him into trouble, despite the company he kept.

"Don't play innocent with me. I hear that you're still cavorting with Maddox and Tenmeter's sons, and I have it on good authority they're using Bright's powder, screwing prostitutes, and making a general nuisance of themselves with omegas at school."

"They are, but I haven't done any of those things, Uncle. I swear."

Heath's eyes narrowed and he took a sip of his wine, considering. "It's a good thing I believe you. But proximity to sin and criminal activity doesn't reflect well on you either, Ned. It makes it look like you condone it at the very least, and then it reflects badly on *me* because your behavior makes it seem as if you haven't been raised with any sense of morality."

Ned cleared his throat, unsure what to say to that.

"Which seems a bit unfair to me, wouldn't you agree? Since I didn't raise you. No, that was on my idiot brother, and no doubt he's at the heart of this continued friendship with these spoiled brats. Am I right?"

Ned fiddled with the napkin in his lap and wished the waiter would return with their food, or at the very least come back with a water for him to drink. His mouth was dry.

"Talk to me, Ned. Why do you continue to hang out with those bastards?"

Ned groaned. "If only they were bastards in the literal sense, then I wouldn't *have* to hang out with them at all."

"Oh? So Lidell's trying to extract money from their fathers in some way? What's the game?"

"There isn't a game. He has contracts—legitimate ones—with Braden and Finch's fathers, and they're all that is keeping us afloat."

"Your trust money that I put aside for you? It's gone?"

"No, it's still there. I haven't given it to him. He's asked, but..." Ned flushed.

It'd been embarrassing when his father had pleaded for help, and scary to turn him down, but Ned knew that if he gave in, they'd be destitute. "Father found another way to fatten his wallet before he wore me down enough to agree."

Luckily. Because he would have agreed eventually. He didn't want to see his father lose their home, nor did he want to lose it either.

However, he'd have at least talked to Heath first before giving his father anything. While Heath wouldn't have given Lidell any more money, he *would* have given Ned good advice.

But, in the end, the contracts with the Maddox and Tenmeter families had come through, and none of it had been necessary.

"Hmm." Heath frowned. "Are you are obliged to be friendly with these peerage brat hoodlums in order to secure the contracts?"

"That's it, yes. No one even *likes* Finch, and Braden's awful. But his omega brother, Ashden, has his heart set on me, and until recently Father wanted me to entertain that courtship." Ned flushed again and looked down at his hands twisting in his lap.

Heath saw the truth. "But you're not interested in the omega brother?"

"Ashden is very handsome and sweet, given his family, but no. I don't want him. Still, Uncle Heath, I *have* to play nice. If Ashden and Braden get angry, and if they tell their fathers to cut ties with my father, then we'll be in financial ruin. Again."

"Lidell always does put his eggs into rotten baskets."

"I'll graduate in a few years," Ned said, hoping to reassure Heath. "And when I start my career it'll be under your guidance. I promise, I won't make the same mistakes he did."

"No. You won't," Heath said. "I'll see to that. I'll take you under my wing and teach you what you need to know, and I have friends who can help you, too. But Lidell has to be kept separate from all of that. He isn't trustworthy if money is involved."

"I know."

"In the meantime, I want you to sever your friendships with those boys, and if the worst happens, then you're to come to me. I'll sort things out. For now, salvage what you can of your tattered reputation, because I won't have you working with me in the future if everyone thinks you're a bully, an addict, and a reprobate."

"I understand, Uncle." A weight lifted from Ned's shoulders. He could walk away from Braden and Finch. His uncle had said so. He could be free. "Thank you." Ned's phone pinged. He glanced down at it, heart leaping with hope.

*Thank you again for your help with a place to stay. I promise to pay you back for your kindness.*

But the name attached to the message wasn't the one Ned was hoping for. It read *Amos Elson.*

Not Ezer. Why hadn't Ezer reached out? Why hadn't Amos insisted on it?

"Ah, here we are. I took the liberty of ordering for us both while I waited," Heath said, as the waiters appeared and placed dishes in front of them, and a water was delivered at Ned's hand, along with a glass of a sparkling wine. "Thank you, Dreyden," Heath said to the waiter at his elbow. "This looks wonderful."

"Yes, thank you," Ned echoed, salivating at the eggplant caponata Heath had chosen for him. He hadn't been hungry, but with the prospect of being done with his asshole "friends," and the wonderful food now before him, he was eager to eat.

They ate their food in companionable silence, and when they were done, both of them sent their compliments to the chef. Over a fluffy chocolate and raspberry dessert, Heath said, "Someone texted you earlier, and your face went on quite a journey. What was that about?"

"A 'journey'?"

Heath smirked and then twisted his own expressions through a parody of excited hope sliding into mock despair. "So? Tell me."

"Ah, well, it's a strange story. Kind of long. We probably don't have time for it."

Heath examined his full plate and then flicked a glance at his watch. "We do. Tell me."

Ned didn't know where to begin. With his crush or his association with Ezer's bullies, or what to say about everything most important to him right now, so instead he summed it up with, "I was in Roughs Neck when the apartment building exploded last night."

Heath's brows flew up. "Excuse me? What were you doing in Roughs Neck? Were you with those peerage hoodlums?"

"I was there because an omega…well, *the* omega I like is sometimes there." He blushed, and Heath's lips twisted in amusement.

"You? The boy who got caught at orgies last year, are now sitting here blushing over an omega? He must be something else."

"He is. He's complicated and fierce and—" Ned swallowed hard. "Beautiful."

"From a good family?"

"Yes."

"Then what was he doing in Roughs Neck? They're reporting the apartment blew up due to an illegal Bright's powder lab inside. Was he there buying that crap?"

"No, no! He lives there."

Heath's head cocked. "In the apartment building?"

Ned rushed on. "His da does. Ezer was visiting him—ah, visiting his da, I mean, and…" Ned cleared his throat.

Heath tilted his head. "Wait, is this one of Amos Elson's sons?"

"Yes sir."

"George Fersee was terrible to the man, but he's still part of the peerage." Heath pondered, "Yes, a son of his is a good option for you. The boy's devoted to his da?"

"Yes, and I was in Roughs Neck because I was hoping to run into Ezer there." It wasn't true, but it'd become true in a way. He wasn't going to admit to his uncle that he'd been there with Braden and Finch while they bought Bright's powder. No way.

"I understand." Heath waved it off. "You wanted to see an

omega you like. Nothing new about that under the sun. So what happened?"

"Just I got to his da's apartment, before I could go inside, the building exploded." Ned swallowed hard, remembering the deafening boom and the way the earth under his feet had shaken. "I was so scared, Uncle Heath." Ned took a gulp of water, trying to get his voice back under control. It'd gone all high-pitched and tight. "But I ran toward the building, hoping to, I don't know, help him or someone else, but the police wouldn't let me in—"

"Thank fuck." Heath swiped a hand through his hair.

"So I went around the back, looking for another entrance, and I found them."

"Your omega and his da?"

"Yes. Well, he's not *my* omega, but, yeah, I found them. They were both in shock."

"I'm sure."

"Yes." Ned let out a sigh. "Because of complicated reasons *I* don't even understand, neither one of them had anywhere to go or any money at all."

"George Fersee is a cruel man." Heath frowned.

"I arranged for them to go to a hotel. I paid for their car ride and called to have the hotel's expenses put onto my credit card, and this morning I called again to tell the hotel to let them stay for as long as they need to, all of it on me. So I'd *hoped* Ezer would contact me. To thank me."

Heath took a bite of dessert. "He hasn't?"

Ned shook his head. "No."

"How rude."

"I think it's because he hates me?"

"He hates you?" Heath's gaze narrowed again. "Why?"

"Well, Braden and Finch…" Ned's phone pinged again. He jumped to check the text. This one was from his father saying he'd be out late tonight, and not to wait up for him. Which meant Lidell had decided to go gambling, most likely, which meant a lot of other bad things, too.

Ned's stomach dropped.

Plus, still no Ezer.

"So, Braden and Finch, the peerage thugs," Heath prompted. "What'd they do to him?"

"They've bullied him. Relentlessly. Horribly." Ned swallowed hard. He wasn't going to admit to the fact that they'd threatened to rape Ezer. He was still so ashamed.

"Ah." Heath took a slow sip of his wine. "You didn't stop them."

He said it like a statement. Not a question. Because he knew Ned well, and he knew Ned was a coward. Ugh. It should have made him feel even worse, but he already felt so bad about it, that it only made him feel nauseous again. He put down his fork.

Ned nodded. "I didn't stop them."

"So the boy hates you for that. It makes sense." Then his eyes sharpened again. "Or did you participate?"

"I was there. I didn't stop them. Ezer thinks I participated."

Heath shook his head in frustration. After a long, humiliating moment, he asked, "You're set on this kid?"

Ned swallowed hard. "Yes, but right now I just want to make him like me."

Heath sucked his teeth, contemplated the ceiling for a long moment, and then checked his watch. "You were right. This is a more complicated problem than I'd anticipated, and we may not have time to deal with it all right now. Here's what I know: Fersee hates his ex-omega. It's demented and complicated, but if Ezer is staying with his da, that tells me that Fersee has disowned him, too."

Ned nodded. It seemed probable.

"If Fersee has disowned him, then for most alphas he won't be good marriage material, because there'll be no money in it for them, or for you. You'd be left right where you are now."

Ned's throat tightened, his mind going back to the insane conversation he'd had with his father just a few nights prior. He should tell Heath all about that now, inform him that he'd been offered a great deal of money to take Ezer off George Fersee's hands, so long as he did it *now*.

"But, then again, you have me." Heath's brows lifted meaningfully. "I've always promised to make sure you have what you need to live a good life, so long as you keep your father's hands away from my money and stay out of trouble."

"I've done that, sir. Since you helped me last year, I've done both of those things."

Heath scoffed. "You may have kept Lidell from gambling away your trust fund, but I'm sure you've been snorting Bright's powder alongside Maddox and Tenmeter."

"I swear I don't snort Bright's, sir. I promise. On my da's grave."

Heath sighed. "You're so young."

"Sir?"

Heath ran a hand over his head again and then sat back. "You only call me sir when you're afraid of me. Are you afraid right now?"

"Yes, sir."

"Good. Because I want you to do what I say this time, Ned. Stay out of trouble. Get away from the Maddox and Tenmeter boys, and don't let your father pull you into any more of his schemes."

"Yes, sir."

Heath sighed. "He should never have asked you to involve yourself with immoral and corrupt people in order to safeguard his contracts. Exposure to rot leads to rot. Do you see what I'm saying?"

"I haven't let them rub off on me."

Heath scoffed. "They've rubbed off on you plenty."

Ned looked down at his hands again.

"I believe you're trying to straighten things out. Also I believe you're in love with this omega, and, oddly, I support this attachment despite Fersee being a rancid piece of crap stuck to the bottom of far too many shoes in this city."

"You do?"

"Yes, because I like his omega parent, and I can tell you want to be a better man for this boy."

"I do."

"If you can make it right with this boy, then do it. When the time comes to handle his first heat and breeding, even if Fersee has disowned him, I'll support you in it. *If* you don't fuck it up…" Heath pointed a finger at Ned and said with scary calm, "So don't fuck it up, Ned."

"I won't, sir. I promise."

Heath seemed skeptical, but an alarm on his watch went off. He tapped the screen and sent a message. "I'll be a little late. Don't hold tea." His attention turned back to Ned. "I need to go. Repeat to me what I've told you."

"Ditch Braden and Finch. Do whatever it takes to make Ezer forgive me. Stay out of Father's schemes."

"And?"

Ned searched his memory, finding nothing. He shook his head.

"And trust in me."

"Yes. Trust in you, Uncle."

Heath smiled, and it was more frequent now than it used to be before Heath had met Adrien, but it was still an unusual expression to see on his face. "I don't have time to deal with this until after Adrien's given birth. But, when things settle, I'll return to Wellport, and I'll see what I can do to help smooth the way for you with this Fersee kid. All right?"

Ned's heart lightened. "You'd do that?"

"If you do what I tell you, yes."

"I will! Thank you, Uncle. Thank you."

"But in the meantime, I'd like to see you step up and become more of a man. It's time you put away childishness and folly. It's time to make your own decisions about what's right and wrong."

Heath rose and motioned for the waiter to put the meal on his tab. "Stay and enjoy whatever you like. Another dessert, a little more wine, whatever you'd enjoy. It was good to see you, Ned." He patted the top of Ned's head, something he'd never done in the past either. "Hang in there, kid. We're going to build a wonderful future for you. Don't doubt it."

After he swept out of the room, Ned did as Heath suggested and ordered a second dessert and a nice wine to go with it. He ate the chocolate confection, checking his phone, and scrolling social media for updates on the apartment explosion.

There were no more messages from Amos or Ezer.

Somehow, his disappointment made the dessert taste less sweet.

# Chapter Twelve

"BACK SO SOON?" George said, leaning back in his leather seat behind the wide desk in his home office. His eyes were closed, as if he couldn't even be bothered to look at Ezer standing in the doorway.

Ezer collapsed into the seat across from his father—no, *George*, because that was how he was determined to think of him now that he knew the truth—without invitation and buried his head in his hands.

On a typical day, Ezer knew, his father would have left hours ago for his office downtown, but since Pete was large with child, he stayed home these days to keep his omega safe and satisfied.

In fact, Pete was perched naked on George's knee, his expression still drowsy, and his head resting on George's shoulder. He'd probably just enjoyed a morning's tumble with George on the desk.

"I knew you'd come around after a night in Amos's dump of an apartment," George murmured, eyes still closed.

Ezer hesitated. What he had to say was not for Pete's ears.

Pete woke up more as he took in Ezer's scruffy state. Blinking with worry, he leaned to whisper in George's ear.

George's eyes popped open, raking his gaze over Ezer's uncombed hair, stinking clothes, and unshaven face. A frown marked George's brow, and he pushed Pete from his lap, leaning forward with an air of apprehension. Was the concern for Ezer real? Or faked for Pete's benefit? Ezer didn't know for sure, but George sounded genuinely bothered as he asked, "What's wrong? What's happened?"

Pete, swollen and calm, pulled on his soft robe and came around the desk to put his hands on Ezer's shoulders, touching him with kindness. Ezer didn't shrug him off. It turned out it wasn't Pete's fault George hated Ezer, or that he'd kicked Da out. All this time, he'd blamed the pretty young omega for something that Pete had nothing to do with at all.

"There was an explosion," Ezer gritted out. His throat was tight, and he didn't know if it was from breathing in smoke the night before, or because he felt like crying. "Da's apartment. Everything and everyone inside. Gone."

Pete gasped, squeezing Ezer's shoulders, and then he slipped his arms around them from behind to hug Ezer, rocking him side-to-side. That was a bit much. Ezer tugged free of Pete's embrace and scrubbed his hands through his hair.

"And Amos?" George asked. If Ezer didn't know better, he'd think George was scared for the man he'd cast aside. Maybe he still held a bit of care for him in his heart after all. Whatever the case, George didn't want Da dead.

Pete slipped a hand through Ezer's hair, cooing soothing sounds, and Ezer wished he could appreciate it. He resisted the urge to toss Pete's hands away.

"He's alive," is all Ezer shared about Amos. "He's safe."

George caught Pete's eye and then jerked his chin toward the door. Pete seemed to hesitate, but then he bent to kiss Ezer's cheek, whispering, "It'll be all right, sweetheart," before leaving the room.

Ezer lifted his hand to wipe away the sticky residue Pete's soft lips left on his cheek.

"Tell me," George said, his voice tight and rough. "Everything."

Ezer dropped his head, trying to think of where to start. His breathing still came in ragged gasps, and he worked hard to get it under control.

When Ezer thought he could get through the telling of it without bursting into tears, he lifted his head and explained what he knew about the apartment: a Bright's powder lab explosion, no internal sprinkler system, flammable materials everywhere, and a poorly kept apartment building. It'd been a tinderbox. He didn't tell his father about the help he and Amos had received from Ned; it was still too strange, and he had other things on his mind.

"And where's Amos now?" George asked.

"Like I said, he's safe. I'm meeting him at ten." Ezer clenched his fists. "I'm just here to sign the contract. Like you wanted."

George stared at him, jaw ticcing, eyes searching.

"Father, I…" Ezer swallowed hard, and his eyes filled with tears against his will. His voice came out rough and weak. "Da has nothing now. I know he hurt you, but…he has *nothing*."

George whispered back, "He has *you*. And you were all he ever truly wanted. He wanted you enough to ruin everything."

Ezer wiped at his eyes with his palms. "I love him, he's my da, and I know some part of you must still love him, too."

At that, George bristled. "Pete is my omega now."

"I know. And he's a good person. I like him. I do."

George scoffed but said nothing.

"I also know Da made a mistake, and that mistake led to me, and I *understand* that you don't want…that you can't…" Ezer shook his head, tears slipping over his cheeks again.

"I can't what?"

"You can't love me. Now that you know the truth."

George leaned back and let out a slow breath. "He told you

then."

"Yes."

He huffed, his lips curling up at the edges, ugly and harsh. "And you're still siding with him?"

"What would siding with you look like, Father? You want to be rid of me. I get that, and I understand now why you do." Ezer tossed his hands up. "I'm here to sign the contract. You can have me out of your sight once and for all. I just ask two things of you. One—keep your promise to give Da what he needs to make a new life. And two—make it so that I don't have time to regret my choice. Let's do this as soon as possible."

George continued to stare at Ezer as if he were a madman. The sound of the clock over the dark fireplace permeated the room—*tick-tock, tick-tock*. Ezer took a deep breath; he couldn't even smell the odor of his father's cologne with the scent of smoke from the night before still stuck in his nostrils.

George's expression softened as he opened a drawer to retrieve the paperwork from his desk. He pushed the pages and a pen over to Ezer. "I've flagged the places that need your signature."

The words, as always, swam as Ezer's gaze moved over them. He could make no sense of any of it, but he found the flags and started to sign his name as he'd been taught, but he hesitated. "Wait, I do have a third request. I know the ownership of the apartment by the lake won't transfer to Da until I've borne a child—" He blinked, hurtful disbelief at his own words and their meaning shocking him silent for a moment. God help him.

Ezer calmed his wild heart. "But, please, add a sentence that allows him to stay in the lakeside apartment starting tonight. He has nowhere, Father. He has nothing."

George pulled the paperwork over the desk and wrote a few lines. "There. I've added an immediate monthly stipend for him, too, so long as you stay with the alpha I've chosen for you."

"Thank you." Ezer wiped at his tears again.

George shrugged. "Ezer, you realize I'm not trying to hurt you. I do care about you, son, and I believe in this life for you. You'll be happier this way. I know it."

Ezer shuddered.

"Do you want to know what the contract says? Who the alpha is?" George asked, after Ezer signed by all the flags and the newly written additions. "I can read it to you."

"What does it matter?" Ezer said. "I've signed it already. I'm officially his. It's too late to back out now."

George nodded and pulled the paperwork back across the desk. "It's done then."

DA SAT ON the bench across the street from the ruined apartment, staring up at the smoking remains of the building. His shoulders shook, and when Ezer came around to grab him in a tight squeeze, Da's eyes leaked tears.

"I don't know what to do," Da said, his voice quivering. "This shithole was all I had."

Ezer swallowed hard. "Father said he'll help you."

Da wiped away his tears with the back of his hand. "That's where you've been? With George?"

"Yes."

Da snorted. "What's the catch, Ezer? Why would he do that? He's made it clear he doesn't care what happens to me."

"He does," Ezer said with a strangled voice, remembering the expression on George's face when he'd thought Amos might be dead. "He cares. And he's going to give you back the apartment by the lake. He said so. He gave me the keycode to pass on to you." Ezer pulled the paper out of his pocket and handed it to his da. "And some cash."

"Why?" Da said, suspiciously, taking both and trying to make sense of his full hands.

"Because he's sorry that he's been so cruel. His pride was hurt, and he was wrong." Ezer wished that was all there was to it, but his da would put the pieces together soon enough.

Da's eyes narrowed. "That can't be all. I know him, Ezer."

Ezer went on staring at the smoking building, watching the wind take the dark ash into the spotless blue sky. He shivered. "Other alphas have been giving him the cold shoulder for what he did to you. They say it's unseemly. They've been cutting him off—"

"Socially or in business?"

"Both," Ezer went on, lying through his teeth. Though many alphas thought George's treatment of Amos was reprehensible, most of them had taken it as a sign that George could not be moved and had no shame, so they didn't risk their business deals by pushing for better terms with him. "He's got to make it up with you to save face for himself."

Da still examined Ezer skeptically, and then shifted his focus to the smoking building. "No one I knew inside was killed or injured at least," he said. "Except the rats."

"That was lucky."

"I'd grown rather fond of those rats."

"Da."

"George really said I can have the apartment by the lake?" In that moment Da sounded so young, like a hopeful child.

Ezer nodded.

"When?"

"Tonight."

"Ah." Da huffed a laugh. "I see. You've signed the papers in exchange for getting me into the apartment. You agreed to be bred."

"And wed. If the alpha wants that." Or so Ezer assumed. He hadn't read the details of the contract after all. He couldn't. It made Ezer's hair stand on end think of becoming a baby-making machine for some unknown alpha, but he'd do anything for his da.

"Oh, Ez," Da murmured. "As much as I think this is the right thing for you, I know you didn't want it. I don't know what to say."

"Say thank you."

"That seems wrong given your initial resistance to this plan."

Ezer shrugged. He couldn't help but agree.

"For what it's worth, I think you could be happy with this boy."

"So you've said. And Father, too."

Again Ezer didn't ask who the boy might be. He was too afraid to know. The decision was made. He'd have to learn to live with it. But for now, ignorance seemed closer to bliss.

"I suppose I need to thank George for this generosity," Amos said. "Last night, for the first time since George forced me to leave, I was scared, Ezer. This apartment wasn't much, but it was all I had. This and you."

"It's okay, Da," Ezer said, wrapping his arms around Amos.

He was still full of questions about his biological father, Finn, and about why Amos had risked so much for so little. But he held it all back. What did it matter now?

Ezer was going to be bred and as good as married, and his entire life as he knew it was over. He concentrated on comforting his da instead. "You're going to be safe. I promise."

Amos shivered in his arms and turned into his hug. His cheek was wet with tears when he pressed it against Ezer's.

*Yes*, Ezer thought, *I'd do anything at all. With anyone.*

*For Da.*

# Chapter Thirteen

"LIDELL IS WAITING for you," Earl said when Ned arrived back from his meal with Heath. "In his office. Hurry on now."

Ned rolled his eyes. If his father was waiting for him, then there was more scheming about money afoot, and he'd already been warned by his uncle to stay out of it. And he would. There was no way his father was going to convince him to stay friends with Braden and Finch or coerce him into befriending any other jerks for his contracts, either.

Ned was pleasantly stuffed full of dessert and loose with wine, but he was determined, too. Nothing Lidell said or did could get under his skin or make him waver. He had Heath's backing and promise of help, and he wasn't going to lose it for anything.

"This is it, Ned! This is what we've been waiting for!" Lidell shouted, waving a glass of bourbon around, and already flushed with it. "Sign here." His finger came down on a piece of paper on his desk. "That's all you need to do, and, boom, we're set for life."

"What in the hell are you are you talking about?" Ned didn't bother curbing his language. Not today when he had Heath's permission to do what he wanted and be free. "Sign here for what?"

"For your rich omega," Lidell said with a smirk. "He's already signed, and, according to Fersee, he's eager. Hot for it."

Ned blinked, trying to parse what his father was going on about. He'd had a whole bottle of wine on his own, yes, but was he so intoxicated he was passed out and dreaming? He must be misunderstanding something important.

Ezer hadn't even texted him a thank you after last night. There was no way he'd signed a heat and breeding agreement. Had he?

Ned strode across the room and grabbed the papers from his father's desk and read the entire contract all the way through. At each important juncture, there it was—Ezer's scrawled signature. He recognized it from the group projects they'd worked on together in class.

"What the hell?"

"George had already told me not to worry about it. He always said Ezer was up for this—or would be after some persuading—and it seems the boy is. Can you believe our good luck? Between this income and the contracts with Maddox and Tenmeter, we'll finally be able to start fresh and put our bad financial luck behind us. The tides have turned! And with no help from my asshole brother for him to hold over our heads."

"But..." Ned's head swam. If Ezer had signed, and if he signed in return, then they'd...

During heat...

And it'd be amazing, he had no doubt, but also...

They might make a baby.

A baby.

He'd be a father.

He was only nineteen!

"Father," he said, swallowing hard. "I'm not sure I understand. You really want me to breed Ezer Fersee? We're too young for children, aren't we?"

Lidell waved his hand. "Oh, you're overthinking it. You

won't be raising the child. Read the contract. You'll have plenty of money, and you can hire a nurse, like Earl's been to you. I never had to put myself out to be your father. It's nothing in the end. A bit of pain for the omega, sure, but assuming he's healthy and lives through it—" Lidell did blanch a little at that, which was the only thing that spoke to him having any conscience at all, as far as Ned could tell. "Well, if he lives through the births, then you'll get even more money. There'll be nothing at all to worry about. Leave the raising of the babes to the omega and whatever legion of nurses you hire. That's what makes omegas happy, you know. Raising babies. They all live for that." He huffed a laugh. "*Actually* they live for heats and the sexual attention from their alphas they require to sustain a healthy pregnancy. *That's* the thing that keeps them happy and content. It's what drives them. You'll see. This Ezer may be a devil at school now, but he'll be an angel when he's full of your child."

Ned scratched at his sweaty head. He didn't want Ezer to be an angel—and he didn't agree that Ezer was a devil. If anyone was a devil between the two of them, it'd have to be Ned. But if Ezer became placid and sweet when pregnant, like so many omegas tended to be? Ned didn't think he'd like that at all.

He liked how Ezer fought back like a kitten with sharp claws—going for the eyes and the soft bits. He liked how Ezer challenged the world around him when it came at him the wrong way. He just wanted Ezer to let Ned stand by his side while he did it. To help protect Ezer from the world's blades and bites.

He snorted. Like he'd done very well at that so far.

He'd been the worst.

As for being a father, well...

Ned had never imagined himself as the kind of man to leave all the childcare to his omega and a nurse. Sure, that was how *he'd* been raised, but it wasn't as though Lidell was a very admirable man, or an aspirational figure in his life. Ned wanted to be more like his Uncle Heath—who, as he'd witnessed last summer, adored his son, played with him, and cared for him.

"Sign it," Lidell said, pulling a pen out of his desk drawer and foisting it on Ned.

He took it. "I…I need to think this over."

"You can't mean to say no to this? It's the chance of a lifetime. Rich men don't ever pay to have their omega sons taken off their hands—especially not omegas you already have a thing for." Lidell tilted his head. "Or did you lose your taste for the boy already?"

"No! I just didn't think he'd really choose me," Ned said.

There'd been no indication in their brief interactions yesterday after the apartment explosion that Ezer liked him, or that he'd been even remotely happy to see him. What would make Ezer want to commit to Ned now? And not just for a smile or a friendship, but for heat, a breeding, and probable marriage? It was hard to understand.

Ned cleared his throat. "I think I should talk to Uncle Heath about all this first."

"What? Why?" Lidell snarled. "He doesn't have anything to do with us, or with your romantic inclinations. This is a brilliant opportunity for you, for *us*. You won't see one like it again. And if you don't take it, son? Well, I hate to tell you, but *someone* will. Fersee isn't planning to let this boy continue to embarrass him. If you don't sign, you're not saving this omega from anything, just so you know. All you're doing is passing this money and this boy over to some other alpha. And who knows what *that* alpha will do with him…"

Ned's head spun. He couldn't stomach the idea of Ezer with anyone else. Plus, the contract called for breeding. There was no room for confusion. George Fersee wanted Ezer pregnant as soon as possible. He wanted it so badly that each baby came with bonus money. Unreal.

The idea of Ezer pregnant with another alpha's child made him feel dizzy.

Ned took a breath and said, "I just think Uncle Heath wouldn't—"

"Heath doesn't own you!"

"Father, I'm calling him." Ned tugged his phone free of his pocket and pressed the contact. It went straight to voicemail. "Uncle Heath, please, if you can, get back to me as soon as possible. I have an urgent issue that I need help with. Thank you."

"Ridiculous," Lidell said, rolling his eyes. "I'm telling you that—"

The door to the office opened and Earl came in, seeming harried and a little scared. "I just heard from Simon," he said, breathlessly. "Adrien has gone into labor early. It's not good news for the wee one. It's too soon…" He clucked his tongue. "And before you ask, yes, Heath has been contacted. I've been told he left his business meeting at a run."

"Heath was here? In Wellport? On business?" Lidell asked, having the gall to look wounded that he hadn't known.

Earl nodded. "Yes, and he's gone again now, of course. I've never heard Simon sound so frightened," he said, wringing his hands. "We've been married for three decades and…" He shook his gray head. "I think I should go to him."

"You're needed here to prepare Ned for his first—"

"No!" Ned interjected. "Go to Simon. Help if you can."

"Thank you. I think the wee one, that sweet Michael, might need me. He's always at his da's heels, and I worry that…" Earl teared up. "Well, Simon will have his hands full with Heath if anything goes wrong with this delivery."

"Oh, I'm sure Heath will be as dramatic about it as ever," Lidell said, rolling his eyes. "He'll make everything about him, I'm sure. He always does." He turned back to the dreaded stack of papers and began to read over them again. "Well, go on then. Ned can prepare without you."

"'Prepare'?" Earl tilted his head, confused.

"Don't worry about me. Go on," Ned said, moving to the door and putting an arm around Earl's shoulders, steering him away from Lidell and the contract still unsigned on the desk. "Let us know how things go. If Adrien is all right, and the baby…"

"Of course, of course," Earl said, looking warily over his shoulder at Lidell. "Don't get involved in any scheme of his," Earl whispered as Ned released him and started to shut the door. "Whatever you do. Just steer clear of your father's plans."

Ned kissed Earl's papery cheek. "Don't worry about me. I'll be fine. It's Adrien and Heath who matter now."

Earl hugged him and then hustled away.

Ned turned back to the office and re-entered it. He stood with his back to the door, contemplating his father for a moment. Then he pulled out his phone and replied to Amos's message of thanks:

*I'm sure you know what Mr. Fersee and my father are planning. Ezer has signed the documents. I don't know what to do. Does he really want this? I'd like to ask him. Can I have his phone number, please?*

The text message showed a read receipt at once, but Amos took a long time to type in his reply. When it came through, Ned's knees went weak, and he wiped a hand over his top lip.

*Ezer doesn't have his phone on him, and even if he did, he wouldn't text you back. Sign the forms. George is offering him to Finch Maddox next, if this falls through with you, and you know that jerk won't hesitate.*

Ned texted back: *Finch? Why?*

*Because it's easy. So make up your mind, Ned. It's you or Finch. Do the right thing.*

Ned wished he could wait until Heath's crisis was over to talk with his uncle about this choice, but the contract stipulated that Ezer was to be in heat and to be bred within a week. With the crisis at Heath's home with his omega and new child, talking to him now—or anytime in the next few days—seemed unlikely. So much for getting any sort of advice from his uncle.

Ned had to go with his own heart and mind, his own instinct. And, for the most part, it fought him. It told him this was a very bad idea.

Until he considered Amos's reply and his father's words, too, and then it felt like a moral imperative to sign the forms. A force for the greater good.

He couldn't let another alpha—especially not Finch fucking Maddox—touch Ezer.

He stalked over to the desk, lifted the pen, and signed his name. Vomit rose in his mouth, and his stomach flipped wildly. But it was done. The contract was signed by both parties. It was legal, and now he was beholden.

In a week's time he'd be alone with Ezer, servicing his heat, and if things went to plan, he'd be a father four months after that.

He met his own father's gaze and winced at the elation he found there. That was never a good look on Lidell and had only ever foretold disaster in the past. But then he glanced at the message from Amos again, and his resolve solidified. He'd done the right thing. He had.

*Please let me have done the right thing.*

Hours later, after spending all of dinner listening to his father's various plans for where Ned would service the heat, and how the servants should be instructed to prepare the nest, Ned climbed into bed with a whirring mind.

He brought up his phone and read Amos's reply again.

"What have I done?" Ned murmured to himself, tossing and turning in his bed. He couldn't get comfortable no matter how hard he tried. Scraping his nails over his scalp, he took a slow, deep breath, and spoke aloud into the darkness. "I did the right thing."

God, he really hoped he had.

# PART TWO

## Heat

# Chapter Fourteen

NED STOOD OUTSIDE the small house set on the edge of his father's beach property, far from any town, and isolated aside from a single road back to civilization. Dunes came right up to the fence, and a trail led to the beach. He'd walked down there already, some primitive part of him satisfied to see the cove was protected by large cliffs on either side.

Heat houses were always remote. Ned didn't like to think about all the reasons why. Certainly some of it was to protect the omega during a time of extreme vulnerability, and the alpha during a time of extreme distraction. But that wasn't the only implication of isolation and Ned knew it. Consent was a legal requirement, but once given it couldn't be revoked mid-heat. He didn't know how he felt about that, and the part of him that dreamed of a happy, joyfully consenting omega didn't want to examine it too closely.

Lidell stood by the front gate, giving him room to claim the place as his own. Ned had refused his offer of the mountain house where he'd been conceived, and the apartment inside the main house, the one where his father handled purchased heats, was being prepared as a nest in case it was needed.

This small, one-room oceanside house had belonged to his omega grandparent on his father's side. Uncle Heath had gifted it to Lidell as a peace offering years ago after one of their many rows. But it'd sat empty until Lidell had sent servants out earlier in the week to fix it up in preparation for Ned and Ezer.

Thinking of Heath made Ned's stomach flip. Heath's omega, Adrien, had given birth to a sickly, early baby—a beta—and they'd both been devastated by the news that it was unlikely to live. There was still a chance, but it was slim, and so while this news had been sent on to Lidell and Ned in messages from Earl, they hadn't heard from Heath about it.

Given all that was happening at Heath's home, they'd given leave for Earl to remain there helping out with Michael. They also hadn't burdened him with the choices made in his absence to share a heat with and breed Ezer. Lidell seemed opposed to telling Earl, lest it get back to Heath. "We don't want to disturb him during this difficult time."

But Ned selfishly wished they had.

Even now he wondered what his uncle would say about his choice to sign the contract with Ezer. He had a feeling Heath would disapprove, but he also knew Heath would be willing to sacrifice Ezer's well-being for Ned's, and that wasn't something Ned was willing to do.

Which was why he was now waiting for Ezer to come to him, to arrive at the heat house of his own volition, and to share in one of life's greatest intimacies with him.

Ned shivered in anticipation. He couldn't believe that Ezer-with-the-blue-eyes had agreed to be his omega. It was true he didn't know much about Ezer, not really. But he knew Ezer had always made Ned's body sing with expectation and caused his heart to yearn for emotional connection. They'd hardly ever spoken to each other, and still hadn't exchanged a word since that brief discussion outside the burning apartment building. But he'd watched Ezer close enough over the last few months to recognize that Ezer agreeing to this, consenting to all that he'd consented to, went against what Ned knew of Ezer's personality.

That knowledge was what disturbed his peace as he staked out the heat house in anxious anticipation. Part of him was thrilled at the thought of Ezer acting out of character because of him, *for* him. But, deep down, he suspected Ezer had his own reasons for signing, reasons closer to Lidell's than to Ned's own. Still, whatever Ezer's motivation, he felt a breathless, rising, roaring honor that he was the one Ezer had agreed to do this with.

Though Ned wished they'd been allowed to talk on the phone before they met in person. It would have been a relief to hear Ezer say he'd chosen this of his own free will, and for Ned to be allowed to give his apologies for all that had passed between them. But at least they'd have a few days alone in the cabin before Ezer's heat kicked in to get to know each other and clear the air.

Ned wanted to explain *everything*. Before he put a hand on Ezer, he wanted him to know the truth about Braden and Finch. Ned wanted, more than anything, to go into this heat with an understanding of each other in their hearts.

If they were going to be parents together, then that would be an important place to start.

After pacing by the sea oats, he headed back toward the house, his heart hammering and his pulse thrumming. Dust kicking up in the distance alerted Ned to the arrival of a car. His stomach flipped over with nerves. What should he say to Ezer first? He cleared his throat and practiced.

"Hi," he said aloud. "*Hi*," he tried again, stronger this time. He frowned, trying to sound more like a grown alpha, putting a deeper tone toward his next attempt. "Hi."

"They're here!" his father called.

Ned nearly threw up, but he wiped his sweaty hands on his jeans and started walking toward the black, four-door sedan pulling into the drive.

It was time.

EZER HAD NEVER felt anything like the humming heat beneath his skin, burning into his muscles, making him restless and leaving him shifting in wet, soggy underwear beneath his jeans. His nipples ached, his cock was half-hard, and he loathed that he was losing the fight to stay aware and coherent in front of his asshole 'father'.

"It would have been kinder to *wait* before triggering his heat," Pete opined, in a rare instance of disagreeing with his alpha. He sat across from Ezer and his father in the limo, still ridiculously large with child and draped in the softest robe. Normally, at this stage he wouldn't leave the house at all, but George planned to take Pete to the private cabin in the mountains in anticipation of his delivery. There they'd be joined by a dedicated doctor who'd be on hand just for Pete and the new baby.

Recent studies had shown that giving birth in a quiet, stress-free environment and remaining there for several weeks afterward helped mitigate the post-partum drop. Pete was willing to do anything George proposed at this point, so his dissent about the "kindness" of having Ezer crashing on incoming heat waves when he arrived to meet this alpha—whoever it was who'd been given an absurd amount of money to take Ezer off George's hands—was interesting.

Not interesting enough to distract Ezer from the hot, sizzling need making him pant and writhe, forcing his eyes back into his head, so hot it was agony as it washed over him. George pulled a handkerchief from his pocket and breathed through it. "It's a kindness to have him ready and willing," George said, as if educating his spouse. "He's not like you, Pete. He's stubborn.

This will help and, in the end, when he's pregnant, he'll be glad for it."

Pete seemed skeptical.

For his part, Ezer was enraged at being so out of control, so vulnerable, and utterly at the heat's mercy—and soon to be at the mercy of a strange young man chosen for him by his parents. Never mind having his heat triggered in advance was what *he'd* asked for, begged for even, it turned out the *experience* of heat was still terrifyingly lacking in consent. When he'd pleaded for this, he hadn't known what he was asking for. How could he have? Heat was beyond comprehension until it came over you.

At the time, he'd only know he didn't want any way out of his choice, afraid he wouldn't have the courage to follow through if he wasn't desperate for a knot before he'd even met this alpha. But he'd been wrong. The heat being already on him didn't change that he was still terrified, furious, and helpless. And hornier than he'd ever imagined possible.

Ezer moaned as another searing wave rose up.

George coughed and rapped on the partition between them and the limo's beta driver. "How much longer?"

"Just ahead, sir."

Ezer's asshole leaked slick, and his nipples tingled. He wanted to get free of the car, away from his father and Pete before he lost his mind. The need inside grew so unbearable, he was tempted to throw the car door open and leap out, running until he found an alpha to knot him. But as he reached for the lock mechanism, the limo slowed, and his father jumped from the car himself. Ezer peered from of the window, sweat pooling in his pits and crotch, and his asshole quivering wetly.

Dunes. Waves. A pale sun.

Ezer shuddered and rocked, trying to get satisfaction by rubbing his body over the supple leather of the seats. His clothes were too rough, and he wanted to be rid of them, but he still had enough sense to keep them on.

The door beside him jerked open. A man ducked in and pulled back, coughing. "He's in full heat," he barked. "What in God's name were you thinking having him start like this?"

"Calm down, Lidell," George said. "He wanted it this way. Besides he'll make less trouble for your son in this state. I know what I'm doing."

"Trouble for my son? He looks a hundred pounds soaking wet. My son's all muscle. He wouldn't have any trouble with your boy."

"Well, this way there's no question, is there? He'll be begging for a knot instead of running from it."

Lidell—the name seemed familiar but Ezer couldn't place it—huffed, but ducked back in and tugged Ezer out of the car with a gentleness George's men had lacked when shoving him in. "Come on, now. Let's get you inside."

Ezer shuddered under the firm pressure of an alpha's hands. This must be the man his father had contracted him to be with, a bit older than he'd like, but it didn't matter now. It was all he could do not to sway into Lidell's arms and rub against him like a cat in heat. Because he *was* in heat. His first. And, *fuck*, it was overwhelming. Any alpha would do. He needed to feel full and fucked and knotted. No wonder cats caterwauled. He wanted to throw back his own head and wail in needy agony, too.

Instead he fell to his knees and started pawing at the front of Lidell's trousers.

"Shameful," Lidell hissed at George. "You should have given him some time here with my son to adjust." He gripped Ezer's hands in his own, stopping his quest to get to his cock.

Ezer moaned. "Please," he whispered. "Help me. I need it. I *need* it. Please."

Lidell stroked a hand into Ezer's hair soothingly. "Of course you do, sweetheart. You'll have it, too. Come here, son!"

Ezer didn't even look up as a pair of muscled legs encased in jeans tenting obscenely at the crotch came into view. Hungrily, he dove for this new alpha's groin, rubbing his face against his hardness, and wriggling his ass around in desperation. He wanted his clothes off. He wanted to get fucked—whatever that felt like. Ezer shivered, skin too sensitive, heart pounding, and he heard Pete make a sharp sound of disapproval.

"I don't like this, George," Pete said in a small voice. "I'll wait in the car. But, for the record, I do *not* approve of this at all."

Hands gripped Ezer's hair, holding him in place, and he breathed in the delicious scent of ripe, dripping cock. As he mouthed the jeans covering the alpha's cock, he didn't care who it belonged to, only that it was hard for him. He needed alpha cock in his body *now*. As soon as possible.

"The money has been wired to the bank," George said. "If your son can make sure Ezer's no longer a nuisance and embarrassment to me, and if he can get him knocked up sooner rather than later, then you'll never want for anything again. Sums will be settled on you, your son, and each child born that will make dealing with Ezer and his issues more than worth it. You won't need to turn to your arrogant prick of a brother Heath for anything ever again. But, if your son *can't* handle Ezer, and if Ezer returns to his prior inappropriate behavior, ambitions, and affiliations, then not only will the funds be cut off, but you'll owe me reparations. Understand?"

"It's all in the contract," Lidell said testily.

Ezer sucked the bulge in front of him, tasting a tangy substance soaking through the alpha's jeans. He quivered, moaning as he realized it was pre-cum. All for him. Delicious. He darted a glance up, but lust, the pale sun, and another crash of heat blurred his vision. The boy holding onto his hair with a strong grip was golden-blond, muscled, and tall, but that was all he could make out as he convulsed with ungratified need.

"It *is* in the contract," George agreed. "This is more than I want to see already. Let's go."

Ezer closed his eyes and dedicated himself to sucking more of that taste into his mouth through the heavy weight of the jeans. He heard footsteps and the slam of car doors, followed by the rumble of engines, then heavy panting from above him and the distant crash of waves. He whimpered, worked open his own pants, and shoved them down.

Eyes squeezed tight, Ezer turned and presented himself, ass up, face in the dirt. He reached back to spread his cheeks wide to show off his wet hole.

"Fuck me," he begged. "Please. Fuck me."

# Chapter Fifteen

NED'S BALLS THROBBED and his head swam with a lust he'd never known possible. He could only imagine what hunger Ezer must be in the grip of if heat was exponentially more intense than his own need. He couldn't knot Ezer here on the grass no matter how much he wanted to. He didn't know how long his knot would last. He'd never done it before, and from what he understood, sometimes it lasted just a few minutes, and other times it lasted almost an hour.

Ned tamped back rage at George Fersee for bringing Ezer to him in this condition. He'd never wanted it to be like this. In his imagination, Ezer came to him willingly, and they'd have several days of increasing intimacy and forgiveness, earning trust and giving affection, as they introduced the first hormones to trigger the heat, followed by a beautiful joining of their bodies and souls as they tried to make a child together.

Instead, Ezer was so far gone in heat already, Ned wasn't even sure his omega even understood who he was with, or what it meant to be fucked by him. If Ned didn't have a signed contract back in the oceanside heat house, he might not even be sure of true consent. Heat made sluts of every omega—their need became so great that any alpha would do. As was evidenced when Ezer had tried to get to Ned's own father's cock. He shuddered at that memory.

"Please," Ezer begged again, his wet asshole clenching and

releasing. "Fuck me." He shivered and shook, his small body twisting with unsatisfied, heat-driven lust. Slick slipped down his wiry thighs invitingly.

Ned groaned. His cock flexed and leaked pre-cum. Chewing on his bottom lip, he forced himself forward. He removed Ezer's pants, leaving them in the dirt and sand, and lifted Ezer into his arms. Ned needed to fatten him up; he was too skinny to support a healthy pregnancy.

Ezer fell to sucking a hickey on Ned's neck.

Distracted, Ned carried him toward the heat house, walking stiffly, impeded by his engorged cock. The roaring in Ned's ears outmatched the ocean waves, and he nearly sobbed in relief when the pale sun reflecting off the dunes gave way to the dark, cool interior of the house. He could have Ezer here. It would be safe.

"Please, please," Ezer chanted against the wet, aching spot he'd left on Ned's throat. "Help me, please. I'm dying. I *need* it. Please."

If Ezer needed him, then he'd have him.

Nothing about this was Ned's ideal, but with Ezer's slick scent filling his nostrils, and Ezer's lust causing him to wriggle half naked in Ned's arms, begging to be filled, his duty as an alpha was clear. He deposited Ezer onto the massive bed dominating the one-room house. What had seemed almost silly or threatening before—a private, isolated house dedicated to fucking—now made complete sense to him.

Nothing should get between him and Ezer. Nothing and no one.

Stripping Ezer was easy enough. He lifted the soft shirt up and over Ezer's head. When it came to getting his own clothes off, though, Ezer was as much a hindrance as a help, tugging Ned's jeans down and engulfing his cock in hot wetness, sucking so greedily that Ned's head fell back, and his knees went weak.

Gripping Ezer's hair in two fists, Ned fucked into his mouth and felt him gag. When he pulled out, he had to hold Ezer back from gulping him down again, so he could get his jeans, T-shirt, and socks off.

With both of them naked, Ned lost control of the situation. Ezer's pretty cock dripped everywhere, and his pale skin was stained red from his slight chest up to his neck, and into his cheeks. Ezer's eyes were closed, and he swayed on his knees, delirious and lost in need. When he rose, it was only to fall onto the bed, presenting his pink, hairless asshole again, and begging for Ned's cock.

Ned didn't make him wait again. He climbed behind Ezer, skimmed his hands down his slim, heaving back, noting his tiny hips and ass fit into the curves of Ned's palms perfectly, and without further hesitation, he sheathed himself in Ezer's wet asshole. A growl escaped Ned's throat as the fiery tightness of Ezer's body gripped and convulsed around him. It'd been so long since he'd been inside an omega, and never one in heat. Ned threw his head back, reveling in it. It was bliss. It was pure wonder.

And for it to be *Ezer*…

Ned quivered all over, holding himself steady inside Ezer. He felt as frail as a bird beneath him, but inside he was so hot, so incredibly, beautifully hot. Ned cocked his hips, thrusting in and out once, hard and firm, testing the sensation.

"Oh God! Yes! Thank you!" Ezer cried, as cum spurted from his cock to the mattress, and his hole convulsed on Ned's aching dick. "Thank you, sir. Thank you."

Ned realized he hadn't said a word to Ezer yet. He regretted that almost as much as he regretted that Ezer's wild need had precluded him getting the satisfaction of a first, innocent kiss.

Ned gripped Ezer's hips and held him in place. Fuck, it was

just so good. His balls drew up tight, and his own orgasm threatened to burst forth too early. He needed to stay strong, though. He had to fuck Ezer through the worst of this first wave before knotting him. Ned bent low, kissed Ezer's shuddering back. "Calm down now, Ezer. I've got you."

Ezer moaned, twisted on Ned's dick, and came again.

Ned stared in wonder as Ezer clawed at the mattress, riding his cock furiously, as convulsion after convulsion wracked his body. It was clear pain and pleasure ran close together for Ezer. Tears and shouts of joy layered with sobs, and every sensation seemed so easily triggered.

Ned had learned about heat in classes, but nothing had prepared him for the real thing.

Ned's cock felt brand new, as if it had been awakened by pushing into Ezer's body, making all Ned's past experiences pale in comparison. He was obsessed with the way Ezer dripped with sweat and slick, and how cum exploded from his cock with Ned's rougher thrusts, and the way cries of ecstasy burst helplessly from his pink mouth as he rode Ned's dick like he needed it to survive. Ned had never imagined the mindless rapture of it all. Ned simply hadn't known. Now he did.

And he could never give this up.

EZER WAS A raw sheath of nerves reacting to each plunge of his alpha's cock with a helpless roar of gratification. He submitted because there was no other choice. Heat flattened him, rolling over him and smashing his willpower to bits. He was flesh. He was pleasure so close to agony that it exploded in orgasm, again and again.

In moments of near clarity, he felt one with the universe. The identity of the boy fucking him didn't matter. Ezer was Omega being fucked by Alpha—all alphas, the entire universe of alphas—and it was right. It was good. And he *loved* it.

The arrival of a shattering orgasm lifted him out of his body like a shimmering firework, before dropping him down again. His climax was followed by an impressive thrust from his alpha and a wrenching cry.

Ezer groaned as the knot grew inside him. He was pinned in place, his asshole spread wider and wider as hot gushes of cum filled him and made his flat stomach expand with the gushing load. A vague buzzing calm started inside him, beginning with the realization that his alpha was indeed quite young to have filled him so full. As alphas aged, their semen grew less plentiful, and many older alphas used plugs to help the seed stay in and impregnate their omegas.

The gushes of semen continued, until Ezer squirmed from the internal pressure. He cried out and convulsed on the hard knot as the movement triggered another orgasm for him, and he panted through the end of it. Each twitch left him no choice but to surrender again to the raw pleasure of orgasm, though these post-wave climaxes were less intense. Each of them felt like a blessing rather than a trial by fire.

As Ezer came out of the first heat wave, consciousness blossoming in him again, he found himself on his left side, pinned from behind on his alpha's knot, staring out of a wide window at the sparkling sea. He felt drained. All energy spent.

Ezer was tender, inside and out, emotionally and physically vulnerable, with nowhere to go or hide. His skin tingled. His cock twitched in exhaustion. Wet with cum and slick from the back of his knees to the middle of his shoulder blades and up over his chest, he was filthy. And tired. And if he squeezed around his alpha's knot he'd probably come again.

The temptation was great, but he fought it off.

"Be calm now. I've still got you," his alpha murmured by his ear.

Ezer quivered, pleasure pulsing in his groin as another small load choked out from his cock. How could words make him come? Heat was terrible, and amazing, and he rode the torrent of it for another blissful moment.

"That's it," his alpha said. "Give it all to me."

Ezer moaned and convulsed, tingling all over with pleasure. As he calmed again, he wanted to tell the man to shut up, not to say another word, but his order was stopped cold by the realization that he had no idea *who* was inside him at all.

He went very still, suspended on a hard knot of flesh, and the knowledge that if he twisted or moved in an attempt to see the man—boy—*alpha*—then he'd lose himself in another orgasm, and he wanted, no, *needed* a break from that.

A kernel of rage flared inside at his utter defenselessness. This man could strangle him, gut him, do anything at all to him right now, and he'd be powerless to stop him, stuck like a dog on his cock, and raw with over-sensitized nerves.

But the boy only seemed to want to calm him, stroking his arms and back gently, and humming a nursery tune in his ear. He shouldn't have let his father railroad him into this without knowing anything at all about who would be taking him to this very great height. Did his father even care how it ended? If this man destroyed him, would his father do more than tut and say, "What's the loss of one disobedient omega son when I have three more obedient ones?"

Perhaps he did care. Perhaps it was a kind of love—sick, twisted love—to have pushed Ezer into the arms of a boy who was, from all current indications, every bit the romantic his father had promised.

"I'll take care of you," the boy whispered. "I'll take care of you always. Be calm now, Ezer. Calm."

Ezer's heart did slow with the careful strokes and soothing, with the familiar nursery tunes that brought back memories of being cradled in his omega parent's arms. His asshole was stretched tight around the base of the massive knot locking them together; normally this might've frightened him, but it felt right, satisfying. His balls ached pleasantly, a reminder of the blissful oblivion he'd emerged from.

The alpha buried his face in the back of Ezer's neck and groaned, his cock pulsing inside again, sending another hot spurt into Ezer's womb. Ezer shuddered with borrowed pleasure, sighing in relief when it didn't set off another violent orgasm in himself.

The ocean waves moved outside the window, rolling and tossing, sparkling under the pale sun. Ezer rested in the muscled arms of the quiet alpha boy and waited for his sanity to return. Surely it would, wouldn't it? Between waves of need?

As the knot inside softened, and finally slipped free, it did.

With an anxious twist in his stomach, he pasted on a hesitant smile, and turned to take in the face of the alpha whose seed now filled him, and whose child he might soon carry. He froze.

A flash of memories tumbled through his mind: shoves and pushes, kicks and taunts, and the force of a boot against his chest for a long, agonizing moment.

Ned Clearwater stared down at him with a hopeful, anxious expression.

Ezer clapped a hand over his own mouth to keep in his scream.

# Chapter Sixteen

NED FROWNED, WORRY passing over his features. "Ezer? Did I hurt you? Are you all right?"

Nauseous, Ezer stared at him with his hand over his mouth. He'd never thought…

My God, he'd never thought for even a moment…

"Let me get some water for you," Ned said. "Are you hungry? I have yogurt and berries. Oh, but I need to start the hearty stew. It's a family tradition. It's gotten all my family's omegas through their heats for three generations." Ned smiled, tentatively. "I thought I'd have more time. I didn't realize you'd arrive so…" He paused, seeming shy. "I thought we'd have a few days first."

Ezer didn't say a word, just glared as Ned climbed from the bed, pulled on a fuzzy robe, and entered the bathroom, coming back with a warm bowl of water and a towel. Ezer sat, stunned, and Ned cleaned them both off, wiping away slick and cum. Afterward, Ned went over to kitchen area of the room to claim a glass, filling it with water. He brought it over to the bed, his large cock poking between the folds of the robe, swinging between his thighs, and his exposed chest flushed from the intensity of their prior activities. Ezer's asshole ached to have that cock back inside even as his heart wrung with agony at his plight.

Still unmoving, Ezer stared at the glass in Ned's hand.

"It's all right now, Ezer," Ned said again, pushing it toward him. "Your first wave has passed, but we need to prepare for the next one. Drink it. Please."

Ezer did. The water was a blessing on his throat, and it burst with a fresh coolness in his stomach. But that didn't drown out the shock of looking into the warm eyes of one of his regular tormentors, now talking to him with tenderness, as if he were something precious. Was this a nightmare? A joke? A horror story?

Ned's behavior outside Da's apartment fell into place. His da's words that the alpha cared for him. How had he not put together that the alpha knew him? That he wasn't going to be foisted onto one of his father's business partner's sons. He'd assumed George wanted him far away. He'd assumed the alpha would be a wealthy son of a peer in Yeddana or Billepsi City. Not Ned Clearwater.

Ned reached out to stroke Ezer's hair.

Ezer jerked away, unwilling to tolerate his touch now the wave had passed. How long until another wave hit? How long until he was begging this bully to fuck him, this terrible alpha who'd stood by and let Braden and Finch torment him, and even participated sometimes?

He was sharing his heat, breeding with a cowardly abuser.

"Why?" Ezer asked. His throat felt raw from crying out in pleasure.

Ned tilted his head, confused. "Why what?"

"Why are you doing this to me?"

Was it revenge of some kind? A new endless torment? Was it all a horrific joke so that Ned could laugh at Ezer's expense later with his friends? Describe the way the helpless "cocksleeve" had begged for it?

Ned's eyes clouded and he reached out again, but Ezer knocked his hand away. Tilting his head, Ned answered, "Because you're in heat and you need an alpha."

"No! I know that. Why did you *want* to do this?" Ezer wished he wasn't so tired and weak. He wanted to kick Ned in the face, spit on him, and then run out of the door as fast as he could, but he wasn't an idiot. He wouldn't get far. There was a reason heat houses were isolated—many reasons—but this exact scenario was definitely one of them.

"That's why I hoped we'd have a few days before your heat started, so I could help you understand," Ned said. He sighed and sat on the side of the bed.

Ezer scooted away, leaving a gap between them.

"I was surprised you signed the contract. It seemed so out of character. When our fathers first proposed this whole"—he waved around the room and twisted his lips up in a weird smile—"thing, I thought for sure you'd refuse. It seemed like a dream. A fantasy."

"A fantasy?"

"That you might want this with me," Ned said. "The way I wanted it with you. I mean, being with you, not necessary servicing a heat and…and having a baby. I wasn't even sure we *should* do that, you know? Because we're both so young." He swallowed. "And you hated me."

"*Hate* you," Ezer corrected. "Present tense."

Ned blinked, shaking his head. "No, no. You signed the contract. You wanted this."

Ezer was a fool, but Ned seemed to be one, too. Either he was a very good actor—and he was not—or he was more clueless than even Ezer had been about the situation they were now in.

"What makes you think I wanted this? With you?" Ezer asked, his voice unsteady.

"Because your father could have found others to suit his needs—your needs, I mean. So many others. But you signed for *me*, so, I thought maybe…"

"Maybe what?"

"I thought *I* suited your needs somehow. That you understood my feelings for you, or that you just wanted me too?"

Ezer sneered, astonished at this boy's arrogance. Of course Ned Clearwater would assume any omega would want him—handsome, strong, connected as he was. Assholes like him always felt entitled to an omega's lust and believed it was inevitable they would be the object of it. "I signed for my *own* reasons. It had nothing to do with you. I didn't even read the contract between your father and mine before I signed it."

Ned blinked. "What? Why not? That's reckless."

"Dangerous, even. I know." Ezer was very aware of that now. He'd already had Ned's knot in him once, this bully's seed was currently dribbling out of him, and he was going to have to take it again.

And again.

And again.

And, *fuck*, probably bear his child. What had he done? Why had his da wanted him to agree to this? How could he have thought he'd be happy with this bully of a boy?

"Then I don't understand. Why are we here?" Ned asked, and Ezer had never imagined that the brute could look and sound so small. He was hunched in on himself.

"My father wanted me off his hands." *Father?* Ezer couldn't seem to stop thinking of George as such, even after everything, even knowing the truth. Old feelings and habits died hard.

"Yeah," Ned agreed, showing that he knew at least that much.

"My da thought that you were a good choice for me and encouraged my father to arrange this between us." Ezer snorted. "Though why he thought you were the right match, I have *no* idea." Ezer narrowed his gaze. "He saw what you did to me, what you all did to me, what you planned to do."

"I was going to stop them. I swear."

Ezer took a slow breath to still the roiling in his stomach. When he was sure he wasn't going to vomit, he turned onto his side, giving his back to Ned. "Whatever. It doesn't matter now. I did this for my da. So my father would give him a better place to live. He had nowhere to go after the fire, and my father wanted me out of his hair, so…"

Carefully, Ned's hands landed on him, and Ezer decided it was easier not to fight. He'd be handled by this boy for the rest of this heat now, like it or not. Ned turned Ezer over, forcing him to meet his gaze. "You're saying your father *coerced* you into taking this breeding heat with me?"

Ezer huffed. "Don't act like you didn't know all the details."

But it was clear that Ned hadn't known. Or that he hadn't understood. Ned had obviously hoped this heat was about something he'd created in his mind out of a misguided attraction to Ezer. God help him. His father and da were right about Ned—he was a romantic. He'd had *feelings* about this.

Ned tugged a hand through his dark-golden hair. "I *did* know your father wanted you out of his way and settled. But I *didn't* know he'd forced you by holding your da's safety and happiness hostage like that. I swear I didn't know he'd trapped you into this." Ned licked his lips. "I thought you wanted it to be me handling your heat, and I thought that by taking the contract I was rescuing you from something worse. From *someone* worse."

Ezer flinched. "Knowing my father, perhaps you did."

After all, Ned had been kind to him during his heat so far. He'd taken care of his physical demands and satiated his heat wave, and he was being gentle now. Ezer supposed it could have been worse.

Ned's eyes filled with tears, and his lips twisted up. "I don't know how to fix this," he whispered. "I shouldn't have signed. I should have waited for my Uncle Heath's advice. I'm so sorry, Ezer. I don't know what to do."

Ezer blinked as a tear slipped down Ned's face, and he sat, putting a hand on Ned's shoulder awkwardly. "Well, I should have known the details of the contract," Ezer said. Ned's teary eyes and trembling chin got under Ezer's skin, pricking him with a desire to take his pain away. Stupid, really.

"Why didn't you?" Ned asked. "Read the contract, I mean?"

Ezer wasn't about to admit to Ned that he had trouble reading on the best of days, and even more so when he was upset. "I was angry with my parents and the situation. I thought it would be easier if I didn't know who I was being given to, if I just accepted their will and submitted to it, you know?"

Ned tilted his head, his eyes still wet. "No? Can you explain?"

Ezer shook his head, turned to retrieve the glass of water from the bedside table, drank it down, and then thrust the empty glass at Ned. "Not now. I'm hungry."

"Yes," Ned said, leaping up and brushing a hand over his eyes quickly. He assumed the role of a caretaking alpha. "Let me get the yogurt. And start the stew. I'm sorry. I really thought I'd have time to prepare it all for you." He glanced back over his shoulder as he scooped creamy, white yogurt into a bowl and added honey without asking. "And I thought you knew it was me. I believed, for some reason I didn't understand, you wanted this."

Ezer grabbed the yogurt from Ned's hand and ate it like a starving man. As he shoveled the gooey yogurt in and swallowed it down, Ned mumbled approving praise, like eating was a sport, and Ezer was training to be a champion at it.

As soon as Ezer was full, Ned took the bowl to the sink, cleaned it, and began to chop vegetables, keeping one eye on Ezer over his shoulder.

Ezer lay back on the bed and waited. He could feel the next

wave approaching. It was like a storm, shifting something in him as it came on, the intensity palpable but still distant. Part of him wanted to run, but he knew there was no outrunning his skin. It was terrifying to sense the heat coming and be unable to stop it.

Oblivious, Ned continued to babble. "We have so much to talk about, things I need you to understand, but first I need to get this stew going. The heat waves will come stronger and faster. I don't want to be unprepared."

"But you *are* unprepared," Ezer said meanly, watching Ned flinch.

"Yes."

"So am I."

The tremor started inside again, hot and shocking. Ezer wasn't ready. He wasn't ready for *any* of this.

Ned glanced at him again. "Did you talk to an omega about what to expect?"

Pete had tried to give him "the talk," and so had Amos after Pete had gone so far as to ring him up last week to report that Ezer had been unresponsive to his coaching. That'd resulted in an awkward dinner at a Sivian restaurant in the old quarter, tucked away in a private booth where no one except a beta waiter would see pregnant-Pete. They'd dined there, the three of them: Pete, Amos, and Ezer. Both of George's omegas had been jumpy with each other, but they'd also been dead set on making sure Ezer understood what to expect during his heat and all that came after it.

They'd given far too many suggestions for Ezer's taste. Both had urged that he give in and let the alpha take care of him. Both said fighting it was impossible and would only wear him out. Surrender, though, seemed gutless to Ezer, and yet, in the end, that was what he'd done. They'd been right. Heat was too intense to fight. It won no matter how hard he tried to dominate it. In the midst of a wave, he didn't even want to come out on top.

"Yes, unfortunately," Ezer murmured. "I'm well aware of what I'm going to endure."

He didn't just mean the heat, but the pregnancy, and the birth, too. His da and Pete had been brutal in their descriptions. Though Amos seemed as if he were toning down his commentary about the agony of birth, given that Pete hadn't gone through it yet, not wanting to frighten his replacement.

Ned put aside his knife and turned to Ezer again, his robe flopping open distractingly. "I'm sorry. For everything. I know you won't understand, but if you give me a chance, Ezer, I'll make it up to you. I've always thought you were special." He squeezed his eyes shut. "Please, believe me. I'm not like them."

"Of course you are."

Ned met Ezer's stare, defiance reddening his cheeks. "I'm not."

"You had your boot on my chest two weeks ago."

"I was going to kick Braden in the face," Ned shouted, tossing the knife aside and throwing his hands up in the air.

Ezer's blood leapt at Ned's sudden show of temper, and his cock stirred. He jutted his chin out, saying, "Funny how you didn't, though."

"There wasn't time." Ned raked a hand through his hair again, his breath coming faster, and his cock rising, too.

Ezer's asshole leaked slick. He felt dizzy. "There was time enough. You were a coward."

Ned stared at Ezer, his chest heaving, and then he seemed to wrestle whatever he was feeling down. He settled himself.

Turning away, Ned went back to chopping vegetables and hustling to prepare the ingredients for his stew. He threw everything together and dumped it all into the pot on the stove. He moved jerkily now, like he was angry, hurt, or scared—Ezer didn't know for sure. Despite his own aching hard-on and slippery asshole, Ezer tried to ignore him, focusing instead on the impending wave heading his way. It was going to be breathtaking. He could feel it.

But as the hunks of meat, the final ingredients, were added, Ezer's mind came back around to Ned's pleas for forgiveness, and he found he *did* care about some things. He wanted to know why Ned *hadn't* kicked Braden if that was his plan, why he'd let Braden and Finch say such terrible things to Ezer, and why he'd let them bully him at all? Especially if this—mating with Ezer, making a child—was what Ned wanted from Ezer both then and now.

The "romantic" his parents had promised him couldn't be the same boy Ezer had known before. And yet, now, in this moment, romance seemed the more obvious interpretation of Ned's current behavior. But still…

Before Ezer could work up the nerve to demand answers to his questions the stinging, hot sensation broke over him in a relentless crash. His cock hardened fully, and his asshole soaked the sheets with slick.

"Oh fuck," he whimpered as the burning rose harder and faster than it had the first time. "Oh, help. *Help.*"

The heat hurtled down on him, and once again he was lost in its flames. Ned came to him, and Ezer clung to his strong shoulders against his better judgment. He was like a man burning alive, held by the licking fire of lust and need, until he succumbed to it altogether.

And, somehow, Ned was his unlikely salvation.

# Chapter Seventeen

NED FUCKED EZER with a slow, steady beat that pushed him to stunning, writhing orgasms again and again. He loved seeing and feeling Ezer's lithe, slender body, taking his cock easily, and all the evidence of his pleasure: his cum-streaked stomach, his flushed skin, the ecstasy in his dazed eyes, and his sweaty thighs clenching around Ned's waist. Ezer crowed with pleasure as Ned plunged into his sweaty, slick flesh over and over.

The heat wave was intense, and Ned was exhausted, unsure how he was going to keep Ezer satisfied for the rest of the week. His muscles ached already, and it was only the second day.

For his part, Ezer had given up asking questions after that first moment of clarity between waves. Now, when he wasn't riding out the heat, Ezer seemed to viciously snatch the opportunities to sleep and eat, saying little or nothing to Ned, just reaching for him when the next wave came.

He didn't fight it, and Ned wished he could take heart in the way Ezer surrendered to the experience. But he had a nagging feeling it was Ezer's attempt to cope: complete capitulation to the inevitable for as long as it lasted, and not a submission to Ned as his forever alpha.

Putting such worries aside, though, he was in heaven. The sensation of Ezer coming on his knot was Ned's new favorite thing in life. He could tell Ezer's orgasms were strongest pre-knot, during the active fucking phases, when his slick glands and swollen prostate were brutally massaged, but Ned's strongest orgasms came when Ezer worked his knot with his orgasm-convulsing ass. Between these heavenly interludes, he drove into Ezer harder, seeking the peak that would trigger his knot.

Ezer moaned, thrashing and coming. He was beautiful like this, open and undone, no defenses, and Ned felt lucky to be the one seeing him this way. Bringing pleasure to the random omegas he'd fucked in the past had always been fun, and he'd gotten a lot of compliments from the men he'd been with for caring about their gratification, but this vision of Ezer stripped of everything but his desire was a sacrament, and Ned's knot was a pledge. A tie. A promise to care for the child they might be making, and to stick it out through the pregnancy, the birth, and the child's life. He knew not every alpha saw a knot that way, but he found he did, and it rocked his soul whenever he filled Ezer with his hard, bulbous flesh.

Ezer's eyes rolled up and he shuddered, his breath coming in small pants, as he convulsed, another load of cum striping his stomach. Sex with an omega in heat was messy—slick, cum, and more cum all over, and the sheets needed to be changed regularly. It was good that the heat house was well-stocked.

"That's right," Ned encouraged. "Show me everything. I want to see it all."

Ezer whimpered, clinging and hot against Ned's sweaty skin as he rode the wave.

As clarity rolled around again after the next knot, Ned gave them both a sponge bath, and then pulled on a robe before feeding Ezer the stew he'd prepared. Ezer ate greedily, watching Ned with a cautious eye, until he pushed the bowl away and collapsed on the pillows.

"I want to go outside," Ezer murmured as Ned washed the bowl out and prepared one for himself.

"Now?" Ned asked. "The heat will be back soon."

"No," Ezer said, struggling up to his elbows. "I think it's slowing. I don't feel any prickles yet. Please. I just want to see the sky."

"Of course." Ned put his bowl aside and helped Ezer stand. His legs were shaking like jelly, and he struggled to pull on his robe, but Ned helped him with that, too. Ezer leaned against him, weighing almost nothing it seemed, as Ned opened the front door to the cabin and the fresh sea air rushed in, washing away the heavy, musky scents of sex, heat, and stew.

The front porch was small, but there was a rocking chair, so Ned led Ezer toward it, the shade of the covering casting off the warmth of the pale sun but letting the cool sea breeze sail through. Ezer sighed as he collapsed into the chair, his overheated skin still flushed from their last coupling. He opened the top of his robe, exposing his pink flesh, and Ned sighed to see how his gorgeous ruddy nipples peaked.

Ned took a seat at Ezer's feet, daring to rest his head against his knee, as they gazed out across the sandy dunes toward the splashing water, and the soft blue sky sped away into the distance, merging with the horizon.

Fingers entered Ned's hair, soft and timid, carding through it, and it was all Ned could do not to curl toward Ezer, nuzzle his thigh with his cheek, and cry. Was this acceptance? Forgiveness? He didn't know. He held very still and let it happen.

"You keep telling me you want me to understand."

"I do. I want to tell you everything."

"Then I think you should start talking now," Ezer said after a few sweet moments had passed. "The heat will be back, I know. This is just a reprieve. But we have some time now, and I want to hear you out."

"What should I tell you about first?" Ned asked, not wanting

Ezer to disappear into silence again. "I'll tell you anything."

Ezer laughed under his breath. "You know what's crazy? I believe you would." He touched Ned's hair again, then pulled his hand away, tucking it beneath his arm and looking out toward the ocean. "When did you decide you liked me? Was it when you and your pals were harassing me on the first day of school?"

"No." Ned shook, relieved to confess this truth. He'd lived with it on his own for so long. "Do you believe in love at first sight?"

"No."

"I do."

Ezer rolled his eyes. "Oh, no, Ned. Don't even pretend that you—"

"I'm not pretending," Ned said fervently. "I saw you on the first day of school, and my heart…" Smiling, Ned clutched his chest to demonstrate. "Just like that, I fell in love with you."

Ezer frowned. "That's not what I want to hear from you. I don't believe in it for one thing. For another, it just makes the rest worse."

"I know. I'm sorry. I didn't know what to do or how to protect you."

"You didn't know how to protect me?!"

Ned nodded. "From Braden and Finch." He dove in with explaining his connection to Braden and Finch and admitting he loathed them now and always had. "I should have protected you better," he said. "I was afraid if I called more attention to how much I liked you, then they'd hurt you even more."

"You're too much of a coward to tell your father to make better business deals that don't rely so heavily on the opinions of teenage boys?"

"I guess I am."

Ezer sighed, his eyes the same color as the blue sky he was

peering into instead of looking at Ned. "Okay, so maybe you're good in bed, and gentle during a first heat, and that's good, since I'm contracted with you now. But I'm already regretting asking about all this. You're full of excuses."

"Wait, please hear me out."

"No," Ezer said, diverting his attention to the sea. "For now, through this heat, I'd rather pretend nothing about my life existed before I came to this house. That *I* didn't exist. This is my life now, so I should get used to it."

Ned chewed on his lower lip. This house wasn't Ezer's entire life. It couldn't be. This was just an interlude, and he had to make Ezer understand that, so that they could move forward together like Adrien and Heath had, in full awareness of each other, and maybe even with love. He didn't want to raise a child in a loveless home.

An idea came to Ned. Backwards, maybe, but it might help. He turned to face Ezer, sitting between his feet, and he said, "Tell me about the Ezer here with me in this heat house, then."

Ezer narrowed his eyes at him, as if looking for the hidden blade and finding none. "I don't think I can. It's too much."

Ned cocked his head. "Can you try?"

Ezer sighed and reached out to touch Ned's hair again. "Your hair's so soft," he said, and then gave a bitter little smile. "You must like that I can't help but feel tender toward you after everything, and *despite* everything. Fucking alpha pheromones. Fucking seminal compounds. Making me soft for you." He snorted. "You must love that, huh?"

"Ezer, I want us to be friends. We should have been friends from the start. That's my fault."

"Yes." Ezer groaned and squirmed a little in the chair. "Fuck. The heat's coming again."

Ned frowned. He hadn't learned enough about what Ezer

might want or feel, and he hadn't explained himself well either.

"Lick my nipples," Ezer gritted out, gripping Ned's hair tightly and pulling him to his chest. "Bite them."

Ned's cock surged with renewed lust, and he obeyed Ezer's commands as if he was the omega and Ezer the alpha. He bit and licked, sucked and soothed.

Ezer squirmed and sighed, spreading his legs. "Finger me," he demanded. "Make me come with your hand."

Ned didn't hesitate. He slid his hand up Ezer's leg and pressed three fingers into his sopping hole, massaging Ezer's heat-swollen glands and prostate until Ezer's legs were shaking. Ned dropped his head in Ezer's lap, sucking his dick, lapping at the fluid it released, and loving the way Ezer pumped his hips to get it deeper into Ned's mouth while his hole clenched around Ned's fingers.

"Teeth," Ezer said. "Careful."

Ned whimpered apologetically, and then curved his lips over his teeth so that the sensitive flesh was protected as he sucked eagerly.

"Fuck," Ezer said, and then arched his back, whining as an orgasm pumped through his body, causing him to thrash and clench, shooting a load of sweet omega cum into Ned's mouth. It was delicious. Ned gobbled it down, licking his lips to get the last of it.

"Need more," Ezer gasped.

"Inside." He lifted Ezer into his arms. It was easy because Ezer was too thin, too sharp-edged, and in need of fattening. Ned took him back to the bed where he planted his throbbing cock into Ezer's hot hole, and worked Ezer over until he was a sobbing, wet mess of pleasure. Ned didn't stop fucking him until every inch of their skin was covered by slick, jizz, or tears.

Finally, when Ned pushed deep and came too, his knot growing and pulsing inside Ezer, he whispered, "I love this. I wish you loved it, too."

Ezer moaned. "I do love it. I can't help how good it feels."

Ned buried his head in Ezer's neck, scenting his sweetness. "Do you wish it didn't feel good?"

Ezer thumped Ned's back in a wordless, annoyed reply.

"Do you hope it takes?" Ned gasped.

"A baby?"

"Yeah."

"No." Ezer said vehemently, and then more softly, "I don't know. Maybe."

Ned wrapped his arms around Ezer even more tightly. "I hope it takes. I want to see you big with my child, stuffed full of my future. *Our* future."

Ezer let out a groan and rolled his eyes. "This heat must be receding because I already know that's some serious schmaltz you're spewing. You really are a romantic, aren't you? You don't even know if we can like each other."

"I know we can, and you do too."

"I sure as hell don't know that."

Ned rubbed his face against Ezer's sweaty neck, loving how he could feel Ezer's voice through his body, vibrating on his knot whenever he spoke. "Then why do you 'maybe' want it to stick?"

"Because I have nothing else now. I sold my whole life for this with you. Plus, each child helps my da more."

Smoothing Ezer's hair back from his face, Ned kissed his forehead. "You said that before. That you did this for your da."

"Because it's my fault he's been treated so badly."

"I doubt that."

"Let's not talk about this now. I'm still…" Ezer squirmed and came again, his skin flushing and fresh sweat breaking over him. "Oh fuck. It's just so good." He said it desperately, as if he might cry.

"You smell delicious when you come," Ned said. "I want to cover myself in your scent."

"You're supposed to. It's natural," Ezer murmured, but he sounded drowsy. He must be right about the heat receding. Normally, they'd have another wave or two before there was a break. Ned felt an odd sense of loss over it.

"Ezer?"

"Mmm?"

"I think I'm in love with you."

Ezer's eyes scrunched tight, not bothering to open. "That's fucking absurd. Don't say it again."

"Ever?"

"Ever."

Ned frowned, a bloom of sadness over his heart, but he nodded reluctantly.

"You're just going to agree?" Ezer said, squinting one eye open to glare at Ned.

"I'm going to respect your wishes."

Ezer huffed. "Is this some trick? A roundabout way to, what, *prove* that you quote-unquote love me, or something?"

Ned smirked, moved his hips, and watched as Ezer came apart on his knot again.

Oh, so beautiful, such a delight to see Ezer's ripe mouth fall open, and his body tense and release all over in glorious spasms, all caused by Ned, by the way he was nestled so firmly inside he could feel Ezer's heartbeat around his knot.

"Is it?" Ezer demanded again when he could breathe almost normally.

"I can't talk about that," Ned teased, kissing the edge of Ezer's jaw. "You asked me not to, so I won't."

"Argh, you're already so annoying. How am I going to stand

you?" Ezer said, kicking against Ned's ass and pounding on his back, but a smile teased his mouth as the movement sent them both into spasms of pleasure again.

"I almost don't want it to stop," Ezer said, his eyes dazed, as he peered at the ceiling just past Ned's shoulders. "I can forget when the heat's got me in its grasp."

"What do you want to forget?"

Ezer smirked. "Everything." He ran his hands into Ned's hair again, smoothing it down, and then down to his ass where he gripped him and held him firmly. "This becomes the whole world, and all the other things, all the pain and confusion, just slip away."

Ned kissed Ezer's chin and jaw again, wanting to relieve Ezer of this burden forever. "You never have to be afraid with me. Never again."

"So you say. But what happens when Braden and Finch—"

Ned growled. "I'll kill them if they look at you. I'll gut them."

"Wow. Calm down," Ezer said laughing, and then cursing as that ricocheted into small orgasms for both of them. "That's a little over the top," he panted as they passed. "We don't need to add murder to the list of problems in our lives. I've got plenty. Thanks."

Ned's knot started to go down, and Ezer moaned as Ned slipped free. He pressed four fingers inside and briefly considered fisting him, certain that his hand would fit easily after the stretch of his knot, but he knew Ezer needed to rest between waves, not play more. So he massaged his heat-swollen prostate with his fingers, until Ezer hissed and kicked at his arm, and then Ned pulled free, rising to cover Ezer with his body.

"You're too small to carry a child healthily," Ned murmured. "I'm going to make sure you eat better now. In the nest at my father's house, we'll have the best food for you. I'll make sure of it."

"Maybe," Ezer said noncommittally. "But you can't make me eat it."

"No, but I can entice you to eat."

Ezer frowned. "How?"

Ned shrugged. "I don't know yet."

That made Ezer tense up. He pushed against Ned's chest. "Please get off me. I can't breathe."

Ned rolled to the side and Ezer pulled away so that they weren't touching any more. "What did I say wrong? Tell me, so I can apologize and take it back."

Ezer huffed a small laugh. "If Braden and Finch saw you being so nice to me, what would they think?"

"They *will* see me be nice to you and more. I'm your alpha now. I have to protect you and our child from assholes like them, no matter what my dad thinks." Ned smiled, realizing this arrangement relieved them of the financial obligation to be kind to Braden and Finch anyway. They didn't need their fathers' contracts or approval now, not with Fersee money backing them. He dreaded telling Ezer that, but he supposed he should know.

"My father's very controlling," Ezer murmured. "I don't do well with being controlled."

"No?"

"No. I tend to rebel." It sounded like a warning to Ned's ears, and maybe it was. "I wasn't supposed to visit my da after he was kicked out. But I did. Father didn't want me leaving St. Hauers. But I did."

Ned got more comfortable on his elbow so that he could gaze up at Ezer as he lay naked, letting the breeze from the open door waft over his skin. Ned decided he'd open all the windows later, air the place out, and really cool them down.

"He wanted me to work out with my brothers, get bigger and stronger, so that I could be a tool for him. He doesn't see us as real people—just tools. We're only omegas to sell off for his own purposes. So I didn't eat much. Stayed small. Useless."

Ned sat, adjusting the sheet over his cock, and sitting cross-legged. "Omegas are more than tools."

"Yes," Ezer shot Ned a sharp look. "Braden and Finch think we're also cocksleeves."

"They don't. Not really."

"Oh, yes, they do."

"Maybe. But they have omega brothers. They don't see *them* like that."

"Yeah, well... they're like my father. They probably see their brothers as tools, too."

"How so?"

"My father thinks omegas exist to make his life better. His new omega Pete does—he's sweet and eager. My father takes a lot of pleasure in him physically. Pete's pregnant and so they're often together, fulfilling those needs, which I think my father enjoys. And my brothers make his life better because they're smart, handsome, and are going to bring in nice prices for their heats and marriages. But I make his life worse."

Ned shook his head. "How?"

"I'm the reason his life fell apart. I'm the reason he's so bitter." Ezer stood, his skinny frame glinting with sweat in the lowering sun. "I want a shower. I feel gross."

Ned blinked. He'd thought another wave would be coming soon, but it seemed that maybe the heat had well and truly passed. Ezer seemed more and more clear as the seconds ticked by, and a desire to wash and get out of bed were two signals for the end of heat. Or so his father had said. He truly wished he'd had more preparation for this entire event. At least Ezer didn't seem dissatisfied with his performance.

"Let me help you."

Ezer turned to him then, his blue eyes striking at Ned's heart. "I can manage."

"You're tired. What if you fall?"

"If I get dizzy, I'll sit down. I want to be alone."

Ned nodded, his throat closing up with hurt, but he let Ezer go into the bathroom and shut the door. He waited on the bed until he heard the water start up, and then he rose, taking in the wrecked sheets and the dishes in the sink.

Then he got busy cleaning up for his omega.

# Chapter Eighteen

THE CABIN WAS clean when Ezer finally came out of the shower after using every drop of hot water. He'd wrapped a towel around his waist, and the mirror across the room showed his hair curling with dampness.

Ned was nowhere to be found.

Ezer felt a strange panic to find himself alone in the heat house by the sea.

Finding a pair of sweatpants and a hoodie Ned must have left out for him, he slid them on. The pants were too big, being Ned's, and he had to tie the drawstring incredibly tight to keep them on his body. They bunched oddly, but they stayed put at least. The hoodie was soft and clean. He tugged it over his head and walked out onto the small porch.

Ned wasn't there, either.

He was on the beach, a long way down the strand. A man against the backdrop of the waves and water. Ezer felt the distance, and the vast aloneness of the heat house. He stuffed his hands into the pocket of his hoodie and, barefoot, stepped out to join Ned. The walk over the dunes was slow going, but by the time he reached the water, Ned was heading back.

As they drew close, Ned held out his hands. "For you." Sheets of mother of pearl almost as big as Ned's palm, and two perfectly formed tiny conch shells rested there.

Ezer raised a brow. The attempt at courting was sweet, but he still hadn't settled in his mind whether he was willing to accept it. He was only nineteen; he'd never given much thought to what it meant to be someone's omega. He hadn't ever wanted to do more than auction his heats. He'd never planned to breed, or to have this sort of attention from an alpha, much less one he had such a difficult past with.

"I thought they were pretty. Like you."

"God, Ned, stop with the flirtations."

Ned's shy smile slipped off his face as the shells slipped from his hands. They landed in the sand at their feet, and he didn't stoop to pick them up.

Neither did Ezer.

Finally after a long moment of staring into Ezer's eyes, Ned said, "I guess I should start dinner. I'm tired of stew. We'll want to wait here at least a day to make sure the heat really is over." Then he walked past Ezer and toward the house, the wind, the waves, and the sand dunes muffling his steps.

"Wait," Ezer called. "I'm sorry."

But Ned didn't return. Ezer squatted and picked up Ned's small offerings. What was wrong with him? He was being a jerk. Ned had been so tender during the heat, so kind, and generous, keeping him hydrated, fed, and pleasured beyond his wildest dreams, but Ezer couldn't even take a few shells as a gift and endure a compliment?

He cradled the tiny conchs in his palm, and then admired the sheen of the sheets of mother of pearl. Carrying them back up to the house with him, he entered and put them on the counter next to where Ned was preparing rather large and messy sandwiches.

Ned glanced at the shells and then at Ezer, a glimmer of hope passing over his features before he schooled his face and asked, "Do you like mustard?"

"Yeah."

"Me, too. I like the spicy kind. You? I have the yellow stuff if you don't."

"Spicy is good."

Ned's heaviness seemed to lift slightly with each agreeable comment from Ezer's mouth, which boded well for him being an easygoing alpha, but also seemed to prove Ezer's point that alphas only liked omegas when they made their lives better. Though he had no idea how him being marginally polite made Ned's life better as a whole, but he supposed it wasn't hard, and being polite was fair, so he would continue with it. For now.

Sitting down with their sandwiches, Ezer picked at his before saying, "I guess we should discuss a few things."

"Like what?" Ned asked, letting Ezer take the lead.

"Like what we expect from each other. Heat is heat. We know what happens during that. But now it's over…so what do you expect from me?"

"Well, a lot depends on if you're pregnant," Ned said. "Did anyone review that outcome with you?"

"I've seen it up close and personal with Pete these past few months. The real question is are you ready for it? Because there's a lot expected from you as well."

"My father told me that it's just keeping you satisfied." Ned took a big bite of his sandwich.

Ezer laughed. "Oh, God. Okay. Maybe you should get a book on it. Fatherhood, I mean." He took a bite of his sandwich, too, the mustard bursting tangy across his tongue. As out of control as he felt, he was surprised he wanted to eat at all. But heat and the aftermath left him no space to ignore the demands of his body, so his bites were big and messy. Ned didn't seem to care.

"A book on fatherhood," Ned repeated.

"Yeah, because there's more to it than just fucking me sated for months, and then doing all this again once they manage to trigger another heat in me." Ezer had no doubt they would, too. There was too much money in each pregnancy not to.

Ned picked at his sandwich, pulling pieces of lettuce free and scattering them around his plate. "I know, and I want to be a good father. I'm willing to learn and read, for sure. I want a happy, loving home like my Uncle Heath has with his omega and their children." He frowned, and then seemed to shake something off, turning back to Ezer. "How about you?"

"Me?"

"What kind of da do you want to be?"

Ezer swallowed hard and shrugged, avoiding the question for a moment by chewing several more bites of food. The truth was he hadn't thought about it. He'd never planned to be a teenage father. Unable to delay longer, he gave the only true answer. "I don't know. I want to be a good one. Just because this wasn't my plan doesn't mean I won't care for my child."

"Our child."

Ezer ignored that. "I should get a book too, I guess." God, was he really going to give birth to Ned Clearwater's son? Was he having a baby with one of the boys who—

Ned interrupted his spiraling thoughts with a question. A very scary question. "So you also think it took, then? It's not just me?"

Ezer's heart thumped. "I don't see why it wouldn't. I'm fertile, and you had plenty of semen." He let out a slow breath and tried not to panic. He touched his stomach. Were there even now cells multiplying and making a small human? He felt claustrophobic. There was no way to escape it, if so. Another thing to submit to, another experience to endure.

"Wow." Ned looked down at his plate and picked apart the rest of his sandwich, looking a little green.

"'Wow'?" Ezer's pulse jumped.

"I don't know. It's a lot. Being a father and being your alpha. I thought I was ready, but what if I'm not?"

Ezer stared at him and started to laugh. "You're saying this to the nineteen-year-old boy you probably just knocked up, the one who's going to undergo massive hormone changes, body changes, and then excruciating pain during delivery. You realize that, right?"

"I know!" Ned exclaimed. "And I need to be there for you, and I will, but—" He glanced up at the ceiling, wincing. "What if I'm scared?"

"What if *you're* scared? You're the alpha. I'm the omega. You should care that *I'm* scared!" God, he'd already figured out that Ned was a coward, but this was ridiculous. "Because I am. I'm terrified."

Ned pushed his plate away. "Let me hold you."

"No."

"It'll help."

"It won't."

Ned reached for him, and Ezer found himself falling into his arms.

Fuck, it felt good, too. Ned smelled so right, so comforting. What the actual hell? His body was betraying him in every way. This boy had bullied him, or at the very least had allowed him to be bullied, and now—whether Ned had knowingly done it or not—had participated in the stripping away of Ezer's autonomy. But the post-heat and probable pregnancy hormones coursing through his system meant none of that mattered. All Ezer wanted was to rub all over Ned until his alpha scent coated his skin again, and he could calm down. As if being near Ned was the only key to his peace of mind.

Holy shit. Ezer hated being an omega.

"We need to sort it all out," Ned said, stroking his scruffy cheek against Ezer's less scruffy one. "But don't worry, we'll be all right. I'll take care of you, Ezer. No matter what. I promise, from now on, I'll take care of you forever."

Deep down, beneath his disgust and rage, Ezer was comforted by that assurance, and he hated that he was. He *hated* how much he wanted Ned to be telling the truth.

Hell, he hated *Ned.*

And he needed him.

"Take your clothes off," Ezer said firmly.

Ned didn't need to be told twice. He released Ezer and stripped. He stood there in the light from the windows, his body muscled, with strong thighs and arms, a chiseled stomach, and all of him dusted with glistening hair.

Immediately, Ezer's body responded to the sight of him. Slick released, and his nipples tingled as they brushed the softness of his hoodie. He shucked his own clothes and pressed his body against Ned's. Their hard cocks were rubbing together and smearing pre-cum all over both their bellies.

"Don't touch me," Ezer ordered when Ned gripped his ass cheeks and tugged him in tightly.

Ned seemed to struggle for a moment, but then he released Ezer and stood there while Ezer rubbed on him, soaking in his scent, getting it on his skin, and then taking hold of Ned's cock to stripe his own stomach, hips, and ass with heavy streaks of pre-cum.

Ezer's heart pounded, and his asshole released gushes of slick, but he stayed strong. After he was certain he was scented all over, he pulled away and collapsed onto the bed. "That's all," he said as Ned moved to approach. "No more than that."

Ned stood shaking by the bed, naked and hard. The light streamed in and highlighted every beautiful thing about him. Ezer waited for Ned to break, for him to turn into the bully Ezer knew he was. He held himself rigid on the mattress, expecting Ned to pounce on him, to force his legs up and apart, to push inside against Ezer's will…

But Ned didn't. He put his clothes back on and said over his shoulder, "I'll be back," as he walked out of the door.

And Ezer? Was disappointed.

His gut dropped like a stone. He ached all over to call Ned back. Dumb. Stupid. He didn't want sex. He *didn't.*

But he wanted it desperately.

Ezer rose and went to the window, watching as Ned walked toward the sea and stared out at it. He waited for a long time before climbing back into bed alone, but still smelling of Ned. He touched one of the dried streaks of Ned's pre-cum on his skin, rubbing his fingers against it. He wanted more of that. He wanted Ned to shoot cum on his body, and *in* his body, and in his *mouth*—

Ezer's cock thickened where it rested on his stomach. He wanted…he *wanted*…he wanted so much.

But he wasn't going to give in. Not until Ned had suffered too.

Submission had been his only route during heat, and, if Ned wanted to turn back into a bully, it would be his only option, going forward. There was no way Ezer could fight off Ned and his strength. But if Ned wasn't going to force him, if he was going to play it like this…

Then maybe Ned would find out what it meant to be the one out of control.

Maybe they could both learn about submission together.

# Chapter Nineteen

NED WATCHED EZER sleep. Normally, once a heat was over, the omega went home to his family, or back to his life—school, job—until it was ascertained that a pregnancy had taken root.

But because Ezer's father wanted nothing to do with his son anymore, and believed he was better off out of sight and out of mind, Ned was supposed to take him home right away to his and Lidell's house.

Ned knew that a heat nest had been arranged for Ezer in his absence, and he knew it would be safe and secure. Yet he still chafed at the idea of making Ezer endure the rigors of pregnancy—such as the extreme horniness and intense nesting instincts—with Lidell around, likely reporting every move they made back to Ezer's father.

Assuming the heat had produced a child…

But Ned was sure it had. Otherwise, he couldn't explain the protective feelings swamping him with their intensity, a wild rage burning in the deepest part of his heart when he thought about anyone outside of the family seeing Ezer now, or touching him, or even breathing at him the wrong way.

Nor could he otherwise explain why Ezer, who still resented Ned, kept stepping into his space and touching him, bringing them both to a trembling, aching need before ripping himself away and telling Ned to go without allowing either of them to climax. It was torturous.

They hadn't had sex again since the final heat wave had receded. Ezer hadn't said why or explained it, but Ned understood. This was Ezer's way of taking control back, and Ned was willing to give him that space for now. But he wasn't sure how long Ezer was going to be able to hold out. His body craved connection to Ned, and Ned *burned* to fill Ezer with his compound-laden semen that would help calm Ezer, relax him, and promote his body's ripening to accommodate the rapid expansion of a growing baby.

Four months. It was such a short time for omegas' bodies to cope with the extreme changes required to carry and birth a child, and for anyone to prepare for a new life. A life that until last week, neither of them had thought to plan for.

It sent Ned's head spinning.

So, yes, he felt sure Ezer was pregnant. Otherwise, Ezer should be able to tolerate distance from Ned better than he did, and he wouldn't feel compelled to get naked before bed and press against Ned again and again. It was torment for them both. It was delicious, too. Ned lived for the command he undress. Ezer might be putting out clear signals sex was unwanted now, but Ned knew it was only a matter of time before Ezer would be desperate for his cock and cum, and Ned was willing to wait for it.

In fact, he *liked* waiting for it.

He enjoyed feeling aroused and frustrated. It was exciting.

Still, he knew if Ezer kept fighting their nature, it would be harder on Ezer than on himself, but Ned wasn't going to take away more of Ezer's autonomy by forcing the issue. He wasn't going to be a bully in their life together. He was going to redeem himself in Ezer's eyes. That meant letting their unions going forward being on Ezer's terms as much as nature allowed.

Ned might be an idiot about a lot of things, but he knew that much already.

Ezer sighed in his sleep and shifted toward Ned. The scent of slick rose from his body, and Ned's cock swelled in response. He was horny, but he held back. A release of slick in Ezer's sleep due to proximity to the alpha who'd impregnated him wasn't permission. It was just natural.

Holding very still until he had his urge to touch and fuck under control, Ned watched Ezer's chest rise and fall steadily. When he had his fill of Ezer's sleeping beauty, he rolled onto his back, away from Ezer's hot body, and let the breeze from the open windows wash over his nakedness.

He thought about the future, both near and far.

Ned knew he'd have to return to school in a week or two. He'd service Ezer when he could, but, as an alpha, he was required to continue with his responsibilities even if his omega was pregnant, and until he'd graduated, his responsibility was school.

But Ezer wouldn't be going back. Not ever.

And that was, Ned supposed, unfair. He knew Ezer struggled in some subjects, that he had a learning problem, but he also knew from the group projects they'd done together, and from secretly watching him work math problems for fun, that Ezer was not only a smart guy, but that he enjoyed learning.

Ned knew Lidell would tell him, and no doubt Ezer's father would agree, Ezer could learn about child-rearing now. Or he could learn about how to be an omega to an alpha of the peerage, meaning how to make seating plans for dinner parties, and which omega friends to suck up to to further Ned's future ambitions. That would be the normal way of it, if they had been older, and not teenagers, and were further along in their lives, like most couples when they brought a child into the world.

But for teenagers like them, that wasn't an option.

Ned didn't have a career yet. He didn't have dinner parties. And he'd be damned if Lidell used Ezer as a substitute omega spouse for *his* career and dinner parties. No, Ezer was his omega now, and he wasn't going to share him with his father or demean him by treating him like a means to an end.

Ned frowned, thinking about how to occupy Ezer after the baby came. He knew that the period of pregnancy required rest, indulgence, relaxation, and fucking, but he couldn't imagine Ezer being happy in the long term as just a da, just an omega waiting at home for his alpha's life to begin.

Ezer was going to demand more from him.

Ned twitched, wondering how to solve that problem.

Now he understood why Ezer's father had promised additional money for each child birthed. Handling Ezer wasn't going to be easy. He was smart and hard to please. It was going to take a lot of thought and planning.

Good thing Ned hadn't wanted an easy omega.

Because he sure as hell hadn't gotten one.

# PART THREE

## Nesting

# Chapter Twenty

"THIS IS *IT*?" Ezer asked, turning around in the spacious living room with three comfortable couches making a U within a big wall of windows showing off a view of the cliffs and sea. "This is where I'll be for the next four months? This one room?"

At home, George had a two-story nesting area built in for his da and then Pete. And with only omega and beta sons, no alphas to threaten or see, George's omegas had always enjoyed the full run of the house.

This nest was tiny in comparison.

Earl, the beta servant who'd been Ned's nurse in childhood stiffened at Ezer's harsh tone. He almost felt bad for the old man. It wasn't that it wasn't a nice room, a beautiful nest by many standards, but as the days at the beach had passed, Ezer had found himself feeling more and more claustrophobic and anxious whenever he was inside.

By the end, he'd demanded Ned let them sleep with the windows and doors open, and had even then felt too trapped, too hot, too full of Ned's unwanted child to breathe properly.

Here, in the basement-level room on the edge of a cliff, he was literally below ground with only a glassed-in view of the outside world to let him know he wasn't buried alive. No balcony, no garden, and no windows that opened to let in fresh air.

"There is a kitchen and a bedroom, sir," Earl said, motioning off toward a hall leading deeper into the cliff, to what had to be an even more oppressive, windowless area.

Sweat slipped down his back. Ezer sucked in a breath and let it out.

"Where's Ned?" he asked, again, though he already knew. It irked him that he'd feel so much better if Ned were with him now. It enraged him that he knew he'd be all right with being trapped in this claustrophobic nightmare of an underground nest if he'd just give in and let Ned fuck him, or allow him to come in his mouth, or at the very least, drink his cum from a glass. But he refused to give in. He was not going to lose control again. And if he gave even an inch, he would. He'd lose himself in the sex and the lust and the contentment that settled on all pregnant omegas, and he'd lose himself. He'd lose *Ezer*.

He'd be the happy horny slut his father wanted, and while he knew it was inevitable—he'd have to give in—he needed to resist and stay himself for as long as possible. He didn't want to forget that he hated Ned, and his father, and being pregnant. Not yet.

But he also didn't want to suffer and grow sick, nor did he want to lose the baby which—for some insane reason—he felt a strong urge to keep safe from harm. Unwanted but wanted. The poor child was going to grow up as confused as Ezer had been if he wasn't careful.

Had been? Try was. Ezer had never been more confused in his life.

Yet another sensation that would evaporate if he gave in and asked Ned to shoot a load down his throat. But he wasn't ready yet, so he'd been making do with rubbing his naked body against Ned's until they were both panting and dripping, and then he always put a stop to it.

He had to admit there was a beauty in Ned's face when Ezer

left him hanging—his dick veined and throbbing, his breath coming in harsh sobs, and his balls drawn up tight, along with his pebbled nipples.

All of that needing and yearning for Ezer.

And all of it rejected by Ezer, too.

The power of denying Ned was almost as hot as he suspected the consummation would be.

"Ned is with his father," Earl said, and it seemed like he was repeating himself. "Are you all right, sir? Should I get him for you?"

Ezer tried to get his mind out of the gutter and remember what he and Earl had been talking about. Weird that the thought of Ned before him, naked and dripping, seemed to both soothe and irritate him all at once. But it did. "Uh, what? I'm sorry? What are you asking me?" He ran his eyes over the nest again, feeling the walls closing in. Even the glass of the windows seemed to push at his skin and hurt.

"You asked where Ned was again, sir, and I told you he's with his father. Should I get him for you?"

"No, no," Ezer said, rubbing at his arms and shifting awkwardly in his jeans. His clothes were constraining, too. He couldn't breathe in them. He couldn't breathe at all in this room and in these garments. He wanted to be back at the beach; he wanted to be running naked on the sand. He wanted Ned to catch him and throw him onto a sandbank and shove his—

"Fuck!" Ezer whimpered, squeezing his eyes closed.

"Sir, I think it's time you were rid of those clothes," Earl said. "Let me help you take them off."

Ezer gritted his teeth, but let Earl help him remove his hoodie, his T-shirt, and his jeans. His underwear was wet from both slick and pre-cum, but Earl said nothing as he slipped them down Ezer's thighs and pulled them from his feet. He didn't look up at

Ezer as he collected the clothes in his arms, saying, "Wait here, sir. I think I know what you need."

Ezer wanted to argue, but he was naked as the day he was born, aching all over, dizzy, angry, scared, oppressed, and so horny he wanted to cry. But there was no privacy afforded a pregnant omega by beta servants. He was supposed to feel safe and comfortable with his nudity, with his hard on, his wet asshole, and his flushed skin in front of Earl.

Which was upsetting and not true, and yet he could feel that it *would* be true. He would soon stop caring, losing all sense of shame. Yet another part of him lost to this experience that he'd never even wanted. With an alpha he despised.

"Please," he whispered to the empty room. "Help me."

The door opened and this time it wasn't Earl who returned. It was the man he most and least wanted to see.

Man?

No, they were both still boys.

It only added to the cruelty, Ezer thought, that they were both so young. And yet when Ned wrapped his arms around Ezer, he was awash with relief.

"Let me help you?" Ned suggested.

Ezer squirmed against him, trying to imprint Ned's scent enough to not need more, but he knew it was useless. With tears sliding down his cheeks, he nodded.

"Yes. Help me."

STANDING IN HIS father's study, Ned was still thinking about the expression on Earl's face when he'd arrived with Ezer. The disappointment, the irritation, the anger. He hadn't expected the old servant to be home from his uncle's house yet. Even if he'd considered the possibility, he'd assumed Lidell would have explained everything to him, and Earl would understand.

But no. It was clear Earl did not.

For a moment Ned had thought his nurse would scold Ned in front of Ezer, take him by the ears like he had when Ned was a naughty child, and tell him off for this choice of his. But he'd underestimated Earl. The man had shuttered his glare toward Ned and proceeded to greet Ezer with the respectful, polite distance of a well-trained, high-class servant.

After a few awkward moments, Earl had suggested he take Ezer down to the nest that had been prepared and told Ned that his father was in his study waiting to be debriefed about the heat. Lidell was smart enough not to greet them at the front entrance the way Earl had. An alpha would not easily tolerate another alpha near his pregnant omega, even if that alpha was his own father.

Still discombobulated, wondering when he would get a chance to explain himself to Earl, Ned listened to his father's report: Heath's beta son had survived, though he was still sickly. Also, Earl had been very angry when he had returned and found out what Lidell had arranged. "I was been tempted to fire him," Lidell said. "But I figured you'd want his help with your omega and a baby, if one is going to come."

Ned didn't know what to say, which was fine since his father kept talking. "If Heath's new baby wasn't still so sick, I have no doubt Earl would report all this to Simon, who'd tell Heath, and we'd have him on our doorstep with his judgment and threats. Well, there's nothing he can do about it now, is there? What's done is done."

"Yes," Ned agreed.

"And what is done?" Lidell asked. "Can you sense any changes? Did it take?"

Ned nodded. "I think it took."

Lidell stood, coming around to embrace Ned. "Another wad of cash for us, then, assuming he delivers safely."

Was the money all his father cared about? No excitement about becoming a grandfather, no worry for Ezer's health?

"About delivering safely," Ned said. "Ezer is quite small. I'm worried that—"

"Nonsense. He'll be fine. We'll have the best doctor on hand for him. You must remember omegas are designed to give birth. It's natural. So don't fret."

Ned stared at Lidell. "But how can you say that when my own omega parent—"

"That was a horrible thing, but, overall, quite unusual." Lidell put his hand over his heart, raised his eyes to the ceiling and said, "Bless you Sandrino." His attention returned to Ned again. "I figure you'll be restless with me, another alpha, staying here so near your omega's nest. I think I'm going to get out of your hair, take a little of that new money and get out of town for a while. You won't mind if I leave you and your omega with Earl."

"Father—"

"Sir," Earl's voice cut into the room. "Ned, I think your omega needs you."

That was all that was required to break Ned free of his father's mercenary glee and set him off at a near run toward the nest, which he hadn't had a chance to examine yet for himself. He hoped it was to Ezer's liking and that he was happy with it.

Earl trotted along behind Ned, not able to keep pace. "Sir, I would dearly love to scold you for this mess you've gotten yourself and this boy into, but I suppose now isn't the time. He's nearing a panic. I think your last issue of semen is wearing off."

Ned ran faster, leaving Earl and his disapproval at the top of the stairs leading down. "I'll handle it."

Once he had Ezer in front of him, naked, and the verge of hysterics, Ned wasn't sure he *could* handle it actually. Ned knew what he *wanted* to do—everything, anything to please his omega, even if that meant giving him space and control. But he also knew Ezer *needed* Ned's semen in his system more than anything else in order to settle his mind, to protect his body, and to help the pregnancy progress safely. He also knew Ezer hadn't even eaten a handful of grapes before they'd left the heat cottage that morning and hadn't eaten anything else all day. Not only was he needing his alpha, but his blood sugar was low, and given how wild-eyed and trembling he was, Ned knew there was no way he was going to convince Ezer to eat if he didn't help him reach a state of ease.

"Kneel for me," Ned said with a firmness that belied his inner anxiety. He saw Ezer's resistance for a moment in the tension around his mouth and eyes, but when Ezer dropped to his knees, the knot of anxiety in Ned's chest began to come undone. "Open."

Ezer's cheeks flushed, and he glared up at Ned, but he unclenched his mouth and held it open with an air of defiance.

"Good," Ned encouraged. "Stay just like that."

Ezer snarled, but opened his mouth again, holding out his tongue, eyes closed, waiting. Ned wanted Ezer's eyes directed at him again, even if they were full of panic, rage, and fear.

"Look at me," Ned murmured.

Ezer shook his head.

"No?"

Ezer stuck his tongue out more, and then pulled it back in, saying, "Just do it. Please. I can't breathe in here. I can't take it. Just fucking help me. Shoot in my mouth. I'll drink it."

When Ezer stopped talking and opened his mouth again, Ned didn't want to risk losing his trust by taking more than he'd been offered. So he didn't touch Ezer. Instead, he got his cock out of his jeans, pumped it a few times until it was fully hard, and then jerked off rough and fast, staring at the pulse in Ezer's throat, and the way Ezer's lashes lay against his red-flushed cheekbones, and how the light from the windows trailed through his dark curls.

"Ugh," Ned grunted, shooting hard and fast, the first orgasm he'd been allowed since the heat ended. It ripped through him like a bomb going off.

White cum striped Ezer's red tongue, and Ned moved his hips forward so that his cockhead was inside Ezer's wide open mouth but touching no part of him. Holding himself steady, he shot and shot until his knees quaked. He moaned as Ezer's mouth filled up and he greedily gulped down Ned's jizz.

After wringing one more pulse from his orgasm, Ned started to draw away, but Ezer flicked out his tongue, swiped over the damp head of his cock to get the last bead of cum and wiping him clean. Sweat slipped down Ned's cheeks from his temples, and his hands shook as he put his dick back into his pants and stood back, waiting.

Ezer stayed on his knees, eyes closed, hands resting on his skinny thighs. His cock jutted up hard and red, looking painful and forlorn above his small, tight balls. A tear slid down his cheek, but he didn't say anything, and he didn't move.

Ned stayed silent, too. Ezer was still in many ways a stranger to him, but he'd grown to know his body language well enough to recognize that touching him now would be considered a violation.

Finally, Ezer opened his eyes, glared up at Ned with a hot anger that cut to the core, and took hold of his own dick. He jerked it twice—crying out as he came hard. Cum jetted out onto Ned's jeans, painting him with splatters from the knees down.

When it was done, Ezer stood, pressed himself to Ned again,

and held tight. It didn't feel like affection. It felt like rage. Ned wrapped his arms around him, trying to contain it all, hoping to find a way to turn that red-hot fury into something softer, gentler, and healthier.

"Better?" he asked after another few moments of holding Ezer's nakedness against his clothed body.

Ezer nodded and pulled away, turning to gaze around the room. His shoulders fell.

"What? Is something missing? Do you hate it?"

"No," he whispered. "It's fine now."

He sounded defeated as he sat on the nearest couch, gorgeously naked and still flushed from his orgasm. His eyes drifted toward the wall of windows.

"Yeah. It's fine now."

But Ezer didn't sound fine at all.

# Chapter Twenty-One

"MY FATHER SENDS his regards," Ned said as he moved around the kitchen area of the nest while Ezer sat and watched him. Looking a little calmer, Ezer had still already complained about the size of the nest, the darkness of the bedroom, and the kitchen being windowless, tucked away as it was behind the living area.

Ned had tried to reassure him there was plenty of airflow in every room of the nest, due to a complicated ventilation system which pulled air through and provided constant white noise and an internal breeze throughout.

Ezer wasn't relieved by that. Ned was starting to worry the nest here at his father's house wasn't a good fit for his omega.

"Lidell won't come down into this area, and he's planning to leave shortly for an extended stay away to give us privacy."

"I won't have to see him?"

"Not unless you want to leave the nest in the next few days and go up to the decks for sun and swimming. We have a pool and I've heard that water can be soothing as your body changes and the baby grows."

"What about the servants?" Ezer asked.

"We don't keep any others. Just Earl."

Ezer's fists clenched in his lap, as he murmured, "I'd like to see the pool. Yes."

"In that case, my father might be around until he's left town.

If you're uncomfortable with that, then we can always warn him when you'll be—"

"It's fine."

"He's an alpha," Ned said, stating the obvious to Ezer's clear irritation which soon dissolved away reflecting a dull, loose calmness.

*The semen is doing its work.*

"Will it bother you?" Ezer asked without much emotion. "Do you trust him with me?"

Ned pondered and then nodded. "He's terrible with money, but he's never had a weakness for omegas, and I do trust him. Yes."

"You could handle him seeing me naked? And pregnant?"

Ned frowned. Ezer sounded so distant and a little numb. He didn't love that. He'd wanted Ezer to be calmer, yes, but not like this.

As for his father seeing Ezer naked and pregnant, he didn't love that idea either, but he didn't think his father would linger. So long as Ezer was comfortable with the possibility of being seen, then Ned could cope. Probably.

"You're welcome to use the pool whenever you want," Ned said. "This is your home now. I'll take you up after dinner to show you the way."

Ezer's mouth lifted at the corners, but just barely. It was like he was made of glass: fragile, breakable. His stomach growled.

Ned was finished with their meal. He needed to add garnish and—there. He was done.

"Let's eat in the living room," he suggested. "It'll be more comfortable."

Ezer took the plate from Ned with a relieved half-smile and followed him out into the bigger room. They sat on the sofa facing the wall with the large television and other technology screens. Ned noted that Earl had scented the nest with lavender to help soothe Ezer's nerves. It mixed well with the scent of the pasta, and all-in-all, Ned felt the nest was very homey, very comforting in vibe.

"There's internet access," Ned said, using his fork to indicate screens. "If you want to contact friends or family at any time. You're not alone here."

"I don't have a lot of friends," Ezer said shrugging. "But I guess I might contact my brothers."

"You should!" Ned encouraged.

He knew many omegas grew happily introverted while growing a baby, but he had a feeling Ezer was going to need contact with people other than himself, especially once Ned was at school. Earl didn't seem to have made a wonderful impression on Ezer, given the way Ezer avoided looking at Earl whenever he came into the room.

Ned should ask about that. Nip at least one problem in the bud.

"Do you want a different servant? Someone from your home, maybe? I could talk to your father about having one transferred for the duration if—"

"Does Earl dislike me already?" Ezer asked, taking a messy bite of his pasta and frowning when some of the oil drizzled onto his chest.

Ned admired the pink of Ezer's nipples and fought the urge to lean forward and lick the oil away. Arousal flared at the sudden realization that before long, those nipples would grow puffy, Ezer's chest would make milk, and he'd grow round with their child—

It was so much. Too much.

They were too young.

Ned had to stop thinking that, though, because, young or

not, they'd done this, they were doing it, and they'd have to keep on doing it. A baby was on the way.

"He hasn't said one way or another," Ned admitted. "But I can't imagine he wouldn't like you. It's just I got the impression *you* don't like *him*."

"Oh." Ezer shook his head. "He's fine. He's already seen me naked. I don't want to start new with anyone else. Earl will be fine."

"You don't have a problem with him?"

"I have a problem with this!" Ezer said, motioning around the room, then down at his body, and then between the two of them. "I'm not like you. I can't just act like this is all okay or that I'm not scared or upset." He took a bite and chewed it angrily. "I know you want me to let you fuck me into stupidity, and I have no doubt before long I will, but I don't *want to* yet. I want to stay *me*. I want to stay mad."

"All right," Ned agreed.

"That's it? Just 'all right'?"

"I'm not going to fight with you about it."

Ezer flung his fork down on the plate and glared at him. "What if I want you to fight me? What if I want you to argue?"

"Well, then you'll be disappointed."

Standing, Ezer threw his plate and the pasta onto the tile floor, the pasta coiling in an oily mess and the plate ringing. Ned gaped at it, shocked to silent stillness.

But Ezer wasn't through yet. He stalked over to Ned, grabbed his dinner, and threw it too. This time, both of them stiffened when the pasta splattered all over the wall and the plate broke.

"Do something!" Ezer said. "Do anything! Just don't act like this is okay!"

Ned blinked between the pasta on the wall and Ezer's enraged expression. He had no idea what to say or do. There was silence in his head, a buzz of white noise he couldn't think around. But it wasn't silent for long.

Ezer picked up the glass he'd been drinking from and threw it against the wall, too, watching it shatter. Again with Ned's glass.

Then, with a scream, Ezer seemed to shatter, too.

Before turning on Ned and trying to break him as well.

"HEY," NED SAID, both hands up. "Let's—"

"Shut up," Ezer shouted, shoving Ned's shoulders back into the sofa. "Just shut up."

Ned did just that, and Ezer felt a rush of power, like he had in the heat house when he'd made Ned wait, when he'd left him hungry for his body but restrained by Ezer's fierce denial. Head spinning with rage and need, Ezer reached for the buttons of Ned's jeans, ripping them open. He smacked Ned's thigh as punishment for lifting his hips, making it easier for Ezer to jerk his underwear halfway down his thighs. This wasn't supposed to be easy.

Ezer wasn't at all surprised to find Ned's cock erect. Of course he wanted to fuck. Of course he did.

"Fight me," Ezer demanded. "Push me. Hit me."

Ned stared at him and stayed motionless, his breaths coming in rough pants, and his hands clenched into fists at his side.

"C'mon," Ezer whispered, pushing hard against Ned's shoulders, shoving him back on the sofa. "Damn you, *fight* me."

Ned's cock pulsed and leaked pre-cum at the rough treatment. Ezer wasn't surprised by that at all either. But he *was* angry.

He was still *so angry*.

After climbing onto the sofa, Ezer crouched with his feet on either side of Ned's hips. Face-to-face and breath-to-breath, he took hold of Ned's hot, hard cock.

"Do you want this?" he gritted out.

Ned blinked and said nothing.

"I know you do. You *want* me to let you fuck me. You want to push your cock up into me, don't you?"

Ned's brows quirked, but he kept his silence.

"Well, I'm not going to let you. I'll fuck myself. Understand? I'll fuck *myself.*"

Ned swallowed, and Ezer could see his pulse pounding in his throat. Ezer's dick throbbed, having grown hard as he'd poised himself over Ned's cock.

"Don't you get it? I hate you," Ezer said, as he lowered himself. His head fell back as perfect pressure flared against his hole, and he moaned as Ned's thick, fat cock moved deep inside, rubbing his slick glands perfectly, stroking his prostate, and filling him in the most flawless way imaginable. "I hate you so fucking much."

Ned held still as Ezer rode him, used him, and pleasured himself on his dick. He didn't thrust, he didn't take hold of Ezer's hips, and, with his eyes on Ezer's face, watching, staring with intensity Ezer didn't understand, Ned didn't seem close to coming.

Whimpering, he clung to Ned's strong neck and shoulders, working himself up and down, wringing unsatisfactory pleasure from his own body. It was so close to what he needed—but it wasn't enough. It just wasn't enough. "Please," he whispered. "I need…I need you…"

But Ned refused, playing the part of a flesh and blood statue.

"Ned," Ezer groaned. "I can't…I just can't…" He rode harder, his thighs burning from the effort, his dick aching and straining with every rub over Ned's stomach, and his nipples almost stinging with tightness. "Help me."

Ned murmured. "Beg me for it."

Ezer shook his head, stubbornness rearing his head again. "No. Take it. Be a bully."

Ned kept still, his cock rigid inside Ezer, rubbing all the right places as Ezer writhed.

"Fine," Ezer bit out. "Come inside me, Ned. Make *me* come. Touch me. Fuck me."

Ned smirked. "That wasn't begging."

"Do it!" Ezer shouted, desperation mounting in him, along with that now ever-present rage that seemed to catch light even when he didn't want it to, even when he wanted to escape into this pleasure like he had into the heat.

"Such a sweet, submissive boy you are," Ned teased, taking hold of Ezer's hips and stilling his frantic ride. He stood; Ezer wrapped his legs around Ned's hips to stay impaled and clung to his neck. "Let's see how you like it now."

He moved them to a wall and pushed Ezer's back to it, gripping the backs of Ezer's thighs, and demonstrating his superior strength by using that pressure to hold Ezer up on the wall, cock buried deep inside. His grip pinched at Ezer's skin and hurt a little, but Ezer didn't want sweet and nice—so it was fucking perfect.

"Goddammit." Ezer said, clawed at Ned's shoulders. "Fuck me."

Ned did, and the vulnerable, gravity-defying position left Ezer with no defenses. His ass was plowed hard by Ned's thick, gorgeous dick, and his hands gripped onto Ned's firm shoulders, and his asshole flexed wide with each plunge in. Ned was stupidly fucking hot—how had he not seen it before? And being fucked by him felt so goddamn good it blew his mind. Ezer wanted to hate it, he wanted to stay angry, but almost instantly he was far too lost to the sloppy-good-slick-wetness to manage.

His asshole was a fount of slick, his legs shook where Ned held them back, and his insides spasmed with orgasm after orgasm, as his cock painted Ned's stomach, and his own. He was almost as mindless as he had been in heat, but he wasn't sure how much more of this he could take. Unlike heat, which had seemed gorgeously endless and transcendent, this was a continual crisis—he needed it over with, and then he needed it again.

"That's it," Ned said. "That's what you wanted."

Ezer wanted to scream, to pound his fists against Ned and deny it, but instead Ned's words made him come again, helplessly crying out, and shaking with pleasure.

"Such a good boy," Ned crooned. "I love fucking you."

Ezer's eyes filled with tears as unwanted satisfaction filled him at those words. He didn't want this. He didn't *want* it, but he needed it, and he loved that Ned desired him, and he couldn't deny that he desired Ned, too.

"Here you go," Ned grunted. "This is going to help you so much."

Ezer clung to Ned's shoulders at his rough thrusts grew faster, tighter, and then ended with a smashing, groan-soaked, and sweat-perfumed climax. Ned's body shook and his arms threatened to drop Ezer for a moment, but then he leaned in, pinning Ezer's body to the wall with his full weight, and he kissed his neck, his collarbones, and his shoulders, avoiding his mouth and nipples.

"Tell me," Ned whispered, when he finished coming in Ezer's convulsing ass. "Tell me to kiss you."

Ezer shook his head. He wouldn't. He would never.

But within moments, he felt the impact of Ned's semen deposit inside him, the way his emotions calmed, the gentle affection trickling into his heart and mind. The unfairness of his biology tricking him into saying, "Kiss me."

Ned nuzzled his neck and hair, and then, sweetly, like it was their first kiss—and, in a way, perhaps it was, since the others had been during the mindlessness of heat—he took Ezer's mouth with his own. Ezer groaned at his tender lips, the sweetness of his tongue, and found that he couldn't stop himself from chasing Ned's mouth when he pulled away.

"There now," Ned said, lowering Ezer to his feet and holding him steady. He felt the precious cum start to leak out, and he reached down to push it back in. He needed it inside…or else he'd want this again too soon.

Ned's eyes followed his frantic attempts to push the cum back up, and he scooped Ezer into his arms, carrying him out of the bright living area and down a dark hall to an even darker bedroom.

No windows.

One door.

The bed was soft, smooth, and cool against Ezer's back.

"Tell me," Ned said as he lay on top of Ezer. "Tell me what you need."

"Do it again," Ezer said, betraying himself with his next words. "Make it go away. Make *me* go away. Fill me up with only you."

Ned, it seemed, was happy to comply.

NED LEFT EZER in the dark bedroom sleeping and spent.

It had taken three times, with each fuck growing longer and more intense in the heated darkness of the room, for Ezer to give way to his nature and let himself feel their combined bliss. He'd swallowed Ned's load, then taken it in his ass again, and with each deposit he'd grown looser, calmer, more intimate and reciprocal.

It'd been the best sex of Ned's life outside of the heat, but he knew it still wasn't as good as it could get. Even though the seminal compounds were working on Ezer's mind, in his heart there was still resistance, and it wasn't true affection. Not yet.

There was still too much between them. If he could keep Ezer calm long enough, they'd have some good, honest talks soon about the past, about the present, and about their future. Hopefully, he'd given Ezer enough semen now he'd stop fighting him every step of the way at least.

Ned pulled on a robe and went out to the living room to find Earl clearing up the shattered plates, glasses, and the food mess Ezer had made earlier.

"He's frightened, I see," Earl said, as Ned knelt down next to him and began to help.

Ned nodded. He wanted to tell his old nurse that he was frightened too, but he remembered Ezer's damning commentary at the beach: he was the alpha. He was supposed to be the one to help Ezer through his fears, not indulge in his own.

"What are you doing to help him?"

"The usual."

Earl scoffed. "Obviously." He motioned at Ned's appearance, and said, "A shower would be in order before you go anywhere or see anyone else."

"It's a nest," Ned said, defensively. "What were you expecting?"

"Nothing less, nothing more. I just don't know if you realize how you look right now."

"That's the least of my problems," Ned said, running a hand through his hair. He stood with the collected pieces of plate, and took them to the garbage can Earl had dragged in.

"What is your biggest problem? Let's tackle it first."

"He hates me."

"Ah…" Earl went wide-eyed. "So you haven't been able to explain to him about the way things were before, with Braden and Finch, and your father?"

Ned sat down on the sofa, scrubbing his hands through his hair. "I did tell him about it, but he wasn't impressed."

Earl scooped up the pasta and dumped it into the garbage can. "Your behavior with them was unimpressive, so I understand his point of view."

"I do too. It's just that it's been hard to get him to *try* with me. Even during the heat. He either refuses to talk to me, or he wants to fuck, or he doesn't want to fuck, but then he throws our food on the floor, and he fucks me anyway." Ned waved at the mess.

Earl started to scrub at the stain on the wall, remaining quiet, listening. Like how Ned wished Ezer would listen.

"Just now, I wanted to have dinner and talk, but *that's* what happened instead. So, I fucked him until he passed out, and now I don't know what else to do." Ned's shoulders drooped.

"He should be calmer now then," Earl said, as if he could personally vouch for the effect Ned's semen should have on Ezer. "Things will be better now."

"He's a fighter. I think he's trying to fight how all this works. He wants to be angry."

"It gives him power."

Ned thought about how Ezer had seemed to enjoy denying him, the way his lips would twist up smugly after making Ned shake with need and then saying no. "Maybe so. What's the solution?"

Earl came to sit by Ned and patted his knee. "Patience. Time. You can't rush this, Ned. Let him get there on his own."

"There's no way to skip to the happy ending?"

"No, darling. There's just real life." Earl stood and went back to clearing up the mess.

Ned's mind continued to turn over the way Ezer had behaved on the sofa earlier, challenging him, trying to provoke him to violence, and then taking what he'd needed without any thought to Ned's preferences. But, in the end, he'd required Ned's pleasure, too. He hadn't been able to come or ejaculate until he'd felt Ned's rough reciprocation.

Ned continued to think, and Earl finished cleaning up their mess.

"Let's solve a smaller problem first," Earl said. "Should I bring a new dinner, sir? I can bring something down from upstairs."

Ned nodded. He was tired, hungry, and needed to develop a plan before his omega woke up in who-knew-what state of mind.

He had to be ready for anything.

So that meant he needed sustenance.

"Bring whatever you have. I'll eat it."

Earl disappeared to do as he'd been told.

When Ezer did come out of the dark back room, Ned was ready for him. He'd eaten enough for two men, so he'd better be.

# Chapter Twenty-Two

"IS THERE ANY food left?" Ezer asked, twisting his hands together in front of him, and keeping his eyes on the floor.

He'd woken feeling calm, rested, and embarrassed by the way he'd behaved earlier.

Top to bottom it was all mortifying: pitching a fit, throwing the plates, and then fucking Ned. Hell, needing Ned was humiliating enough. It was even worse to fail in every attempt to control himself.

"Of course," Ned said, standing in his fluffy white robe. "Why don't you get comfortable here, and I'll bring you something."

Ezer did as he was told without fighting for once. Not because he didn't want to, but because the shame of earlier was still so fresh. He waited on the sofa for Ned to return with food with his stomach growling and his heart aching. The view from the windows was a beautiful one, all gray, blue, and brown with the cliff, sea, and sky mixing in a gorgeous color palette. He took it in quietly.

The air of the nest was scented. He didn't know why he'd just realized that, but it was. He breathed in and out slowly trying to place it. Ah, yes. Lavender. It was supposed to have a calming effect. He remembered now how his da used to spray it over his pillow at bedtime to improve his rest.

This scent was yet another attempt to modify him, to control his emotions. Ezer hated it.

"Here you go." Ned's voice pulled Ezer from his reverie, and he turned to accept the plate held out toward him. It was piled high with a cheesy casserole, and his mouth salivated.

"This isn't what we had earlier."

Ned took a seat at his side. Ezer wanted to lean into him, breathe in the scent at his neck, at his groin, and cover himself with it. He held back.

"It's from upstairs. It's left over from what my father had for dinner."

"Oh." Ezer ate the casserole, the flavors bursting over his tongue. It was so delicious, as if he hadn't eaten in days. He found he couldn't control himself, stuffing it in faster and faster until it was gone.

Ned watched, his arm stretched across the back of the sofa, his fingers brushing the back of Ezer's neck in a tantalizing way that sent shivers up and down Ezer's spine. He said nothing until Ezer's plate was scraped clean, and then he offered seconds.

"No," Ezer said. "I'm full now."

In fact, he'd never been quite so full in his life. He didn't know how he felt about it. He probably hated that too. But in the post-fuck, post-meal haze, he was feeling fuzzy about why he was so angry. The food had been so ridiculously good. He didn't know why it tasted so much better than any food had before, but his hunger felt different too: ravenous, uncontrollable. He'd always been able to control it in the past. Another change he hadn't asked for.

"By the way," Ned said, taking the plate from Ezer and sliding it onto the small, low table in the middle of the sofa. "I've asked Earl to keep our kitchen down here stocked with all the things you like most."

"Oh," Ezer said again.

"So, you'll need to help him with that. Make him a list of your favorite fruits, meals, soups, pastries, whatever you like. You need to eat."

"Yes," Ezer agreed. He looked down at his nakedness—how had he become accustomed to it so quickly?—and smoothed a hand over his still-flat stomach. Even now he could feel a strange tension from inside, almost as if he were still full of Ned's semen, a bulging pressure.

"I know you're angry—"

Ezer cut a glare at Ned; he couldn't help it. Angry was an understatement. But he'd realized as he'd drifted into consciousness in the dark, warm bedroom of his nest that he'd *chosen* this—maybe he'd been coerced, but it'd been his choice all the same. He could have done many things differently and had another outcome.

So he needed to make the best of it. The way he'd made the best of the heat. Fighting Ned every step of the way for the entire pregnancy wasn't going to help him or help the baby. He snorted. That was probably the seminal compounds talking, but it didn't make it untrue.

"I know you're angry," Ned began again after a small pause. "But we need to stay calm and talk about a few things. We're going to have a child. We should have some understanding between us."

Ezer nodded. He pulled his knees up to his chest, resting the flat of his feet on the sofa, and wrapped his arms around his shins. He wasn't cold, but he was vulnerable, and he felt better holding himself this way. At least his genitals weren't so exposed. Why didn't alphas suffer from the sensitivity that made garments unbearable to omegas during pregnancy? Why was he the one to suffer so much indignity? God, or whoever had invented this game of life, was unfair. Definitely an alpha.

Ned sat with his legs wide, his arms relaxed at his side, and he didn't seem to be at all affected by the fear stringing through Ezer's muscles and sinews again. Ezer took a slow breath, trying to calm himself, but it was useless. Was Ned's semen wearing off already? He didn't see how. Most omegas could go hours and hours between if they needed to. That was how their alphas were able to get any work done at all during these pregnancy months.

But maybe it was that he *didn't* need to wait? Ned was next to him, after all, covered in nothing but a fluffy robe with his beautiful cock *right there* beneath—

No! He had to keep calm for this.

Ned wanted to talk. And he was right. They needed to get some things straight. Like the fact that while Ezer might give in and play his part the way he'd agreed to do when he'd signed the contracts, and he might try to make this 'work' in terms of parenting a child together, Ned should never misread any of it as liking or friendship. Ezer was still going to hate Ned deep down for the rest of his life. Ned needed to know he should never mistake Ezer's physical pleasure for affection, or his compliance for love. Everything he did, every move he made, was for his da's safety and happiness—and, now, for this new innocent life they'd created. Nothing more, nothing less.

Ezer's head spun. A few weeks ago, his life had been so different. He'd been a brother, a son, and a student. Now and into the future he would be this… He touched his stomach again.

Ned went on, assuming Ezer's agreement. "I think, to reach that understanding, I need you to forgive me for how things were in the past, and how I didn't speak out or do more to protect you from Finch and Braden."

Ezer clenched his jaw but said nothing. He listened as Ned spoke about his prior status as Heath Clearwater's heir, and the loss of that inheritance when Heath had a late-born son. He told

Ezer about his father, Lidell, and how he had a way with money—a way of losing it. Ned told him about the dire financial straits his father had kept them both in most of his life, teetering between wealth and ruin, with no comfort or safety.

Ned also revealed everything about the money and contracts Lidell had with the Maddox and Tenmeter families, and how Ned had been told to make nice with them, how he'd felt powerless to say no.

Then Ned confessed to getting in over his head with those assholes, doing Bright's powder, fucking omegas—why did Ezer's stomach clench with sickening jealousy over that?—and getting in all kinds of trouble, to the point his uncle, Heath Clearwater, had had to step in and bail him out.

"And that's when I swore to myself that I'd stop being such a putz," he said, chewing on his bottom lip before smiling ruefully. "Turns out I lied. As you know."

"Coward," Ezer ground out. How had he ended up connect-ed to such a cowardly alpha? *This* was the man who was supposed to take care of him and their offspring for the rest of their lives? What good was a romantic if he was also a wimp?

But Ned wasn't insulted. He nodded and shot an apologetic and shame-filled glance at Ezer before saying, "I should have cut them out. I should have done more to protect you. I'm sorry."

"They were going to rape me."

Ned's face twisted with rage, but he shook his head. "No. I was going to kick Braden in the face. I was going to—"

"You were going to do *nothing*. If my da hadn't showed up with a gun..." Ezer lifted a brow. He wondered if they'd be arguing about this forever, even when they were old with grown sons. Probably.

"I wouldn't have let them hurt you. Like I told you at the heat house, I've loved you since I first saw you. I was just trying to figure out how—"

"How to what? How to say, 'Let's not fucking rape Ezer because I'm in love with him, and you all suck, and I hope you die in a firebomb?' How to say that?"

"Yeah. Pretty much." Ned sounded like he was holding back a laugh, but the topic was so far from funny that Ezer wanted to spit in his face. He could still feel the panic surging through him that day, the bruising hands on his body, the weight of Ned's foot resting on his chest for a brief moment.

Had Ned really been about to kick Braden? Or was that a pretty story to tell his pregnant, horny, desperate-to-believe omega so they could get on with fucking and making babies and building a life together without any hard feelings over times past?

God this situation was so absurd. So messed up.

Ezer gazed out of the window at the waves crashing white onto the brown cliffs. How had he ended up here, naked, and already feeling like he needed another dose of what Ned had to offer, when just three weeks ago he'd been dying from angst over his Literature oral exam?

Literature. Biology. Physics.

All classes he'd never attend again.

*Why* had he attended them anyway? Omegas never went on to have careers. Not when they were from wealthy families. The only omegas who got to have careers were those who are poor enough to be allowed to auction off their heats, rather than have them arranged privately. They got to live however they damn well chose. That was why Ezer had wanted that path for himself.

That was why…

It didn't matter now. He had a new path ahead. He needed to find a way to follow it without wanting it to end on that cliff with a long jump to the rocks below. He turned his gaze from the view out of the window and back to Ned's annoyingly handsome face.

Ned was still talking. "Just before this—" He gestured between them. "Like, just a few days before, I'd had a meal with my uncle."

"Heath Clearwater," Ezer clarified.

"Yes. He told me he'd support me in cutting Braden and Finch out of my life. He said he'd make sure it wasn't a financial hardship for me to do that. So it's all right, you see?"

Ezer blinked. "Are you saying that you'd still be friends with them if Heath wanted you to be?"

"Well, there's no need to even think about that because he doesn't want me to be. And with the money from your father…"

Ezer snorted. "With the money from my father, you don't need to suck up to those shits anymore. I get it. So my body and my father's money have paid for your peace of mind. You get the rewards while I pay the price."

"No, I just mean—"

"You just mean that you'd still suck those assholes' dicks if you thought you had to for the money. To live like this," Ezer said, waving around at the nest, the view, and the part of the city they were in. "You'd sacrifice your pride, the omega you claim to care about, the—"

"Stop," Ned said. "Please stop interpreting everything I say in the worst light possible."

"How else should I interpret it?"

"I'm saying that you're safe now!" he exclaimed. "That you're with me, and I'm done with them, and we have money, and a nice home, and the support of a man like Heath Clearwater. That's what I'm saying and that's how you should interpret it."

"Ah." Ezer hated that his cock was getting hard as Ned's cheeks flushed with passion while he was defending himself. He hated that his hole was leaking slick, that his nipples were tightening. He hated that he knew what came next.

"'Ah' what?" Ned challenged.

"I just mean that *you're* safe, so you think I'm safe."

"You *are* safe. It was me or Finch. They were going to offer you to Finch!" Ned yelled, standing up, his face going redder. "Fucking Finch!"

Ezer swallowed hard. "Is that true?"

Ned pulled his phone out of his robe pocket and pushed it into Ezer's hand. "Read for yourself."

Ezer stared at the screen. The letters swam. He had no idea what it said.

"Fucking Finch," Ned said again, raking a hand through his hair. "So yeah. You're safe compared to that. I know you don't love me, or maybe even like me yet, but…I'm not fucking Finch."

Ezer looked back at the screen for a few seconds willing his brain to unscramble the letters. Nothing. He handed the phone back to Ned.

"Are you satisfied?" Ned said, still flushed, but calming a little. He put his phone back into his pocket and sat down again. "You see that I did the right thing, don't you?"

Ezer cleared his throat. "I see that we both had our reasons for this arrangement. Whether either of us was 'right' or 'wrong' to contract for this"—he put his hand over his stomach—"doesn't matter anymore, does it?"

"So you forgive me?"

Ezer shrugged. "No."

"Why not?" Ned sounded desperate.

"Because you let people treat me horribly, you *were* a bully, and even this situation is fucked up. There's nothing beautiful or right or romantic about it, is there?"

"Fucking you is beautiful and right," Ned said adamantly. "You have to agree with me on that. You love it."

Ezer's stomach flipped, and his cock filled. He *did* love it. And he hated it. And he needed it. And he *wanted* it. And he loathed it. Like everything else about this situation, there was nothing pure or perfect in what they did with their bodies. It was, none of it, his idea.

He'd done what he'd had to do, sure, but he wasn't arrogant enough to claim what he'd done was right.

Unlike Ned.

Privileged, spoiled, bully Ned.

Ned's chest heaved with uncontrolled breaths, and Ezer saw that Ned's cock was hard, too, poking through the opening in the robe. Ezer crawled across the sofa to him and fell to sucking Ned's cock hungrily.

Ned gasped, arching up.

The taste of Ned's pre-cum exploded over Ezer's tongue, the most delicious thing he'd ever tasted, better than the meal he'd had, better than anything, and he worked the engorged flesh with his hands and mouth to get more.

"We're supposed to talk," Ned panted, but his hands were buried in Ezer's curls, and he didn't tug Ezer up and off. If anything, he held him down, making him take his cock deeper into his throat. "We're not supposed to be doing this. We're supposed to *understand* each other first."

Ezer didn't stop sucking to tell him he understood Ned perfectly. He just didn't forgive him. Forgiveness wasn't necessary for them to move ahead with this baby, this life of theirs. It was better if Ezer didn't forgive Ned, didn't forget who he'd been. Because people never changed, and Ned would be back to his cowardly behaviors before long. It would always fall on Ezer to be brave.

It was good to remember that.

Ezer gulped down Ned's seed, squirming in resentment as he

felt the first hints of calmness returning to his system.

Falling onto his back and licking his lips to get every bit of Ned's cum, he twined his hands in Ned's hair and brought him down to suck Ezer's dick in reciprocation. Humping up into Ned's hot, silky mouth, straining for release, Ezer vowed to never forget.

Never forgive.

NED WOKE IN the night.

The room was pitch-black. The darkness was pricked with even more blackness, that was how endless it felt. But the room was warm and smelled of sex and Ezer. He nestled against Ezer's back, the big spoon, having fallen asleep immediately after fucking Ezer into a state of exhaustion deep enough that he'd passed out as soon as Ned had finished coming.

Ned nuzzled the back of Ezer's hair, and scented him, a wash of contentment coming over him that he wished would last. He knew far too well it wouldn't.

Ezer's father had been right. Ezer was difficult and stubborn and terrifying. Ned understood better now how George Fersee would not have liked being confronted by his brutally honest omega son.

Ned had wanted Ezer just the way he was, *of course* he had, but he hadn't realized how much energy it took to manage an omega like Ezer. It was draining to argue with someone smarter than himself, someone angrier by far, and someone who was determined to hate him. He almost wished he could pull the I'm-the-alpha-and-I-say-so card, but Ezer would never put up with that, and Ned didn't have it in him to use a firm hand on Ezer. He was no brute, no matter what Ezer believed.

Ned wallowed these thoughts around in his head, only to go still, understanding what had woken him as the sensation started again. Ezer was pushing back to him, his slick-wet and open asshole riding the tip of Ned's cock. Was Ezer awake? Did he know what he was doing? Or was his body seeking Ned's in his sleep, knowing better than Ezer's rebellious mind what he really needed?

"Ezer?" he whispered.

Ezer moaned and tilted his hips so the tip of Ned's cock nearly pushed inside.

"Do you want this?" Ned asked. "I know you need it, but do you want it?"

Ezer whimpered and shoved his hips back. Ned reached down and held his cock steady, letting Ezer work himself onto it. The tight, hot, wet sensation on the head of his cock as he thrust in took his breath away. He loved the first press into Ezer. It was one of the most beautiful parts of fucking. The joining of their bodies. The two becoming one.

Now though, he did nothing. He simply let Ezer's hot ass consume his aching cock, and then held still as Ezer seemed to fall back to sleep, impaled on his hardness. For some time, Ezer's body went limp and loose, his breathing evening out, and aside from the thump of his pulse around Ned's dick, there was no movement or attempt to escalate the situation.

Ned held himself in place, nipples tingling, balls aching. He desperately wanted to thrust in and out, fuck Ezer until he cried out again. He burned to do all the things he knew Ezer liked, and a few he wasn't sure Ezer liked at all, but which always elicited gorgeous sounds and a powerful orgasm from his omega.

But Ned restrained himself.

Time passed slowly—his cock in Ezer's body, hard and yearning—until he, too, fell into a restless, horny sleep. Short moments or long minutes later, he didn't know in his half-conscious state, he woke to Ezer grinding back on him, whimpering, and clawing at the sheets.

In his snatch of sleep, Ned had dreamed of fucking Ezer over a table in the middle of their school cafeteria while Finch and Braden had cheered him on. It'd been upsetting, but at the same time, hot, and he'd been just about to come in his dream when he'd woken.

Ezer moved eagerly, working himself on Ned's dick. Ned groaned, the hot, slick heat on his cock making him tremble. He threw his arm around Ezer, breathing in the scent of his sweat, and Ezer tensed, grunted, and then, with a high-pitched cry, convulsed hard in Ned's arms. The scent of Ezer's cum filled the dark room.

"Oh, fuck," Ned gritted out, his own balls drawn up tight, and on the verge himself. Ezer panted and moaned, still trembling as the scent of cum grew stronger in the air. Ned wasn't going to hold back now. He rolled Ezer onto his stomach, wrapped his arms around him, and buried his face in Ezer's sweaty hair. He moaned, fucking into him with sharp, fast thrusts, and as the pleasure crested unbearably, he bit Ezer's shoulder, making him cry out. Ned shot his load deep, his body pulsing with pleasure and mind-numbing, spangled bliss. As it passed, he released the bite and licked Ezer's skin, feeling the imprint of his teeth.

"Fuck," he whispered. "Sorry."

But Ezer reached back, tugged Ned's ass to draw him in deeper, and quivered beneath him with a wild whimper. He'd liked it.

Ned's cock pumped again, sending another burst of cum into Ezer's body. Ned sucked on the bite mark on Ezer's shoulder until his heart rate slowed. Then he rolled off Ezer's back and pulled out.

Ezer panted in the darkness, shifting so that they weren't touching. "Don't fuck me in my sleep," he said, after the long silence between them—filled only with the sounds of their labored breathing—grew almost painful.

"I woke up and *you* were fucking *me*," Ned defended. It was mostly true. He'd just held his dick in place to help Ezer get onto it. He hadn't moved at all until the end when he'd taken Ezer's ass hard.

"Mm," Ezer said. He didn't sound like he thought Ned was lying, but he didn't sound like he believed him either.

"You pushed your ass onto my dick," Ned went on. "I thought you wanted it."

Ezer sighed and rolled closer. Ned wished he could see his eyes in the darkness. Even when they stared at him in hatred or rage, Ned still loved Ezer's gorgeous eyes.

"I can't hate you when you've filled me with your cum," Ezer murmured. "I *want* to hate you, but every time it gets harder. Did you know that my body assimilates your cum into a kind of physiological drug? It makes a person feel like they're in love to promote bonding."

"You feel like you're in love with me?" Ned asked, and he was ashamed of his eagerness and obvious hope.

"No. But right now I don't hate you, and, worse, I feel like one day soon I'll even like you."

"You think that's just from the cum?"

"Yeah." Ezer scooted closer and rested his head on Ned's shoulder, trailing his fingers up and down Ned's abdomen and chest, feeling him all over. "And in the dark, it's easier, too. I can't see you, so I can just give in. Drift here with you and all your fleshy goodness."

"'Fleshy goodness'?" He *did* sound a little high.

"Mm," Ezer muttered. "I'm the omega my father wanted me to be now," he said drowsily. "Pregnant, well-fucked, sated but sure to be horny again soon. I'm distracted, and out of his hair."

"I'm glad," Ned said.

"You would be."

"I just mean that I'm glad you're not around him anymore. He didn't appreciate you or love you the way you deserve. He didn't see how precious you are."

Ezer laughed. The sound was more wonderful than windchimes on a sunny day. "Ah, I see. God, you really are a goner for me. That's absurd, but true I guess."

"I was a goner the first time I saw your eyes. They're so beautiful."

"Are we supposed to have this much sex?" Ezer asked, ignoring the compliment. "Should I *be* this horny? Why can't I get satisfied?"

Ned felt Ezer's cock push against his hip again. He wasn't sure how much was too much. He just knew that he'd been told pregnant omegas needed it a hell of a lot, and Ezer was living up to that expectation and then some.

*It's a good thing I'm young,* Ned thought. His downtime was shorter than an older man's.

"Climb on top of me," Ned said, directing Ezer into position. He smiled into the darkness, as Ezer's hot hole engulfed his cock again. "That's it. You're doing great. It's going to be okay, Ezer. It's all going to be okay."

That seemed to be what Ezer needed to hear, because he fell to Ned's chest, kissing his collarbones and pecs, letting Ned fuck into him slowly. They made it last, and when Ned did come again, his balls ached from the strength of his orgasm.

Ezer moaned and fell asleep on top of him, full of Ned's cum with his hard little stomach pressing against Ned's flat one.

He'd grown rounder already.

Amazing.

# Chapter Twenty-Three

THE NEXT DAY Ezer woke with a sense of calm that had been missing from his entire life. He knew what it was. He was supposed to be fighting this exact thing. But it was pointless because he was going to keep fucking Ned, and each fuck would lead to an even heavier blanket of calm until he faced the agony of delivery.

If he rejected the sex, he'd suffer, the baby would suffer, and one or both of them might die. It was the way omegas were made and there was nothing to be done about that. Even more confirmation God was a sadistic alpha.

He rested his hand on his stomach, feeling the hardness starting where the baby grew inside. He stroked the skin and wondered who was in there. Someone smart and funny? Someone brutal and arrogant? Someone sweet and quiet? Beta, omega, alpha? Time would tell.

Fuck, he still couldn't believe he'd made a child with Ned Clearwater.

Or that he was riding Ned Clearwater's cock willingly.

He also couldn't believe he hadn't heard from anyone in his family. Not a single one of his brothers, not his da, not his father, and not even Pete. He was truly alone here.

He couldn't believe this was his life.

"Do you want to get in the pool?" Ned asked as he watched Ezer clear his plate of a third helping of breakfast. He seemed pleased by the number of eggs Ezer had put away, and the multiple slices of bread and jam. "I think you'll like it. My father has left, so we can swim without him being around."

"Oh, yeah, sure," Ezer said, licking the plate to get the last drop of jam. His stomach gurgled, and he reached for another strip of bacon. "That sounds nice."

"The pool should help you feel more comfortable as you get bigger," Ned said.

"Mm," Ezer replied, stuffing his face with another spoonful of yogurt. Finally, *finally* he felt full, and he sat back with a heavy sigh. He was eating more every day than he had in a week before. Still, he didn't seem to gain weight, just girth around his waist. "Thank you. Breakfast was good."

Ned smiled. "It was all Earl's doing. He cooked it and brought it all down. I just kept it warm for you."

"Oh." Ezer still wasn't sure how he felt about Earl.

He'd grown up with plenty of beta servants around, but he hadn't ever had one assigned to him the way Ned had while growing up, and he wasn't accustomed to having an old man around who tried to predict his every whim and need. It was invasive and unnerving, but he knew it was only Earl's duty.

"I'll get a swimsuit—"

"If I'm going up there naked, so are you," Ezer said firmly.

Ned looked like he might argue for a moment, but then he shrugged. "All right. There's nothing Earl hasn't seen before on either of us."

"Exactly."

As soon as Ned had washed and put away their dishes, they left the nest, heading upstairs into the main house and then out to the pool.

Ezer wasn't that impressed with Lidell Clearwater's home. After all, he'd grown up as George Fersee's son, so he was accustomed to luxury. But it wasn't a step down for him either. The stylistic choices of the house were different from his father's taste, which tended toward the heavy, dark, and wooden. Meanwhile, Lidell's home was modern, sleek, and open-air everything. It was three stories, including the basement nest area, and all of it was white on beige, and shiny where possible. Ezer didn't hate it. It was somehow soothing in its blankness, if stark.

The living room hosted a fluffy white sofa and a glass table, along with matching chairs and a few overflowing bookcases. Ezer had no idea what was in any of the books, of course. The letters on the spines moved around unhelpfully, so he supposed he'd never know. But his da always said educated families were better than wealthy families when it came to marriage, so Ezer hoped he was right.

Not that he and Ned were married just because of the contract they'd signed. No, he owed Ned his body and his children for life, but he hadn't committed his heart, and that was what marriage was about, wasn't it?

He was *never* going to commit to that.

The living room opened onto the pool deck, and for the first time since he'd arrived, Ezer felt like he could breathe. He stepped into the sunshine, naked as he'd ever been, and lifted his arms. He heard Ned's surprised hitch of breath before he realized that a huge smile had broken over his own face. The first one, he suspected, Ned had ever seen.

"Not a smirk, not a bitter lip grimace," Ned muttered. "A smile. A real smile. This is what it took? I'd have brought you up here the moment we arrived if I'd known that."

Ezer ignored him, turning to face the sun, breathing deeply. When he opened his eyes again, he took in the sparkle of the blue water against the white-and-beige-tiled interior of the pool, and the brown-painted concrete pool deck. The rails of the deck were a tan wood, and he could see the cliffs and the sea beyond them.

It wasn't a boiling hot day, but it wasn't cold either. It was like being given a delicious piece of cake after being denied a dessert for far too long. Ezer was, in this moment, satisfied and settled like he hadn't been in weeks. Since way before all this had begun with Ned. Probably since his da had been forced out of the house.

"Fucking semen and sunshine," he muttered to himself. He knew what it was, that it was what everyone wanted of him, but it didn't make the peace humming through his veins feel less true.

"There you are!" Earl's voice rang out.

Ezer jumped into the pool in a fit of shame, embarrassment, and modesty. He cried out as the cold water engulfed him, and then swam to keep his head above water, finding the pool was deeper than he'd expected.

"Oh!" Earl exclaimed, seeing that Ned wasn't alone. "I'm sorry. I thought it was just you out here, darling," he said, holding out a robe to Ned, as if his ward had come out here naked in a fit of forgetfulness.

Ned waved the robe off. "If Ezer's naked out here, then so am I," he said, with a huff of a laugh.

"Oh, is that the case?" Earl smiled. "If you prefer not to be naked, sir," he said to Ezer. "I can ask my Simon where he got the robe that Heath's Adrien preferred to wear during his first pregnancy. He was very modest back then."

Ezer gave a tight, close-lipped smile, not sure what answer to give. He didn't think he'd mind being naked in front of Earl eventually. He'd never seen omegas who preferred to be in a robe. His da and Pete both preferred to be naked. Pete, when he wore the robe, always said it felt too confining and scratchy, though the time Ezer had touched it out of curiosity, he'd thought it'd been as soft as clouds.

"That's not his real smile," Ned informed Earl. "That's a fake one. I saw the real one earlier. It was beautiful."

Ezer rolled his eyes.

Earl laughed. "Alphas always go weak for their omegas," he said.

Ezer thought Ned was plenty weak before they'd come together.

"So should I ask Heath?"

"We don't want to bother him right now," Ned said, with a small frown. "Not while he's dealing with…" he trailed off as if he didn't want to mention Heath's troubles in front of Ezer. Probably because he was pregnant, and it was considered very bad luck to say anything at all about omegas dying in childbirth, or babies not making it, or anything negative at all in front of a pregnant omega.

"Oh, so you haven't heard? Simon called this morning! Heath's son will live!" Earl's smile was big and genuine. He was pleased by this infant's survival, and, in principle, so was Ezer.

It was objectively good news. He continued to swim in place, keeping his body beneath the blue water.

"They're going to call him Laya."

"A beta called Laya," Ned said, softly. "That's a good outcome."

"Yes, better than they thought."

Ned bit into his lower lip and his gaze shifted from where Ezer was still swimming, over to the cliffs and the ocean. He frowned.

"What's wrong?" Earl asked.

"Nothing," Ned was quick to say, but Ezer could see that Earl didn't believe him, and, frankly, Ezer didn't believe him either.

Earl's gaze shifted away from Ned down to Ezer, and he said, "Oh, of course. Yes, well, we'll have to see what happens won't we? I'm sure Heath will understand and, if not, then we'll blame your father. It's the right thing to do."

Ned shook his head. "No, I'll take the blame. It was my choice."

Earl didn't argue. "Well, it's time to start lunch. I'll go see what we have. Would you like more of those sweet potatoes, sir?" he asked Ezer. "I noticed you enjoyed them last night."

"Yes, please," Ezer said, surprised that he could even think about eating again after his big breakfast.

"Then you'll have them."

Earl left the pool deck and entered through the open wall to the living room, disappearing into the depths of the house, where the kitchen must be. Ezer supposed he'd know this house inside and out like it was his own one day. Because it would be his home until Ned decided they'd move elsewhere.

But this was his home now.

Weird.

So very weird.

Ned jumped into the water, too, once Earl was gone, and a cry of shock flew from his mouth as well. He bounced off the bottom, and came up shaking his head like a dog, spraying water everywhere, including in Ezer's face.

Ezer wiped at his eyes, and nearly choked.

"Hey now," Ned said. "C'mon, this way." He tugged at Ezer's elbow until they bobbed across the pool where it grew shallower, and he could put his feet on the bottom. "There. See? Better, yeah?"

Ezer didn't bother agreeing. The answer was obvious. He ducked into the water, though, up to his shoulders, crouching so that he was covered. He noticed the sun illuminating something red on his shoulder, and he glanced at it, surprised to see a bite mark. Then he remembered the night before. The way Ned had fucked him into the mattress and then bitten him.

It'd been…

Hot.

He'd loved it.

And he'd been mad about loving it.

He sighed. That seemed to be the story of his life now.

"So your uncle, the one that you were so proud to tell me had given you permission to cut Finch and Braden out of your life?"

"Mm." Ned flinched. "What about him?"

"He doesn't know about me, does he?"

"No." Ned paled, all the more evident by the sun illuminating his freckles.

"What's he going to think when he finds out?"

"That it was a terrible idea."

"And is he going to cut you off again?"

"With the money from your father…" Ned trailed off, looking embarrassed.

"Tell me."

"It won't be a problem either way. My father wanted this because it'd make us independent from Heath once and for all."

"The money George is giving you to keep me pregnant and fucked silly frees you from being obligated to your uncle. I see. Another win for you in this arrangement."

"I did it to keep Finch from—"

"Right. To keep Finch from having me."

Ned clenched his jaw. "Would you have liked that? Would you have wanted him to do to you the things that I do?"

Ezer snarled. "I don't know. I didn't want *you* doing them either, and yet I seem to like it just fine."

"He wouldn't be like me. He'd hurt you. He'd…" Ned wiped a hand over his face. "Why do you do this? You twist everything up. You make it sound ugly just so you can fight with me."

"I make it sound ugly because it's ugly," Ezer said. "This isn't some grand romance. I signed the contract for ugly reasons. You signed the contract for mostly ugly reasons, and a mistaken idea of one noble one—"

"'Mistaken'? You wanted Finch's body on yours? You wanted to be stuffed with Finch's baby?"

"I didn't want to be stuffed with yours either!" Ezer yelled, standing up, and shoving Ned back against the edge of the pool. He saw Ned's erection just as he felt his own. What was *wrong* with them? Why did fighting always make them hard? More evidence that this wasn't love and would never be. "But I am now, so I make the best of it! And I'm sure I'd have made the best of it with Finch, too."

"No! Because he wouldn't have liked any of this—" he waved at Ezer. "This backtalk and arguing. He'd have dealt with it."

"Then maybe you should deal with it," Ezer shouted. "Go on. Deal with it. Deal with me."

"What if I did deal with you?" Ned loomed over Ezer now, his eyes furious, snarling lightly. "Is that what you want?"

"Yeah," Ezer said, breathless, and shaking. His cock was hard now, his nipples aching, and his heart pounding. He didn't know what he was saying, or what it meant to be dealt with, but he suspected it was going to feel really fucking good. Or horrible. Or both. "Deal with me. I dare you."

Ned claimed his mouth. The kiss wasn't passionate so much as enraged, and Ezer gave as good as he got. He tasted blood and wasn't sure if it was his own or Ned's, and he didn't care. He was hauled to the edge of the pool, the concrete scraping his back and ass, as Ned sucked biting kisses down the front of him, skipping over his nipples and heading straight for his cock.

"Oh fuck," Ezer gasped, as hot, wet suction took him in deep, and he threw his head back, bucking up fitfully. "That's…it. Deal with me."

Ned was good at giving head, Ezer realized, and he also realized he wanted more of it, whenever he wanted it. "You'll suck me any time I want," Ezer said, sharply. "You'll suck me until I come."

Ned groaned around Ezer's cock, and then pulled off with a wet slurp. He stood in the pool glaring at Ezer with red, puffy lips, and a brutally hard cock, but he steeled himself and backed away, hands raised.

"Get it from Finch if you think he'd be so good at it."

Ezer let out a bark of a laugh. "'Good at it'? He'd be a nightmare. But so are you. In a different way."

"A better way," Ned insisted.

Ezer's cock thudded. He wanted to get fucked so much. He wanted to slurp on Ned's dick until it spurted in his mouth. He wanted to calm down and ride out the little bit of peace Ned's semen provided. "Fine. A better way."

"So I did the right thing," Ned insisted.

Ezer didn't think either of them had done the right thing, or that a right thing even existed in their world, not with their complications, but he stared at Ned's stubborn jawline and then nodded. "Fine. You did the right thing."

Ned caved then, grabbing Ezer by the waist, hauling him into the pool with him. They kissed wildly—sucking and biting lips, necks, nipples, and frotting against each other until orgasm was so close they were both desperate for it.

"Fuck," Ned groaned, heaving himself out of the water, and then reaching to pull Ezer out, too.

He directed him to a heavy wooden poolside chaise and bent Ezer over it, positioned so he was holding onto the back for steadiness. As Ezer panted and begged for Ned's cock, Ned fingered him open.

"Please," Ezer crooned, shocked by his own desperation. "Please fuck me."

"Tell me I did the right thing."

"You did the right thing," Ezer said. He'd have told him the sky was red and the earth was pink if it got his cock into his ass immediately. "You did the right thing. You saved me."

Ned groaned and pushed his cock against Ezer's wet hole. It was loose from the fingering, the semen deposits, and his own pregnancy hormones. They still hadn't had him tested, but it was clear. They could feel it between them in the changes to Ezer's body, and the way he behaved. There was no doubt.

"Fuck," Ned said, sinking in balls-deep in one fluid motion. "You feel so good on me."

Ezer didn't want compliments, though. He wanted to get screwed again, so he wriggled his ass, and then crowed in pleasure as Ned railed him. It ended too fast and when the orgasms hit, they were less intense than they'd been earlier in the day.

"We need to take a break," Ned said, when they were done, and they lay in one chaise lounge with Ezer's back pressed to the wooden arm, and his head on Ned's chest. "We need to stop fucking long enough to get past the refractory period for good."

Ezer nodded drowsily. He felt satisfied again, though he didn't know how long it would last. He loved the way Ned smelled, and he rubbed his face near Ned's armpit trying to get as much of his odor as possible. He felt good. This was how he was meant to feel as a pregnant omega.

Maybe if they didn't talk about anything important, they could stay in this state of calm for a longer time. It didn't seem to do them any good to communicate; they just fought. And when they fought, they fucked. So they should cut straight to the fucking and be done with it.

Ned stroked Ezer's back, and the sun beat down on them,

making them warm and sweaty together.

*I won't fight him anymore,* was Ezer's last thought as he drifted off to sleep. *I'll let him think he's won me over.*

That resolution lasted until the moment he woke.

# Chapter Twenty-Four

NED CAME AROUND to a sensation he was being watched. He didn't want to disturb Ezer, who needed his rest to grow the baby healthily, but the sensation didn't go away and his alpha urge to protect his omega was stronger than his urge not to disturb him.

Ezer was sound asleep, though, and when Ned rolled out from under him, and eased him back down onto the chaise, Ezer snuffled and turned his face the other direction.

Ned spotted a robe on the other chaise and realized that Earl must have returned and found them asleep, left the robe for Ned in case he changed his mind, and then left again. Still, Ned felt eyes on him. He scanned the house and the windows and found nothing. It wasn't until he turned his gaze toward the gated path leading up from the garden that he recognized the intruder. His heart started to pound.

After checking that Ezer was asleep, he began toward the gate. He'd just reached it when it swung open, and Braden poked his head through, giving Ned a smarmy smirk. "What's up, little Nedkins? We've missed you at school."

Ned pushed him back through the gate and into the front garden. He glanced around for Finch but didn't see him. "What are you doing here?"

"You've been absent. No explanation. No replies to texts. I got curious." He smirked again. "Was that a piece of ass I saw you with by the pool?"

"You need to go, Braden."

A dark look passed over Braden's face. "You think you can tell me what to do?"

"I think this is my property and you can get the hell off it."

"What the fuck? I was worried about you, and you're acting like we aren't even friends."

Ned took a deep breath. This was his moment. "We aren't."

"Excuse me?"

"I said we aren't friends, Braden. Tell Finch the same. And both of you leave me the fuck alone, all right? I don't want to talk to you here or at school or anywhere else."

Braden took a step forward, but when Ned went into a fighting stance—left leg back, fists up—Braden backed off with his hands raised. At least the idiot was smart enough to know he couldn't take Ned in a fight. "Whoa, whoa. This isn't any way to handle a problem between friends. Just tell me what I did, how much cash it'll take to fix it, and we're cool again. No worries."

"There's no amount of money that can fix someone as damaged as you," Ned said.

"No?" Braden cocked a brow. "What if I decide I need talk to my dad about this conversation?"

"Go ahead."

"And if he doesn't want to do business with the father of a shitty alpha bully who doesn't know his place?"

"'Bully'? I'm bullying you?"

"Sure sounds like it."

Ned blew out a raspberry. "Fine. Then your father'll be left with a reputation for breaking contracts for petty reasons, and my father and I will be just fine."

"Just fine? You need those—"

"Needed. Past tense. We don't need them anymore."

Braden's shoulders snapped back, and his gaze darted toward the gate again. "Ah, I see. You've got a rich omega in there, someone who's promised you a lot of money in exchange for something. What's he want?" Braden frowned. "I legit can't think of anything a wealthy omega would want from *you*? But it must be something good."

"Go, Braden," Ned said. "I've put up with you for too long. Get the hell away from here."

Braden's head tilted. "You know who else has gone missing from school?" His smirk turned crueler. "Finch and I thought maybe he'd died in that explosion, or gone back to that school for stupid kids, but now… Now I have another idea."

The casual way Braden referenced the explosion that'd taken people's lives, and very well could have taken Ezer's, made Ned see red. He reared back with his fists clenched and said, "Get the fuck out of my yard or I'll knock you out of it."

"Come on out, Cocksleeve!" Braden called, stepping sidewise and lifting his chin so his voice would carry. "Come out and give my dick a big, wet kiss!"

Ned grabbed Braden by the collar and shook him. Ned's robe was loose and started to fall open, which made him feel vulnerable and no doubt look ridiculous, but Braden still had the sense to be intimidated by Ned's size and strength. Ned could see the fear in Braden's eyes, despite the smarmy twist to his mouth.

Braden jerked free and backed away. "Fine, fine, I'll leave. But fucking a sloppy cocksleeve bastard of George Fersee's isn't going to get you what you think it will. Notice I used the word bastard, right?" He shook himself free of Ned's hold. "Yeah, bet you didn't know that, huh? He's not Fersee's kid. So, whatever that cocksleeve has promised you for your, what? Protection? From me and Finch? He can't deliver."

Ned's mind reeled. If what Braden was saying about Ezer was

true, then it explained so much. It explained why Fersee wanted Ezer out of his house, why he'd treated Amos so badly, why he'd paid Ned and his father to get Ezer off his hands and out of his life…why he didn't seem to give a damn about what happened to Ezer now. Fersee hadn't even checked in on Ezer once during the heat or since they'd been back in Wellport. At least, not as far as Ned knew.

"Ah, see? I'm smarter than you think I am. I figured you out."

"You haven't figured anything out," Ned said with a snarl. Though, of course Braden had. He'd dug up a body all right. Just not the body he thought he'd exposed. "Get out of here before I bust your face in and your daddy has to pay for more plastic surgery to fix it."

"Fuck you, Ned. I'm telling you, whatever he's promised you? He can't give you. And here you are spitting in the face of the guy who's been your biggest champion."

Ned shoved Braden back. "Go. Get the fuck away from here. Never come back."

Braden flipped him off. "My father *will* hear about this. There *will* be consequences."

Ned spat after him. He would have spat in Braden's face if he could have, but by that time Braden was too far away. He watched as Braden climbed the back fence and left down the driveway. No doubt he had a driver waiting on him.

Why had Braden snuck into the garden? Why hadn't he come up the drive to ring the front bell like a normal person? Why had he been spying on Ned and Ezer? And how long had he been there? What had he seen?

Ned would ask Earl later what he knew about it. All he knew now was that he had a headache, a sick stomach, and his jaw hurt from clenching his teeth. He also knew now that Ezer was an outcast from his own family just as he'd claimed, and thanks to

Braden's nasty jibes, now he knew why. He wished Ezer had been the one to tell him the whole of it.

But Ezer didn't trust him. That much was clear. Of course he hadn't said anything. He was protecting himself from a perceived threat. But how were they supposed to continue on together? How were they supposed to raise a child…?

They needed to talk, and they needed to not fight, and not fuck.

Ned had to find a way to make that happen because their future happiness depended on it.

EZER WOKE ALONE with the sun dazzling his eyes. His skin felt tender all over, as if he might be getting a sunburn, so he rose to stretch and find a place in the shade. If he was also looking for Ned, he didn't want to admit that to himself.

But of course he *was* seeking Ned already. He wanted to know where his alpha had gone to, leaving him alone and vulnerable. Ezer assumed Ned was getting food for them, or helping Earl with something, or maybe had been called away to take a phone call from a friend, or his father, or maybe that uncle—Heath—who was going to give him a harsh talking to for impregnating an omega at his age.

But, as Ezer stretched in the sun, he heard the voices.

Too familiar. Too sickening.

His stomach turned over, and for a moment he thought he'd vomit for real.

"Cocksleeve, come out and give my dick a big, wet kiss!"

Braden's voice slashed through the air, and then Ned's came after—lower-pitched and unclear. Ezer's heart pounded. He wanted to run, but he didn't know where to go. Back to the nest?

They'd corner him there.

Down the driveway? Where would he go? He was naked.

Fuck.

He'd started to believe in Ned, started to trust him—

"Sir," Earl's voice came from behind and startled him.

Ezer nearly burst into tears, but instead he grabbed his chest, gasping for breath, feeling dizzier by the moment. Earl's expression turned frightened, and he took hold of Ezer's arm and guided him in through the living room and onto the fluffy sofa.

"There, now, what's happening? Are you all right? Are you an asthmatic, sir? Do you have an inhaler?" He seemed on the verge of panic himself.

Ezer couldn't get enough breath to reply. He simply clutched his chest, shaking his head, and tried to inhale.

"Ezer!" Ned called out.

If Ezer didn't know better he'd think Ned sounded worried, but he knew better now. Ned had been talking with Braden, they'd called him Cocksleeve, and they'd been planning...planning to...

Ezer's head spun, and he collapsed back on the sofa, breathing too fast and shallow, his pulse racing.

"Sir! He's in here! I don't know what's wrong! Sir, does he have an inhaler? Should I call an ambulance?"

Ned rushed to Ezer's side, falling to his knees next to him, but Ezer tried to pull away from Ned's seeking hands. His breathing was too fast and shallow to get many words together, but he managed to pant out, "Stay. Back."

"What's wrong?" Ned asked. Then his expression darkened, and his eyes lit with rage. "Was it Finch? Did he get into the pool area?" He turned, looking all around, a snarl on his lips. "Did he touch you?"

Ezer closed his eyes, pulling in gulps of hot air, terror grabbing hold. Finch had been here, too? The three of them...

He nearly passed out.

"Here, sir," Earl said through the haze of panic. "It's an old-fashioned treatment, but I don't know what else to do."

Ned tried to help Ezer sit up, but Ezer fought him off, not wanting his hands on his skin. "Please, baby, please. Just breathe in this bag. Just breathe."

Ezer grabbed the paper bag from Ned's hand and put it over his mouth. He remembered now seeing in old movies and television shows that somehow this helped. As he shallowly puffed in and out, he started to feel like he was able to take a solid breath again.

"There," Ned said, stroking Ezer's hair, his face scrunched with worry. "What happened? Talk to me. Was it Finch? I'll kill him if he touched you. If he even thought about touching you."

Ned's voice was so savage that Ezer thought he might stand up, go find Finch—wherever he was—and do that. Which was weird since Ned had been planning with Braden to...to...

Or had he?

Ezer didn't know what Ned had said to Braden. He had no idea what had happened, really. He'd assumed, and terror had grabbed him around the throat like a familiar, horrible, strangling sweater.

"Braden," Ezer said, pulling the bag away from his mouth to speak. "You were talking to Braden."

Ned's eyes burned with rage again. "I was gonna punch him out, but, yeah, I guess I talked to him. Is that it? You heard us talking? He scared you?" The way Ned's voice was so deep and his eyes so bright with fury, Ezer could imagine he would either take Ezer apart for being frightened, or Braden apart for scaring his omega. Experience told him one thing, and logic and learning another.

"He called for me." Ezer's voice sounded puny next to Ned's terrible anger.

Ned's lips creased in a vicious snarl. "Your name is Ezer. He didn't call for you."

"He yelled out for—"

"Cocksleeve, I know," Ned said darkly, but his hand had crept onto Ezer's thigh, and he stroked his skin. "But that's not your name. Remember? You told him so yourself."

Ezer nodded, his hand drifted to his bare stomach, caressing the hardening swell that was just beginning, but seemed to be more and more visible by the hour. "I remember."

Ned's hand slid from Ezer's thigh, joining him in pressing the swelling of his stomach. "Braden came here because I haven't been in school. Confidentiality prevents the school from telling anyone why I'm not there. I'll get to make up my class work later, but…" Ned leaned in and kissed Ezer's knee, then lifted up off his haunches, to kiss Ezer's stomach. It tickled and Ezer fought the urge to comb his hand through Ned's messy hair. "But Braden got curious, and he came here—"

"I didn't let him in, sir. He rang the bell, but I sent him away," Earl offered. "I didn't think you or Ezer would want to see him."

Ned didn't glance at his servant, instead keeping his gaze on Ezer's stomach, which he bent to kiss again before saying, "I didn't. We didn't. Right, Ezer?"

Ezer nodded.

"He didn't leave, though, he sneaked up the garden path and spied in from the gate. When I caught him, he said some ugly crap. I threatened to punch him. He threatened my dad's contracts, and I told him none of that mattered to me and to get off my property. Then he guessed the truth about you and me. That you were here with me. He told me—" Ned's brow creased.

"Told you what?"

"Earl, leave us now."

"Are you sure, sir?"

"Go."

"Ezer, sir, are you going to be all right?"

Ezer's heart still tumbled faster than he thought could be healthy, but if Ned wanted Earl gone for whatever he was going to say next, then it was best if the old man left. "Yes, I'm fine now."

Earl looked doubtful, but he left the room as Ned had requested.

Ned kissed Ezer's stomach again, pressing Ezer's hand with his own, and then he met Ezer's gaze.

"Tell me," Ezer urged. "What did Braden say?"

"He told me about George Fersee not being your father. He thought that might make me 'come to my senses' about what you could realistically offer me. He thinks you're bribing me to protect you from him and Finch. But…yeah, now I know."

Ezer's chin wobbled. So what if Ned knew he was Amos's love child with another alpha? So what if Ned now understood the real reason George had gotten rid of him? And yet, somehow after everything, it was too low a blow. It took the breath from him again, and tears welled over, spilling down his cheeks.

"If my father had turned your father down, and your father had gone to Finch, he'd have taken you. The money is that good. He wouldn't have hesitated. And he wouldn't have been kind during the heat, or gentle after. He's a sadist, just like Braden, and you know it," Ned said. "Worse, if he'd found out after the fact, *after* you were pregnant with his son, that you weren't who you seemed to be…"

The implications hung between them.

"He'd have hurt you. He'd have made your life miserable."

Ned nuzzled Ezer's throat, sniffing and kissing in quick alternation. "I saved you."

"You expect me to be grateful?" Ezer choked out.

"I just want you to understand. I protected you then, and I'll protect you always."

"I hate you," Ezer whispered. "I hate you so much."

Ned got up from his kneeling position on the floor, and slipped onto the sofa, putting his arm around Ezer's shoulders, and pulling him close. "I know you do."

They didn't fuck. They didn't even talk.

They just sat in silence, Ned holding Ezer until he relaxed against him, both watching as the sun glistened on the pool outside, and listening as the birds chirruped cheerfully. They stayed that way until Earl came back and announced that lunch was ready.

# Chapter Twenty-Five

EZER'S THIGHS WERE slick-wet and trembling as he collapsed onto the sofa with Ned behind him, cock still buried deep. He still missed the delirious fullness that came with a knot, and how it kept the crashing post-sex clarity at bay for a longer period of time.

Now he lay pulled tight to Ned's body, feeling him shrink in size until he slipped out, wondering if Ned was going to force him to confess everything now, to own up to what Braden had told him.

Minutes ticked by with Ned playing with Ezer's hole, pressing the leaking cum back inside, pushing fingers in to massage the glands and prostate until Ezer squirmed enough for him to stop.

"We don't have to talk about it," Ned said, pulling his fingers free and wiping them on Ezer's stomach, the cum sliding over his skin like a stripe of ownership. "Not tonight. Not even tomorrow."

"We don't?" The cum was doing its job, calming and soothing him, and at Ned's words Ezer's hopes lifted.

"No. But we *do* have to talk," Ned said. "About ourselves. About the things we like and who we are. Like…like new friends."

"Friends," Ezer scoffed.

Ned shrugged. "I don't know how else to do this, baby. We either try, like actually *try* to make this work, or we just go on forever misunderstanding each other, and being intimate strangers."

Ezer rubbed a hand over his face. *Intimate strangers? Is that a new word for slave and owner?* He almost bit the bitter words out, but he held them in. Hadn't he promised himself as he'd fallen asleep by the pool that he'd stop fighting Ned at every turn? He didn't want to raise his son in a house where his parents couldn't carry on a civil conversation.

"All right. What do you want to know about me?"

Ned smiled and flipped Ezer around as easily as if he were a doll. Brushing Ezer's hair off his face with soft fingers, he asked, "What's your favorite TV show?"

"I'm not much of a TV person. I prefer movies."

"All right, your favorite movie then."

Ezer hesitated. "*Knotting Hill.*"

"I've seen that a few times. What do you like best about it?"

Ezer shrugged. He wasn't about to admit that he'd always found the situation the omega finds himself in—a famous actor omega, lost in heat, taken in by a bookstore owning alpha he hardly knew—titillating, and the sweetness of the unexpected romance heartwarming. Instead, he offered an indisputable fact: "The alpha playing the lead is handsome. What's your favorite movie?"

"I'm a TV guy, and lately I love the show *How to Catch a Cow Thief.*"

Ezer blinked, trying to see a glint of humor in Ned's eyes, revealing this confession as a joke. "Please tell me that show isn't literally about catching cow thieves?"

Ned grinned. "That's for me to know and you to find out when you watch it with me later."

Ezer rolled his eyes, and started to flip back around, but Ned's hand on his hip stayed him.

"Okay, what's your favorite book?"

Ezer shrugged. "I don't have one. What's yours?"

"Superhero comics."

"Figures."

Ned, who had seemed relaxed with post-sex afterglow, jerked when his phone pinged. He sat from the sofa and reached over Ezer to pick it up from where it rested on the coffee table. Glancing at the screen, his expression went tight, and his lips drew into a thin line. Ezer wondered who the message from was from. His father, or Uncle Heath, or maybe Finch and Braden sending him taunts or threats?

Ned ran his eyes over the text once more and then passed the phone to Ezer, saying, "Look."

Ezer stared down at the screen for a moment, his cheeks getting hot, and then he handed it back to Ned. "What does it say?"

Ned's brows furrowed. "You didn't read it?"

"I can't read." Ezer's gut churned at the admission. His biggest shame.

Ned stared at Ezer. "You can't read?"

Ezer shook his head. "No, and I can't learn how to."

"I could hire someone to teach you," Ned said, clearly dumbfounded.

"I said *I can't learn*. The doctors say I have a brain problem." He tapped his forehead with two fingers. "I can't ever learn to read."

Ned shook his head. "But I've seen you in school, working math problems."

"Numbers are different."

"How?

"They don't move around. They stay put on the page." Ezer's throat tightened. "Numbers are friendly that way."

Ned considered that for a long, quiet moment. "So that's why you were at St. Hauers?"

Ezer nodded. "But my da arranged for me to switch over to Doubleton, and to take my exams verbally. So…yeah. I can't read. Not the message you showed me, not a book, not the contract I signed, not anything. I'm sorry."

"It's all right," Ned said, but he still sounded uncertain. "Is that why you didn't read our contract? Because you couldn't?"

"George offered to read it to me," Ezer admitted. "I declined."

Ned stared, his brain working overtime.

"Who's the text from?" Ezer asked, bringing him back to the present.

"Uh, it was from your da. He wanted to know about you." He opened the message again and read from the screen:

*How is my Ezer? Give him my love and tell him to call me when he can. Please tell him to forgive me. He'll do what you say. You're his alpha.*

Ned huffed a laugh at that. "You'll do what I say? Yeah right."

Ezer reached out his hand for the phone again. "It really says that?" he said, looking at the swimming letters. "He says to give me his love?"

"He does."

"Oh…" Ezer looked helplessly at the message a little longer and then handed it back to Ned. "Can you…will you tell him that I'm pregnant?"

Ned sat, pulling Ezer along with him. Then together they watched as he punched letters in. "Here's what I'm saying: *Ezer is settling in slowly but surely. He's pregnant and doing what he can to make sure the baby is healthy. We're starting to get to know each other now. I think he'd like it if you called him instead. The number where he can be reached is…* And then he put the number that rang the screen there in the nest.

"Have you sent it?"

"Not yet."

"Don't give him that number."

"Why?"

"I don't want to talk to him yet."

"But you'll want his comfort later, won't you? When the time gets closer?" Ned cocked his head. "In class they said omegas like to have their omega parent with them when they give birth."

Ezer shrugged. "I don't know what I'll want by that time, but I can't talk to him right now."

"Why?"

"Because I *haven't* forgiven him, and at the moment I'm using up all of my forgiveness on you, on trying to not hate you."

"Is it that hard?"

"Yes."

Ned huffed and took out the part about the number. He reread the entire message and asked, "Should I send it?"

"Tell him that he was wrong. Tell him that I don't like you at all."

Ned frowned but started typing dutifully.

"Stop," Ezer interrupted. "Don't add that." Ned wasn't as bad as Ezer wanted him to be. Not here and now in their nest, not when he looked at Ezer with that sweet little smile, and his eyes glowing with suppressed amusement.

Even though nothing about this situation was funny. Nothing.

"All right. How about I tell him that you're not taking calls right now to keep your peace of mind."

"Tell him that I'll call him when I'm ready."

Ned typed and then read it all once again. When Ezer agreed it was okay to send it, he did. Putting the phone aside, he stretched and then chuckled when Ezer's stomach growled. Ezer hadn't even realized he was hungry yet, but suddenly he was ravenous. "Lasagna or spaghetti?" Ned asked.

"Spaghetti."

"Apple pie or peanut butter ice cream?"

"Uh…peanut butter ice cream? I guess?"

"Then what's your favorite ice cream?"

"Mint chocolate chip."

Ned grabbed the phone again and typed in some words. "Earl will buy it for you." Then, before he could put it down again, it buzzed in Ned's hand.

"It's your da again. He doesn't believe me that your mind is at peace, but he understands why you don't want to talk to him, and he says you'll forgive him one day. *Then* he tells me that he hopes I'm taking good care of you." The phone buzzed three more times. "Um, he sent a few pictures of his new apartment. And he says thank you for giving him this fresh start."

Ezer put his hand out and Ned passed it to him. Taking in the photos, Ezer noticed they were taken by the lake and inside the beautiful lakeside apartment. As he studied the apartment's posh interior, well-maintained like all his father's properties had always been, another photo came through. It was of Da with his arm around a man Ezer recognized as Finn. It'd been sent along with another flurry of swimming words.

"What does this one say?" Ezer asked, passing it over to Ned.

Ned frowned at the words. "It says that this alpha, Finn, has come to visit him in his new apartment, and plans to stay for a bit. Um, well, he seems to imply that this man is your real father?"

Bitterness swelled, overtaking the satisfaction Ezer had felt at seeing his da's new circumstances. "Finn's not my 'real father.' I don't have one of those. He's the person my da decided to risk *everything* for just to share a single heat with him."

"Amos must have really loved him."

"I guess," Ezer said. "I met him once. Right before everything changed."

"Oh..." Ned tilted his head. "You look like him."

Ezer nodded.

"But you have your da's eyes." Ezer almost choked as Ned added, "I love your eyes. They're the prettiest eyes I've ever seen. Prettier than your da's somehow, even though they're the same. Maybe it's because the rest of your face is so..." He looked up then, caught Ezer's bewildered expression, and blushed. "It's just that your eyes are my favorite eyes in the whole world."

Ezer said nothing. What was he supposed to say? In another situation, if there had been love and understanding between him and his alpha, he'd have returned the compliment. He'd have said that Ned had the most handsome face and most beautiful body he'd ever seen, because he did. But as it was, he didn't want to share the thought.

"Do you wonder about how things are at your old home?" Ned asked. "How your brothers are doing? Your father?"

"Yeah. I wonder if Pete's had the baby yet. How that went. If they're safe."

Ned looked up. "I can find out. Let me just text—"

"No. I don't want to know from you or from gossip. I want to be told by my family." Ezer rolled his eyes. "Petty, huh?"

"Do you want me to message one of your brothers?"

"If I decide I want to talk to anyone there, I'll call Shan and Flo. They'll pick up." He didn't know if Yissan would, and Rodan was still too young to have his own phone. "I wanted to wait until..." Ezer bit his tongue as a weird sting of tears came to his eyes. What was wrong with him?

"Wait until what?" Ned prompted.

"Until I'm not ashamed of what's happening to me here. I don't want Father to think he won. I don't want my brothers to think I've been defeated."

Ned seemed to restrain himself from whatever his initial reply was going to be. Instead, he asked, "Can I help you feel less ashamed?"

Ezer shook his head. "It's just that I don't want to call them feeling meek, you know? I want to be proud and defiant and prove to them all that despite this—" he motioned at his stomach and then Ned—"they didn't beat me. I'm still myself."

"You are."

"No, I'm not. Not really." Ezer's throat tightened. "I'm not myself anymore at all. This is changing me. And I *am* ashamed of that. My father wanted to show me my place and I guess he did."

Ned stayed quiet long enough that Ezer spoke again without being prompted, which surprised Ezer as much as it did Ned. "My father never loved me. I was always his problem kid, but when he found out I wasn't an accidental by-blow from an unexpected heat, but the planned offspring of my da's first love…" Ezer's voice gave out.

Ezer hadn't loved his father in a long time, not since George had tossed his da out, but there'd been a time when he *had* loved the man, and it still hurt to have lost that.

"He was humiliated to find he'd been cuckolded so thoroughly. His hate turned on Da, and then on me. Being *weird* didn't help my cause. I'm not beautiful, or obedient, and I can't read. I'm damaged goods. He wanted me gone, and now I am."

Ned listened so well Ezer forgot he wanted to keep some pride and not spill *all* his guts. "And it worked, because here I am pregnant and tamed, just like he wanted."

"'Tamed'? That's hilarious," Ned said. "'Pregnant'…well, yeah. But you're still you. You still can't read or obey an alpha worth a damn."

Ezer hiccupped a surprised laugh. He wasn't sure why that struck him as funny, but it did. He rolled his eyes. "But I'm here, aren't? Content to fuck and suck and lay around napping in the sun. I'm just like Pete."

"Did you dislike Pete?"

Ezer thought about it. "I liked him fine. He was the man who replaced my da, so I didn't like that. But he was kind to me. Young. Kind of naïve. But he was nice. I hope he delivered safely. I hope he gave my father the alpha he's always wanted. If he didn't…I mean, Father seemed very enamored with Pete, but who knows?"

"He's young with plenty of heats left."

Ezer shrugged.

Ned looked at his phone. "I did some searching online. There's an announcement for the birth. *The Wellport Star* says a babe was born to George Fersee and his omega Pete Wilson last week. The baby came while you and I were at the heat house. No gender given. No name either. No further announcement."

Curiosity pricked Ezer. "Must not have been an alpha. Father would have been crowing that from the rooftops."

He thought back to when Rodan had been born and the subdued celebrations they'd hosted after Da's post-partum drop had passed. If Pete's baby was an alpha, there would be massive parties planned, and announcements all over the place. The Fersee line finally being saved by the birth of an alpha would be huge news.

"Another omega or a beta, then," Ezer said to himself. "I'm sad for them. I shouldn't be but I am."

Ned shrugged. "All the focus on alphas… It doesn't make sense to me. A child is a child. Each of them is valuable. I wish our culture was different."

Ezer rested his elbow on the back of the sofa and his chin in his palm. "So you wouldn't prefer an alpha?"

Ned shook his head. "I don't care what we have, so long as you're safe and the baby is healthy."

"What if it's an omega?"

Ned looked confused. "That's okay?"

"How will you handle his future?"

"Meaning?"

"Will you let him choose his life for himself, or will you pay an alpha to take him off your hands if you don't like his behavior?"

Ned put his spoon down. "Ah, there's my Ezer. See? That hostility in your tone? You're not tamed. You don't need to worry about that."

"Right now, I'm worrying about the future of any omega child I have with you and what arrangements you'll make for him."

Ned shifted back in his chair, crossed his arms over his chest, causing his biceps to bulge.

These were the kinds of questions Ezer had always wanted to ask in advance of a breeding. It was one of the reasons he'd always planned to auction off heats *without* breeding attached to get through his life. Having children hadn't ever been included in his dream, no matter how much he craved them, because of how complicated and ugly the world could be, especially for omegas. He'd never wanted to bring an omega into the world to live at the whim of alphas. So, if he were being honest, he hoped he gave birth to an alpha or a beta. Then he'd know for sure that his son's life would be much easier than his had been so far.

"I promise I'll never make an arrangement for one of our sons that you don't approve of in advance."

Ezer narrowed his eyes. "That's almost a good answer, but not quite good enough."

Ned huffed. "Why? How'd I fall short this time?"

"Promise to never make an arrangement for one of our sons that *they* don't approve of in advance."

Ned smiled then and wagged a finger at Ezer. "See? You're smart. I like that. And it's a deal. I promise."

Just like that? Ned wasn't going to give him pushback or suggest that alphas had a better grasp of the world than omegas, or…

"Is this just because you want to make nice with me?"

"It's because I never wanted an omega who didn't want me," Ned said sharply. "This isn't how I dreamed my life would go either. I mean, yes, I wanted *you.* I wanted you from the start, like I've said, but not like this. In my dreams, you wanted me, too."

Ezer swallowed hard. "I…do…" He took a deep breath, feeling shame inside, but also having to admit the truth. "I do want you. Physically."

Ned rolled his eyes. "That's not the same. You'd want any alpha who'd stuffed you full with his kid. It's biology. Nature. You can't even help it. I wanted you to want *me* to be the one to do it. Before we did it."

Ezer didn't know what to say to that. As the days passed, he was becoming… not fond of Ned, per se, but something very close to fond. He could no longer imagine doing the things he was doing with Ned with another alpha. He wasn't even sure there was another alpha out there who would take the insults Ezer hurled at Ned, or would let Ezer lower himself onto their cock while declaring how much he hated him, and all without violence. Alphas were, in general, not known for being patient and understanding of mouthy omegas. There was a reason submissives like Pete were considered so desirable…

"You signed the contract, too," Ezer said. "You agreed."

"Like I've said several times before, I thought you *knew* who you were contracting with, and I hoped…" Ned rubbed his hands through his hair. "I don't want to talk about that anymore. It is what it is. You want me physically. I guess I have to be satisfied with that."

"I *do* want you," Ezer said, surprised as his urgent desire to reassure Ned that he was a desirable alpha in Ezer's eyes. "Physically, we match well."

"And in every other way?"

"I think you're growing, and maybe I'm growing too." He touched his taut stomach. "And not just here, but in here, too—" he touched his chest. "And here." He touched his temples.

Ned's gaze trailed down to Ezer's belly. "I swear, the babe is growing so fast. You look bigger than you did at lunch."

Ezer nodded. His skin was starting to feel tight, and he recognized the mild withdrawal symptoms as his body processed the nutrients and compounds in Ned's semen and now needed more. "When you go to school, what will I do with myself?"

Ned frowned. "I don't like leaving you. I'd stay here if I could."

"You really can't?"

"No. I have to return to school. It's the way things work. If I had a job, it'd be the same."

Ezer frowned, thinking of his father and Pete. "Though, with our status, you'd work from home."

Ned nodded. "But school doesn't come to me."

"It should."

"Most people don't do this so young," Ned said.

"No. They don't."

The heaviness of what they'd done together hung between them. The responsibility of a child. The difficulty of doing something so outside of the cultural norm.

Ned asked, "What will I tell people at school? What do you want them to know about us?"

Ezer felt a hot burn of shame scour him on the inside. It was nauseating. "Tell them...tell them I went into heat unexpectedly and you helped me. Tell them that you're a hero. You saved a desperate omega."

Ned blinked at him. "Not the truth?"

"No, definitely not. I don't want them to know you're being paid to make me placid. I don't want them to know how my father decided to break me." Ezer shuddered.

Ned's eyes grew sad. "Do you feel broken, Ezer?"

"Sometimes. Not always. But who knows? I've got the rest of my pregnancy ahead. And the birth. I hear birth alone can break a man."

"You won't break. You'll always be fierce."

Ezer snorted. He didn't want to talk about that anymore. "Just tell them you're a hero who helped me with an unexpected heat. That's a prettier story. You come out looking good, and I look unfortunate, but lucky. It's a good cover."

"All right. I promise."

Ned tugged Ezer down next to him, sniffing his skin, and kissing his neck. The softness of his lips was arousing, which was frustrating, and exciting. "When will Earl bring our dinner?"

"Soon." Ned slipped his hand down, sliding his fingers around the slickness of Ezer's rim. "We have time for another quick fuck."

Ezer wanted to decline, to say he didn't need it yet, but then Ned flipped him onto his stomach, and all he could think of was getting Ned's thick dick inside him, rubbing all the right places, and leaving another wet spot on the blanket beneath him.

Afterward, panting and sweaty, Ezer muttered, "When do you go back?"

"To school?"

"Yeah."

"Tomorrow."

"Oh."

Ned kissed Ezer's temple. "I'll bring you something special, though. What do you want? Name anything?"

Ezer didn't know how to express what he really wanted, what he'd fantasized about as they'd fucked—a way to turn back time and meet Ned in a different way, in a different place, and to choose each other freely—so he said, "A new Advanced Calculus workbook. Mr. Shein should have one put aside for me. He'll give it to you."

"I'll bring it. No problem."

No problem for Ned, but Ezer was going to be so bored and so alone. It was enough to make him almost panic, but he held it in, and let Ned finger his cum-filled ass until Earl's footsteps sounded on the stairs down to the nest.

Dinner was served.

# Chapter Twenty-Six

HAVING NEVER HAD an omega in residence and being an only child, Ned had never realized just how much sex went into maintaining a pregnant omega.

As he left Ezer sprawled sated in bed, and got up to dress for school, he worried his balls were so drained from the last many days of fucking and coming that he'd been unable to leave Ezer full with enough semen to satisfy Ezer's growing needs while he was away.

But what was done was done. He had to go, or risk being late, and that would bring more attention to him than he wanted on his first day back after his unexpectedly long break.

In the upstairs kitchen, Ned ate the breakfast Earl had prepared, though he had a knot in his stomach that made it hard to swallow the buttered bun down. He didn't want to leave Ezer. He knew he'd be safe enough, and his omega seemed to have accepted his situation, so he didn't think he had to worry about Ezer deciding to take off out of the nest. But he'd still been tempted to ask for a longer reprieve from school, at least until Ezer was well and truly showing, because there was no way Ezer would be able to leave the nest on his own then.

But right now…

Well, Ned didn't think Ezer had anywhere to go. He was still angry with his father and his da, and while he seemed interested in connecting with his brothers, he also seemed ashamed of the idea he might appear weak to them. He didn't know the dynamic Ezer had grown up with in the Fersee household, but he suspected Ezer's older omega brothers had all warned him at least once to comply with their father's demands or to expect certain consequences.

Now, pregnant with said consequences, Ezer clearly felt shame.

"Son, I'm glad I caught you."

Ned jerked at the sound of Lidell's voice. He'd been so overwhelmed with Ezer the last many days, and his father had been gone so long, he'd almost forgotten he lived in the house, too. Amazing how his world had narrowed to Ezer, the nest, sex, and little else. This unexpected meeting was like the world cracking open again. Just in time to leave for school.

"You're back," Ned said, standing up to clasp Lidell in a hug. He had problems with Lidell, but he loved him, and in the face of Ezer's complicated family relationships, he felt lucky to have only an entitled spendthrift as his father.

Though Ned was still unsure about a lot of choices they'd made lately—like how things had gone down with Ezer—he was at least sure Lidell loved him. Maybe not as much as he loved spending money, but more than a father who'd paid to have his son taken off his hands.

"How's your omega?" Lidell said, taking the empty seat at the table next to Ned and pouring some coffee from the carafe Earl had prepared for Ned.

"He's pregnant."

"Doctor confirmed?"

Ned shook his head. "He's supposed to come today. I wanted to be here for it, but..." He winced, hating how he'd let Ezer down on that front too. "I should have told the school I wouldn't be back until next week. I should have insisted."

"Is your omega still fighting you?"

"No. He never really fought *me*. He just fought the circumstances." Ned was trying to convince himself of that anyway.

Lidell smiled. "This experience will teach him, don't worry. All omegas live for heats. You'll see. This baby will come, and in no time at all, he'll be asking the doctor to trigger another so he can do this all again."

Ned worked his jaw. He didn't know what to say to that. He didn't know if that was true of Ezer, or "all omegas," or if that was just what alphas were told to believe so it was easier for them to take the pleasure they wanted, without care for the omega's true needs and desires. If "all omegas" lived for heats, then alphas could feel like they were right and good to fill them with babes endlessly, because omegas were "just like that".

"He isn't happy, though," Ned said. "He's struggling."

Lidell frowned. "Are you fucking him enough?"

Ned scoffed. He didn't think he could fuck Ezer any more often. His balls would drop off.

"Okay," Lidell said with a chuckle. "If you're fucking him enough, what do you think's wrong with him?"

Ned dismissed that with a wave of his hand. "What if there's nothing wrong with *him*? What if there's something wrong with me and my semen?"

Lidell wrinkled his nose. "That's not possible."

"Why?"

"Because alphas don't have problems with things like that. He must be unnaturally saturnine, just like his father said."

"Maybe. Or maybe it's not true that all it takes is plenty of alpha semen to calm an angry, pregnant omega. Maybe there's more to it all than that."

"Like what?"

Ned rolled his eyes. His father was clueless. After Ned's omega parent had died, Lidell had never been close with an omega again. He'd shared heats, gotten his own needs met for a price, but he'd never looked at an omega as an equal, or considered that an omega might have needs outside of sex and children. Ned knew all that about his father, and yet it was still disappointing to have it confirmed.

"I'm not going to school today," Ned said, standing up. "I'm going to stay for the doctor's appointment. I'm going to be there for Ezer."

"If you don't trust your omega to let the doctor know the truth of what's going on with him physically and emotionally, then you must, of course, supervise the appointment."

Ned's jaw clenched again. That wasn't at all what he'd meant, but his father would never see it like that. "Call the school for me?"

"I'll have Earl do it."

"Thanks."

Ned headed back down to the nest, irritation with his father flaring beneath his skin and threatening his mood. When he opened the door to the bedroom, Ezer sat, confusion on his face in the low light, and Ned's heart almost exploded into starbursts of joy when Ezer's face broke into a strange little smile.

Who cared what his father thought? It only mattered what Ezer needed.

"What about school?" Ezer said, opening his arms to welcome Ned back into the mess of their bed, embracing him. He rubbed his bare skin over Ned's school uniform shirt and pants and nuzzled his neck.

"I want to be here for you."

"You have to go back to school, though. It's how it works…"

"Tomorrow. After the doctor's appointment."

Ezer stopped nuzzling and pulled away. "You don't trust me?"

"I have some questions for him, too. About myself."

"About you?"

Ned nodded, and tugged Ezer into a spooning position. He kissed the back of his neck and his shoulders, enjoying the way Ezer let him, and didn't stop his hand from drifting down to take Ezer's hardening cock. "I'm not perfect. I know that."

Ezer let the subject drop as the usual lust escalated between them.

Ned buried his face in Ezer's hair, breathing in his scent as they fucked, and prayed that he would find a way to make Ezer happy one day.

And not just from the strength of his semen's compounds.

Truly, honestly happy. Because he was Ned's.

"I DON'T LIKE this," Ezer said faintly, as they waited for the doctor to come back into the room that had been prepared for the exam, complete with exam table. Ezer lay back on it now, legs in the stirrups, covered by the softest blanket he could find. "He's going to put his hand in me?"

"Just his fingers," Ned said, and it was all he could do to keep his own outrage at the proposition of that invasion from breaking free. He didn't want anyone, much less old Dr. Savage, putting fingers into Ezer's body. "He needs to check the opening to your womb. But after that, it'll be over, and so long as there isn't a problem, then that sort of intrusion will be over until closer to the birth."

Ezer frowned, rubbing his arms. His tummy was bulging more already, and Ned wanted to ask the doctor about that, too. He knew that pregnancy only lasted four months—and they were over three weeks in now, but he'd thought the majority of growth happened in the later stages.

Ned twined their fingers together.

Ezer didn't seem comforted by the action, but he also didn't pull his hand away either. Ned smiled at him, and Ezer's lips tightened in the opposite of a smile.

"Hey, it's going to be all right," Ned said, reassuringly. "It's just that there could be possible complications, and this will help rule them out."

"And if there is a problem? Then what?"

"There won't be," Ned said with certainty.

That wasn't the right answer, because Ezer tugged free and turned his face away, too. "You can't know that."

"What if there's a problem with me?" Ned said. "What if I'm not making the right proteins in my semen?"

"Why would you say that?"

"You should be more settled than you are."

Ezer's turned back to glare at Ned, and he opened his mouth to speak, but the door to the improvised exam room opened, and Dr. Savage walked in again.

"Well, well, you're looking sour," Dr. Savage said with a huff of a laugh. "You should be floating away on a raft of alpha seminal compounds at this stage, well-satisfied and blissful. Are you doing your job, young man?"

"He is," Ezer answered for him.

Dr. Savage's brows rose at Ezer's presumption to speak for his alpha, but he didn't scold him for it. "Well, then, we'll have a little look and feel of you, and then we'll talk about what to expect going forward. You're both young, healthy—"

"Actually," Ned interjected. "I'm not so sure that I am healthy? You mentioned that Ezer doesn't seem as satisfied as he should be. I wondered if that could be my fault."

"You're fucking the boy? Then it's not your fault."

"My semen. What if the proteins and compounds aren't sufficient?"

Dr. Savage's lips tilted up in amusement. "I see. Well, it's possible. *Unlikely*...but, good for you for thinking of it at all. The times I've had to deal with an alpha who wouldn't even entertain the possibility that he could be the problem in cases of insufficient satiation." He looked Ned up and down. "You look healthy enough, though. Lack of protein compounds is usually a problem in old men. But if your omega is in distress, then it's worth considering—"

"I'm not in distress," Ezer hissed. "I'm just not happy."

Dr. Savage laughed. "Oh, I see. He's a spitfire." He grinned at Ned. "You like that, don't you?"

"Yes, sir."

It was obvious Ezer didn't enjoy being talked about as if he weren't there, but he just clenched his jaw and glared more.

"I'll tell you what," Dr. Savage said. "Let me do the exam, and if we can't locate an issue, then we'll consider testing your semen." He turned his attention to Ezer. "Lie back, please. I'll be putting my hands on your abdomen, chest and nipples to check for proper development for milk, and into your body to feel your womb. Your penis may react. Don't be embarrassed."

Ezer's eyes blazed, and he looked as if he might rip Dr. Savage's head off for suggesting his cock might react to his ass being stimulated by the doctor's touch. But he said nothing, lying back with a resentful air, despite his obedience.

Dr. Savage met Ned's gaze again and chuckled. "You have interesting taste, but to each his own." He then touched Ezer's arm gently, before sliding his hands over to Ezer's belly and pressing. His head tilted. "When did you say the heat was?"

"Three weeks and two days ago."

"Hmm."

Ezer grew pale, and Ned saw the worry growing in his omega as Dr. Savage pressed with an intense expression.

"Is there a problem?" Ned asked.

"No, I don't think so..." Dr. Savage said, but he didn't sound convincing. "I'll know more after the internal exam." He nodded at Ned. "Hold his hand. They don't like this part."

Ned's jaw clenched as he did as he was told. Ezer's face went incandescent at his outrage at having been referred to in the third person, but he closed his eyes, and turned his head away as Dr. Savage parted his legs and put three thick fingers inside.

"Sorry," Dr. Savage said as he worked his hand until he was shoved in up to his wrist, twisting his arm in a way that made Ezer grunt.

Ned snarled.

Dr. Savage met his eyes and said, "Down, boy. This is just a check. His womb tilts back, making him harder to...ah, there. Good." Carefully, he withdrew from Ezer's body.

Ezer covered his face with his elbow, but not before Ned saw the tear leak out and down his cheek.

"Well, the good news is his womb is closed tight, so the pregnancy isn't in danger of ending early. At least not at this juncture. The bad news—well, the *complicated* news is...well, let me confirm something first."

Ned's stomach churned, and Ezer's chest heaved in and out with small, struggling breaths. Ned soothed Ezer's curls. "It's all right," he murmured. "It's all going to be all right."

Dr. Savage took out a stethoscope and listened at Ezer's stomach. "Normally, I'd suggest we bring him in for an ultrasound, but this is easy enough to confirm." He closed his eyes and then smiled before putting the stethoscope away and feeling Ezer's stomach again. "Yes, well, it's as I thought." Dr. Savage caught Ned's eyes. "Your omega is quite small with narrow hips, so I do have some concerns, but perhaps we'll be lucky. They might be small like him."

"'They'?" Ezer said, his elbow coming away from his face, his beautiful blue eyes still shining.

"Do you have a history of twins in your family?" Dr. Savage asked.

"Yes," Ezer whispered. "My brothers, Shan and Florentine."

"There you go." He nodded as if that meant everything. "And now you'll be carrying on that tradition. You've got two babes cooking in there, young man. Congratulations."

Ned felt dizzy. "'Two'?"

"Yes, and that means," Dr. Savage continued, turning his full attention to Ned again. "It's not a problem with your seminal proteins not being enough to counter his sour moods. It's just that the need is essentially doubled for him. For *you*, I'll prescribe some vitamins and semen enhancer, but his dissatisfaction isn't because you aren't making enough, son. It's that *he* requires more."

Ezer squeezed Ned's hand so hard it hurt. Dr. Savage smiled at Ned and then at Ezer. "Well done, boys. This is more than you bargained for, I'm sure, but with luck, we'll see you through to a healthy delivery." Dr. Savage held Ezer's gaze and smiled reassuringly. "Don't worry about that. Your alpha and I will take good care of you."

"Twins," Ezer said to the air, his eyes searching the ceiling as if it was full of clouds and he could read oracles in them.

Ned couldn't free his fingers from Ezer's grasp to escort the doctor out; he stayed with Ezer as Earl did that work.

Ned didn't know what to say. He was tongue-tied and shocked, and grateful as hell he'd come to his senses and stayed back from school today. He couldn't imagine how any of this would have been for Ezer without him here.

Wasn't that what alphas were for? Supporting their omegas?

"I'm scared," Ezer said, suddenly. "I'm really, *really* scared."

Ned sat on the table next to him and pulled him into his arms. Ezer didn't fight, but he didn't hug him back either. He let Ned hold him as he stared at a spot on the wall and trembled.

"Twins," Ezer repeated again. "Twins."

Ned kissed his curls and tried to keep his own heart from pounding out of control. Was his omega strong enough to deliver two? Time would tell.

"Yes, twins," he confirmed.

*Twins.*

# Chapter Twenty-Seven

SCHOOL WAS DELAYED by a few more frantic days after that as Ezer tried to calm himself by fucking Ned relentlessly. Multiple times they went at it until they were both dizzy and dehydrated, and Earl had to force them into drinking liquids and taking rest in separate rooms. Lidell left for another trip away, rather than be subjected to their displays on the pool deck and in the main living areas of the house. Ezer was shameless now, and Ned seemed happy to satisfy him anytime, anywhere.

The vitamins and supplements the doctor had prescribed for Ned had increased his seminal load massively, and he said each orgasm felt almost like a knot now, with *tons* of semen pumping from his cock. Ezer loved it. It was glorious to feel so full of Ned's cum. It sent him into space every time, and within two days of the doctor's visit, he understood what other omegas loved about this part of the whole process. He was high as a kite, relaxed and happy, his body and mind floating away on semen and satisfaction.

Glowing, floating, relaxed and easy-going. These were all words that applied to the sensations of his heart and body.

Ned seemed happier, too, and when Ezer laughed at something he'd said, Ned's eyes gleamed as if Ezer had declared him the best alpha in the world and sworn his undying love.

Ezer had enjoyed that expression so much he found himself wishing to see it again. He didn't even feel shame about how this desire was a clear sign he was giving in, becoming the thing his father had wanted. He didn't *care*. He *liked* it. He wanted to feel this good *forever*. It was so much better than being sad and scared.

The morning when Ned truly left for school for the first time, Ezer got up too, ate breakfast with him, sucked his dick one last time, and waved him off, before heading up to the pool area to nap. His stomach was rounder than ever before. There were small movements coming from inside—slight pops and thumps—though it seemed soon for that.

Sitting naked in the sun, he giggled over the fact that he was finally the round, happy omega everyone had wanted him to be. Okay, so maybe not *happy*, but he was cheerful, calm, and way too well-fucked to be argumentative now. In fact, he thought he was ready to do the thing he'd most wanted and dreaded doing since he'd first arrived.

If he could just figure out how to operate the damn tablet.

He fiddled with the device Ned had left with him, telling Ezer he could use it to call his brothers or Amos whenever he wanted. But the initial set-up included reading a little, and that was defeating him. Normally he would have felt frustrated and angry about it, but the seminal proteins had seeped so deeply into him, tamed him so thoroughly, he couldn't be bothered to get mad. Maybe he'd take a nap instead.

"Do you need help, sir?" Earl said.

Ezer almost jumped at his voice. Did the man have cat paws for feet? "I can't set this up," he said, holding the tablet up to Earl. "Take it back to the nest, please. Ned can set it up later."

"I could help."

Ezer wasn't sure what to say. If he accepted, then Earl would guess that Ezer couldn't read. If he didn't, then he'd look like a fool who couldn't figure out simple tech. "All right."

Earl put the pitcher of lemonade he'd brought for Ezer down next to a glass to pour it in. "Here. Let me see." He started the set-up process and glanced at Ezer with questioning eyes only twice before handing it back. "My brother had dyslexia," Earl said. "The swimming letters? The moving words?"

Ezer lifted his eyes to him.

"He was one of the smartest men I've ever known, but he could never read a full sentence."

Ezer's throat tightened. "Yeah?"

"Yes, sir. Now, should I help you with anything else?"

Ezer examined the tablet. The calling app seemed easy enough. He checked, and the numbers were solid and still as ever—he'd long lived in dread that they'd start moving too. Experimentally, he pushed in the number he'd memorized for his brother Shan.

"I think I'm good."

"All right. Just call out to me if you need more help. I'm here for you, sir."

"Thank you."

Ezer waited until he was sure Earl was back in the house. Not just in the open-air living room, but farther inside behind closed walls, before calling Shan. He was surprised when his call was answered on the first buzz.

"It says it's Ned Clearwater calling," Shan's voice cut through, as a chaotic scene of a ceiling, and then a floor, followed by a cluttered vanity table came into view on the tablet screen. Ezer recognized Flo's room. "I think it's Ezer!"

"It's me," Ezer said, as the screen continued to show sincere excitement from his brother, based on the way the camera careened around, one moment covered by a hand and the next showing the floor again.

"It's him!" Flo's face filled the screen. "Ezer, are you all right?

Are you safe?"

"Yes," Ezer answered. "I'm safe."

Shan grabbed the phone from Flo and then his golden-brown eyes peered through the screen at Ezer. "Are you sure?"

"Yeah. Ned treats me well."

"Good," Flo said. "If he didn't, he'd have to answer to us."

A silly threat, but it warmed Ezer's heart all the same.

"Pete had the baby," Shan said. "They named him Prince."

"Prince?" Ezer scoffed. "What kind of name is that?"

"A name for an alpha," Flo said.

"Really?" Ezer gasped. "Pete had the elusive alpha?"

They both nodded miserably.

"Why are you sad about it?" Ezer asked. "Isn't Father over the moon?"

"He is, but…now he wants to breed Pete again, as soon as possible."

"He'll have to wait a year or two at least," Ezer said. He knew this from his own conversation with the doctor by phone the other day. He'd called after the examination to check in, and Ezer had found he had more questions. It'd been a relief to hear he wasn't going to be expected to birth two babies and then turn around and birth another right away. The doctor had said that would be very risky to his health.

"Yes, but in the meantime, Father wants to get rid of all the omegas in the house. He says when he gets home from the mountains, after Pete's safely past the post-natal drop, he's going to contract each of us off to an alpha, one by one."

"He said he'd replace us with alphas with Pete."

"Fuck him," Ezer said. "He won't do that."

"Yes, he will," Shan said. "He can and he will. Yissan is terrified. You know he's never wanted to be contracted against his will, and now he has no time at all to find an alpha of his own choosing."

"Well, tough for him," Ezer said, a little bitterly. "At least he has some time to look. I wasn't given that chance."

"You're naked," Flo observed.

Ezer looked down at his bare chest. The growing swell wasn't visible on the screen, but all omegas knew what it meant to be naked weeks after a heat. "Yeah," Ezer said. "It's weird. But I'm getting used to it."

"Does he use you daily?" Shan asked, crowding onto the screen. "Is it horrible?"

Ezer frowned. He hadn't realized Shan thought about sex with an alpha that way. "He doesn't *use* me," Ezer explained. "We have sex. A lot more than daily. About every hour or so."

Shan grimaced, but Flo was intrigued.

Ezer went on, "When he's home, that is. He's at school today, so I'm on my own for a bit."

"School," Flo said with a sigh. "I so wish Father had let you finish school."

"Is he always horny? Your alpha? Does he demand it all the time?" Shan asked.

"He's not like that. He's not a bad person," Ezer said. "He's trying to be a good alpha. He's young, though. Like me."

"We know," Flo said. "Father told us everything. After it was too late to do anything to help you, of course."

Ezer was doubtful Flo or Shan would have gone out of their way for him. They still relied on their father too much, and they'd always thought Ezer brought trouble onto himself. "Well, it's done now."

"You're pregnant?"

"With twins."

Flo and Shan exclaimed in excitement. Ezer wasn't surprised. They loved being twins, but they weren't the ones facing the carrying of two, or the prospect of giving birth twice within a few minutes. "Did it hurt?" Shan asked quietly.

"What part?"

"Heat. Knotting."

"All of it," Flo said. "Any of it."

"Um, well, it hurt my pride the most. Physically, it all feels really good."

Shan wrinkled his nose, but Flo seemed fascinated. "How good?"

Ezer laughed. "Let's put it this way, I forgot who I was and what I was all about during heat. It was so consuming. Now? It's good enough to make me forget I didn't want this life."

"But you chose it!" Shan said. "Father said you signed the contract of your own volition. He said he didn't make you."

"He didn't *make* me," Ezer agreed. Though he wouldn't say he'd done it of his own volition either. "There were circumstances, though. Involving Da."

Both of them rolled their eyes. "We told you to stay away from Da."

"I know."

"If you had, maybe you'd still be home with us right now," Flo said.

"Maybe." Ezer didn't think so, though. His father had wanted an excuse to get rid of him—and the eyes that had reminded him of Amos's betrayal.

"Rodan was asking after you," Flo said. "Father told him that you were gone, like Da, and to stop with the questions."

"He hasn't mentioned you since," Shan went on.

"Oh." That hurt more than it should have, but maybe it was for the best. "Well, I'm not sure what the future holds, but if Father thinks I'm going to just be a quiet, pregnant omega happily tucked away in Ned's house, he's wrong. I don't plan to present Ned with children like I've plucked them from an apple tree. I'll have these two, and then we'll see what I do with my life."

The twins looked at each other. "Is that safe? Won't your alpha punish you?"

"Ned? Punish me?"

They nodded.

Ezer felt an odd, warm sensation in his chest—was it security? Was it even maybe a subtle joy? "Ned would never punish me."

"Never?"

"Never."

*Yell at me, fight with me, fail me, or fuck me silly, yes, but punish me? No.*

Ezer didn't know why he felt so sure of that, but he was.

"Yissan said this alpha of yours is better-connected than you would have gotten on your own. He says Father did you a favor."

Ezer chafed at that. Ned claimed to have wanted him even before this was all arranged by their parents. He used to not believe Ned's romantic nonsense, but now after the way Ned tenaciously stuck to this story, he thought maybe he was telling the truth. Ned had been horrible at knowing what to do with that feeling, but it wasn't as though Ezer couldn't have made this connection on his own. But he couldn't explain that to his brothers. They wouldn't believe him.

"Ned is Heath Clearwater's nephew, and former heir. He's still close with his uncle." Ezer did wonder, though, what would happen when Heath found out about the choices made in his absence. He got the impression that Heath was not the type of man to take kindly to being left out of big decisions like this one.

"Father wants to sell us off next," Shan said, darkly. "There's a businessman interested in Flo. I don't like him."

"You don't like the situation," Flo corrected. "You've never even met him."

"Have you?"

Flo flushed. "Yes, and he was handsome."

"When did you meet him?" Shan screeched.

"Why does it matter? I met him. I liked his looks."

"An alpha needs to be more than handsome, Flo. You're thinking with your hole."

"What's an alpha need to be then?" Flo challenged.

"Mature—"

"Ezer's alpha is still in high school."

"Ezer's alpha isn't your alpha," Shan said. "You're special."

"Wow, thanks," Ezer muttered.

They ignored him. "An alpha needs to be mature, handsome, patient, gentle, kind, heroic, and *very* rich. And this man Father is looking at for you is only a little rich." Shan lifted his nose. "Not good enough for you."

"I want him," Flo said. "I saw him, and I wanted his knot. That's good enough for me."

Shan paled and went silent.

Ezer was feeling a little dizzy now. He didn't want to see the twins fight. "I'm sorry, guys, but I have to go take a nap now." He was so tired. The conversation had drained him.

"Call us again soon," Flo said. "We've missed you. And I want to know everything about being with an alpha during heat. All the details. I can count on you, right?"

Shan stood and left the room, slamming the door behind him. Flo rolled his eyes. "He's going to have to get used to it. For me and for him, for all of us. At least I'm ready. I want a family of my own. Shan doesn't."

"It's a big commitment," Ezer warned.

"You went into it blind enough," Flo said. "And look how well it's turned out for you. Sitting by the pool, napping in the middle of the day, getting fucked so well you're glowing. I want that. It's not fair that you got it first when I'm older than you."

Ezer sighed. He wasn't going to try to explain to Flo why his point of view on all of this was immature. No one believed the realities of heat, pregnancy, and contracting with an alpha until they experienced it for themselves. And if Father wanted Flo to contract with this businessman? Then he'd be contracted with him. His father would see to it. Ezer's own life was a case in point.

"Go rest," Flo said. "I have to go comfort Shan now."

"I miss you," Ezer said, but what he really meant was he missed home the way it had been before Da had been expelled. He missed being a child and not knowing any of what he knew now.

"Love you too," Flo said. "Bye."

Then he was gone. Ezer hadn't even been the one to disconnect the call. Oh well, that was typical of his brothers.

Ezer rubbed a hand over his stomach, surprised that it felt even tighter and rounder. The little ones inside were not wasting any time in growing. He shifted, an urgent prickling feeling starting beneath his skin.

Great. Now he was horny, and Ned was at school.

He'd just have to wait.

"FUCK!" EZER CRIED, his head thrown back, and his cock spurting between them.

Ned licked Ezer's neck and held on to his hips as he drove into Ezer one final time and convulsed with pleasure. The powerful bursts of semen took his breath away, and he was shaking all over by the time he was done with his orgasm.

Between them, Ezer's growing belly rubbed at a different angle than it had before. Their skin was shiny with sweat, and Ezer moaned in Ned's ear as he convulsed on his cock again.

"I missed that," Ezer huffed. "Thank you."

Ned almost chuckled. He hadn't ever thought he'd hear Ezer thank him for anything, much less for a good fucking, but he managed to hold the laugh back. He knew it would elicit a response in Ezer that would kill the moment.

"Now," Ned said, lifting Ezer up and off him, quickly rolling him to his side so the semen deposit would remain in his ass to be absorbed. "Believe it or not, I have homework. Remember that pesky stuff?"

Ezer nodded, his eyes glazed and full of bliss. He closed them, and seemed to drift away on slow, gentle pleasure as the semen did its work.

Ned headed into the bathroom attached to their bedroom and washed himself off. He checked the mirror. No signs of the humiliation he'd endured at school were written on his face. That was good. He didn't want Ezer to know anything about that.

When he came back, Ezer had emerged from his blissed-out state, and was propped up on an elbow, still dreamy-looking but lucid, waiting for him. "How was school?" he asked, almost like he'd read Ned's mind and come up with the question Ned most didn't want to answer.

"Good," he said. "I have a lot of work to catch up on, though. Mostly math." He wrinkled his nose. "Ugh. I'm going to fail, I think. I just can't figure out what the hell they want me to do with all those formulas, and that was before I missed a ton of classes."

"I could help," Ezer said, sitting up, and then making an "ugh" face as his asshole gushed with a combination of slick and Ned's cum.

Ned rushed over to push him back down, and then used his fingers to scoop some of the cum back inside, rubbing at Ezer's rim until it trembled, and Ezer squeezed it tight.

Breathless, Ezer muttered, "I'm good at math."

"I know, and, uh, Mr. Shein sent that advanced calculus book you wanted. It's in my backpack."

Ezer flopped onto his stomach and pushed his ass up in the air. "Finger me first, and then I'll help you with your math problems."

Ned bit his lip to keep from letting another chuckle escape. He could get used to Ezer being like this. It was adorable and sexy. He loved it.

Pressing his fingers into Ezer's slick ass, rubbing the glands, and making sure to hit his prostate, Ned worked until Ezer was shifting around on the bed, sweating, and mumbling curses into the pillow.

Ned removed his fingers to a hiss of protest, sidled up behind Ezer, stroked his own cock a few times and then pushed inside.

"Fuck," he whimpered. Somehow Ezer felt tighter. He'd noticed it earlier, but he *really* noticed it now when Ezer should be loose and open. Suddenly, there was a slide against his cock, and it took only another moment to recognize that the tightness was from the weight of the babies, and the movement he'd felt was one of them shifting in Ezer's womb.

"Oh," he whimpered. "He moved. One of them *moved*."

Ezer moaned, and nodded into the pillow, not lifting his face. "I felt him."

Ned took hold of Ezer's slim hips and pulled almost all the way out, and then pushed back in, his legs trembling with an otherworldly excitement. "Fuck. He did it again."

"Mm."

The pressure on his cock was delicious, but he wanted to get

Ezer off again first. He needed to make sure his omega was pleasured. He twisted his hips to a position that usually let him fuck Ezer hard, but kept him from getting too much friction, but now Ezer was just so tight inside, so full and rapidly getting fuller and fuller.

Their sons. Their flesh and blood.

"Can you come for me, baby?" Ned muttered. "Let me feel you come."

Ezer moaned again, his hips twitching back and forth on Ezer's cock, and then he grasped beneath himself and began to stroke.

"That's it. I want to feel you come."

Ezer stroked hard, his hips flexing, and his hole working around Ned's dick. Ned held it steady, feeling the shifts of Ezer's body—both from the babies and from Ezer's tensing muscles as he reached for orgasm—and then it arrived. The glorious, spasmodic clenching of Ezer's release.

"Fuck, you're amazing, baby," he whispered, massaging Ezer's slim back as he twisted on Ned's cock. "That's beautiful. You're beautiful."

Ezer quivered and shook. Ned shoved deep, feeling the ripples of the babies moving, and the unbelievable glory of that—of what they'd made—raked him like a machine gun. He collapsed on Ezer's back, shuddering as he shot inside.

"That's it," he muttered. "Take my cum. Use it. That's it, baby."

Ezer squeezed around him, and Ned felt as if he was going to lift out of his body and go to Heaven. This was so beautiful. He wondered if Ezer thought so too.

After another few minutes, Ezer sighed. "Go on and clean up. Then go out to the living room and get your math homework out. I'll come help in a few minutes. I just need to rest first, and wash up."

"Are you all right?" Ned asked, tugging free of Ezer's body and sitting by him on the bed. "Was I too rough?"

"'Too rough'? You made me do the work." Ezer chuckled, and the sound was like bells to Ned, the best sound in the world.

"Earlier I mean, during the first fuck." He hadn't meant to screw Ezer so hard, but how could he hold back when Ezer had been waiting for him, slick and ready as soon as he'd walked in the door of the nest? He'd gone wild on Ezer during that first fuck after being away all day, slamming into his body as hard as he could, leaving a full day's worth of pent-up semen inside. But as Ezer got bigger, he'd need to be more careful with how hard he took him.

"I'm fine," Ezer said. "I'm just tired. It's been a long day."

Ned almost teased him, asking what had been long about a day snoozing in the shade by the pool again, but he held it back. He was sure Ezer would be quick to remind him that he had no other choice after all. "You rest," he said, kissing Ezer's butt cheeks. "I'll get started on this homework, and then we can have dinner."

"I'll help with the math," Ezer said as he drifted off. "Wait for me..."

Ned smiled as Ezer fell asleep. He wouldn't wait for him, but it wasn't like he was going to get anywhere with the math problems anyway.

"Ezer talked with his brothers today, sir," Earl said, when Ned was seated at the big table in the living room of the nest. He'd had it moved there when it became clear Ezer had no desire to eat in the windowless kitchen. He was working on his Literature homework. He hadn't even read the book, but he could fudge his way through the essay pretty well, and he knew the teacher would go easy on him.

"He did?" Ned asked, looking up to gauge Earl's opinion of the phone call. "How did it go?"

"He seemed tired after. A little sad. But no more than he has sometimes been in the past, I suppose. Did he mention it to you?"

"No."

"I wasn't eavesdropping," Earl said defensively.

"Of course not," Ned reassured him, though he suspected Earl had absolutely listened to the entire call and on purpose.

"His father's omega had an alpha."

"Really? That's good, I suppose. Fersee wanted one."

"And now he plans to get rid of his other omega sons. The twins are next in line for it, it seems. I don't know why he delays with the oldest, but there you have it. Ezer seemed…"

"He seemed what?"

"Tired."

Earl had said that before.

"He's growing twins. Of course he's tired."

"No, it was different. I think his family grieves him, but he loves them anyway. I think they don't love him the way he wants to be loved."

"Whose family does?"

Earl nodded thoughtfully. "Anyway, I though you should know, sir, in case he's exceptionally taciturn tonight."

"Me? Taciturn?" Ezer's voice cut into their conversation. He trailed out of the bedroom with a silky sheet wrapped around his shoulders and his eyelids weighed down with sleepiness. "I'm always a bundle of cheer, Earl. I'd think you'd know that by now."

"Of course, sir. Always laughing. Always smiling."

That made Ezer actually smile, but he didn't laugh. "I'm fine. My brothers are exhausting is all. And I thought you were in your rooms when I made that call."

"I wasn't eavesdropping, sir. I just wanted to check on you."

Ezer sighed. "In the future, I want my privacy, and I mean it."

Earl bowed like some old servant of yore, and Ezer sniffed haughtily like a prince. "I might have nothing left of my old life, but I have some pride still, and I deserve my personal privacy, and I won't be the subject of gossip between my alpha and his servant."

"I'm sorry, sir," Earl said. "I overstepped in my urge to protect you while Ned was at school."

Ezer's anger deflated, and he sat at the table. "I'm too tired to stay angry. Just don't do it again." He turned to Ned. "Show me those math problems. I'll help you."

Ned wordlessly pushed his math assignments over, and Ezer grinned as he took them up. "Oh, these are fun ones, Ned. Look..."

Ned dismissed Earl with a wave and bent over his omega's shoulder to see the problems. The solutions still didn't make a lick of sense even when Ezer was done working them out, but he loved seeing Ezer so happy.

"Let's do the next one."

Ned agreed.

He wished things could stay this easy between them forever, but he also knew that was too good to be true. Post-partum drop was a real thing, and Ezer was likely to be handful during it.

But Ned would handle him.

Ned loved him.

# PART FOUR

## The Break

# Chapter Twenty-Eight

EZER'S ENTIRE BODY ached, and his hole was constantly dripping with slick and Ned's cum. He was exhausted and enormous, and horny, and he spent most of his time sleeping, eating, or fucking. *And*, if he wasn't too tired, doing math problems for Ned's homework and for himself for fun.

Ezer hadn't called his brothers again, and no one in his family had reached out as far as he knew. He trusted Ned to tell him if Amos had texted. So, given the lack of care shown for him, Ezer figured he was alone in this world outside of Ned's devotion. His brothers hadn't bothered to check in, and his own da, for whom he'd done all this, was presumably too busy making love to the man he'd shared an illicit and life-altering heat encounter with, safe in his nice lakeside apartment, to make sure that Ezer was all right, to see if his pregnancy was progressing well, to see if his "favorite son" was safe.

Sometimes Ezer thought he was a fool.

Other times, he knew he was.

"Please," he begged, clinging to Ned's hand. "I just need it one more time before you go."

Ned laughed and kissed his hair. "I would, baby, but I have to leave now—like right now—because I'm already late."

"So what?"

"It's important. I have too much going on at school right now, and I can't afford to bring attention to myself," Ned said, and then stood to go. "I'll be home as soon as I can. Rest."

Ezer stayed in the soft blankets, feeling the babies moving inside him. They flipped and kicked, and sometimes it seemed they wrestled each other like puppies, though surely not. Sibling rivalry couldn't start in the womb, could it?

Ezer ate and napped by the pool for the rest of the afternoon. Earl had gone to the grocery store, and he reveled in being alone in the house. It was the best way to be, in his opinion, if he couldn't have Ned with him. He loved the silence of it, and the fact he could let down his guard entirely, just breathe.

It was only after Ezer's first nap by the pool that Ned's words fully registered: *"I have too much going on at school right now, and I can't afford to bring attention to myself."*

There'd been something in the way he'd said it. He wasn't talking about classes. He wasn't talking about schoolwork. He was talking about people. And Ezer knew exactly which people he was obliquely referring to: Braden and Finch.

Were they harassing Ned now? Tormenting him the way they'd tormented Ezer? But how? Ned was enormous. He could take both of those assholes down easily. But Ned was also a softie. He was gentle on the inside. Braden and Finch could easily hurt him with their words alone.

Because Ned was, at heart, a coward.

Sure, he'd been enraged when Braden had confronted him by the garden gate, but that was the reaction of any alpha when his pregnant omega was threatened. Ned would never do anything to protect *himself*. Ezer was sure Ned would let Braden and Finch bully him.

But what could Ezer do to help him? Nothing. He was pregnant, small and huge at the same time. Unwieldy. That was what he was now. Not to mention so very trapped. So Ned would have to deal with it all on his own. There was nothing Ezer could do to relieve any pressure or discomfort his alpha might be facing at school.

The week before when Earl had been at the store and Ned at school, Ezer had taken the opportunity to snoop. He'd perused the whole house, looking into Ned's room still decorated with his childhood things, and the guest rooms, and even Lidell's bedroom…

He needed to ask Ned what the plan was for his father's residence when the babies came. Were they going to live here with Lidell forever? Or was Lidell going to stay gone and find his own place? Or was he planning to return to live with them after the children came?

Ezer wasn't sure about the idea of living with a man he hadn't even met yet while trying to care for two babies. It wasn't like he was an old pro at baby care, though he'd helped with Rodan. He knew post-partum drops could be rough, and he didn't think it would help to have a stranger around for it.

But those were worries for another day. Today, his mind was preoccupied with what sorts of troubles Ned had been keeping from him. What sorts of issues he'd been facing on his own. They were a team now, or were becoming one, anyway. They should work as a team in all ways.

Eventually, Ezer got tired of chasing the circles of his own thoughts and went back into the house and down to the nest to get his advanced calculus book.

As he settled back at the table by the pool, starting on some math problems that appeared deliciously complicated, he heard a noise from near the garden gate. He glanced in that direction, and, seeing nothing, decided it must be the squirrels he'd seen earlier in the day chasing each other.

He squinted at the equation, noting that the letters didn't move around on him, and he wondered why that was. It always seemed unfair that they wouldn't just stay still like that when they were in actual words.

"Well, look at you, Cocksleeve, ripe as a peach, and still full of a nut, too, I bet."

Ezer's blood ran cold. His heart thumped so hard he saw spots and felt the sudden restless movements of his babies inside, jolted by his adrenaline flooding their tiny bodies as well.

Lifting his head, Ezer took in Braden leaning against the garden gate, insolent and tousled in his school uniform. He must have climbed the fence in the garden and not landed cleanly, because the knees of his pants were grass-stained, and his blazer had dirt on it.

Ezer opened his mouth to call for help, but Braden said, "Don't bother. I know you're alone here. Ned's family has always kept a distressingly low number of staff, don't you think? Bet you're regretting that right about now."

Ezer swallowed, and his tongue was dry.

"Ned's been holding out on us at school," Braden said, casually. "Refusing to talk to us, telling us nothing. But no one goes absent from school that long without consequences, not unless there's an omega in heat involved."

Ezer's throat spasmed. He could barely breathe. He'd assumed that Ned had told everyone at school the story about being the hero alpha to handle Ezer's surprise heat. Though he supposed it shouldn't be too unexpected that Ned had simply offered no explanation, and no excuses. That was like him, too.

Braden opened the gate and crossed the threshold. "What happened, Cocksleeve? Did you realize he was in love with you, and you figured that by letting him knot and breed you, he'd save you from your miserable, shitty life?"

The babies kicked hard inside.

"Or did you go into heat early, like so many trash omegas do, and he was the closest alpha when the time was right? Serendipity and all that."

Ezer's jaw felt wired shut. He wanted to yell, to call for help, even if there was no one in the house, maybe a neighbor might hear. But his throat wouldn't cooperate. He remembered rough hands on him, holding him in the dirt, and Ned's foot on his chest. He remembered the way Braden had tugged on his pants, getting them down, trying to…

Not taking his eyes off Braden, Ezer felt around the table for the tablet Ned had given him. It wasn't there. He must have left it down in the nest when grabbing the workbook.

Braden drew up alongside the table, loomed over Ezer and took one long, deep inhale. "You smell amazing. Always have. I wonder why? Never thought I'd like to fuck trash until you came along, and since then I've wanted to find out what'll make you squeal. I've got a good imagination, but it's never as good as the real thing."

Ezer choked.

"And now you're all round with a baby and sexier than ever. Do your nipples leak yet? Do you let Ned have a taste? Suppose I have a suck and see what I get, what do you say?"

Ezer's head swam.

"How will Ned feel after I've used you? He won't mind if I sample that ass and leave a deposit of alpha semen to ease you through the long day without him home, will he? It'd be like a favor right?" He smirked. "The babe won't know the difference between his cum and mine. You'll like it, too. I promise." He reached out to touch Ezer's chin.

Ezer knocked his hand away. "Don't touch me."

"Oh, look at you, still have some fight in you? That's sweet. Ned clearly hasn't been doing his job properly. You should be bending over to offer me your hole by now." Braden's lips twisted. "But I like a challenge."

"I will kill you."

"Kill me?" Braden leaned close. Ezer could feel his breath on his face. "With what? Your glares? Your weak little arms?"

Ezer lunged, aiming for Braden's throat, but he wasn't fast or strong enough. Somehow, he ended up with his back to Braden's front, one arm twisted behind him, and Braden's hand on his throat. He felt exposed and vulnerable, his rounded belly sticking out and his groin unprotected. His heart pounded, his vision swam, and his stomach shifted wildly as the babies wrestled.

"I'm going to bend you over this table," Braden said in his ear, "and teach you a thing or two about being fucked. Make some slick, Cocksleeve, while you still have a chance."

To Ezer's horror, his body obeyed. He didn't know if it was the scent of Braden's alpha pheromones, or the dread of what was to come, but his body produced a rush of slick, even as his eyes filled with tears. He struggled, but Braden was stronger than he was, and ruthless, too. He dug his fingers into Ezer's neck and squeezed.

"Go on and pass out," Braden encouraged. "Wake up with my dick in your ass. You'll be aware for enough of it. It'll be a good message to Ned, won't it? He's too egotistical these days. Thinks he can ignore me? Deny me what I want? I'm a fucking Tenmeter, and I can just *take it.*"

Ezer was forced over the table, his chest against it, his stomach taut with gravity and still moving with the agitation of the babes. He felt their reaction to his fear, and it amplified his terror. Struggling just earned him a smack on his ass so hard that tears fell down his cheeks.

"Get ready for a real alpha cock. I've got a thick one," Braden said, opening his pants. Ezer felt the hot, slick head of Braden's dick on his buttocks. He fought again and earned another harsh slap to his already smarting ass cheek.

"Please," Ezer whimpered. "Don't. Please. Stop." He hadn't meant to beg. But the words tumbled from his mouth all the same. "Please don't do this—" Braden's cockhead touched his hole. "Oh, fuck. Please! No!"

Braden pushed lightly, testing his entrance. Ezer braced himself.

"What the fuck is going on here?" an unfamiliar and deadly-dark voice came from the living room of the house. "Get your hands off him. Now."

Braden flinched and then raised his hands, backing away from Ezer.

Flicking his gaze up, Ezer saw a tall, bearded alpha with dark eyes and an enraged expression standing beside a handsome, young, shocked-looking omega with a baby in his arms. The baby started wailing.

The babies inside Ezer kicked angrily. His knees went weak, and he collapsed to the rough concrete. Braden stood there, cock out, eyes wide, and a terrified expression on his face.

"What's going on here?" the alpha asked again, stalking forward, eyes cutting between Braden and Ezer.

"He wanted me to," Braden said quickly. "He begged me for it, sir."

Ezer shook wordlessly, a cold rage racing through him. He felt helpless, like when he was trying to read and the letters wouldn't stop swimming, only now it was language that wouldn't come to him.

"Is he yours to fuck?"

"Yes!"

Ezer shook his head.

The alpha's eyes grew blacker. "He says he's not."

"Well, no, but…but!" Braden sounded confused, but when

he spoke again, he was more confident. "Sir, he begged me to fuck him. Pleaded for my semen. He said he needed it. Couldn't live without it. I mean, he's pregnant and in need of alpha semen. His alpha neglects him, so I was doing him a favor."

The alpha took an inventory of Ezer and glared at Braden again. His omega whispered something, and the alpha nodded. Braden kept babbling, zipping his cock away, now sounding completely at ease and nonchalant. "Anyway, as I said, he wanted me to do it. C'mon, he bent over the table and exposed himself to me. I'm only nineteen and an alpha. All those hormones, you know? What else was I supposed to do?"

"You're Tenmeter's son," the alpha said.

"I am," Braden said, imperious, as if the reminder he was a Tenmeter gave him the assurance that he would definitely get away with this.

Ezer wanted to vomit because he suspected that he would. Even if Ned believed Ezer, no one else would, and what could Ned do against the Tenmeter family?

"And who are you?" Braden asked, running his fingers through his hair, and straightening his blazer.

"Heath Clearwater."

The name rang in the air and Braden seemed to lose some of his pomp, but he maintained his air of coolness, sticking out his hand. "Good to meet you, sir. I hear you have many business deals with my father."

"Is that what you hear?" Heath said, darkly. "Perhaps that won't be true for long."

Braden sniffed. "Who else would you do business with, sir, if not my father? There's no one at his level."

"I could put someone at his level," Heath said, but at another whisper from his omega, he changed the topic. "What do you think your father will say when you're arrested this afternoon for the attempted rape of a pregnant omega?"

Braden scoffed. Then, as Heath's gaze didn't waver, and the omega typed something into his cell phone with one thumb, while juggling the infant in the other arm, Braden paled. "You don't need to do that, sir. Like I said, he wanted it."

"I don't think he did," Heath said. "I heard 'no' very distinctly, and you had him restrained."

"It was a game," Braden said. "You know how some omegas are, they want to cry and scream no while you take them. It gets them hot."

"Have a seat until the police arrive."

Braden's face turned from white to purple. "Sir, you will not involve the police in this," he commanded.

Heath strode toward Braden, all muscle and much taller, a fully grown alpha. He took him by the shoulders, steering him onto the chaise lounge. As he did, his omega—Adrien, Ezer thought he was called—came rushing over with the baby and knelt at Ezer's side.

"Are you all right?" he whispered, and when Ezer nodded—though he doubted his own answer was true, because he was far from all right—Adrien asked, "The baby? It's all right, too?"

"They're fine."

"Heath," Adrien said, taking hold of Ezer's arm and helping him to his feet. "I'm taking him inside. Surely, he won't need to talk with the police? Lidell will be upset enough that you saw his pregnant omega, and even more upset if the police do."

"He isn't Lidell's," Heath said.

Adrien blinked, confused. "Then whose…oh."

"Ned's," Heath said, not taking his eyes off Braden where he sat in the chair, looking perplexed and scared. It was an expression Ezer had never seen on Braden's face before, and he wished he could see it for longer, but Adrien was leading him away. The baby in Adrien's arms fussed and whined, and the sound made Ezer's heart pound even more.

"Come inside," Adrien said. "Where's your nest? Downstairs?"

Ezer nodded, but he didn't want to go down there now. Not to that restricted area with nowhere to run, no way to get out except for the way he came in. He started to breathe shallowly, and Adrien noticed, and seemed to understand exactly what was happening.

"Just to the sofa in the living room, then," he murmured. He had a lovely voice, very soothing and sweet. It matched his handsome face, and his baby was pretty too. Ezer just wished he would stop crying.

Ezer covered himself with a soft throw from over the sofa. He didn't want to be naked if the police decided to question him, and he had no doubt the police were coming. He was shaking and had a hard time breathing, but he glanced toward the clock on the wall. "Ned will be home soon."

"Where's Earl?" Adrien asked kindly.

"He went to buy groceries. Sometimes he meets his husband for dinner afterward."

Adrien nodded, and Ezer remembered that Simon was their servant, their sons' nurse, and Heath's long-time companion. Like Earl was to Ned.

"Why don't you tell me what happened?" Adrien said after he'd calmed the baby by lifting his shirt and placing a swollen tit in his mouth. "I can tell Heath, and he'll let the police know."

Ezer took in a shaky breath. "He—Braden Tenmeter—has tried to rape me before."

"When?"

"One time before this, about four and a half months ago now, I suppose. It was at my da's old apartment. He found me alone there. My da came home in time—"

"Dear God."

"Today, Braden came when he knew I was alone here, and he tried again."

Adrien's mouth tightened. "I don't want to ask this, but the police will want to know: do you have a history with him? Is this a jealousy thing or a lovers' quarrel?"

Ezer's head pounded. "No, I don't have history with him. Not like that. I went to his school, and he liked to bully and scare me." He licked his dry lips. "Over time, it escalated." Ezer's voice went small, and he stared at the nursing baby, watching his dark head bob as he drank. "I thought it was over. It should have been over. I did everything they wanted."

"Everything who wanted?"

"Them! All of them! I'm here, aren't I? Stuffed with children, just like my father wanted. Just like Ned's father wanted, too! And they promised me in exchange for giving it all up, for doing…for doing this—" he pointed at his stomach "I'd at least be safe. They said I'd be safe. Why wasn't I safe?" His voice cracked. "Ned said he'd protect me."

Adrien reached out and squeezed Ezer's fingers. The baby nursed a little longer, and then the sound of tires on the drive below and the ringing of the bell let Ezer know that the police had arrived.

"I'll let them in," Adrien said. "You wait here. If they want to talk with you, they'll need Ned's permission first. Hopefully we can skip that unpleasantness. Right?"

Ezer covered his face.

"But don't worry. Heath and I will handle everything with the police. Then I'll make tea for you. You need to rest. This has been a shock to the twins, I'm sure."

Adrien disappeared for a long time, and thankfully took the

again-crying baby with him. Ezer waited alone in the living room. The shadows danced over the floor as the breeze shook the ornamental trees outside. Eventually, Braden's shouts and denials from the pool drifted in on the breeze. Lies, all of them. Ezer wanted to defend himself, but he couldn't.

He didn't move.

Finally, Adrien came back with tea and a murmured explanation that he needed to speak with the police some more on Ezer's behalf and that he'd be right back.

Ezer didn't drink the tea.

The babies twisted inside him. They felt like they were tangled up and trying to undo the knot of their bodies.

Out of the corner of his eye, Ezer could see movement, heard a tussle, and then Braden's undignified scream of rage.

The clock chimed.

It was almost four. Ned would be home soon.

Ezer's stomach turned over and he staggered to the open area just outside the living room and vomited into the bushes out of sight of the police, Ned's uncle and his omega, and Braden.

Then he went back inside, curled up on the sofa, and waited.

Numb to the bone.

# Chapter Twenty-Nine

"YOU HAVE A lot of explaining to do."

Heath's voice took Ned by surprise as he opened the garden gate and stepped into the pool area, where he'd expected to find Ezer sunbathing or napping.

"Uncle," Ned said smiling anxiously. "You're here? I wasn't expecting you."

Heath glared.

"I, uh, has Earl—"

"Earl isn't here. Your omega is here, and he's been assaulted."

Ned's stomach dropped, and a sour taste lurched into his mouth. "Assaulted? What? How?" He didn't wait for Heath's answer, though, rushing through to the house to find Ezer curled up on the sofa, covered with a soft blanket, and with Adrien and the new baby in the loveseat beside him.

Ned didn't take the time to greet Adrien, instead dropping to his knees beside Ezer.

"Ezer? Are you all right?" He was met by a dark grimace. His mind raced and he knew without having to be told. "I'll kill Braden Tenmeter. I'll *fucking* kill him." He rose, his heart thumping, his blood rushing with white rage, fist clenched, and murder in mind.

Heath took hold of his shoulders and shook him. "He's been arrested. I saw to that."

Ned huffed in and out his nose. "I'll kill him."

"I know," Heath said, almost like he thought Ned should. "But I also know that right now you can't get to him, *and* I know that you need to see to your omega."

Ned looked down at Ezer, his blue eyes shut, and his cheeks pale. He sat next to him, relieved when Ezer didn't flinch away. "Baby, are you okay? Did he hurt you? Did he hurt the babies?"

Ezer shrugged at the first question and shook his head at the second.

"We should go," Adrien said, standing.

"No, there are answers I want from Ned," Heath said, darkly.

"Not today."

"I'm not leaving them here. They're children."

"They're nearly the age I was when you gave me Michael," Adrien said.

"And you were too young!" Heath shouted. "At least I was a grown man. They're *both*—" He broke off and then added, "They're too young!"

"Shh," Adrien said. "You'll wake Laya. We can't stay here, Heath. This is his home, he's the alpha here, and this problem is his duty to deal with. Now is not the time to interrogate Ned. Think." Adrien took hold of Heath's arm. "Ezer needs his alpha…"

Heath shot Ned another glare and then said, "Take good care of him. He's your responsibility. Those babes in his belly? Your responsibility, too. You let him down today and it almost cost you—and him—everything. It may well still have." He snarled. "How you allowed your greedy, rotten father to talk you into breeding an omega at your age—"

Adrien interrupted him. "Heath, not now."

It seemed to be all his uncle could do not to launch into a rant. Ned wanted him gone, though. He needed to attend to Ezer.

"What on earth?" Earl's voice rang in the room. "Oh, Mr. Clearwater, Adrien, sirs, let me get you tea, and what is Ezer doing upstairs, oh, what's...what's this?" he asked, seeing Ezer's face, and everyone else's expressions as well. He dropped his grocery bags and rushed over. "What's happened? What's the matter?"

Adrien sighed.

"I'm going down to the nest," Ezer said, dully, standing and moving with a slowness that struck fear into Ned's heart. Had he been violated? Was he hurt? Was there damage? Rage almost felled him again, and he fought the urge to storm the police station until he reached Braden to wring his puny neck.

Assuming Braden was still there. He was a Tenmeter, after all, and would be released as soon as money had passed hands. And then Ned would kill him. He'd murder him. He'd watch his face turn purple and then—

"Ned," Adrien said softly. "Your omega needs you."

Ned caught his uncle's eye and said, "I'll explain everything soon."

Heath nodded.

Adrien had pulled Earl aside and seemed to be informing him of the events of the afternoon. First fear and then anger slammed over Earl's face.

Ezer, though, was gone. He'd already left and taken the stairs down to the nest.

Ned followed him, his emotions a wail of extremity.

EZER DIDN'T WANT to be in the nest, but he couldn't be up in the living room with all those people either. Adrien had been kind, and Heath had been too, in his own way, but it was all too much.

Earlier, he'd been forced to bend over for Braden Tenmeter, and he'd felt the monster's cock against his hole. He'd been helpless to stop him. If Ned's uncle hadn't arrived—and why had he even come by?—he'd have been raped and violated, and not only himself but his unborn children would have had Braden's vileness forced on them, too.

He wanted to seal himself up into the nest.

He wanted to smash out the windows and jump to freedom.

He wanted to run away.

He wanted to hide.

Ezer stood stock-still in the middle of the room. He sensed Ned's presence behind him, advancing on him, about to touch him.

He screamed.

The sound echoed off the walls and ceiling and floor.

"Oh God!" Ned cried, flinging his arms around Ezer. "You're hurt. You're in pain. Baby, let me help you!"

Ezer yelled until his lungs were empty and then he slumped back into Ned's strength. Tears spilled over his cheeks, and he whispered, "He wrenched my arm. He pushed me over the table. He put his cock against my hole."

Ned growled and the sound was so loud it rattled Ezer's body.

"I was scared. He almost—he nearly—"

"I'll kill him," Ned said again.

Ezer shrugged off Ned's arms, and turned around, dropping the sheet he'd been draped in since Adrien had covered him with it earlier. "You should have dealt with him before now," he rasped. "You knew he was a problem. But you let him just keep on. You're a coward."

Ned's eyes widened. "He's Braden *Tenmeter*. What was I supposed to do?"

"Report him for attempted rape—"

"Heath already did that! And I'll back him up!"

"I meant the first time," Ezer said, cold creeping into his veins. "You told me I'd be safe as your omega. Your father promised my father the same too, didn't he? And yet you let a monster go without facing any repercussions for what he did to me, what you saw him do—"

"He was just—"

"He was just what?"

"I didn't think he'd try again!"

"With me? Or with any other omega?"

"With...with you. I was only thinking about you."

"Selfish. But even that wasn't enough, was it? Because he came here looking for me when he knew you weren't around, when he knew Earl was gone. What's been happening at school? What haven't you been telling me about? Why did he come hunting me today? Why?"

Ned's skin paled, and he swallowed hard. "Let's sit down. You're tired."

"I don't want to sit!" Ezer shouted, beginning to pace the room. "I hate this nest. There's no room to breathe, no air, no freedom. I want to go, but..." He jerked his hand toward the stairs. "Up there is too much to handle. Too many people, and *he* came for me up there. He was going to put his cock in my body, force our babies to be exposed to his cum, and there was nothing, nothing I could do to stop him! *You* could have stopped him, Ned! You could have stopped him ages ago!"

"If I'd turned him in after what happened in Roughs Neck for the Bright's powder and assaulting you, I'd have incriminated myself too!" Ned shouted, throwing his hands up.

Ezer pointed at him. "There! See? You weren't thinking of me. You were thinking of yourself."

"I was thinking of both of us."

Ezer shook his head. "Not that day. Not the day you put your foot on my chest. You were thinking of how you were going to get me out of it without impacting *your* situation. That's not thinking only of me. And at school…there's something going on. You look so ashamed. What's been happening at school? Tell me."

"He's been hounding me. I've been ignoring him. But he wouldn't let it go. Coming up to me every day. Wanting to know if *you* were the reason I'd been gone so long. He's obsessed with you—and me, but mainly you."

"'Obsessed'?"

"Yeah, he came up to me saying, 'I thought Co—" Ned seemed to choke. He changed what he was saying, but Ezer knew the truth. "He said, 'I thought Ezer switched back to St. Hauers.' But he'd had a friend check it out, and found out you weren't there. And then he was all up in my face, all snarly and smarmy, saying, 'He's not there. It's like he's nowhere to be found at all. Like an omega after a heat, when they're confirmed pregnant.' I just walked off, but he wouldn't shut up about it. Always coming up to me and asking, 'How was his tight ass? Was it sweet? Was it good? How was his first heat, did he scream for your dick?' It's been endless. He's obsessed. I just wanted him to stop."

"So you did what?"

Ned flushed. "I ignored him."

"Ned, you did nothing." Ezer pointed his finger into Ned's chest. "You. Did. Nothing."

"I'll do something now," Ned said, turning his back on Ezer, and starting for the stairs. "I'll kill him. With my bare hands."

Ezer almost let him go. He almost let him walk out of the room and do whatever it was an alpha did when he wanted to destroy another man.

But he couldn't.

Not now.

Not when he hadn't been fucked since that morning.

His body was already rebelling. His heart was racing. His womb felt tight. He felt like he couldn't breathe properly.

"Wait," he said, and his voice was faint enough that he was surprised Ned heard him and stopped. "You have to fuck me first."

Ned turned to him, eyes dark, and a kind of fear on his face that Ezer hadn't seen before. "You'll let me?"

Ezer sneered. "I have no choice, do I?"

Their coupling was fast, the way Ezer demanded but didn't actually *want*, and it left him feeling broken inside in a way he wasn't sure would ever heal.

After, he fell asleep on the sofa, curled on his side, a blanket draped over him, and Ned's cum left deep inside.

# PART FIVE

## Courage

# Chapter Thirty

NED DIDN'T KNOW how to fix things.

Nothing was as it was supposed to be now. Ned still fucked Ezer, and left him satisfied and filled with his cum, but the burgeoning trust and friendship between them had been severed again. He didn't know how to get it back.

As the police had proceeded with prosecuting Braden, the atmosphere at school had become intolerable. If Ned wasn't certain Ezer would accuse him of being cowardly again, he'd just drop out and change schools.

Instead, he trudged along, going to classes, enduring his new outcast state. He was infamous. He'd knocked up an omega and taken down Braden Tenmeter, and all the wealthiest, most entitled alphas were nervous around him now. Betas avoided him, too, though he didn't know why. Maybe it was his impending fatherhood? He didn't know for sure.

But it was the wary eyes of omegas that hurt him the most. They all stared at him as if he'd taken one of their own against his will. As if *he'd* raped Ezer. Ned supposed the idea of being pregnant in high school was terrifying to them, too. And they should be afraid, because what he and Ezer had done was no joke. It was enormous and terrifying. None of it had ever been a joke. Not even a little bit, not from the start.

They'd been misled by their parents and his hormones, and now they were in a position that no person—no alpha, beta, or omega—envied. At least Ezer got to stay home, sheltered from all of this shame and humiliation, this social outcast status. At least he was spared that.

At night, Ned came home and did his homework, doing math problems with his quiet, withdrawn omega who showed him the solutions with no enthusiasm. Ezer was someone else now. Someone he'd never been before, and Ned hated it. He even told Ned to pick the babies' names. Ezer didn't fight him anymore over anything.

It was exhausting.

"I don't know what to do," Ned said, his head in his hands, and his father's hand on his shoulder. "He's so unhappy. All I want is for him to be happy."

"Omegas are like this," Lidell told him, in exact opposition to what he'd told him before about the happily pregnant omegas of the world. "They're hard to please."

"You really have no advice for me?"

"I'm afraid not. But I'm going to be leaving town again. This time for the islands. Tropical drinks and omegas wearing little thongs and nothing else. I can afford it now, so why not?"

Why not? Because his son was facing a trial with Lidell's former business associate—because, yes, Tenmeter had ended those contracts—and was dealing with an unhappy omega who was pregnant with twins and was only a month away from giving birth to them.

"When will you be back?"

"Oh, before too long. You'll barely have time to miss me."

Ned took in Lidell's anxious expression and realized his father couldn't be the man he needed him to be right now. Lidell was incapable of allowing any attachment to form with an omega, even with his son's, for fear of losing them. Losing Santino had destroyed his heart, and he didn't have the courage to risk what was left of it, even to support Ned and Ezer. It was yet another way in which his father had been, and perhaps always would be, useless in his life. Hadn't he just been congratulating himself on having a father who loved him? What good was love if it had no courage behind it?

"Yes, you should go," Ned said. "Enjoy yourself."

Lidell rubbed his hand over Ned's hair affectionately. "Earl will take care of you, and if you have any problems with the boy, just call Heath. He's got his fingers in this pot now, might as well let him stir it."

Ned followed his father to his room and watched as he finished his packing. Before he knew it, Ned was on the front porch waving goodbye to Lidell again. Or rather, standing there with his arms crossed watching his father go.

"He's always thought of himself first," Earl said, from over Ned's shoulder. "I'm glad you've grown into a different kind of man."

But that was not what Ezer thought, was it? Ezer believed Ned thought of himself first and Ezer a distant second, and Ned still wasn't sure how to prove that it wasn't true.

Maybe because it was. After all, even now, he was more focused on what he wanted—Ezer's trust—and less on what Ezer wanted—to feel safe again.

He went down to the nest and found Ezer asleep. He was sleeping more and more these days, which the doctor said was appropriate. Growing two babies was very tiring work.

Ned watched him sleep on the sofa, his dark curls against a white pillow, his lips stretched into a mild grimace, and his beautiful eyes hidden beneath silky-smooth eyelids. Even in rest, he didn't look peaceful.

How could he fix this?

For weeks, he didn't know.

IT WAS A rainy Tuesday when Ezer's oldest brother, Yissan, reached out to Ned asking for a meeting at a local park. Ned had never seen Yissan before or talked with him and was surprised by his boldness in reaching out to an alpha, but he agreed to meet him.

"Did you have to skip school to be here?" Yissan asked, motioning Ned beneath the wide umbrella he held up to the relentless pitter-patter from the sky.

Ned didn't resist the tug but felt uncertain being so close to another omega. Yissan was undeniably beautiful with wavy dark hair, ebony eyes, and a lush mouth many alphas would fantasize about. He was also tall, well-built, and held himself with a confidence Ezer lacked except when he was angry. Ned tried to hold his body away from Yissan's, not wanting to show too much impropriety, and unsure how Ezer would feel about him being snug under an umbrella with his omega brother. Though Ezer wasn't a possessive type, at least not of Ned, given that he didn't seem to care about him much at all anymore.

Ned said nothing, waiting as Yissan lit a cigarette and blew a plume of smoke into the air. The gray sky hung low, and the duck pond they stood beside echoed it in steely, glittering misery. It fit Ned's mood these days. The season had turned, and so had his hopes for his life with Ezer.

"How's my brother?" Yissan asked, picking a bit of tobacco from his tongue, and flicking it away.

"He's…" Ned wasn't sure what to say. Miserable? Scared? Enormous? Resigned and defeated? "He's going through a lot and could use some support from his brothers."

Yissan nodded. "You must think I'm very cold, that we all

are."

"I don't know how brothers are supposed to act. I'm an only child, but what I do know is Ezer's hurting, and I'm not enough to fix it."

"Aren't alphas supposed to be enough? Isn't that the point of the nest?" Yissan challenged, his dark brows drawing low.

"Maybe that's how it is when an omega is older, when the pregnancy was wanted, but with Ezer neither of those things were true."

"He's been abandoned by his family and forced to carry a child—"

"Twins."

"Oh." Yissan's brows twitched. "I hadn't heard." His expression grew even more cloudy. "I'm the only one who remembers Shan and Flo's birth. None of the others were born yet. I was five." His voice trembled. "Da was in agony. I could hear his screams through the entire house. He begged to be killed, to be put out of the misery of it."

Ned shivered. "It was that bad?"

"All births are hard. Twins aren't what we were designed for, our bodies aren't meant to handle it. And Ezer is small, much smaller than Da. He's going to be in danger, you realize."

Ned's knees trembled. He'd assumed that Ezer would be fine. Sure, Dr. Savage had mentioned being worried, but it'd been so offhand that Ned hadn't thought any more about it afterward. But that was how people were in front of omegas, weren't they? And Dr. Savage probably hadn't wanted to scare Ned either. Unlike Yissan who seemed bent on terrifying him.

"Why did you call me out here?" Ned asked, crossing his arms over his chest and resisting the urge to step out from under the umbrella and allow the rain to pour down on him.

"I should say it was out of concern for my baby brother,

shouldn't I?"

Ned frowned.

"It's a lot less virtuous than that. I need your uncle's help. As an omega, I can't reach out to Heath Clearwater and beg for his intervention in my life, but as my brother-in-law and his nephew, you can."

"What kind of help do you need?"

"I need out of this contract my father is setting up for me." Yissan shivered, and Ned didn't know if it was from the cold wind that cut over them both at that moment, or the idea of whatever heat/breeding/marriage arrangement George Fersee had cooked up for his eldest.

"Who's it with?"

Yissan's eyes went darker than Ned thought possible. So dark they shone like polished ebony. "My lover's father."

"Your..." Ned paused to gather his thoughts. "But you're supposed to be a virgin for your first heat. It improves the price."

Yissan gave him an exasperated look. "You are so young, aren't you? Naïve. My poor brother. Stuck with someone as innocent as you." He shook his head. "Yes, I'm supposed to be many things, but omegas aren't dolls that exist to please alpha cocks. I'm a human being, and I have motivations and urges that exist outside my father's plans for my asshole and womb."

"Uh, yes, of course." Ned's mind reeled.

"My lover is a beta," Yissan said quietly. "John Stone."

"Of the *Trace Stone* Stones?" Trace was a powerful alpha out of Summerton, who summered in Wellport and sent his sons to school here.

"I've been in love with him for years. We met in high school."

*Like me and Ezer*, Ned thought.

"We tried to resist each other." Yissan's lips twisted into a bittersweet smile. "Well, he did. I was insistent that we take advantage of what alone time his status as a beta afforded us. I wanted him from the start."

*Like I wanted Ezer.*

"We always knew it wasn't going to last between us, that one day I'd have to move on to an alpha who could give me the children I want, and my father the money he wants, but neither of us ever imagined that the alpha would be John's own father."

"You'd imagined someone your own age. A son of the peerage."

"But it turns out Trace Stone has wanted me for a long time. He had my father put a pin in my mating and heats until he was ready to negotiate a proper price for me."

Ned wrinkled his nose. "That's disturbing."

Yissan nodded. "He's been through four omegas. Two sons each and then ditched them. My father refused to give me to him unless he promised to treat me differently. The contract states five sons and a minimum of twenty years with me as his only omega."

The sheer misery in Yissan's voice made Ned's blood run cold.

"Your father has a habit of this," Ned said. "Putting his sons in horrible positions with no way out."

"There *has* to be a way out. I won't go through with it."

"They'll make you. Somehow, they'll find a way to make you."

"Consent still matters. It's still the law," Yissan said, tossing aside the half-smoked cigarette and turning to grip Ned's forearms. He pulled him close enough for Ned to smell his tobacco-laced breath. "Your uncle has to help me. *You* have to help me."

"How can I help you when I can't even help Ezer?" When everything Ned did to help him just made his life worse and ended up with him stuffed full of two babes who might, according to Yissan, be too much for him to handle, who might steal his life?

"You need to set up an appointment for me. With Heath Clearwater."

Yissan sounded so sure. Wasn't not talking to his uncle where Ned had gone wrong with this thing from Ezer from the start?

"All right," Ned agreed. "I'll see what I can do, but I'm not going to promise anything."

Yissan drew back, satisfied, his face stamped with emotion. Not relief, but some kind of hopeless hope. "Thank you. Please, just—thank you."

"It doesn't mean anything will come of it."

Yissan nodded, and then lifted his umbrella away from Ned's head. The rain was bitterly cold as it hit his scalp and slipped down his face. Ducks floated on the water, uncaring of the drizzle.

"Wait," Ned said. "I helped you, now I need you to help me."

Yissan stopped and turned around, his jaw tight. "All right. Quid pro quo is fair."

"What does an omega want from an alpha? What do they want most of all?"

Yissan pondered Ned, then scrutinized the sky, letting rain hit his face for a moment before righting the umbrella. "They want to know they're safe with them. Safe to love and be loved. Safe to be real."

"Ezer knows he can be real with me. He's never been fake. He fights and argues and gives as good as he gets." Until recently. Until his safety was stolen from his nest.

Yissan's mouth curved into an amused smile. "Sounds like Ezer. Then make sure he keeps on feeling that way. That's all an alpha can give an omega. Love, affection? That's all too much to ask, unless you were already a love match. Omegas need respect.

They need empowerment. They need to be allowed to decide."

Their conversation was at an end, and Ned let him walk away. Heading back toward school, ready to face the consequences of skipping out for half the day, Ned turned over what Yissan had asked of him and what he'd said about an omega's needs. He needed to reach out to his uncle. But more than that, he needed to make a plan.

Operation Make Ezer Safe.

Now if only he knew where to start.

# Chapter Thirty-One

EZER SAT BY the pool, wrapped in a heavy blanket, watching the blue water ripple in the wind coming in off the sea. The season had changed and so had he. He was tired, monstrously so, and bigger than he'd ever imagined being. His stomach bulged so much he had a hard time sleeping, and getting fucked was becoming an exhausting burden he felt compelled by his hormones to bear.

He was daring himself right now. Sitting in the place where the crime had taken place. Letting himself be exposed to the elements, letting himself be vulnerable.

After the attack from Braden, he found it hard to leave the nest, but he also hated it down there. So airless, so lifeless. All walls keeping him contained and safe, and with far too much silence. He never listened to music now, or watched television. Sometimes he didn't even know what he thought about all day. It was a wall of white noise in his head until Ned came home, fucked him, ate dinner with him, and then broke out his homework.

Ezer didn't even work problems for fun anymore. Just for duty to his alpha. And those were very easy, very boring problems.

Unlike the problems of his life. Those were complicated and unsolvable. Equations that piled up on top of each other and couldn't be untangled, turning the math of his life into letters that heaved around and refused to make sense.

Perhaps that thought made no sense.

He didn't care.

But for some reason today he'd woken up, and a flicker of his old self spoke to him. "I won't let them take it all from me." So with Earl's help, he'd made it up the stairs with his enormous belly, and now he sat outside, exposed to the elements. A cold summer rain was coming.

The babies twisted around inside. He put his hand on his taut stomach, feeling their feet and hands press against his skin. He wasn't sure what he thought of the life inside him. He was afraid in too many ways to know whether he loved them or not. He wasn't sure he was going to survive this. The doctor made increasingly dark noises whenever he came for a check-up, muttering under his breath about the smallness of Ezer's hips, and then he'd smile at Ned and tell him everything was fine.

Ezer didn't think everything was fine.

Nothing had been fine since his da had been kicked out, since he'd signed that contract without having it read aloud to him first, since he'd sacrificed himself on the altar of another person's happiness. And for what? Where was his da now? Was it worth it to have sold himself to a man who hadn't fought for him, only conspired to work within the system for an outcome pleasing to everyone but Ezer?

Ezer didn't know how to contain all his feelings and dread, all his disappointment and disillusionment. He sat alone knowing that Ned would come home eventually. Maybe looking forward to his arrival, and maybe not. He didn't look forward to much of anything. He definitely didn't look forward to giving birth.

The skin beneath his hand jolted again. Terror vibrated just beneath his consciousness. He could lean into it or lean away. For sanity's sake, he leaned away.

The gray of nothing was better than the fire of panic. He breathed in and out. He tried not to think. He was outside. By his own choice. He'd won this much at least.

The rain came down.

NED MET UP with Heath at Sivian, skipping school again in order to enlist his uncle's help with Yissan's situation. Ned had gone into the meeting optimistic, only to be dressed down before the drinks had even arrived for absolutely *everything*.

"You have no career, no future planned," Heath stormed. "You planned to what? Rely on the boy's father's money forever? What kind of alpha does that?"

Lidell's name hung in the air between them.

"What you've done to this boy is life-changing, life-creating, and life-destroying all at once. I don't know what to do with you."

Adrien was at the luncheon, too, wearing a scarf and nursing the new little one under it. He put a hand on Heath's arm to calm him down. "Ned didn't come here to be scolded. He came here for help."

Heath scrubbed a hand over his head, took a calming breath, and then said, "What he needs is *not* help! What he *needs* is a swift kick in the ass."

Adrien sighed and turned to Ned saying, "I'm sure you're overwhelmed right now, but you understand that Ezer is scared. Just give him time. Be there for him. In time, he'll understand you better." He smiled up at Heath. "Just like I did with your uncle."

"Don't believe that," Heath said, rolling his eyes. "He ran away. Ran off back to college and took Michael with him. Don't let him fool you."

It was Adrien's turn to roll his eyes. "Well, you'd kept a very important secret from me, and I was going through a heavy post-partum drop."

"Exactly," Heath said, turning back to Ned. "Omegas aren't as easy as all that. I know people like your father like to believe otherwise, but he's never lived with one, so what would he know? Omegas are difficult creatures."

"Humans," Adrien corrected. "And we're not difficult. We just have minds of our own, which troubles alphas more than it should."

Heath stayed focused on Ned and went on, "Which is why *you* had *no* business getting one pregnant at the age of nineteen."

"Adrien was twenty when—"

Heath raised a dark brow at him, and Ned went silent. There was apparently a difference between a rich, older alpha impregnating a twenty-year-old omega, and a dependent and stupidly young alpha doing the same to a nineteen-year-old.

"If you want to salvage this situation, then convince Ezer you're worth sticking around for," Heath said, jabbing the tip of his forefinger at the table. "Figure out how to do that, and then *do it*. No matter what it takes. Otherwise, contracts be damned, he will leave you. And he should."

"But how can I prove that to him?" Ned asked. He hadn't asked Heath here to talk about Ezer. He was here to talk about Yissan's request, but Adrien had asked about Ezer as soon as they'd sat down, and Ned had been too honest. That had set Heath off scolding, and now here they were. Ned was as lost as ever about how to make things right with his omega.

Heath shrugged. "If you can't figure it out, the other option is to let him leave."

"What?" Ned asked, his heart in his throat.

"He never wanted this—you, the children, the contract, correct?"

Ned nodded.

Heath sighed. "Then, if you care about his happiness, you have to give him the option to go."

Adrien snorted. "Like you gave me an option?"

"Oh please. As if you really wanted to go."

"I was at my dorm with our son. I think it was clear I wanted to go. At that time."

"He was in a box. You had our baby in a box in your dorm room, like he was a pet rabbit."

"Heath—"

"You didn't want to go, or you wouldn't have come home with me."

Adrien shrugged. "You made a compelling argument, what with the begging and pleading and—"

Heath shot him a look and Adrien stopped talking, but a chuckle remained on his lips.

"You have to accept, though, that if you give him the right to go, he might take it."

Ned felt dizzy at the thought. He didn't know how to be a good alpha yet, and he didn't know anything about fatherhood, but the idea of Ezer leaving, of him going away and leaving him with twins to care for was overwhelming. But if it was what Ezer needed…

Heath went on, "For what it's worth, you'll have to be willing to lose the children, too. Omegas are attached to their offspring." Adrien snorted again, but Heath ignored him. "If you tell him the contract is void, that he can go, he'll take the babies with him."

Ned felt even sicker at that thought. He didn't know his sons yet, but he loved them all the same, and he wanted to do right by both Ezer and them. He was a kid, but he was brave enough to face this.

Heath continued, "As hard as that might sound, if you aren't up for the rigors of fatherhood yet, and if he's not interested in being with you seriously as your omega mate, then it could be for the best. End things now."

Ned's stomach swam up his throat.

A waiter approached and Heath waved him off. Ned was glad to have longer to collect himself before having to place an order for food he no longer wanted.

"But where would he go? His father won't take him in," Ned said. "He'd be penniless with two babies. He can't leave if he doesn't have a place to go." It made him sweat to imagine it, but he knew that if he were to make a true offer of freedom from this mistake they'd made, then he had to offer him the means to gain that freedom, too.

Heath regarded him with a stony, serious expression. "There are ways. The children will be my great-nephews. I'll settle money on both them and on Ezer. I'll even provide a small home for him in Fellson, so he can start fresh in a new city. He can claim to be a widower. No one will be the wiser unless he prompts someone to dig."

Ned wiped at his face, his heart pounding and feeling as if it would rip in two. "All right," he whispered. "Thank you."

"You don't want him to take the offer," Heath observed.

Ned shook his head. "I love him. But I love him too much for him to be with me out of obligation. I want him to be *happy*, even though I barely know what that looks like. I had it for maybe two days before it was destroyed again by Braden showing up at our nest. I'd rather he be happy without me, than miserable with me."

Adrien touched his hand. "That's beautiful, Ned."

Ned shrugged. It didn't feel beautiful. It felt awful, wrenching and world-ending, but he wasn't going to hurt Ezer more than he already had. Ezer had deserved autonomy and consent from the beginning. It was like Yissan had said, an omega should be allowed to decide for himself.

Speaking of Yissan—

"Thank you for doing all this for Ezer, Uncle, and I'll let you know what he says and how it progresses with him. But the main reason I asked you here is to discuss another problem. I was approached by another omega recently—"

"Another omega!" Adrien said, scandalized.

"It's not like that," Ned hastened to explain. "It's Yissan Fersee, Ezer's eldest brother. He's in trouble and wants help."

"What kind of trouble?"

"This is confidential?"

Heath scoffed, offended.

"I'm sorry. I just don't want to endanger him."

"Go on," Heath said. "Omegas who seek out an unrelated alpha for help have big demands. Bigger than can be accommodated, but let's hear it." Adrien took a little breath, and Heath patted his hand. "Not that I won't entertain the problem. Of course I will."

Adrien checked on little Laya beneath the nursing scarf and, finding him asleep, removed him from his teat, cradling him close and keeping his face shielded from the light. Adrien looked content and happy, and Ned took a moment to wish he could ever see Ezer just as content with their children.

"Yissan's problem is complicated."

"As I said it would be."

After Ned spelled out Yissan's situation, Heath sat back from the table, arms crossed over his chest, and a deep frown on his forehead.

"I thought you said this was complicated. This is straightforward. An omega has compromised himself, feels no guilt for it, and wants to shape his own future without his alpha father's hand in the matter."

Adrien looked up sharply, but Heath didn't seem to notice.

"Consent is the law," Ned pointed out. "Ezer didn't give true consent. He was coerced, and I believe Yissan will be coerced too."

Heath nodded. "Well, as abhorrent as I find his behavior with the beta, I can't say that I approve of the match his father is contemplating. Trace is known for the callous treatment of his omegas, and his omega sons as well. He also indulges in..." Heath caught Adrien's eye and then glanced away. "*Activities* that aren't always enjoyable for his partners. He likes that they don't enjoy it, from what I understand."

Yissan was in more danger than Ned had realized, but even if Trace Stone had been as pure as the driven snow in his intentions and treatment of omegas, the simple fact was that Yissan didn't want him.

"I have some lawyers on retainer who've dealt with omega rights cases in the past. I'll reach out to one of them tonight, and I'll fund Yissan's case. But what I cannot do is fund his life afterward. I have deep pockets, but I can't have every omega in Wellport and the known world coming to me for support."

"No, of course not," Ned agreed.

"But this young man is your family now, which makes him my family."

"Uncle?"

"Yes?"

"Is there an organization dedicated to helping omegas in situations like this? Lawyers who work to help them out of coercive situations, or worse?"

Heath tilted his head, meeting Ned's eyes. "Is that something that interests you? Helping omegas?"

"I love Ezer, and if he will stay with me, I want to make everything right for him, but how we got here wasn't okay. It wasn't true consent. I don't think it's right for other omegas to go through this. I'd like to stop it from happening again to someone else."

"I know some attorneys, yes, who're involved in fighting for omega rights. I can introduce them to you. Once things have settled in your life, perhaps you could do some volunteer work with their office."

Ned smiled, relieved at having a concrete way of making things happen. "Thank you, Uncle, for all of this. You have no idea how relieved I am to hear you can help Yissan." Ned had dreaded having to tell Ezer his older brother was being forced into a situation as bad or worse than the one Ezer had been coerced into.

"I can't promise the boy will be delivered from his fate, but Jeger Forest, one of the attorneys I mentioned, will know where to start."

Heath waved the waiter over, and they ordered their luncheon while Laya slept in Adrien's arms. After they'd eaten, and when they were on their way out of the door, Heath gave Ned a big hug.

"I'm stern with you because you need it."

"I know, and I do."

"You'll let Yissan know to await a call from my attorneys?"

"Yes."

"And I'll wait to hear from you about your omega. Don't let him go easily, Ned. If you love him, it'll be worth making sacrifices to make sure he stays."

Ned's throat tightened. "I'll show him how much I care for

and respect him somehow," Ned said.

"'Somehow'," Heath snorted, turning to relieve Adrien of Laya's weight, so Adrien could grab a hug as well. "'Somehow', he says."

Adrien scolded Heath again, but as Ned left the restaurant, he couldn't help but think back over all the discussions he'd had with Ezer, all the times Ezer had called him a coward, or questioned his motives. He couldn't stop himself from remembering his own father packing up and leaving.

Ned knew what kind of future he wanted to have, but he also accepted that he may not get it. Ezer made up half of the outcome, and he wasn't a doll. He couldn't be controlled. Ezer had made that clear from the start.

Ideas began to form, slowly but surely, and Ned made additional plans. There wasn't much he could do right away. Everything was set to a wait-and-see pattern, even the trial against Braden Tenmeter, but when the time came, he needed to have the plan in place.

Instead of going straight home, Ned took a seat in a sunny part of the nearby park to brainstorm the next steps. He wished Ezer could be there with him. He'd love the bright colors of the flowers.

Summer had arrived. Change was on its way.

# Chapter Thirty-Two

"YOU HAVE TO help them," Rodan's voice was small and his eyes bloodshot, as he stared at Ezer through the screen. "They're all scared, Ezer, and Father is *so angry*. Pete is scared, too. He hides from Father with the baby."

That was not the greeting that Ezer had expected when he'd picked up his tablet to answer a video call from the Fersee house. He'd expected Shan or Flo, or maybe Yissan, if he'd been recently contracted with an alpha. He'd expected their worry over his pregnancy, or questions about what to expect during their heats, or even questions of where to find Da.

But Rodan? Never.

"Rodie, what's going on?" Ezer said, shifting to get more comfortable in his body. The babies pushed against everything now. He was hungry all the time because they took up too much space inside, leaving too little for his stomach. His back ached. His *bones* ached. Pain was the only thing keeping him from sleeping his life away.

"Ezer, it's bad."

"Start at the beginning."

As Ezer listened to his brother lay out the dramas that had unfolded in the Fersee house over the last few weeks, his heart pounded. The twins had rebelled. Or Shan had, rather. The alpha Flo had been interested in had changed his mind on meeting Shan and insisted on having his first heat and breeding instead.

Shan had refused.

Flo had supported Shan's refusal.

Father had blown his top, trying to force Shan to sign the contract by threatening to give Flo's first heat to an elderly alpha who wouldn't have the stamina to satisfy him. Shan had still refused. Flo had as well.

Father had stormed and raged.

Then Yissan's turn had come. He'd delayed and made excuses until Father trapped him in a room with the alpha he'd chosen, and Yissan had to fight off the man's advances.

"Father said Yissan embarrassed him. There was shouting. Tables turned over. Yissan got a black eye. And Shan is leaving tomorrow with another alpha Father forced on him."

"How?"

"By threatening to punish both him and Flo. He said he'd trigger their heats and not allow them an alpha at all. He said that would teach them."

Ezer sucked in a horrified breath.

"Shan doesn't want to go. Flo has been locked into his room. He pounds on the door and screams to be let out constantly. Pete is hiding with Prince. I snuck into Father's library and found the number to call you. I don't know what to do. Do you, Ezer? Do you know?"

Ezer chewed on his bottom lip, listening to his baby brother's shaking voice, trying to come up with a plan. Any plan.

"Is Father there right now?"

"He's drinking in Pete's old nest, yelling about ungrateful sons."

It was madness to think he could change anything, but if he didn't act then he was condemning his brothers to a life like his own, and the very least his father deserved was to be confronted with the ugly fruit of his actions toward Ezer.

"All right. It might take some time, but I'm on my way."

"You can't leave," Rodan said, wide-eyed. "You're pregnant."

Ezer nodded, wondering where he could find something to wear that would fit over his swollen belly. The robe was enough for getting around the main part of the house if he was feeling shy, but it was insufficient for the street.

He'd need Earl's help. He fingered the soft blanket on the sofa. Or would he?

"I have a plan." It wasn't a good plan, but it was as good as Ezer could do right now, and it was the first thing he'd felt galvanized by in weeks. "You just keep yourself quiet and safe. It's going to be okay."

He had no idea if that was true, but everyone kept telling *him* that these days, including his doctor and alpha, so he decided it didn't hurt to spread the lie.

First, he tied the softest robe he had onto his body, and then he took the softest blanket, the one from the sofa, and cut a hole in the middle of it. This he put his head through. He gathered the edges around his body and tied it together with a ribbon from one of the presents Ned had stacked up in the corner of the room. He'd brought them into the nest hoping to lure Ezer into caring about the oncoming birth with gifts of baby clothes, baby seats, toys, and books. Hoping to lure him into caring about anything really.

Then Ezer had to sit and rest.

His feet ached, and he could feel his ankles already expanding, but after a few moments to catch his breath, he hauled himself up. Finding his shoes, which he hadn't worn in months, he struggled to get them on. The stairs proved a challenge. Usually, if he were going to head up to the pool, Ned or Earl helped him manage, and he always had to stop in the middle of them to rest.

On his own, with his enormous belly, he was struggling by a third of the way up. He paused, breathed, and, with the force of willpower, continued.

The main house was quiet. Ned was out meeting his uncle, and Earl had gone to the store. Since Braden's attack, Ezer spent times like this holed up in the nest, preferably behind a locked door. But he pushed his feet onward, rage burning like an ember in his heart. He felt alive. It was the first time he'd had any sensation in his dead soul since the attack and his subsequent confrontation with Ned.

The babies had gone still inside him, which was a relief. He didn't have the energy to deal with their energetic ways, not when he had to focus on getting out of the house, down to the bus stop, and onto the big, heaving vehicle without anyone stopping him or doing more than looking at him oddly.

Which plenty of people did.

He'd covered himself, but it was clear he was pregnant.

People on the bus shifted away from him. Omegas watched with a hint of terror in their eyes as he tried to maneuver his big belly into the bus seat, barely fitting. Alphas twitched, some were angry, some concerned. One hero tried to approach but an omega blocked his path, saying, "He's pregnant. His alpha won't like it if you talk with him."

"He's in public!"

"I'm sure he has his reasons."

The standoff lasted longer than Ezer would've liked, but the alpha backed off and the omega took a seat behind him, acting as a kind of guard against any other alpha or even beta who might get the idea to approach.

"Where are you going?" he asked.

"My father's house," Ezer said, knowing it sounded almost reasonable. One of the only halfway reasonable reasons a pregnant omega might give for being out in public at this stage of the pregnancy.

"Your alpha will come for you there, you know. There's no getting away from him." The omega's voice trembled, as if he too had once run back to his father's home while hugely pregnant, perhaps running from an alpha he loathed.

"I know."

Ezer counted on Ned finding him. There was no way he'd have the strength to get back home if things *didn't* go exceedingly badly with his father today. A certainty that he was walking into a tornado came over him. Was he strong enough to survive the storm? He touched his stomach. Would his father hit him? As pregnant as he was? There was no way to know.

"Are you going to be all right?"

"I hope so."

"You look ready to birth at any moment."

"Twins."

"Oh," the omega breathed with relief. "You should see yourself. I thought you might deliver right here on the bus."

"I have time yet."

The omega smiled encouragingly. "You're going to do great. Don't worry." But then his eyes flickered over Ezer's body, and Ezer knew exactly what the omega was thinking: if there was more time yet to go, what room did the babies have to grow? Ezer's body couldn't handle much more.

The bus came to a stop downhill from the Fersee mansion. The walk was impossible. Ezer sat on the bench at the bus stop looking up toward the house he wanted to reach, seeing the sharp edges of the roof protrude from the neon-green leaves.

Between the summer heat, the robe, the blanket, and the pregnancy, he was huffing and far too hot. The material felt worse and worse the longer he wore it. His skin was hypersensitized, and the weight of the fabric was claustrophobic and itchy. Trying to put his discomfort aside, Ezer waited for the anger inside to generate enough energy for him to rise and attempt the climb. It was taking its sweet time.

"Ezer?"

The voice was familiar but for a moment he couldn't place it. But as Ezer turned his head toward the car that had slowed and stopped in front of him, he recognized Pete in the backseat peering out at him. He was handsome and young, almost as young as Ezer himself now that he thought about it. Had he really disliked Pete? For what? For being what the world insisted he should be?

"Pete."

"What are you doing here?"

"Going to Father's house."

Pete blew out a rough breath, panic lighting in his eyes. "Ezer, things at the house are tense. Let me take you home." He got out of the car, and it was strange to see him without the big baby belly. He was slim and seemed taller than Ezer recalled. But he still had a baby face. "That's it, let me help you."

As Ezer got into the vehicle, he insisted, "I won't go home. Take me to see Father."

Pete gazed at him, bewildered. After he climbed in next to Ezer, he studied him a moment more. "I can see that you're as stubborn as ever. Your alpha hasn't managed to tame you."

"Not yet."

"Not for lack of trying, I'm assuming."

Ezer shrugged, cradling his stomach, relieved the babies were still behaving.

After a few more moments, Pete nodded and told the driver to head on to the house.

"Where's Prince?"

Pete flushed. "I left him with my parents for the night. Things are very unsettled, Ezer. I felt it was safer to take Prince away for a few days."

"Father would never hurt his precious alpha." Ezer didn't mean to sound nasty, but there it was all the same.

"He's out of control," Pete whispered, shivering.

"But you're going back?"

"He's my alpha. My father says I belong at his side."

"No doubt my father will say the same to me. But I'm done listening to him."

"Is he very cruel to you then?" Pete asked quietly, taking hold of Ezer's hand and squeezing his fingers. "Does he beat you? Abuse you in other ways?"

"Who?"

"Your alpha. The boy your father gave you to."

"Oh, Ned." Ezer thought of Ned's hazel eyes, his earnest attempts to make him happy. "No. He'd never hurt me."

"Then what are you doing trying to come home? Have you lost your mind?" He scanned Ezer's face. "Are you unwell?"

"I'm dressed in a blanket," Ezer pointed out. "And I'm out of my nest. Clearly I'm not well."

Pete fretted. "Are you sick, or have you gone crazy?" He asked the question so sweetly that it didn't sound like an insult, but a genuine concern.

"Angry," Ezer said. "I'm just angry."

They rode in silence the rest of the way up the hill. When they arrived, Pete helped him into the house, keeping his voice down as if afraid to attract attention. "Let me find your brothers. Yissan will talk sense into you. He'll take you home."

"Is Father still in the nest?"

"The library, sir," a servant said, gaping at Ezer in astonishment.

"Thank you," Ezer said, pulling free of Pete's 'helping' hands. "I'm going to talk to him."

"Please don't," Pete said. "He's not in a good place right now, Ezer. He's sent your brother Shan off with an alpha. There was violence involved."

"From Flo?"

"From Shan."

"Where is Flo now?"

"Locked in his room."

"Is it too late to stop this with Shan?"

"Your father triggered his heat early like he did with you. It's not full-blown yet. The alpha has time to get him somewhere safe, but Shan fought. He spit on your father." Pete sounded so scandalized he might vanish into the air. "He clawed and bit."

Ezer's heart pounded, remembering the way his da had fought being kicked out of the house, holding on to the walls, biting his father and the men who forced him. The blood.

Shan hadn't wanted this. Shan dreaded everything to do with heat and breeding and alphas.

"Where's Yissan?"

Pete looked away. "Your father plans to trigger his heat next. He has an alpha ready for him. Yissan will be gone by the end of the week." Pete shifted awkwardly. "It will be just me, Flo, Rodan, and Prince then. I'm worried for Flo. He hasn't endeared himself to his father in all this."

Ezer swallowed hard, and when he took a step forward, the room swayed. He was too pregnant for this. It had been too many hours since he'd had Ned's seed, and his frame was too small to support the weight of the babies inside.

He fought off the exhaustion. Tugging out of Pete's hands and starting toward the library, he put one foot in front of the other, hoping that he could reach his father before he fell to the floor.

Ezer had no idea what he wanted to say, or what he planned to do. He just needed to reach the library door, fling it open, and confront his father. The words would appear for him. He was certain.

George was at his desk, head in his hands, and a bottle of whisky next to him. At the sound of the door opening, he muttered, "Pete, love? You're back?"

"He's back," Ezer said, waddling forward, hands on his big stomach, and his blanket-tunic burning on his skin. "And so am I."

George lifted his head, eyes bleary, and took Ezer in for a long, silent moment. "You. This all started with *you*."

"It's too late for Shan, isn't it? He's lost in his heat by now."

George sat straighter. "None of you boys are right in the head. Being given to a prestigious, wealthy alpha is everything an omega could possibly dream of."

"Some of us have dreams beyond being a baby incubator and sex machine for our alphas."

"There it is! This *is* your fault. You got into their heads, didn't you? You convinced them they needed more than a perfectly happy, normal life as an omega. Now Shan wants to be a musician, and Flo wants to sell his heats, and Yissan is saying he's in love with a beta for God's sake. A beta!"

Ezer tilted his head. He hadn't heard that from Rodan. He wasn't sure how that would work for Yissan's heats, but surely there was a creative way to deal with it. His brother was smart, and he'd figure it out. "You can blame me all you want, but the fact is, I'm the only son of yours who willingly complied."

"There was nothing willing about it," George bit out. "If I hadn't had the upper hand with Amos, you'd still be in my hair."

One of the babies jumped, as if he'd just woken up. Ezer took a sharp breath at the kick in the ribs. Closing his eyes, he puckered his lips to exhale out the pain, the way the birthing coaches did in the videos Ned had been making him watch.

Steadier, Ezer went on. "You knew I didn't want this life, didn't you?"

"Many omegas say they don't, but they all come around."

"Did Pete want this life?"

"Of course. He was docile from the start. I learned my lesson after Amos. Never choose an omega with opinions."

Ezer nodded, plucking at his blanket-clothes, and wanting to peel them off before his skin was scoured away by the roughness of the fabric. "And you knew I didn't want to share my heat at such a young age or get pregnant with any alpha's child at nineteen."

"Of course I knew. It changes nothing. You should be contented by now. Look at you. Swollen large with two of his whelps." George hesitated, a flash of anxiety crossing his face. "You'll be strong enough for it," he rushed to assure Ezer. "Is that why you're here? Because you're afraid you can't do it? You wanted to make sure I knew you held me responsible to the end?"

Ezer swallowed hard. He hadn't thought of that at all. In fact, he tried not to think too much about the likelihood his body wouldn't withstand this birth. But if his father felt guilty seeing the possibility of Ezer's death staring him in the face with the bulging of his stomach, then so be it.

"You did this to me. You took away my youth and my choices. And all because you didn't want to look at my eyes. My da's eyes."

George picked up the whisky and swallowed a mouthful. "You also look like the man who bred you, in every way except for those eyes. Scrawny and ugly. I was grateful to that man for years. Believed he'd saved my Amos a world of agony, saved him from being raped. But it was all a scam. You were a scam."

"I was a baby."

"And a very disobedient omega." George swallowed another mouthful of whisky before using the bottle to gesture at Ezer. "Look at you. What are you doing out of your nest? You're *pregnant*. This is disgraceful. Your alpha will punish you after he rips the head off any other alpha who's been near you." George glared. "Is that it? Do you want that alpha to be me?"

"I want you to admit you put me in a position where I had no real consent."

"Why? What difference does it make now?"

"Because you did it to Shan, too, and you're about to do it to Yissan."

"Omegas should be with alphas. They should be pregnant and happy."

"Do I look happy?"

"You could be if you stopped thinking ugly thoughts."

"You knew I couldn't read the contract when I signed it."

"I offered to read it to you. You declined."

"You knew I didn't know what I was signing."

"I did. I knew a lot of things. I knew the Clearwater boy wanted you, I knew you needed to get out of my house, and I knew the less you knew about it all the better. But, for what it's worth," George gestured to Ezer's stomach. "I didn't know you'd have two." George's face grew pale and his eyes cloudy. "Your da—Amos—he struggled with the twins."

Ezer rubbed his stomach, his feet aching and his knees feeling as if they might collapse under the weight of him. "I'm smaller than he is."

"You're just here to frighten me?"

"Does it frighten you? That you set one of your sons up to endure a situation that might cause his death?"

"You aren't my son."

"I am. In the eyes of the law, on my birth certificate, I'm very much your son. You once considered me one."

"What do you want from me, Ezer?" George asked. "More money? I can send your alpha more cash if he's spent it all already. Do you want something expensive? A birthing present of some sort? Jewelry?"

"I want you to let Yissan out of whatever contract you've designed for him. I want you to let him make his own choices."

"Yissan? My firstborn? The one I've wanted, since childhood, to find the best possible match for? Why on earth would I let him make his own choices? He is in love with a beta. He's an idiot."

"And Flo, too. I want you to promise me that both of them will be allowed to choose."

"Or what?"

Ezer shrugged. "Or I'll file a failure to consent suit, and my alpha will file a contractual abuse suit, and we air this filthy laundry in public. Assuming I'm alive to do it. If I'm not, then I suppose you'll win after all."

George studied him, scoffing as he scrubbed a hand over his face "You're not bluffing, are you? You'll file the suits."

"I will."

"And if I back off for now? Tell Yissan he can have a year to reconcile himself to this contract so that he signs without so-called coercion?"

The walk and the movement had taken its toll. Ezer hurt all over, and when one of the babies gave an especially violent kick, his back spasmed. He gasped and shifted, trying to get comfortable, but it was no use. The spasm wouldn't let loose.

George narrowed his eyes. "I'm calling your alpha."

"Go ahead," Ezer said, as George reached for the phone. "I'm not afraid of him." As the spasm released and vanished, he said,

"Father, please, swear it. Swear to me that the others won't face what I've faced."

What Shan was facing right now.

A pain like none Ezer had ever felt before lanced across his body, a popping sound come from within, and the babies jolted inside him. Vomit churned in his throat, as Ezer slumped and cradled his head. The room spun. "Swear it," he demanded, determined to get his way, to save his brothers even if he couldn't move his father's heart. "Promise me."

"Damn calling your alpha, I'm calling an ambulance."

Ezer heard George's voice, and then his shouts for Pete. The room was spotted and swirling, and vomit made its way up his throat.

"Don't pass out," George's voice said from quite close.

Ezer realized he was held in his father's arms, spread out on the floor, his limbs shaking and jerking.

"Ezer, son? Stay with me. Show me your eyes. Show me Amos's eyes."

Ezer didn't hear any more.

# Chapter Thirty-Three

"HE SHOULDN'T BE out of his nest," the hospital doctor, a tall, dark man named Urston, said irritably.

Grim and miserable, Ned nodded, gripping Ezer's hands in his, watching as fluid dripped into his arm, keeping a close eye on the monitors strapped both to Ezer's chest and his stomach.

"It was foolish of him to leave the house. Has he been having psychotic episodes?" Dr. Urston asked. "Some omegas don't wait for the post-partum period, a few experience a serious drop and psychosis while still pregnant."

"He's been depressed," Ned murmured. "He's felt unsafe."

Dr. Urston glanced around the room, taking in the worried faces of Heath, Adrien, George Fersee, and Pete. "You're both young. It's hard for an alpha of your age to fully satisfy the safety needs of an omega. It's time for you to grow up, young man. You must put him first. This is already a dangerous pregnancy. He will undoubtedly need a cesarian to even hope to survive this."

Ned's stomach dropped. The food Adrien had convinced him to chew and swallow, once it'd been confirmed Ezer and the babies were all right, threatened to come back up.

"Are you understanding me, young man? This is beyond serious; this is life or death."

"I understand," Ned whispered. "I'm doing my best, but I'll do even better." He kissed Ezer's fingers and prayer filled his heart. "I'll do anything to make him feel secure."

"Good, because he won't be ready to have these babies safely until he trusts you." The doctor tsked, and then turned to George Fersee. "It's a shame when young omegas and alphas make poor choices, enjoy a heat, and end up in a situation like this."

Ned didn't miss the assumption that this was his and Ezer's fault, that none of the adults in the room had anything to with it.

"With hips as narrow as Ezer's, I'd have recommended waiting a few more years before he was impregnated at all, and the twins just complicate things. Did he have a heat-readiness exam?"

"He did," George confirmed. "They said he was fit."

Dr. Urston shook his head, making a note. "Unreal. I couldn't disagree more. But what's done is done." He turned back to Ned. "If you care for this boy at all, and I can see that you do, then his every wish will become your world until delivery is over. Nothing should prevent you from being near to him. I'll write an excuse for your school."

"Thank you," Ned said, squeezing his eyes shut.

He still wasn't sure what'd happened. He knew only that Ezer had gone out on his own, wearing a blanket and a robe, and somehow made it to his father's house. There he'd passed out after exhibiting signs of pain and enduring a seizure. But why Ezer had left, what he was doing at George Fersee's house, Ned didn't know.

"Why was he even there?" Ned asked, when the doctor had left the room, and the only people left were so-called family.

Heath crossed to put his hands on Ned's shoulders, squeezing reassuringly. "Yes, George, what was the boy doing at your home instead of being tucked away safely in his nest?"

"That's a question for your nephew," George said, crossing his arms over his chest. He smelled of whisky and looked exhausted. "He's the one who says my boy doesn't feel safe enough with him."

"Ezer is safe with Ned," Heath stated.

"I don't see how, when he's recently been assaulted in his own nest—" George had heard about that during the interview with the doctor when Ned had been asked if Ezer had had any shocks recently. "And he was able to leave the house on his own without anyone noticing. Not even a servant."

"He came to talk to George about his brothers," Pete said quietly, arms crossed protectively over his chest. "He wanted to stop George from doing to them what he's done to Ezer."

George scoffed. "What I did *for* Ezer, you mean?"

"What you did for yourself," Pete said tightly. "Please don't be angry, George. I'm proud to be your omega, and I love you, but when I see how you're handling your omega sons, it scares me. What if our next son is an omega? Will you do the same to him? I chose you, didn't I? Of my own free will, I chose to be with you. Ezer here—" Pete shook his head. "I was in the car. He was out of his mind in heat before he even saw the boy."

"Pete," George said warningly. "Love, do keep your mouth shut."

"No, I'm rather interested in what he has to say," Heath said. "Go on. I'd like to know more."

Pete's eyes lingered on George's angry face, seeming to reconsider saying more, but then his gaze flitted to Ezer in the bed, swollen with children, sick and unconscious. "He's so young…"

"My other boys are older. They've waited long enough. Omegas are meant to be bred," George said. "Everyone will agree to that."

Pete and Adrien met each other's eyes, and Ned saw the complicated look exchanged between them.

"I chose you," Pete whispered.

"I chose Heath," Adrien said.

"No, you didn't," Heath corrected. "I bought your heat and a breeding at auction."

"But I *chose* to sell those things to you. I could have made a different choice."

"You were broke," Heath argued. "You—"

"Heath, I *chose* you!" Adrien whisper-shouted, throwing his hands up. "Would you rather I hadn't?"

Heath stopped talking after that, and turned back to Pete, lifting his thick eyebrows to urge him to go on.

"Ezer didn't really *choose*, George. I heard you say that you were aware he didn't even know who he was contracting with when he signed the contract, that he couldn't read it, and you didn't insist on reading it to him. You knew he felt coerced. I heard you admit it."

George's jaw ticced, but he nodded once.

"Ezer doesn't want this for his brothers," Pete motioned at the bed. "He wants them to have a choice. Shan was hysterical today. He hurt himself trying to get away. You forced him to go with that man." Pete was shaking now, and George's face grew a livid purple. "He begged. He begged *me* for help. Me. And I let you do that to him."

"Pete," George said, frowning. "You have too soft a heart. Shan needed to learn that he and Flo can't be together forever. Harrison will take care of him. He's a strong, no-nonsense alpha. He'll tame him in no time."

"Not all omegas can be tamed," Ned said. Ezer's fragile eyelids looked bruised in the fluorescent light of the hospital. "Some of them have minds of their own."

"All of them," Adrien corrected.

"Right, all of them," Ned agreed absently, unable to take his gaze from Ezer's pale face. It seemed to grow paler by the minute. "He's a fighter. He can do this. He will do this."

"I say take the babes now," George said after a moment of

silence filled the room. "I watched Amos go through it, and he was a bigger, stronger omega than Ezer. Take the babes. If they live, they live. If they don't, then this wasn't meant to be."

The silence in the room was suffocating. No one even moved as George's words blanketed the room with the weight of a thick snow.

Ned bowed his head, pressing his temple against Ezer's hand, breathing brokenly. He tried to find the courage to agree, to tell the doctor to cut his Ezer open, take the babies they'd made together. It would save Ezer's life, so it'd be worth it. They'd made these lives before they'd been wise enough. Before they'd known what they were doing.

"Okay," Ned said finally. "We should do that."

"No—" Ezer sounded exhausted, but his eyes peeled open halfway. "Ned, you are *such* a coward. You aren't taking the babies just because you're afraid I'll die."

Ned stood up, adrenaline pumping through him. "Ezer? You're awake."

"Yes." His dazzling eyes were shaded by his lashes, but he licked his lips and said again, "Don't be a coward, Ned. Be brave."

"BEING BRAVE DOESN'T have to mean letting him risk his life," Heath said in the corridor half an hour later after Ezer had gone back to sleep. "You're his alpha. You can say what happens next."

"Go against him?" Ned asked.

"If you want him to live."

Ned scrubbed at his face. There had to be a middle way, like inducing or taking the babies before they endangered Ezer's life, but waiting long enough to allow them to grow more first.

Holding off until their lungs were fully formed, and their hearts were stronger.

"He suffered an acute pancreatitis attack. There isn't enough room inside his body. His other organs are being crushed." Heath was brutal in his outlining of the problems.

"But he doesn't want to give up on the babies yet."

"Ned, he's delirious, on pain medication, and he's not in his right mind. Look, I know you don't want to violate his consent any further in this relationship. He's been through enough. But part of being brave, of creating a safe space for your omega, is also knowing when you need to make him safe even against his will."

"I can't," Ned said. "I won't."

Heath simply stared at him a moment, then said, "When you lose your omega and your babies, you'll see that I was right."

"What an awful thing to say," Adrien said. "Apologize."

"No. He's being an idiot."

George Fersee and Pete stood off to the side, whispering. It seemed clear to Ned that Pete had the upper hand in the conversation, and despite all his rage and hostility toward George, he felt sorry for the man. He was clearly in love with his young omega and was now startled to find Pete had more of a mind of his own than he'd imagined.

"Fersee," Heath called, turning away from Ned and walking toward George. "I have attorneys on retainer who have already reached out to your son, Yissan. I suggest, if you want to save face, you do whatever your omega here suggests, or it's going to be a shit show."

George caught Heath's eyes. "You were always too big for your britches, Clearwater. You shouldn't get involved in other alphas' business."

"When they're abusing their sons and violating consent laws? I beg to differ. I think I have an obligation to get involved. And, from the sound of it, you'll be lucky if not one, but two of your sons don't press belated charges of coercion against you."

"Abusing my sons!"

"Yes. Trace Stone is known to violate his omegas, to take pleasure in that. All men of my age know of his proclivities."

George paled.

"You didn't?"

Ned saw the moment George knew he'd been defeated, whether it was by this new knowledge, Heath Clearwater, or the omegas in his life, it didn't matter. He'd lost this round, and he knew it.

"Yissan will be allowed to choose his own destruction, but surely I won't be expected to fund it."

"Men have cut their sons off for less," Heath agreed. "But after your treatment of Amos, do you really want to foster the reputation of being an unreasonable, selfish, and cruel alpha? It's up to you of course."

George snarled. "I hope you're cursed with a dozen omega sons. Then you'll see what it's like."

"So far, we just have an alpha and a beta. I look forward to an omega. He should be interesting if the omegas in my life—and yours—are any indication."

"Both our sons are interesting," Adrien defended. "Michael is quite the philosopher already. He told me the other day that God lives inside us all."

"And then he suggested he cut you open so he could look for him. I was there."

"Speaking of cutting open," Pete whispered, coming closer to Ned. "He won't forgive you, you realize? Even if what you choose ensures he lives? He'll leave you if you take his sons now."

"Why? He didn't want them," George said. "Surely he'd prefer to have his own life?"

"You've never carried a child," Pete said. "That much is clear."

All the debate in the room was unnecessary. Ned had made up his mind.

"He said no. And that's enough for me."

EZER WOKE UP to a mouth so dry he couldn't swallow. He tried to sit up, but he was unable to manage with the size of his belly. He was confused by that at first, but then he felt the movement inside.

Right.

He was pregnant.

He peeled his eyes open and took in the gray light of morning seeping through the window near the hospital bed. Ned was in a chair next to him, one arm crossed over his chest, and his chin propped on the heel of his other hand.

The kicking in Ezer's belly drew his attention again.

He placed his palms on the taut skin.

Images flashed through his mind. The bus. An omega asking where he was going. His father's house. George with a whisky bottle. Pete's worried eyes.

What'd happened?

Struggling, he managed to prop himself up more, and find the controller to move the bed and, in doing so, woke Ned.

"Ezer!" he sat up straight, his dark eyes wide and his hair a mess. "You're awake again."

Ezer didn't remember being awake the first time, but he nodded. "Water," he managed to cough out, and Ned hopped into action. Within seconds his throat and mouth were soothed by cold sweetness pooling in his belly. The twins kicked again.

"What happened?"

"You went to your father's house," Ned said, his brows furrowed. "The babies are hurting you, Ezer. They're growing too big, too fast, and your organs are struggling to accommodate them."

Ezer's brain clicked. A vague memory of someone saying the babies should be taken. He grabbed his stomach again, pierced by a sudden fear that he'd imagined the bulge and the movement. But, yes, there was a foot pushing up, and someone inside had the hiccups.

"I don't think you can birth them safely," Ned went on. "The best we can hope for is that they'll grow well in the next week, get stronger, and then we take them out via cesarian, here in the hospital."

Ezer frowned. "But what about the nest? I want to go home."

Ned's brows lifted. "Is the nest your home?"

"Yes. Why wouldn't it be?"

"I thought maybe you'd gone to your father's in part because you weren't comfortable in the nest anymore. That you were seeking your real 'home' to have the babies there."

Ezer scoffed. "My father's house as my home? No." He rubbed his forehead. "But what was I doing there? Why did I leave the nest?"

"Pete said you wanted to help your brothers."

"He's trying to sell them off. I won't let him do it. He can't."

"He's not going to. Between you, Pete, Heath, and the potential rumors, he's put those goals aside for now. I can't say for how long, but Pete isn't the pushover George thought he was. He's not pleased to see him use chemical and other coercion on his omega sons."

Ezer let these words soothe him, though he wasn't sure how long his father would allow his sons and his new omega to defy him. But if it saved Yissan and Flo from an immediate contract, then he was relieved. So were the babies, apparently, because one seemed to be patting him from the inside. Such an odd feeling.

"Ezer?"

"Yes?"

"We have to talk."

Ezer almost laughed. "Talk or fight?"

"Talk." Ned put his hands up. "I want to do what's right from now on. It's important to me."

Ezer tilted his head. "Go on."

"These babies. I love them already, but not as much as I love you. If I had to trade their lives for yours, I'd choose you."

"We don't have to choose, do we?" Ezer asked, his voice wavering.

"The doctors are concerned." He took hold of Ezer's hand. "I don't want to, but if the time comes, I need you to know that I'm choosing you." He glanced down. "You can call me selfish and cowardly, but it's not about that. It's not to make my life easier. It's to save yours."

"Ned, is it really that dire?"

"The doctors say you're stable now, but they aren't sure how long that'll last. You're a small omega, and the twins are big."

"They have their father's build," Ezer said, a dry laugh on his lips.

That didn't seem to reassure Ned or strike him as funny at all.

"Ezer, this isn't the life you wanted for yourself. You never wanted these babies. Why should you die for them?"

"Am I going to die?" His voice shook.

"What I'm saying is that if it comes down to it, if your life is at risk, I'm choosing you."

Inside Ezer, there came a firm kick. It was true he'd never wanted this, that he'd done all of this against his will in many ways, but now he was carrying these new lives, and it was his instinct to protect them. But at what cost? His own life?

"You'd choose me?"

"I don't know if you realize it, but I chose you from the start. I was misled but I wasn't coerced the way you were. I wanted to have you as my omega from the moment I saw you. I wanted you, but not the way I've had you. I wanted you to choose me. I wanted you safe and happy."

"I know."

"That's not what we've been allowed to share." Ned put his hands on Ezer's stomach. "These lives aren't more precious than yours. Do you understand? Not to me. And they shouldn't be to you either. You don't even know them."

"I feel them," Ezer murmured. "I feel who they could be."

"I need you to tell me now. If things get worse, and I choose you, then how bad will it be? I'd rather you lived and left me for this choice, than have you die. You deserve to have a chance to live out some of your dreams. The ones you had before so many choices were made for you that led to all this."

"Shh, stop."

"What? I'm telling you now, so you'll understand why I intend to betray you if I must, in order to save your life."

"It's not betrayal if you've told me it's coming." Ezer took Ned's hands in his own and squeezed. His throat tightened and tears filled his eyes. "I'm scared."

"Me too."

"I can't imagine going through all of this and not coming out the other side with both these babes alive and well."

"I know. Me either."

Ezer swallowed against the painful lump. "But we're too young to be parents, aren't we?"

Ned nodded. "I think we might be."

Silence hung between them, and they breathed in and out, both trying to find calm in the mess they dwelled in.

"Ned?"

"Yes, baby?"

"If we make it through this—me and the twins, I mean—we're going to need help. It can't just be me, you, and Earl. We need people in our lives we can rely on and trust."

"Flo? Yissan?"

"No. They'll want to focus on their own lives. We need people older than us. Someone more experienced to guide us. Like parents." Unfortunately, they couldn't rely on their own parents at all. They'd all three betray them profoundly while claiming to want the best for everyone.

Ned's brow wrinkled thoughtfully. "Heath and Adrien?"

"If they even want to help us? They have their own family and lives."

"They will. I know it."

Ezer hoped so. They sat together in another long silence, Ezer's enormous belly shifting with the babies' movements.

"Ned?"

"Yes?"

"I'm sorry."

"For what?"

"I mean, I forgive you."

"All right, but for what? There are a lot of things you could forgive me for," Ned said shamefacedly.

"I forgive you for being a coward in the past." Ezer touched his stomach. "And I also forgive you for being braver than me right now." Tears slipped down his face. "I don't think I have it in me to do the right thing if it comes down to me or the babies. But you do. I trust you."

"You do?"

"Yes."

"But why? After everything?"

"Because I know you love me. There's no one else in the world I can say that about with real certainty. You love me for *me*, the *real* me. Not some vision of me you used to have in your head. You love the bratty, angry me, not just my best self. I'm not even sure you've ever seen my best self. So, I know you'll still love me even if we lose them." He touched his stomach.

"But will *you* love me?"

Ezer touched Ned's cheek, running his finger over the days of stubble. "I'm working on it. I *want* to love you at least. It's a start."

"Wanting to love me is good." Ned hesitated and then asked, "How can I make you want to love me even more?"

"Just keep on being brave."

Ned kissed Ezer's cheeks, his eyelids, and his nose. "I'll show you that I can be brave enough for you."

"I know you can," Ezer breathed, exhaustion falling over him, but with Ned next to him, determined to take charge if the worst occurred, he finally felt as if he could truly rest.

# PART SIX

## Birth

# Chapter Thirty-Four

SHOCKINGLY, EZER RECOVERED better than anyone expected.

To Ned's distress, the hospital saw no reason to keep him admitted, even though Ezer's organs were still being crushed by the babies, unless they wanted to proceed with the cesarian now. Since they'd both agreed to give the twins a chance to get bigger and stronger, so long as Ezer wasn't in imminent danger, they were obliged to return home.

Ned was an emotional mess about it, but there was nothing to be done. He'd do his best to make sure Ezer stayed on strict bedrest, remained unstressed, and agreed to call an ambulance at the least indication there was a problem.

Ned *was* relieved, though, that after the confrontations with Ezer, Pete, and Heath, George had indeed backed off from his plans for his other sons. In fact, he took his omega, his alpha baby, and Rodan out of the city for a retreat in the countryside to *"re-establish equilibrium in the household,"* as he put it. This was reported to Ezer and Ned by Yissan who came to stay with them, purportedly to "help out" during this delicate time of Ezer's confinement. But he spent most of his time by the pool, sucking on his beloved cigarettes, and making dreamy escape plans with his beta lover, John Stone.

For his part, John was currently hiding out until his father got over being denied Yissan, then they both planned to leave town. To do what? Ned had no idea. But given Yissan's general uselessness, Ned didn't care so long as he didn't stress his brother out with any of it.

Flo stayed on at their father's home but visited from time to time over the final weeks of Ezer's pregnancy. However, he was so depressed and despondent over the situation with Shan, Ned typically sent him home after only a few hours. Ezer's health was too fragile to be brought down by Flo's stories of Shan's sad phone calls and the dissatisfaction Shan expressed over his new alpha.

Ned *did* put Heath's lawyers on it for Shan's sake, but after five days they came back saying the contracts were airtight, and, besides, Shan was likely pregnant. Like with Ezer, unless Shan decided to file a suit, there was nothing to be done about it now.

Rodan, as a beta, seemed safe with his father, but everyone agreed it was worth keeping an eye on him all the same. At least Pete had taken the boy under his wing and was bonding with him. So the House of Fersee seemed to be calming down, even though Shan was left suffering.

As far as Ned could tell, the only other person who needed to be more present in Ezer's life was his da, and that was up to Ezer now. Amos had made it clear that he'd wait for his son to reach out to him. Amos knew he'd betrayed him, and until Ezer was at peace with the situation, and with him, then he'd bide his time.

That seemed selfish as hell to Ned, but he was learning that few people knew how to love unselfishly. It was something he was desperately trying to learn himself.

"Are you going to be okay?" Ned asked, kneeling beside Ezer who was on the sofa, struggling to get comfortable with his giant stomach. "I don't want to leave you."

"You don't really have a choice. You've been subpoenaed, and you need to testify since I can't."

Braden Tenmeter's trial had been fast-tracked thanks to his

father's money and influence, and the rumor was that unless there were airtight witnesses, he would get off. The Tenmeter legal team was counting on Ned being too embarrassed to testify, both because of his failure to protect his omega, and because of his own prior behavior with Braden and Finch. That would leave only Heath's testimony, which was considered less than airtight since he hadn't seen the beginning of the incident. Braden still claimed Ezer had sought his advances, both at school and that day, and he had Finch's testimony backing him up.

There was no way Ned wasn't going to testify. It would be his word and Heath's against Braden's and Finch's. Since omegas weren't allowed to give testimony in a court of law, unless they had brought suit against their own alpha or father for consent violations, their team had moved to allow a written, sworn statement from Ezer, but there was no guarantee the judge would allow it.

"I shouldn't have allowed Earl to go visit with Simon. Or I should have insisted they both come here," Ned fretted.

"He'll be back in a few hours. Earl deserves time alone with his husband. They barely see each other because they're so devoted to you and Heath."

"And our omegas and children."

"Yes, we've taken over their lives. Just let them have a romantic day on the beach. Besides, Yissan is here."

Ned tried not to frown, but he must have failed.

"He's not going to let anything bad happen."

"He spends no time in the nest with you. How would he even know if you needed his help?"

"I would use my tablet and call his phone. He's sure to be on it with John."

"He's obsessed with him."

"Aren't you obsessed with me?"

Ned shrugged. “Yes, but it’s different. We’re alpha and omega, and they’re…” He didn’t want to say an abomination, that was too loaded a word. But they were hopeless, weren’t they? John could never give Yissan what he needed.

“Don’t be gender-ist. It’s gross.”

“But what about his heat?”

“Leave it to them to settle that.”

“He can’t put off having a heat forever. The suppressants will stop working and then—”

“It’s not our business.”

“I know, but…” Ned tried to stop worrying about what mess Ezer’s brother—well brothers really—might get into with their Fersee stubbornness, and instead turned back to the worry at hand. “I shouldn’t leave you. I wish Adrien had come to town with Uncle Heath. He could stay with you.”

“With those babies? I mean, they’re cute and all, but they’re loud, and I’m tired, and they make me question my life choices even more when they’re running around screaming. The last time they came, Michael scribbled on the wall, and I can’t stop looking at it and seeing clown faces in the mess.” Ezer rubbed a hand over his eyes. “We need to paint over it.”

“I’ll have Earl do it. You should have told me.”

“One of the faces has teeth.”

“Baby…”

“You’re going to be late. Go. Yissan is here. I have my tablet.” Ezer held it up. “I’m going to nap and let these babies grow some more. I’ll probably just be waking up when you get back.” Ezer licked his lips and batted his gorgeous eyes. “Just in time for you to put another load in my throat.”

Ned brushed the hair back from Ezer’s face. “All right.”

Ezer puckered his lips, and Ned gave him a wet kiss.

The trip into the city wasn’t bad since Ned took the subway.

He wanted to get his license so he could drive from now on, but he hadn't had the time. As he approached the courthouse, he saw his uncle waiting on the front steps, looking at his watch, and seeming impatient. Typical.

"You're almost late."

"We have thirty minutes," Ned protested.

"My attorney wants a word with you before we start, about those contracts you wanted drawn up."

"Yeah?"

Heath gazed at him. "Are you sure about this?"

"About testifying, yes. Of course."

"No, about the papers to nullify your contract with Ezer? He might not opt to sign a new one with you, you realize. He could choose to leave."

Ned's throat dried up. "I know. If he wants to leave, then he should be allowed to go. Didn't you tell me that yourself? An omega needs to choose."

"I think that was Ezer's idiot brother, Yissan, who said that, but, yes, an omega needs to at least think he's being allowed to choose."

"Don't let Adrien hear you say it like that."

"He's got a heat coming on soon. He'll forget everything bad about me during it, and then when he comes out of the pregnancy haze, he'll remember, and he'll be mad at me for a few weeks, and then it'll pass. He's predictable as a clock."

"That doesn't bore you?"

"Adrien? No," Heath barked. "He could never. If you ever saw him in heat, you'd know."

Ned laughed. "Is that all, though?"

"No, of course not. I adore him. His smile is the whole world." Heath's eyes took on a dreamy gleam. "The hold these omegas have on our balls is horrible." He sighed, tugged Ned's sleeve, and said, "Let's get all this over with. Come on."

EZER WOKE ON the sofa with a powerful need to get to the bathroom. It felt as if his guts were going to turn inside out, and he didn't know which end they would spew from.

Moving as fast as he could with his unwieldy body nearly toppling him over with every step, he headed into the bathroom, and discovered that his breakfast intended to come out both ends. He cleaned up as best as he could, got into the shower, and washed off as well. Then, as he dried himself with a towel, the first true pain came.

"Holy fuck!" Ezer's body tensed as he bent double, groaning and gritting his teeth. The massive contraction took his breath away. He'd been enduring much tamer and smaller ones off and on for over a week, but the last time Dr. Savage had come to check on him, he'd said that was common with all pregnancies, but especially with twins.

"It's just your body practicing for the big day," he'd assured Ezer after putting his whole hand inside Ezer's ass again to check his womb, finding it still closed and high in his body. "But don't worry. You'll never even have to know what the real ones feel like. We're going to take these two before it comes to that."

And Ezer had believed him.

But this felt different.

This agony felt as if his entire being was forced to condense down to a hard, hot knot. The strong contraction bound him in its grip. He groped along the walls of the bathroom, trying to move out into the main room before falling to his knees and panting until the pain left him.

Ezer crawled at first, using the wall to lever himself to standing. "Yissan!" he cried, but his voice was quieter than he wanted it to be. He took a big breath and yelled, "Yissan!"

There was no answer. He knew his brother was probably by the pool deck, and he also knew there was no way he could heave himself all the way up there.

There was the tablet, though. He'd call for Yissan or an ambulance. He'd call for help.

A yearning for Ned's solid presence flooded him, leaving him hollow and mildly panicked. He wanted Ned here now. *Needed* him. He was scared, well and truly terrified, and the only thing he could imagine would fix it was Ned's presence. His scent, his voice, his hands on Ezer's skin.

But Ned was giving testimony against Braden, and his phone wasn't allowed in the courtroom.

Carefully, Ezer pointed his feet toward the sofa where he knew the tablet rested, but another wave of nausea hit him, sending him back to the bathroom where he heaved up bile into the sink. Splashing his face, he breathed in and out slowly, and then turned back to the main room.

He had to call for help.

Ezer almost made it to the sofa before another agonizing contraction hit him, leaving him sweating and sobbing in its wake. His knees had given out during it, and he rested on the floor a moment, curled on his side, cradling his belly. The twins were strangely still. He closed his eyes, reaching inward for some sign they were all right, but another contraction forced a shout from him. Spots swam in front of his eyes.

Agony. Pressure. Pain.

He could breathe again. In and out, he sucked breaths through the respite. But then…

Again.

"Yissan," Ezer called faintly. "Yissan?"

No reply. In his mind, Ezer could imagine his brother, cigarette between his elegant lips, leaning over the railing, looking out to the sea. His back tanned and glistening, the pool shimmering behind him.

Ezer crawled around the sofa, reaching for the tablet and pulling up the call screen. He'd call for an ambulance. He knew he should, but suddenly all he wanted was to hear his da's voice. What if he never heard it again? What if he didn't survive this? There was a chance. He knew it. Ned knew it.

Ezer knew he should have called Amos before now. He should have made amends with his da. Ezer pushed in a number he'd memorized as a very small child. The call rang.

"Just a moment, I think it's Ezer," his da's voice said, warm and familiar, and Ezer's heart melted in relief. Thank God.

Amos's beloved, handsome face filled the screen, tanned and so much healthier than the last time Ezer had seen him. "Is it really you? I was beginning to think you'd never forgive me. I've been longing for your call." Getting a good look at Ezer, Da's expression changed from joy to concern in a heartbeat. "It's time?" A beat. "You're in labor?"

"Da, I'm scared," Ezer panted. "It's bad. It's so bad."

"Where's Ned?"

"Out." It was too difficult to explain. "I need help."

"Can you call for an ambulance? No? All right—" He turned his head away from the phone, saying, "Call for an ambulance. Have them go to Lidell Clearwater's estate. It's urgent." Then he was back soothing Ezer. "Darling, it's going to be all right. Just hold on. I'll be there. I'll be *right there.*" He could see his da's apartment flashing in blurs over Amos's shoulder, and he heard a worried voice that must have belonged to his da's lover Finn, Ezer's biological father.

"You didn't tell me," Ezer whispered, tears in his eyes. "You never said it would hurt this bad."

"It's sheer hell. But you'll forget soon enough, and then you'll want more."

Ezer shook his head. "Don't try to manage me."

"No, no, of course not. It's just—"

"Stop. I won't ever want more. These two are enough."

Da's movements stopped short. "Two? Twins?" His voice went very soft.

"No one told you?"

"No, my sons don't contact me."

Sweating, Ezer groaned, another contraction beginning. Before he knew it, he was screaming, tablet on the floor, and on his hands and knees, blinded with pain.

"Ezer, I'm on my way."

"I need Ned," Ezer said. "He should be here. Get Ned. I need him." He keened in agony, clutching his stomach, and bending over. He was going to die if the pain got worse than this. He was going to die, and Ned would never know that he almost loved him. That he very well might. That he probably did.

When he came back from the most intense pain he'd ever felt, Yissan was there, flushed and wide-eyed. He cradled Ezer in his arms and rocked him.

"There's no time," he said. "We have to prepare in case the ambulance doesn't get here. Where do you want to be, Ezer? Tell me."

Ezer pointed toward the corner of the room, near the back, behind the table. He didn't know why, but he felt it was the safest place. Yissan piled blankets there and helped Ezer reach them.

Ezer squatted in the pile, unable to get comfortable in any other position, rocking away the lengthening stretches of agony.

At first, the time between each was longer than the time of

pain, but quickly, that shortened, and the pain came faster and faster. Yissan sat beside him, holding his hand, but he didn't have the experience to relieve Ezer's mind or reassure him other than to say, "You just have to hold on, Ezer. They'll be here soon."

Ezer didn't know who "they" were—the ambulance, his da, his Ned. But no one came fast enough for him.

Ezer was naked and still squatting with his eyes shut when the ambulance arrived. No longer embarrassed at his nakedness, Ezer didn't mind that these men were checking him over and trying to gauge what to do. Ezer heard bits and pieces of their conversation:

*"His alpha needs to be here."*

*"We need permission to take him."*

*"He's too close now. He's dilated. He's open and near to pushing."*

*"We could sedate him, cut them free—yes—but there's no guarantee he'll live through it."*

*"No, you're right, no guarantee he'll live either way."*

The situation must be dire if they were talking about such a bad potential outcome in front of him.

Yissan was the only one to touch him, the crew holding back, waiting for the alpha permission they sought.

"If anything goes wrong, he could blame us. We need his permission to continue."

Ezer panted, his mind drifting. He visited the heat house in his head, remembered the shells Ned had offered by the shore. He wished he had them in his hand now. Talismans of his alpha's love and hope.

At the time, he'd treated both Ned and his gifts as if they were useless, but all he wanted now was to have them close. Ezer's eyes filled with tears. He wasn't going to make it. He couldn't endure this. No one could. His brother whispered to him to stay strong.

"Ned is coming," Yissan said. "Ned and Da both."

The pain consumed Ezer again, this time accompanied by an intense urge to push. He didn't resist. The men in the room tensed as he did.

Yissan held him upright, but the suffering was all too much.

Dots obscured his vision. Darkness came and went.

Ezer needed Ned. He needed his da. He needed help.

He passed out.

# Chapter Thirty-Five

"I DID, SIR," Ned said, his eyes on the attorney questioning him. "I put my foot on Ezer's shoulder as Braden asked."

"So you were a participant in the brutalization of your future omega?"

"As humiliated as I am by my past cowardice, yes, I was."

"Is it possible that your guilt over this matter, and jealousy that your omega prefers Braden Tenmeter as an alpha, is what has led you to testify against him today?"

"No."

"That's all? Just no."

"Just no, sir."

"That's all the questions I have for now," Braden's attorney said. They'd already covered the accusations around the final attack, with Heath having been the main witness. Though the court had seen fit to allow Adrien and Ezer's sworn, written testimonies to be presented to the judge.

Ned stepped down from the witness stand feeling anxious and cored out. Having his past faults exposed had been embarrassing, but, more importantly, he saw how much more he needed to grow. His humiliation was nothing compared to what Ezer had suffered. Ezer was the victim, and his words should have counted for as much as Ned's and Heath's, but that wasn't how the system worked.

Sitting in the courtroom next to his uncle, he watched as the judge lifted piece after piece of paper, considering them, and making notes. Ned wondered if there would be a verdict announced today—unlikely—and hoped that whatever the Tenmeter family had offered wasn't enough to tempt the judge into a miscarriage of justice. The man was an alpha himself after all; he had to consider the implications for his own omega if someone had violated him in the same way Braden had violated Ezer.

The minutes crept by, and Braden shifted uneasily in his seat next to his attorney. Heath bent over, whispering, "This is good. The judge is giving it a lot of thought. Whatever Tenmeter tried to bribe him with hopefully won't be enough."

The back door to the courtroom opened and a clerk walked in. The judge's brows lifted in surprise but he waited for the young man to hustle up to the bench. He leaned forward, whispered something, and the judge nodded before waving him off.

The clerk caught Ned's gaze with a strained expression as he headed out. Ned's stomach tightened and his fists clenched. Something was wrong. He wasn't sure what, but there was no mistaking that look from the clerk. He cast his mind over everything related to the case but could find no bombshell the clerk could have handed to the judge that would affect the outcome one way or another.

"Mr. Clearwater—the younger Mr. Clearwater," the judge clarified, glancing up from the papers he continued to sort. "You'll want to get home. Your omega has gone into labor there and cannot be transported by ambulance as was planned." The cold, easy speech hit Ned in the stomach, and he rose, sweat breaking over him at once.

Heath rose as well. The judge ignored the impropriety and returned to his papers. Ned shoved his way past the attorneys and ran down the aisle to the door of the courtroom.

Heath grabbed his arm outside the courtroom. "Let me drive you."

Ned nodded. There was no time for a bus. Thank God his uncle was here.

"Why won't the ambulance take him?" Ned asked, fumbling for his phone and other belongings from another courthouse clerk. He looked at his messages. There were many from Yissan, none from Ezer.

As Heath hustled him out of the courthouse, the sun spilling around them like gold, as if there was nothing terrifying or urgent happening, like it was just another spring day, Ned put a call through to Ezer—no answer—and then to Yissan.

"Are you coming?" Yissan asked, breathlessly. "He's asking for you."

"On my way. Why wasn't he taken to the hospital?"

"The EMTs refused. They claimed they couldn't without his alpha's permission."

"I had written permission drawn up weeks ago."

"I can't remember where you put it! I searched the whole nest!"

Ned's stomach twisted. "It's on my father's desk upstairs. I told you and Earl where to find it the day it was done."

"Earl's not here, and, fuck, I panicked and couldn't remember what you'd said, and I'm so sorry. *Fuck.*"

"Fuck," Ned echoed.

The drive took forever, and the whole way there Ned jittered in his seat, feeling sick and miserable. Was Ezer already dead? Had the children survived? What was he going to find when he got to his house? To their nest? Why did everything about this have to be so hard, so painful, so bitter?

"You're spiraling," Heath said. "Understandable. But only

acceptable until you walk in that door. He's going to need your presence of mind, your peace. Do you understand?"

"Yes."

"You've got to be courageous for him. This will be—" Heath swallowed. "Incredibly difficult."

The understatement was evident.

"Did you fear you'd lose Adrien?"

"Every alpha fears that, but I admit Adrien was never as much at risk as Ezer is." Heath put his hand on the back of Ned's seat and then slid it down to his shoulder to squeeze reassuringly. "There's nothing to do now but hope and tell him it's going to be all right. You must pretend for all you're worth."

When Ned reached the house, he raced through the living area and down to the nest. The room was stuffed with people. Yissan was there, of course, and several EMTs. Someone had called Dr. Savage as well, because he was kneeling at Ezer's side, his hand around back, doing something where the babies would exit.

Amos Elson was there, too, holding his son and cooing. There was another alpha in the room, a small man, standing off to the side, who raised his hands instinctively when Ned's gaze landed on him. Clearly aware that strange alphas weren't welcome in a pregnant omega's vicinity, much less a laboring one, fear glinted in his eyes—but then Ned took in the sharp angles of his face, the way he looked so much like Ezer…

Ned turned away from Finn and moved toward Ezer, tugging his shirt open at the collar, and rolling up his sleeves. Ezer squatted in a corner, trembling all over, and his head lolling back as a scream ripped from him.

Spots swam in Ned's vision, but this was it. This was his time to be brave. There was no turning back now. It was too late for an ambulance, even he could see that. It was too late to take the babies. They were doing this.

Ezer was doing this.

Ned had to support him. He pushed everyone aside to get to his love, terror roiling in him, but he composed his expression. "I'm here," he said, as Ezer's wail faded away. "You're okay. I've got you."

EZER COULD SEE through his filmy vision that Ned was sweaty and panicked. He could also see that Ned was just pretending to be strong, and that made him want to laugh, but he had no energy for it.

Even knowing Ned was more scared than he wanted to admit, his voice was still a balm to Ezer's pain and his touch even more so. Ezer struggled to keep his eyes open, wanting to see and touch Ned's flawless skin, but Ned wore a nice shirt, with a pair of pants that fit him beautifully. It was no good. No good at all. Ezer wanted him naked.

"Get it off. All of it. I need your skin," he panted, and then groaned like an animal, rocking back and forth from his toes to his heels, agony taking hold of him. When the contraction passed, Ned was beside him, naked except for underwear and holding him steady, rubbing his back, encouraging him in a soothing, strong tone. Ezer reached out, pawing at him, reveling in his scent.

"That's it," Ned said. "You're doing so good. Right, Dr. Savage? He's doing great."

Dr. Savage harrumphed and didn't confirm anything, bending low to check Ezer's backside.

"He's doing great," Amos confirmed, looking at Ned, and Ezer saw the terror in his da's gaze, too. They were all so afraid. It was funny because now they were all here, in this moment, Ezer felt at peace.

"My alpha, and my da," Ezer whispered. "You're both here for me."

"Of course, darling," Amos said. "I was always here for you. I always will be."

Ezer's eyes dropped closed, but he felt Ned's face press against his neck, nuzzling him, breathing in his scent. It was calming. For a moment.

Ezer threw his head back and screamed. The pain was sharp. Not like the pains before. The babies wanted out, and he was in their way.

As the agony passed, it blurred into another contraction, and once it was over, he sank against Ned's strength. "They're going to rip me in half," he whispered, thinking that he really should be more scared of that, but he was just too damn tired. "I can't do it. I can't, Ned. I just can't."

Ned came around in front of him, lifted his chin, and forced his eyes to meet his gaze. In a calm, certain voice, Ned assured him, "You *are* going to do this, Ezer, and you'll be okay. You'll be strong and healthy, and the babies will be too. We're going to make it through this. You and me. I've got you. Do you believe me?"

Ezer nodded. Ned sounded so sure, like he knew exactly what he was talking about. He was faking it so well. Ezer decided to pretend to believe.

Until another contraction hit.

Then he went back to knowing in his heart that Ned was a fucking idiot.

# Chapter Thirty-Six

NED HAD NEVER seen suffering like this. His beloved omega, his Ezer with the sky-eyes, anguished beyond belief, laboring to deliver their twins. The pain seemed unreal, and Ned couldn't stop himself from slipping into fears of Ezer's death. Could his small frame survive this? Would he live?

But whenever the doubts crept in, he remembered his uncle jabbing his finger at the table and his strong voice telling him to be the alpha Ezer needed him to be. He recalled Heath in the car telling him to pretend for all he was worth.

Using these thoughts as his mantra, Ned calmed himself, and when he spoke to Ezer he did so with authority, reassuring him the delivery was going well, that Ezer was strong and could do this, and that they were all going to be just fine.

EMTs stood around watching, ready, Ned realized, to attempt life-saving resuscitation on Ezer or on the babies after they were born. Dr. Savage was the only one attending to his omega now.

With each word of reassurance, Ned felt in his core that he was lying, but Ezer seemed to believe him, staring into his eyes searchingly and finding something he needed there. Ezer would listen, nod, and then relax, until the next contraction came.

Amos encouraged his son, too, but it seemed that Ned's words were the ones Ezer clung to the most. The reason was made clear during one of the shorter and shorter spells between contractions when Ezer looked at Ned and said, "You may be a coward, but you've never lied to me."

"No," Ned agreed.

"Tell me the truth then, am I going to die today?"

The truth? Ned was trying so hard to be brave, but he didn't know if he could be that brave. Ezer's eyes challenged him, the rebellious omega he'd always been urging him not to betray his trust.

"I hope not."

Ezer's lips quirked. "Not a lie. Thank you."

"I love you."

"I know." Ezer took a slow, deep breath, gazed determinedly at Ned. "All right. Let's do this." He then dissolved mentally back into the space he retreated to in between the pain.

Ned met Amos's eyes and they shared a moment of agonizing fear for Ezer.

Dr. Savage was all business. He kept several gleaming tools handy, saying he might need them later. For what, Ned didn't know and was afraid to ask. Dr. Savage crouched by Ezer, getting a look at Ezer's asshole, which Ned, when he did the same, saw was stretched and distended with the effort to push the first twin out.

Off and on, Amos's eyes went almost black with terror, like when Ezer's scream was so loud and brutal that it seemed it would punch a hole in the roof and expose them to the sky above. Other times, Amos hesitated in his reassurances, his expression shifting between so many emotions Ned couldn't name them all. But always, after steadying himself, he'd put up his chin and say, "Ezer, I'm here. Da's here. You're doing great."

"I know this is the hardest thing you've ever done, but I promise, Ezer, you can do this," Ned murmured, kissing the side of his head after Ezer twisted and screamed his way through another contraction.

"I don't think I can," Ezer wailed.

"You can," Amos encouraged. He caught Ned's eye. "Here now, lean on your alpha. That's right." Amos put Ezer's weight fully into Ned's arms, and then sat at Ezer's side, shakily taking hold of one of his hands. "I'm here, we're both here for you. Your da and your alpha. You're going to be okay."

Dr. Savage did another check and then got up to his knees, nodding. "The first one is fully in the passage." He turned his attention to Ezer. "These next few contractions will be intense, but after that, it shouldn't be long before you greet your firstborn son." He clapped Ned on the shoulder. "Ready, Papa?"

Ned snatched up all the courage he had inside and nodded. "I will be." He turned to Ezer again. "This is it. The first one is coming now."

Ezer didn't need to be told, Ned could see, because he was gripped by another intense pain. He shouted and pushed, straining with effort, his body twisting, his legs and arms, and every muscle working to get the child out. Even his eyes bulged.

"A little more," the doctor said, from where he was now lying on the floor beneath Ezer's butt, staring up at his asshole, waiting. "I can see just the start of his head."

The next contraction turned Ezer's face purple with effort, and silence ruled the room because he was pushing too hard to shout or scream.

"There we go!" Dr. Savage said. "This is it." He got up to kneel behind Ezer, his hands dropping down behind him, as if to catch the baby.

"I'll do that," Ned said, suddenly sure it was the right thing to do. The first hands to touch his son should be his own.

"Hurry then," Dr. Savage said, moving aside and getting Ned into position. "He'll be slippery coming out. Grab him fast."

"Ned?" Ezer said, his voice shaking.

"I'm here." Ned kissed Ezer's shoulder and nuzzled his neck. "I'm right here ready to catch our son."

Ezer reached back, touching Ned's thigh, and then bore into another contraction. His small body shook and strained and then, like a cannonball, their son came free and slid right into Ned's hands.

"He's here," Ned gasped, gripping the baby so that he didn't slip away. "He's here!"

Dr. Savage leaned close, did something to the baby's mouth and nose, and then a scream pierced the room. Not Ezer's. The new babe's.

"Is that him?" Ezer asked, sounding frantic. "Let me see. I need to see." Ezer panted and shook as Dr. Savage helped Ned wrap the baby in a blanket, and then guided Ned around to show Ezer the fruit of his efforts. "This is our son," Ned said, his heart pounding, his throat tight. Ezer reached for the bundle in Ned's arms.

"Let him take him," Dr. Savage said. "He'll be distracted by how marvelous the babe is, and the next contraction won't—"

Ezer shouted, thrusting the baby back toward Ned, who grabbed him quickly, as Ezer grunted, turned purple, strained and fought, and pushed *hard*. A second child was born, this one caught by Amos, who'd taken Ned's position after the first babe was free.

Another scream.

"Oh, he's beautiful," Amos murmured, wrapping the babe up and bringing him around to show Ned and Ezer. "He's perfect."

Ezer reached for both babies and struggled to get them near enough. Tears ran down his face, his breathing coming in harsh gasps. His entire body shook, and he threatened to collapse, having squatted or kneeled for most of his labor.

Tears ran down Ned's face as he and Ezer held their sons. Ezer was coated in sweat, and blood came from his ass. He wanted to lie down, but Dr. Savage encouraged him to wait a moment.

As the babies screamed, confused and scared by this new world they'd slid into, Dr. Savage got on the floor again, this time with some of his tools. He checked on the delivery of the placentas and then, showing them that those had passed as well, thick and purple, he nodded, pleased.

"There's no hemorrhaging," he said, helping them ease Ezer, quaking and small, onto the blankets. "This was a shockingly successful and normal birth. Truly surprising since he's so small. I thought we'd need our friends from the ambulance for sure. That's why I asked them to stay." Dr. Savage helped cover Ezer with soft blankets, and then motioned at Yissan to bring over the water he was holding and which he'd tried to get down Ezer's throat from time to time during the lulls in contractions. "He's got some luck. You both do."

Finally, once Ezer was settled, propped by pillows, and sure not to faint, Amos passed the swaddled, second baby to his son, and Ned did the same with the first. They curled up together as the room around them gradually emptied—first the EMTs, then Heath left, and finally Yissan and Amos went upstairs. The last to go was Dr. Savage who took his job seriously—making sure both Ezer and the babies were truly all right—before saying, "I'll be upstairs. I'm not leaving until tomorrow morning. This has been a miraculous outcome, and I won't leave until I'm satisfied there will be no reversal."

Ned didn't care. The man could stay a year. So long as Ezer and the screaming, red-faced babies were going to live.

Ezer held his children close and, shaking, began to cry himself. Ned wiped at his omega's cheeks, reassuring him, telling him it was all going to be all right now. They were a family. They were going to be happy. It was going to be fine.

As Ezer gazed up at him, shock and relief shining in his eyes, suddenly he laughed.

"What?"

"You're trying to soothe me, but you're crying too."

And Ned was.

# PART SEVEN

## After Birth

# Chapter Thirty-Seven

EZER STOOD BY the window to the nest, holding Ollie in one arm and Sundy in the other. Both babies were betas, and both were, in his opinion, so beautiful. Each shared features of their parents, and Ezer couldn't decide who was more perfect. Ollie with his golden hair but dazzling eyes like Ezer's and Amos's, or Sundy with his dark curls but dark eyes like Ned.

Naming the babies had been a joint effort. It'd been weeks of back and forth until they'd finally agreed on two names that seemed right for the babes and easy on both of their ears.

A month had now passed since the birth. Ezer was healing and gaining strength, and the babies were growing quickly. Both Ezer and Ned kept waiting for the horrible post-partum drop to hit. Everyone had warned him about it, describing it as a depth of despair that could bring on paranoia and rage in many omegas. So far, it hadn't come.

In fact, he felt more and more confident and secure as the days went by.

At first, Ezer and Ned hadn't known how to care for their sons, but Amos had stayed with them a few days, and taught Ezer how to nurse, and Ned how to swaddle, and encouraged Ezer to rely on Ned for more help than he'd previously expected Ned to give.

Ned, for his part, was devoted.

He took even more leave from school and now spoke of never

going back. He told Ezer he had a plan. A big one. Whenever Ezer pushed for details all he got was, "I'm the right alpha for you, and I'm going to prove it."

Which was adorable, and kind of ridiculous, because whether Ned was the right alpha or not, he was indeed Ezer's man, and the father of his children, and he had no intention of dipping out on him now. But Ned said he still had more to prove. More to make up for.

If Ned wanted to work to impress Ezer? Well, Ezer was down for that.

He liked how Ned took every opportunity to be strong for him—emotionally or physically—and he loved the way Ned was showing more courage every day. He'd even gone so far as to inform Lidell that this house was now *his* house, purchased with Ned's trust fund money, and asked him not to return to live here without Ned's permission.

Lidell had taken it well enough, since his plan seemed to be to travel endlessly on the funds Ezer's father had provided at the beginning of their contract. Ned warned that eventually Lidell would use it all up and be back for more. Still, it was a relief to know the man was out of their lives for the time being.

Besides, soon Ezer would leave the nest with the babies and move into the main part of the house. According to Earl, Ned had prepared a lot of changes to the various rooms, making one into a nursery and setting up the master bedroom for Ezer.

"Will I even like it?" Ezer asked the babies, both sleeping soundly for once. "What if I don't?"

But instead of enraging him, the thought of Ned making choices without Ezer's input just made him laugh. He was sure if he hated it, Ned would simply have it changed. That was how Ned was these days; he'd do anything to please his children's da.

Which was something that would have to change eventually.

Ezer couldn't be with a boring yes-man for the rest of his life, but right now, while he was still recovering, it was nice.

Amos was leaving today, though, and he was up in the main portion of the house packing his things. It was time for him to get back to his lakeside apartment and check his bank account for the promised cash from Ezer's father. Two sons meant twice as much money. Amos said it was all he'd need to live on forever.

Sometimes Ezer wondered how much money Ned had received for the twins. Surely his father had given him a bonus too for the extra child? Or maybe the contract was set up to pay per pregnancy only. Whatever the case, he still chafed at the idea that his children's father would accept money for their birth, but, as Amos had told him, "George owes you and the children. Ned may be the recipient of the money, but it will only be used to keep you in the manner to which you've become accustomed."

Coming out of the pregnancy haze, and preparing to leave the nest, Ezer was still trying to understand what manner it was, exactly, to which he had become accustomed, and if he indeed wanted to stay that way.

He and Ned needed to talk. Again. Funny how they always kept coming back to that. This time, maybe it would be productive.

There were footsteps on the stairs, and Ezer's heart leapt. He hoped it was Ned, but he recognized the tread soon enough, and turned from the window to see his da step into the room.

"Where's Ned?" Amos asked, walking over with his arms outstretched for a baby. Ezer passed him Ollie. "I'd like to say goodbye before I go."

"I'm not sure." Sundy started squirming, so Ezer led them all over to the big U-shaped sofa he'd so hated at first. He sat and lifted his shirt—he enjoyed wearing his clothes again—and began to feed his hungry son. "Ned said he had an important errand to run and might not be back for the rest of the day."

"You didn't request more information?"

"Ollie feeding, and I was half asleep."

"Ah. Of course."

"I'm sure he'll be back soon."

"Well, thank him for me, will you? He's been generous letting me stay here so long."

"I think he's enjoyed it. His father didn't bother to come home to help out, so I think he liked having a parental figure here."

"You say that like he wanted his father home. I get the impression he's rather over the man."

"Yes, he's not happy with him right now."

Silence hung between them. There was so much to say about so many things. But neither of them seemed to know where to start. Finally, Da said, "Your father would like to meet the babies."

"George can meet them when hell freezes over," Ezer said.

"I meant Finn."

Ezer paused, remembering the small alpha he'd met that day on the beach. He'd been pleasant enough, but he wasn't sure yet he wanted to invite him into his life or into his children's lives. "What about his omega? His other family?"

Da bit into his lip. "He confessed it all to Young, that's his omega. It went about as well as you might expect, and Young asked him to leave for a few months, to take some space so he could reconcile with the truth. I don't think he knew Finn would come to me, but of course he did. I'd let him know I had my old lakeside apartment back, that I was in a better place, and that I would like to see him."

"So you're a couple then? Living on George's money?"

Da snorted. "I suppose so. For now. Finn will eventually

return home. He misses his family, and he does love Young. He and I have something too fiery to maintain a life together. It's all passion and no substance. He's a good man, and I'm still in love with him. I know I always will be. But he deserves the stability of his home with his omega."

"Don't you think this relationship has caused enough pain?" Ezer didn't have much faith that his da would do the right thing, but he couldn't let it go unsaid. "Continuing on this way is only going to hurt more people."

Da sighed. "It's not as though we wanted this life, Ezer. We did the best we could with what was forced on us. That's why I wanted you with Ned. I knew he'd be a better fit for you than George ever was for me."

"Da, your choices were your own, and they were and are bad ones."

"I hear you and understand that you're still angry. But Finn and I will never truly be over. He'll find time to come to me when his omega permits it. I understand if you can't forgive me for it." He cleared his throat.

"Da, I forgive you for what part you played in my situation," Ezer said, watching his da kiss Ollie's head. "But only because I don't know how else to move on. You and George thought you were doing the best thing for me, even if you weren't."

"You're not happy with your alpha? Ned is so devoted."

"I am. For now. I can't guarantee that I will be in ten minutes, even; he used to anger me so much. But, yes. I like Ned, and I'm growing to love him. He's a good person, and he loves the babies, and he loves me. But I should have had the right to determine my own path. Every omega deserves that."

Da kissed Ollie again, his eyes downcast. "I understand."

"I want to know what you're going to do for my brothers. Father's way of making matches for them can't stand. Now he's abandoned them. It's only a matter of time before he reconsiders and tries again with Flo. But that's wrong. Don't you see? They should be allowed to make matches based on love."

"Your brothers?" Da asked. "What can I do to help? It's not as if I can stop George from his business schemes, and that's all your brothers are to him. Business assets."

"Don't you see how wrong that is?"

"Of course I do, but one day you'll learn too, Ezer. You need to play within the rules of their game. And that's why I planted the seeds in your father's mind that Ned was the boy to handle you. When he came to apologize after that incident at my old apartment, I could see it in him. The potential. The goodness."

"I deserved a life first. I wanted to go to school. Study mathematics. Sell my heats."

"I know. This is better."

Ezer sighed, the baby at his chest had stopped feeding and was now asleep, half-suckling but mostly drooling. He pulled his shirt down, and cuddled Sundy close. He smelled delicious, like baked bread and sweetness.

"Do you want me to apologize?" Da asked. "Because I will if it helps. I'm sorry, Ezer, that I got you a wonderful alpha to—"

"Don't."

Da stopped talking. "You're right. I'm sorry for being petty about this. You had a dream, and I took it from you, and even if your life right now isn't bad, even if you like it, you still had a right to your dream."

"Thank you. That's all I wanted to hear."

He rose and Da followed. They embraced and Ezer said, "I'm sure there's time in my very busy chest-feeding schedule to meet with Finn next week, if you want."

"He'd like that, and I would too."

Their conversation and time together was at an end. Ezer

wanted to follow his da upstairs and wave him goodbye, but he had to take Ollie to change his diaper, and make sure Sundy was sleeping securely on the sofa, with a pillow to keep him from rolling off should he miraculously develop the skill to do so. He turned his attention to those tasks.

"Hey." Ned's voice was quiet and solemn, startling Ezer enough that he almost dropped Ollie's dirty diaper.

"Hi." Ezer turned around after disposing of the diaper, cleaning his hands, and picking up the now fresh baby. He waved the infant's little hand at his father. "Ollie's all clean and happy to see you."

"I'm happy to see him too," Ned said, but he didn't sound happy. In fact, he sounded grim.

"What's wrong?"

Sundy's cry burst from the couch area, and Ezer hastened to retrieve him, soothing the babe with gentle reassurances that Da was here. Ned followed him with Ollie and the four of them sat on the sofa, a snug family, cuddling together.

"Out with it," Ezer said. "You'll have to tell me sometime. It might as well be now."

"Braden's verdict came down today. I went to the courthouse to hear it read."

Ezer froze. "Oh. You should have told me before you left."

"I didn't want you to think about it and worry all day."

Ezer supposed that was fair. He'd been in a good mood that morning, and he'd enjoyed a pleasant day. If Ned had told him about the testimony, then he'd have spent the hours fretting. "Was it—I mean, how did it go?"

"Guilty."

"Thank God."

"Yeah." He continued to frown though. "It's going to be on the news. Everyone will know. There's nothing the Tenmeters can do about it now. But the good news is your name won't be attached. Since Braden's father insisted on this being a closed court, your identity will remain undisclosed."

Relief swept over Ezer again. He'd known that already, but it was good to be reassured that his privacy wouldn't be violated. "So what's wrong?"

"Braden isn't going to get off completely. He has my testimony against him, and Uncle Heath's. Those alone are enough to find him guilty. They're talking about prison, but it won't be the lengthy sentence we hoped. The Tenmeter family's bribes assured that much at least."

"It's still better than I expected."

"Is it?" Ned bit his lower lip. "You deserve so much more."

Ezer sighed. "Why are you so sad? Talk to me."

Ned let out a long breath. "All right. I have to tell you something else—well, several other things—and you might be very angry with me."

"Get it over with then."

"I talked to your father."

"Why?"

"Because I returned the money he sent to my bank account as the payment for Sundy and Ollie." He caught Ezer's gaze and held it. "I'm not for sale and neither is my heart. I love you, and I want you to care for me one day. I don't think you ever will if I'm being paid for handling your heats and for the births of our children. So I'm done with that."

Ezer's heart cracked open, a little light pouring in. He felt free, as if he was a balloon, and someone had cut the string. He was floating away. "But what about money? How will we live?"

"The question is how will my father live? *We* have plenty of money. Uncle Heath has given it to me in trust, and I stand to inherit more from him one day. In the meantime, if things continue as they have, we'll live frugally."

"We can do that," Ezer said. "It's not as though I want to

throw parties every week and fill our pool with champagne."

"My father will be angry." Ned's lips twisted. "No, he'll be hurt."

"You're so soft," Ezer said, touching Ned's chest, feeling his heart beating beneath his button-up shirt. "You're tender-hearted."

Ned took hold of Ezer's hand and held on to his fingers. "I don't want him to think I don't care about him, but the thing is…" Ned shook his head. "I can't let his recklessness endanger our family, and I won't accept money from George Fersee, so there's no other way. To protect you, I have to cut him off."

"What does that mean for him?"

"I'm not sure. But it makes me sad to think about it."

Ezer put his arm around Ned's shoulders, pulling him close, and cuddling him. The babies were sleeping, and the four of them were a pile of souls, huddling for comfort.

"I love you," Ned said. "Don't say it back. I know it's not true yet. But I want to make you proud of me, too."

"I already am."

Ned closed his eyes tightly, seeming to gather his courage. When he opened them, he whispered, "Ezer?"

"Yes?"

"I have contracts, too, that I want us to sign."

Ezer tilted his head. "What kind of contracts?"

"The first dissolves and puts an end to our original contracts, which were signed under duress. It also names me as responsible financially for Sundy and Ollie in perpetuity, and for you, too. It states that my uncle and I will make sure none of you will go without. Heath has already signed. I wanted you to feel secure that even if I turn into a reprobate you despise, you'd still be free and safe." Ned swallowed hard. "After you sign them, and after I do too, you'll be free."

Ezer's heart thudded. "What?"

"You could leave. You could start over without me. You can take the children or leave them here. It's up to you. It's your choice."

Ezer sat straight, hot anger growing in his heart. "What are you saying?"

"I'm saying that I want you to sign these papers so you have freedom of choice. It's what you deserved from the start."

"I thought you loved me, that you were dedicated to me and the—"

"Stop," Ned said, putting a finger on Ezer's lips. "I have a second set of contracts that I'd like you sign when you're ready. I've already signed them because I've always been sure. That set of contracts names me as your alpha, the father of your children, the father of your future children, the handler of your heats, and the man you're married to. You can sign them at your discretion."

Ezer stared at Ned. "But—"

"I've only ever wanted you if you wanted me too. From the start, that's how I felt. We're young. We have a long life ahead. You might not ever love me. You might not ever want to sign these contracts. But you'll always be safe, and I'll always protect you. I'll always love you. Even if you leave."

Ezer's throat grew too tight for words. "Is this real?"

"It's real."

"You want to end our contract."

"And start a new kind of life, yes."

Ezer looked down at their sleeping children. He loved them so much his heart ached. He knew Ned felt the same.

Gazing into Ned's eyes, he tried to imagine a future without Ned by his side. He imagined a future where he moved freely, without an alpha to hold him steady, walking into the world on his own.

A balloon in the sky.

"I don't know."

"Signing changes nothing except for allowing you a choice. I'm not going anywhere until you tell me to."

A niggle of doubt ate at Ezer. "Is this because you want freedom? Another path?" *With a better omega?* his mind whispered.

"I already told you. I'm going to wait for you always. I saw you that first day at school, and I knew you were the only omega for me. But it's okay that you didn't feel the same. Maybe you will one day and maybe you won't. I'll let you find me in your own time."

"I've found you now," Ezer whispered.

"Then be brave with me. Sign the contracts. Be free. Choose me again when you're sure."

Ezer licked his lips, tears welling in his eyes. "I'm scared."

Ned kissed his forehead. "We'll be scared together."

The contracts were on a tablet. Ned read them aloud to Ezer as he nursed Ollie, and then Sundy, and then watched his sons kick as they lay on their backs on the floor at their feet.

"Ready?" Ned said, when the contract had been fully recited. "Or do you have questions?"

"Will you still love me?"

"Always."

Ezer chewed on his lower lip, trying to decide what to do. "What if I don't sign?"

"I need you to sign, Ezer. I want to be chosen, the way I chose you. I deserve that, don't you think?"

Ezer's throat ached as he took the tablet from Ned's hands and signed the blank space by a red mark indicating his signature was needed. Twice more he signed, and then it was done.

They were no longer committed to each other by law. They'd undone the web their parents had woven. Ezer was free. It should feel good. It should feel right.

But Ezer burst into tears and fell against Ned, letting him hold him close.

# Epilogue: Freedom

OLLIE AND SUNDY'S second birthday passed at Heath and Adrien's big home by the seaside. The twins loved to play with their older cousins Michael and Laya, and Ezer and Ned enjoyed being in the company of a couple truly in love with each other.

It wasn't long after Ezer had signed to cancel his and Ned's contract that Heath had fulfilled his promise to introduce Ned to the attorneys whose sole focus was on omega rights cases. These men had taken Ned under their collective wing, encouraging him to switch schools to be nearer to their firm so he could invest in an internship there. It wasn't a hard decision to make. Nothing held either of them at the home Lidell had chosen.

Around the same time, Heath had offered to guide Ned more solidly into manhood and asked for them to move into a cottage on Heath's seaside estate. It was a more modest lifestyle, but they both liked it. Earl and Simon were also delighted to finally live near one another for the first time in years. It also allowed for Adrien and Ezer to become friends, and for the children to learn to love each other. All in all, the change was a good solution to a big problem.

The Fersee family continued to be messy, but one of the attorneys Ned worked with, a man with five brothers, had told him that was how it often was in big families. Still, there were some resolutions and changes that were, in Ned's opinion, for the better.

Flo moved in with Amos to avoid any further attempts by their father to control his fate. Those two were learning to forgive each other for the dissolution of the family due to Amos's choices with Finn.

Yissan had left with John, joining a group near the desert, where a community of beta and omega couples used several alpha "bulls" to handle heats. It sounded titillating and sordid, and Ezer always wanted to know more than Yissan willingly shared. Ned didn't know how he felt about Ezer's curiosity about all of that. He hoped Ezer wasn't tempted to go wild and join them.

Rodan was well, and Pete was pregnant again. Ezer had met with Finn and found him wholly unimpressive all over again. He often told Ned that he couldn't see what his da had found so compelling he'd risked everything for the man, but Ned supposed that was the nature of love—unruly and unpredictable.

As for Shan, the news was thin on the ground regarding his fate. He'd been given to an alpha who lived in a remote mountainous region, and who'd made his fortune in the mining business. The area was isolated, lacking stable internet or phone connections, and messages from Shan were few and far between. Flo fretted over him regularly, worried he'd been impregnated, worried he'd been forced to give birth alone. He passed those fears on to Ezer whenever they talked, and Ned wished there was more to be done, but without legal grounds, they were helpless. And so was Shan.

In these ways, the Fersee family was torn asunder, but in others it was healthier than ever. Everyone knew the boundaries, and everyone stuck to them. The fears for Shan's well-being were the only negative to their current situation as far as Ned could see.

As for his little family, Ned was proud to say that everyone was happy. Ned had mentors in the attorneys he worked for, and in Heath. Heath had a protégé. Adrien and Ezer had support, childcare, and friendship between them—and a plan to start an omega school together. They wanted to support teenage omega parents who wanted to continue their education, and they'd also supply childcare to help make that possible.

The idea was one both men were passionate about, as young das themselves, and which both of their alphas were highly supportive of. Heath in a rather condescending way, of course, calling it their "little project," and Ned wholeheartedly, loving the joy in Ezer's face when he spoke about teaching math. Adrien didn't scold Heath for his mild disdain, though, since he was ponying up the cash all the same.

And then there were the children. Ezer and Ned found they were great co-parents, both of them taking the other's opinions to heart, and both of them feeling secure in the other's devotion to the twins. Their delight in Sundy and Ollie's growth, and the development of their little personalities, was something they shared in and which drew them closer and closer together.

For some time after the traumatic birth, they'd done little more than hold hands from time to time, giving Ezer's body, mind, and heart time to heal. But after moving into the cottage on Heath's estate, they'd found their way into each other's arms, and to the surprise of Ned—who'd started to give up hope that Ezer would ever come to him of his own accord—they'd started sharing a bed, too.

In Ned's opinion, life was good. Everyone he loved was happy. Everything they did together was freely chosen.

Ned had no desire to see any of it change.

Which was why he was surprised one evening to find Ezer in the front garden of their cottage, pensively plucking apart a white rose.

"What's wrong?" he asked, taking a seat beside his lover, worried by the furrow between Ezer's brows. "Is it your family?

Shan?"

Ezer shook his head. They sat in silence as Ezer destroyed another bloom.

"Is it my family? My father?"

"No."

Another long minute passed.

Ned chewed on his lower lip before saying, "Tell me, I'm getting paranoid. Is it me? Have I…are you…is this…?"

"No."

The tension was too much.

Several more minutes passed. "This is torture. I feel like something's very wrong, and you don't want to tell me." Ned whispered, "Are you leaving me?"

Ezer's eyes finally lifted from the third rose he was ruining, and he scoffed, throwing the flower at Ned. "No. Ollie's stopped chest-feeding, too."

That made sense. Sundy had stopped a few weeks before. It was only a matter of time before Ollie did as well.

"They can't stay young forever."

"I swear, Ned, you are so adorable, but sometimes you're just really dumb."

Ned huffed but said nothing. What was there to say to that?

Ezer spoke again. "If Ollie and Sundy are both done with chest-feeding that means there's only a few months left before there's going to be a big choice to make."

Ned's mind spun, searching for what it could be. Pre-school? It seemed a bit early still. And then it dawned on him. "Oh."

"Yes. Oh."

"Well." Ned swallowed hard. "It's up to you. You're free to contract with whoever you want to handle the heat." He knew there was a handsome and unattached alpha who'd been helping Adrien and Ezer with aspects of their omega school curriculum design. What if this mood tonight was because Ezer wanted to share his heat with him instead of Ned?

"I swear to God, I'm going to strangle you one day," Ezer said, but it was mild, with no real anger attached.

Ned sat quietly, waiting for the other shoe to drop. Ezer had something big to say, and it was going to change his life. There was no other reason for all this brooding. It probably *was* the alpha at the school. He was smart, spoke three languages, and loved math. Like *really* loved math.

"I'm ready to sign the contract," Ezer said. "The one you've had on hold? I'm ready now."

Ned blinked. "The contract?"

"Yes, the one that says you're my alpha and that we're married," Ezer looked at him as if he were an idiot. Truly it was a common expression, but this time it seemed unfair. He hadn't mentioned anything about wanting to sign it in all the time since they'd dissolved their initial obligations.

"But what about that alpha at the school?"

"Who?"

"That guy. The one who speaks three—"

Ezer punched his arm. "I swear to God, Ned. I'm so serious right now. I may have to kill you."

Ned chewed his lower lip, thinking. If there was truly nothing with the alpha at the omega school, if it was true that Ezer wanted to sign with him now, he had only one question. "Why?"

"Why?" Ezer blew out a breath. "Because you're my—my—ugh. You're Ned. You're *my* Ned."

"That won't ever change. Even if you wanted to have your heat with that alpha from the school. What's his name? Reynold?"

Ezer stared at him. "Never mind. Forget it. You're too dumb for me to love." He stood up and dusted off his pants. "Let's get dinner ready, come on."

Ned stood dizzily, a dart in his heart. "Really?"

"No! Not really," Ezer said, shoving against his chest. "I love you, you absolute dummy. I want you. I want *only* you. And we're going to share a heat together again. Don't you want that? Aren't you excited about it?"

"Are you?" Ned asked, shocked and confused.

"Yes! I'm looking forward to it. I want your knot. For fuck's sake, Ned."

"Oh, um…wait, let's back up."

Ezer rolled his eyes. "Okay."

"You love me?"

"Yes?"

"Since when?"

Ezer's expression softened as he stepped forward and pressed himself against Ned, peering up into his face with a sweetness that made Ned's knees weak. "A long time now. I think I loved you even before the twins came. Definitely after. And I loved you most when you made me dissolve our contract, and I've loved you every single day since."

"But…" Ned swallowed hard. "You didn't let me touch you for the longest time."

"I was scared."

"Why? I'd never hurt you."

"I was afraid I'd feel too much, and then I'd break." Ezer wrapped his arms around Ned's neck, pulling him close as if to kiss him. "But now I know, you'll never let me break."

"No. I'll always take care of you."

Ezer whispered, "I'll always take care of you too."

His lips were gentle on Ned's own, but heat grew between them quickly. "Where are the kids?" Ned asked, lifting Ezer by the ass, as Ezer wrapped his legs around Ned's waist.

"With Adrien."

"You planned this?"

"Not this, but a conversation. Yeah."

"You want to sign the contract?"

"I do."

"When?"

Ezer bit Ned's chin, and then wriggled until Ned put him down again. "Now."

"All right."

Ezer pulled Ned toward the door to their cottage, his smile growing. "Let's do it."

"Wait," Ned said, pulling Ezer to a stop. "Why were you so angry then? When I got home? Why did you pull apart all those roses?"

Ezer's eyes darted to the garden's path and then back up again. "I want to try for a breeding."

Ned's head was shaking no before the meaning of the word had even sunk in.

"The likelihood of twins happening again is—"

"I can't lose you."

Ezer's smile was tender, and he touched Ned's chin with the tips of his fingers. "I know. It's scary. It's a risk."

"We have two sons. We don't need more."

"They're betas. They can't inherit."

"I don't give a damn. I'll leave it all to them anyway."

"That's not how the law works, and you know it."

"Let's not argue," Ned said. "You wanted to sign, and if we argue, you'll change your mind."

Ezer laughed again. The flowers in the garden bobbed their heads in the wind. "I'm not that changeable, Ned."

"Okay, but I can't. Not this time," Ned said. "No breeding this time."

Ezer tilted his head.

"You have a few more heats ahead. We can take them one by

one. But please, Ezer. Not this time."

"All right. We'll wait. It's not as if the heat won't be fun without it."

"More fun, even," Ned said. "We can just play and not worry about the outcome."

Ezer nodded. "'Play'. I like the sound of that."

In the cottage, sitting at the kitchen table, the tablet placed in the middle, they listened together to the terms of the marriage contract being read aloud. When it was done, and Ezer had no questions, he looked at Ned and said, "I choose you."

Ned replied, "And I choose you, Ezer."

Ezer then took up the tablet and added his signature next to Ned's from two years prior.

*He chose me.*

Ned's heart filled to bursting as Ezer kissed him.

THE ROAD TO the heat house by the ocean was familiar in a dizzy sort of way. Ezer wondered if they might have been better off taking Heath's offer of his mountain cabin. Would the memories of their first heat here mix everything up for them? Would the horror and fear and rage come rushing back in like the tide?

But Ezer found his fear was groundless.

As the days slowly passed and the coming heat drew near, Ezer paced the beach missing his sons, and listening to the music of the waves and the seabirds. Earlier in the day, he'd felt the start of the first wave rising. He'd nearly forgotten the intense beauty of it. Closing his eyes, letting the sensation build and strain against his skin, he recalled that this was what he'd fought before.

But this time, he didn't have to.

This time he could trust that his alpha would find him, take him to bed, and knot him until he couldn't see straight.

Ezer waited, feeling the cool breeze from the ocean on his hot skin. "I love you," he said without turning around, the familiar stride comforting as Ned came up behind him. "It's not just the heat talking. You believe that I love you, don't you?"

Ned turned him around, lifted his chin and peered into his eyes. "I believe it. But why did you wait so long to tell me?"

"It was selfish of me." Ezer felt a splinter of shame over the truth. "It was a cruel test. I was afraid you'd stop striving for me."

Ned's mouth quirked. "I'll prove myself to you until we die."

Ezer leaked slick at the declaration. He was close now. The heat was going to be on him very soon.

"I can smell how ready you are."

"A few more minutes. Just us by the sea."

Ned wrapped his arms around Ezer, and they turned to look at the waves together. The infinite-seeming churning of it, the unknowable depths. The future had no promises for them. The past had already taught them that.

From bully to beloved. From coerced to freely chosen.

The one thing they'd earned that meant more than any other was trust. Between the children, the sex, the home, the grudges, and the laughter, their hard-won trust was the most beautiful thing they shared. It encompassed everything.

"The heat is coming now. It's getting stronger."

"I can take care of you."

"Yes. You can." Ezer took a deep breath, the pinpricks of heat rising beneath his skin. "I'm ready."

"About time."

THE END

If you'd like to read more in the Heat for Sale universe, please pick up Heat for Sale.

# Letter from Leta Blake

Dear Reader,

Thank you so much for reading *Bully for Sale*! If you're looking for more in this universe, check out Heat for Sale.

If you enjoyed the book, please take a moment to leave a review! Reviews not only help readers determine if a book is for them, but also help a book show up in searches.

The absolute best way to keep up with me is to join my newsletter. I send one out on average once per week. There you'll find all my upcoming news and information on releases.

Also I'd love if you followed me at BookBub or Goodreads to be notified of new releases and deals. To see some sources of my inspiration, you can follow my Pinterest boards.

And look for me on Facebook or Instagram for snippets of the day-to-day writing life, or join my Facebook Group for announcements and special giveaways.

For the audiobook connoisseur, several of my Leta Blake books are available at most retailers that sell audio, all performed by skilled and talented narrators. Look for me on Audible.

Thank you so much for being a reader!<br>
Leta Blake

*Another book in the **Heat for Sale** universe*

# HEAT FOR SALE

by Leta Blake

**Heat can be sold but love is earned.**

In a world where heats are sold for profit, Adrien is a university student in need of funding. With no family to fall back on, he reluctantly allows the university's matcher to offer his first heat for auction online. Anxious, but aware this is the reality of life for his kind, Adrien hopes whoever wins will be good to him.

Heath—a wealthy, older man—buys Adrien's heat with an ulterior motive. When their undeniable passion shocks him, Heath begins to fall for the young man. Adrien doesn't know what to make of the mysterious stranger he's spending his first heat with, but he's soon swept away and surrenders to Heath entirely.

Later, Heath secrets him away to his immense and secluded home where Heath grows to love Adrien. Unaware of Heath's history, Adrien begins to fall as well. As their love blossoms, the shadows of the past loom.

Can Heath keep his new love once Adrien discovers his secrets?

*Heat for Sale* is a stand-alone m/m erotic romance by Leta Blake. Infused with a du Maurier *Rebecca*-style secret, it features a well-realized fictional universe, an age-gap, and scorching hot scenes.

*Book 1 in the* ***Heat of Love*** *series*

## SLOW HEAT

by Leta Blake

**A lustful young alpha meets his match in an older omega with a past.**

Professor Vale Aman has crafted a good life for himself. An unbonded omega in his mid-thirties, he's long since given up hope that he'll meet a compatible alpha, let alone his destined mate. He's fulfilled by his career, his poetry, his cat, and his friends.

When Jason Sabel, a much younger alpha, imprints on Vale in a shocking and public way, longings are ignited that can't be ignored. Fighting their strong sexual urges, Jason and Vale must agree to contract with each other before they can consummate their passion.

But for Vale, being with Jason means giving up his independence and placing his future in the hands of an untested alpha—as well as facing the scars of his own tumultuous past. He isn't sure it's worth it. But Jason isn't giving up his destined mate without a fight.

This is a gay romance novel, 118,000 words, with a strong happy ending, as well as a well-crafted, **non-shifter** omegaverse, with alphas, betas, omegas, male pregnancy, heat, and **knotting**. Content warning for pregnancy loss and aftermath.

*Book 2 in the* ***Heat of Love*** *series*

## ALPHA HEAT

by Leta Blake

**A desperate young alpha. An older alpha with a hero complex. A forbidden love that can't be denied.**

Young Xan Heelies knows he can never have what he truly wants: a passionate romance and happy-ever-after with another alpha. It's not only forbidden by the prevailing faith of the land, but such acts are illegal.

Urho Chase is a middle-aged alpha with a heartbreaking past. Careful, controlled, and steadfast, his friends dub him old-fashioned and staid. When Urho discovers a dangerous side to Xan's life that he never imagined, his world is rocked and he's consumed by desire. The carefully sewn seams that held him together after the loss of his omega and son come apart—and so does he.

But to love each other and make a life together, Xan and Urho risk utter ruin. With the acceptance and support of Caleb, Xan's asexual and aromantic omega and dear friend, they must find the strength to embrace danger and build the family they deserve.

*Book 3 in the* ***Heat of Love*** *series*

## BITTER HEAT

by Leta Blake

**A pregnant omega trapped in a desperate situation. An unattached alpha with a lot to prove. And an unexpected fall into love that could save them both.**

Kerry Monkburn is contracted to a violent alpha in prison for brutal crimes. Now pregnant with the alpha's child, he lives high in the mountains, far above the city that once lured him in with promises of a better life. Enduring bitterness and fear, Kerry flirts with putting an end to his life of darkness, but fate intervenes.

Janus Heelies has made mistakes in the past. In an effort to redeem himself, integrity has become the watchword for his future. Training as a nurse under the only doctor willing to tal[illegible] him on, Janus is resolute in his intentions: he will live clea[illegible] the mountains and avoid all inappropriate affairs. But h[illegible] anticipate the pull that Kerry exercises on his heart a[illegible]

As the question of Kerry's future health an[illegible] an explosive head, only the intervention of [illegible] desperate men through to a happy ending.

*Standalone*

## ANY GIVEN LIFETIME

by Leta Blake

**He'll love him in any lifetime.**

Neil isn't a ghost, but he feels like one. Reincarnated with all his memories from his prior life, he spent twenty years trapped in a child's body, wanting nothing more than to grow up and reclaim the love of his life.

As an adult, Neil finds there's more than lost time separating them. Joshua has built a beautiful life since Neil's death, and how exactly is Neil supposed to introduce himself? As Joshua's long-dead lover in a new body? Heartbroken and hopeless, Neil takes refuge in his work, developing microscopic robots called nanites that can produce medical miracles.

When Joshua meets a young scientist working on a medical project, his soul senses something his rational mind can't believe. Has Neil truly come back to him after twenty years? And if the impossible is real, can they be together at long last?

*Any Given Lifetime* is a stand-alone, slow burn, second chance romance by Leta Blake featuring reincarnation and true love. story includes some angst, some steam, an age gap, and, of a happy ending.

*Standalone*

## THE RIVER LEITH

by Leta Blake

**Amnesia stole his memories, but it can't erase their love.**

Leith is terrified after waking up in a hospital bed to find his most recent memories are three years out of date.

Worse, he can't even remember how he met the beautiful man who visits him most days. Everyone claims Zach is his best friend, but Leith's feelings for Zach aren't friendly.

They're so much more than that.

Zach fills Leith with longing. Attraction. Affection. **Lust**. And those feelings are even scarier than losing his memory, because Leith's always been straight. Hasn't he?

For Zach, being forgotten by his lover is excruciating. Leith's amnesia has stolen everything: their relationship, their happiness, and the man he loves. Suddenly single and alone, Zach knows nothing will ever be okay again.

Desperate to feel better, Zach confesses his grief to the facele
Internet. But his honesty might come back to haunt them h

*The River Leith* is a standalone MM romance w
trope, hurt/comfort, bisexual discovery, "first tir
second chance at first love, and a satisfying h

## Other Books by Leta Blake

### Contemporary

Will & Patrick Wake Up Married
Will & Patrick's Endless Honeymoon
Cowboy Seeks Husband
The Difference Between
Bring on Forever
Stay Lucky

**Sports**

The River Leith

*The Training Season Series*
Training Season
Training Complex

**Musicians**

Smoky Mountain Dreams
Vespertine

### New Adult/Coming of Age

Punching the V-Card

*'90s Coming of Age Series*
Pictures of You
You Are Not Me

**Winter Holidays**

North's Pole

*The Mr. Christmas Series*
Mr. Frosty Pants
Mr. Naughty List
Mr. Jingle Bells

## Fantasy

Any Given Lifetime

**Re-imagined Fairy Tales**

Flight
Levity

**Paranormal & Shifters**

Angel Undone
Omega Mine

**Horror**

Raise Up Heart

## Omegaverse

*Heat of Love Series*
Slow Heat
Alpha Heat
Slow Birth
Bitter Heat

*For Sale Series*
Heat for Sale
Bully for Sale

## Coming of Age

*'90s Coming of Age Series*
Pictures of You
You Are Not Me

## Audiobooks

Leta Blake at Audible

## Discover more about the author online

Leta Blake
letablake.com

## Gay Romance Newsletter

Leta's newsletter will keep you up to date on her latest releases, sales and deals, future writing plans, and more from the world of M/M romance. Join Leta's mailing list today.

## Leta Blake on Patreon

Become part of Leta Blake's Patreon community to support her indie publishing expenses and to access exclusive content, deleted scenes, extras, and interviews.

# About the Author

Author of the bestselling book Smoky Mountain Dreams and fan favorites like Training Season, Will & Patrick Wake Up Married, and Slow Heat, Leta Blake has been captivating M/M Romance readers for over a decade. Whether writing contemporary romance or fantasy, she puts her psychology background to use creating complex characters and love stories that feel real. At home in the Southern U.S., Leta works hard at achieving balance between her writing and her family life.

Printed in Great Britain
by Amazon

40364178R00239